On Home

Becca Spence Dobias

This is a work of fiction. Names, characters, organizations, places, events, and incidents are either products of the author's imagination or are used fictitiously.

Published by Inkshares, Inc., Oakland, California
www.inkshares.com

Edited by Avalon Radys & Matt Harry
Cover design by Lauren Harms
Interior design by Kevin G. Summers

ISBN: 9781950301256
e-ISBN: 9781950301263
LCCN: 2021935635

First edition

Printed in the United States of America

To Jonas and Josie:
This is how I give you West Virginia.

CASSIDY

MMMM, CASSIDY TYPED, for the hundredth time that day. It took so little to turn men on, she thought as she took a sip of lime seltzer.

Oh fuck, you like that? NaughtyGuy79 asked.

Cassidy sent back a heart-eyes emoji—the bare minimum required to encourage someone set on having a hard-on—and switched tabs to her chat with Noeli. It was always a bit jarring going from work talk to real-life talk. Jarring, too, was how much more functional regular chat was. The cam site was constantly freezing or changing emojis into random combinations of symbols.

"You working right now?" Noeli had asked.

"Just chat. No video." If she'd been on camera, Cassidy would have applied a bit of makeup, let her blond hair down to cover her undercut, and squeezed her bum into something sexy. Instead she was barefaced and broken out, with too-big cotton panties under her jeans, and a lopsided ponytail.

"So you're all turned on?"

Cassidy laughed.

"By all the sweet tips rolling in? Yes, very turned on," Cassidy told Noeli, and took another gulp of fizzy water, silently cursing the Inland Empire for its lack of fall weather. Locals always talked about the superiority of dry heat, but in Cassidy's opinion, any kind of ninety-degree weather in October was gross.

"You said you actually get off in those videos though," Noeli said.

"Yeah, masturbating feels good. Plus I get paid for it." She stared at the bare wall of her apartment and then out the window beyond to the smoggy peak of Mt. Baldy—brown and dusty in the distance. She didn't miss much about West Virginia, but she did miss green. She'd hoped to live closer to the beach, but rent in LA was outrageous. Actually, she'd wanted to move to the Bay, with its foggy mornings and trolleyed streets, but rent there was even worse.

She needed to decorate for her videos, she thought, remembering some of the cute setups other women had. One had an old-fashioned fainting couch that she lay on for her shows. Another had framed photos of her top tippers and a sign reading *Love* in pink neon. Cassidy was thinking shiplap. Or maybe one of those hanging swing chair things.

"You know I'm not judging you *morally*," Noeli said. "I just don't get it."

"Still want to get tacos later?" Cassidy asked, and Noeli confirmed the time they were to meet. Back on her work tab, her notifications were going crazy.

You there bb?
Girl a selfie pls
Hot and sexy pic just one please
Can I send a pic of how hard you made me

Cassidy smiled, slid lower into the maroon pleather desk chair she'd found by the dumpster, and propped her legs on the books beside her laptop before unbuttoning her jeans. One foot rested on the autobiography of Angela Davis; the other lay atop a guide to self-care for sex workers.

Show me that thick cock, she typed.

Cassidy was so absorbed in a chat with a regular who was promising to purchase several items from her wish list, that when Noeli pulled into the complex's designated visitor spot in her ratty Honda Accord and honked the tired horn, the sound startled Cassidy, though Noeli was ten minutes late. Patting her back pocket to be sure she had her wallet and telling HelloBeautiful she had to run, Cassidy switched her brain back to normal-human-relation mode and skipped down the concrete steps to Noeli's car, letting the door slam behind her. A cat had used the planter in front of the parking spot as a litter box and the smell permeated the windows. She should add some kind of deodorizing spray to her wish list, but she'd have to make it a sexy scent so it wouldn't be weird.

"So, who was he?" Noeli asked as Cassidy buckled her seat belt.

"It's the guy I was telling you about who never actually buys my panties, but gets off talking about how he wants to."

"That's fucking weird." Noeli navigated through the parking lot and around the tennis court, where a woman was rolling a ball under the net for her toddler to wobble after; by the empty clubhouse, sagging balloons and other remnants of a birthday party visible through the floor-to-ceiling window; and past the beige stucco residential buildings that looked like every other beige stucco building in this sorry excuse for a city.

"He is far from the weirdest. I still think the dude with the wedgie fetish wins that one." She smirked, but felt a small tinge of tenderness for MannyBoy27, the plastics engineer. He was always so enthusiastic and grateful, she remembered as she made a mental note to message him later and ask about his day.

Heading south on Haven Avenue, Cassidy looked out at Rancho Cucamonga and its sad collection of strip malls and big-box stores. It was a suburb without a city, like a pronoun without an antecedent. It was middle-aged white women with bleached blond hair and fake boobs and bodybuilding bros with Ed Hardy tanks and backward ball caps.

Once on the freeway, the stucco sped past—interrupted only by palm trees, cell phone towers made to resemble palm trees, and the colorful symbols of capitalism splashed across billboards and boxy buildings. Cassidy felt the car jerk suddenly to the left.

"Did you blow out a tire?" she asked, gripping the armrest.

Noeli tightened her fingers around the peeling rubber of the steering wheel and tapped her nails, with their chipping black polish, against her palms. "The Santa Ana winds get stronger in Fontana."

"That's wind?" Cassidy eyed the towering Amazon truck passing them, its load swaying precariously close to their lane.

Noeli slowed to let the vehicle pass. "I told you we have seasons. Welcome to wind season," she said.

"How's your mom?" Cassidy asked, reminded by the smiling arrow logo. "How's the warehouse?"

"The warehouse is still shit and my mom is still insane."

"I'm sorry." Cassidy looked over at Noeli's bouncy brown bob as they exited and drove south for several minutes in silence before pulling into a parking lot whose entrance featured a large statue of a horse on which three young children scrambled and climbed. Noeli slid into an open spot and pulled the key from the ignition. The Accord let out a sputtering sigh and Cassidy fumbled through her messenger bag for ChapStick before opening her door. She dug around, pushing aside gum wrappers and coffee shop receipts. Her phone buzzed and she fought the urge to check it, knowing it was probably one of her fans and that Noeli would be annoyed if she was distracted during dinner. What would HelloBeautiful end up buying her? She'd put an expensive camera on the list, hoping he might splurge, but she knew it would likely be a collection of smaller, sexier items—cheap lingerie, vibrators, maybe the vanilla fig body gel.

Mariachi music emanated from the restaurant's open patio and the women walked side by side toward the warm glow of the dining area, squinting against the wind. Dirt blew up from around their feet and stuck to Cassidy's freshly balmed lips, which she wiped with the back of her hand. Noeli laughed. "You have things to learn about wind season."

Cassidy made a mental note to add lightweight, fast-dry lip gloss to her wish list.

Inside, the other diners turned to look at the two women briefly, then turned back to their families and friends. Cassidy relaxed against a stucco wall lined with blue and orange tiles, and Noeli began to order in Spanish. The woman at the window looked up blankly from below her black visor until Noeli began again in English. Cassidy saw the cashier had an eyelash stuck to her cheek.

"Make a wish," Cassidy said to the woman as she handed a twenty-dollar bill over Noeli's shoulder. Noeli passed it through the window, wherea few other women and a short dark man stood beside a large wheel, shaping tortillas, and Janelle Monae played from a small portable radio, competing with the sound system in the dining area. The cashier took the money without smiling and returned a handful of change.

A man, squat and white, probably fifty-something, with a white button-down shirt and too much cologne, squeezed past and eyed Cassidy. She gave him a flirty smile, forgetting momentarily that she wasn't on camera. Quickly, she looked away and snuck a glance at her phone. The buzzing earlier hadn't been a fan message, but rather a call from her parents. Cassidy groaned, imagining calling them back. As she followed Noeli to a glass-topped table, she tried to think instead about the sloppy burrito—green sauce, hold the sour cream—awaiting her shortly.

JANE

JANE SAT IN the sterile maroon chair in her room at the old folks' home she'd recently moved to, staring at the ugly blanket on her narrow bed. Her memory was failing, they told her. It was no longer safe for her to live alone. Perhaps they were right, she thought. She had been more forgetful than usual lately, names and words slipping from her grasp right as she tried to speak them, leaving her gaping and dumb.

Most of her life, though, seemed clear as ever—clearer, maybe. These old memories came back to her in waves, reminding her how she'd gotten here, to this room where she was alone with her thoughts and the roaring air conditioner that left her cold no matter how many blankets she piled on her lap.

Jane closed her eyes against the chill and let the memories roll over her.

It was the war again and her brothers were off aiding the Allies, saving the world, while she was stuck at home trying her damnedest to do her part. Most days, doing her part felt an awful lot like keeping her trap shut.

Just weeks earlier, she had walked across the stage, hair pinned neatly, gown rippling like Lady Liberty, to receive her diploma, another moment that had not gone at all how she'd imagined. She had pictured her real life waiting on the other side—college, books, and then a handsome husband. What she'd found instead was a quick embrace from her parents, a newly expanded chore list, and more time than anyone needed to think about the unpleasant state of world affairs.

The war. It was all anyone talked about, wrote about, thought about.

Jane watered the pigs and then stopped for a moment by her favorite tree to give it a quick pat, enjoying the familiar roughness of its bark. That was one thing she could look forward to this fall. This tree's apples were always buttery sweet, their yellow skin snapping under her teeth with a satisfying pop. She could almost taste it now.

Back inside, Arzella was buzzing around the house, fussing as usual over her African violets. The small pot by the door had gotten a new post on the windowsill. The soldier who'd been stationed at the window received his marching orders—it was off to the table with him, and there would be no back talk. Arzella touched her fingertips to the soil, testing the pot's moisture, and caressed the emerald leaves with knotty-knuckled fingers.

"Pigs are good." Jane sat at the table beside her father, Philip, who was worrying over the paper.

He put it down and looked at her. "Thanks, love." Sweat speckled his creased forehead, furrows tilled deeper by the past year. Jane rolled the fabric of her skirt between her fingers. She wanted to ask him to take her into town, but she knew her mother would hassle her, reminding her of the work still to be done on the farm, all the absent brothers who weren't there to do it.

Arzella sat beside them and the three looked at one another, each waiting for someone else to speak first. The war hung between them, heavy as the Hindenburg. How queer it was,

Jane thought, that something could envelop the whole world and yet be so personal, so intimate, such a familiar part of their little home that it seemed to sit right at the middle of their cherrywood table.

No one spoke, and one by one, they looked away: Philip back to his paper, Arzella at her plant, and Jane at the dirt floor. Her brothers' voices seemed to echo in these silences. At moments like this, Jane could hardly stand their absence.

A breeze rustled the short curtains over the sink, bringing the humid summer a step further into the farmhouse. Philip ripped the front page from the paper, then folded it accordion-style, waving it in front of Jane's face and then his own. Jane giggled. "Will you take me into town?" she asked.

"I was planning on makin' the trip anyway. I reckon you could tag along."

Jane smiled at her father gratefully.

"Let's go get the eggs, then," Arzella said, standing. "If you're gonna leave me to make supper on my own, at least help me with that."

Philip winked at Jane from behind the fan. From the accordioned page, a stony-faced housewife glared at Jane, an advertisement she was more than familiar with: *What can* I *do to help win the war?* Jane puffed up her chest, winked back at Philip, and followed Arzella out to the coop.

That was the beginning of the decision that had changed her life, Jane thought now in the maroon chair—the last hour on the farm before her world expanded.

CASSIDY

BACK AT HER apartment, Cassidy threw her bag onto the floor and flopped into her desk chair, surprised HelloBeautiful had left her alone the entire time she was with Noeli. It was MannyBoy27 she was more concerned with. It had been almost a whole day since she'd talked to him, when normally by now he'd have sent her several YouTube links to watch and respond to, bugged her to edit his running Google Doc about the things they would do when they got together, and cajoled her into sending at least a few selfies. She looked at his profile—the picture of him in a plaid button-down, a goofy grin on his bearded face, his bio stating his love for "the courageous and confident ladies who grace us all with the gift of their beautiful bodies," the various thank-you messages from other girls, which had stopped once he and Cassidy had started talking regularly. Cassidy loved that he'd dropped everyone else and become her biggest fan—the one that egged the other tippers on with his large tips and gathered other users for her shows. She loved how he asked her to arrange his weird list in the order she wanted to do them. She always left *give C a wedgie* on top, since she knew how much he liked it, but she'd move the other items around each day, sometimes adding her own items—*massage* or *take C shopping and help her in the dressing room.* Had he moved on to a new girl? Cassidy glanced at the electricity bill that lay half open beside the Angela Davis book. Or what if he had died? Or been in some kind of accident? How would she know?

She scrolled through her chat at the names of her other usual fans—the ones who messaged her when she wasn't on camera. It was quiet. Normal for a Friday night, but still, Cassidy felt restless. She clicked on each name—Timmy, TheDuck, Metallica77—as if opening their conversations might summon them, but no one was around. She considered sending a *hi*, but quickly decided against it. Fans messaged her. They craved *her* attention. They needed *her*, not the other way around.

She could do a show. It wasn't her usual time, but she might attract some new people. Cassidy sat up straighter and began to arrange her mic and ring light, the selection of sex toys next to her chair. She went to the bathroom and brushed her hair out from its bun, put on primer and foundation, contoured her jaw and cheekbones. She eyed the plastic case of magnetic eyelashes on the counter but decided not to bother. This was more for exposure than money. In her bedroom, she laid several sets of lingerie on her unmade bed, looking for something she hadn't worn in a while, and finally selected a purple bodysuit. There was a hole in the lace under one boob but she could angle herself so it wasn't as visible on camera.

Back at her desk, Cassidy went to her settings. She'd set her counts low to draw people in: 50 tokens for a boob flash, 100 for her pussy, 250 to cum. As she hit the button to start the countdown to broadcast, she remembered her first show.

Ten seconds to go. She'd been so sick of driving drunk bros home from bad bars.

Eight seconds. She'd felt so nervous, but she told herself she was just trying it out. She didn't even have to take off her clothes.

Six seconds. What if no one even wanted to see her naked? she'd worried. What if everyone at home had been right? Maybe she *was* disgusting.

She had begun shaking at three seconds. It had to be better than rideshare driving, she'd told herself, and it was definitely better than going back to Buckhannon broke. But was she really going to do this?

When the pink button had announced she was live and Cassidy stared at her own image under the banner reading *NEW GIRL!*, her hesitation vanished. Viewers had poured in and so had the tips. The chat rolled by faster than she could read it and before she knew it, she was naked, giggling, and wondering where the gorgeous girl on-screen with the rosy cheeks and the easy smile had come from. Cassidy liked this version of herself. And she liked how much other people liked her. She'd made several hundred dollars that night. As soon as it hit her account, she spent it on an external mic and a vibrator that buzzed automatically when she got a tip. She'd sold her car to fund an even better setup and never looked back.

The counter before her now reached zero and she was live again. She'd stopped getting nervous weeks ago. Cassidy plastered a smile on her face, already hearing her signature *hiiii-iii* in her mind, like a doorbell. No one was in her room. Cassidy held her smile, her cheeks starting to shake. One viewer entered, then left, then another came in and another. Cassidy asked the room how they were doing that night, what they were up to, what they wanted to see. "I'll give you a freebie this Friday," she teased, removing the straps of her bodysuit, letting her cone-shaped breasts emerge. "A little gift." Two viewers joined and then left, and Cassidy tried not to let her panic show as she absentmindedly played with her nipples, peeking at the other online girls' viewer counts. A few more people joined her room and Cassidy continued rubbing her breasts, occasionally emitting an unconvincing moan. GreenKnobMO tipped 20 tokens and then left. Off nights were normal, she thought, looking toward the self-care guide. They had nothing to do with her talent and especially not with her self-worth. Cassidy rubbed more vigorously and outside, a coyote howled from the foothills. "Anyone want to chat? I love privates," she said, but no one responded. In another tab, MannyBoy27's profile still showed him as offline. Cassidy sat alone in the glow of the ring light, the illuminated circle visible in her pupils on-screen, the lace of her old lingerie pilling in tiny balls she would later snip off with nail clippers, massaging her breasts for four quiet strangers.

JANE

"WOULD YOU LIKE some lotion, Jane?" the health aide offered with a patronizing grin, as if Jane were a child, incapable of moisturizing her own hands.

"No, thank you." The aide left and Jane reached for the bottle of Olay, pumping some into her palm. It was the cold air from the damned air conditioner. Her skin had never been so dry. What had the ointment been at G.O. Young Drug Store that day?

Ah, right. Palmer's Skin Success ointment, *Relieves the IRRITATION of ITCHING, ECZEMA, and PIMPLES externally caused!* She could still hear the advertisement in old Mr. Young's voice as he'd tried to sell it to them. And they said Jane's memory was bad.

Jane and her cousin Ding had peered down through the glass countertops as they slurped their Coca-Colas.

"Too bad it's not ice cream," Ding said. "Now that's a cream I could use."

The girls licked the last drops from their straws and swung their stools to the side and, with a swish, scurried out to the street.

"Maybe I should try that skin ointment," Ding mused, pausing to stare back over her shoulder.

"Ding, you don't have eczema, and I don't think you'd know a pimple if it bit you on the nose."

"But sometimes I have itching."

Jane kept walking and, after a last longing glance toward Young's, Ding rushed to catch up. Grabbing Jane's hand, she skipped next door to Thompson's, pulling Jane behind her.

Inside, bottles and boxes of all sizes lined the shelves, containing tablets, salves, powders, nose drops, and creams—anything you might need for any number of ailments or maladies. Jane took her time browsing, breathing in the scent of newness.

Ding, on the other hand, stormed to the register, where John Hinkle counted nickels, oblivious to her predatory gaze.

John had another year to go at the high school, though he looked older. He also had his pick of local girls from fifteen to twenty, all eager for the attention of one of the only eligible boys around.

Ding plopped a pack of bubble gum on the counter and pretended, as always, that paying was an act of generosity, rather than an excuse to bat her eyelashes at John.

"How's school?" she asked him, her lips curling upward in a coy smile.

"Just school," he said, smiling back politely. He took the coin from her palm, placed it in the register, and turned to count jars of aspirin on a shelf.

Ding left her hand stretched toward him for a moment, as if he might turn back around and grab it. When John failed to realize his mistake, Ding snatched the bubble gum, shoved it into Jane's hand, and huffed out of the shop.

Jane followed, and outside, the girls leaned against the building, staring down the street toward the courthouse, hoping against hope that something interesting might emerge. Jane opened the gum and handed a piece to her cousin, who tossed it into the air and caught it between her teeth.

"Bravo, Miss Victory," Jane said. Ding put a hand to her hip and saluted with the other, lifting her chest like the blond comic book hero. Jane's cousin may have been prone to mood swings, but at least it was simple to lift her spirits.

A baby-blue car approached and for a moment Jane imagined herself chasing it down, rapping on the window, beseeching its driver to take her wherever they were headed—anywhere but this boring little town. Instead she watched as the car rolled by. She opened the bubble gum pack again to pluck out her own piece and an ad fluttered to the ground. Jane bent to retrieve it from the sidewalk.

On the small paper was a picture of a woman seated at a typewriter. Like Miss Victory, the woman's hand was raised in a salute, and a perfect white smile spanned her face. *Victory Waits on Your Fingers—Keep 'Em Flying, Miss U.S.A.*, the ad proclaimed. Smaller text below read, *Uncle Sam needs stenographers! Get civil service information at your local post office. U.S. Civil Service Commission, Washington, D.C.*

Jane had seen the ads for WAVES and for WAC, for SPARS and the Cadet Nurses—all the opportunities for girls to join the war effort—but none of them had struck her like this. The letters her brothers had mailed home from boot camp had left her with little desire to join the service, and she had no interest in wearing a uniform, even if the WAVES did get a Mainbocher hat. She'd heard about the Government Girls, too, had seen *The More the Merrier* with Ding the week it came out, but somehow, until this exact moment, it had seemed like something separate from her and from Buckhannon—a far-off dream for people much more glamorous, from much more cosmopolitan places.

Now, though, she blinked, imagining . . . living on her own in Washington—now that would be an adventure!

"Take a look at this!" Jane said, shoving the ad in Ding's face.

Ding's eyes crossed, trying to make sense of the tiny letters, and she mouthed the words under her breath as she read.

Not a second passed before she grabbed Jane's hand. "Let's go!" she said, pulling her right across the middle of the street. She didn't slow down the whole two blocks to the post office.

The girls got back to Young's just as Philip's truck arrived. "Keep your mouth shut for now," Jane said. She needed a chance to look over the pamphlets, to figure out how to present it to her daddy so that he could do the work of convincing her mother. Ding drew her fingers across her lips in a zipping motion.

The three rode back to the country in a buzzing silence, Ding squeezing Jane's leg. The truck's engine hummed as they drove, and their shoulders bumped at each pothole, Philip's strong and firm on Jane's left, and on her right, Ding's, small and bony.

At Ding's, Jane's cousin hopped down from the truck and blew them both a kiss. "Thanks for the ride, Uncle Philip. I know you love me."

"I feel something about you, Christine. That's for sure."

"You know there ain't no one but you who still calls me that."

"That don't bother me none. You'll always be Christine to me."

Ding stuck out her tongue and slammed the truck door. As Philip turned his head to back down the steep driveway, Jane craned her neck to catch her cousin's eye. Ding winked and again made like she was zipping up her lips.

That night, Jane pulled her quilt tight around her shoulders. From the table beside her, an oil lamp illuminated the papers spread before her on the bed. She sat, studying them closely, her legs crossed in her cotton shortie pajamas. She would emphasize the service part of it all, she decided. She would go to Washington to do her patriotic duty. Certainly her parents couldn't argue with that.

Would it have been better if they had forbid it? Surely not, Jane told herself now, absentmindedly rubbing the lotion into the backs of her hands. If she hadn't gone to Washington, she would not have Ken or Cassidy. And yet—

"Would you like to come to Bible study?" Another aide had poked her head into the room, and Jane's thoughts vanished, gone as if she had never been thinking them.

"No," she said, turning her chair toward the window and the empty field beyond.

CASSIDY

CASSIDY HEARD A buzzing sound, and for a moment her heart leapt at the promise of another tip, her dopamine receptors pinging, until she realized she hadn't felt the vibration in her vagina. It was only her phone, rumbling from within her bag by the door. Cassidy sighed and ended her broadcast, not bothering to say goodbye to the four freeloaders watching her sad show. It was her parents again, as she figured. Cassidy threw her T-shirt on, leaving her lingerie dangling around her waist, and answered the video call.

"It's working."

"No, it isn't. I can't see anything yet." Her parents were arguing, of course.

"It says it's working."

"Do you see anything?"

"Give it a minute."

"Mom? Daddy? I'm here," Cassidy said, louder than necessary.

"Oh! I can see you!" Cassidy's father, Ken, exclaimed as his face came into view. His curly hair was graying, more than Cassidy remembered from their last visit, but his face was animated and boyish as always. "This is the next best thing to having you here with me. How are you, sweet pea?"

"I'm fine." Cassidy smoothed her hair as she looked at her own face on the phone. Her screen was cracked and the fracture divided her left and right halves.

"Are you wearing makeup?" Her mom leaned into the camera's view. "I hate when you wear makeup. You're so naturally beautiful. Why would you cover your face with that junk?"

"What's up, Daddy? How are you?"

A message from MannyBoy27 appeared in Cassidy's notification bar, and she was momentarily distracted. He was alive, at least.

"Grandma Jane . . ."

Cass's attention shot back to her father. Ken's broad grin had fallen. *No. No. No. No.* The word sounded in her head like a car alarm.

And then, to her horror, Cassidy's mind began planning what she would post on social media—what picture, what touching tribute. There was the song from Ingrid Michaelson. She would post it subtly, not make a big deal. If she mentioned it on her show, she would probably drum up a bunch of sympathy tips.

". . .was diagnosed with dementia," Ken finished.

Fuck, Cassidy thought. She was a fucking monster. The fluorescent light from the kitchen thrummed its yellow song and she felt certain her parents could see her bare ass poking through her lingerie, though it wasn't on-screen.

"What does that mean for her?" She tugged her T-shirt down. Her grandma was fine; that was the most important thing. Her grandma was alive. She thought of Grandma Jane and her heart-shaped face, the stories she told about the farm before Cassidy was born—how it used to teem with siblings and cousins and pigs and chickens, how her own mom made dresses from feed sacks, curtains from dresses, and babies out of thin air. How her father, as a boy, would roam it in search of arrowheads while she followed behind plucking four-leaf clovers and remembering her own childhood. She'd usually end up singing then—an old hymn sometimes, or others, a parable tune about a grasshopper and an ant.

Ken took a heavy breath. "She's coherent most of the time. You wouldn't notice anything hugely different. We only got her evaluated because—"

A wave of relief washed over Cassidy and carried her mind back to her whale of a tipper. She should tell him about it privately, before she said anything on the show. He'd be genuinely concerned, wonder what he could do to help.

"Are you listening to your father?" Cassidy's mother's voice cut into her thoughts. "You should come home and see her before . . ." She trailed off.

"Before what?"

"Before it does become apparent. The doctor said she might decline rapidly." Cassidy looked from her mom, stoic and annoyed, to her dad, whose eyes were watering, and said nothing. She really was a monster, but there was still no way she was going back to Buckhannon unless it was absolutely necessary.

"What are you doing out there that you couldn't do here?" her mom asked.

Her dad's voice was softer. "We miss you, Cass. I miss you."

Cassidy rolled her eyes.

"Really, Cassidy?" her mom asked.

"Paloma, can you give us a minute?" Cassidy's mom rolled her own eyes and walked away, leaving Ken alone on the screen.

"Just a short trip," he said. "So you can say goodbye while she's still lucid."

"I couldn't do that." Cassidy's eyes watered. "There's too much pressure. It'd be worse than not knowing. Grandma Jane doesn't want me there. She knows how much I hate Buckhannon."

Ken tilted his head. "This is Grandma Jane. The Grandma Jane who taught you how to sew, who rocked you to sleep when Mom and I were too exhausted."

"I know."

"This is my mother." Ken's voice rose and cracked a little with the last word and Cassidy had to look away.

"I know," she said again.

"It's hard, but don't think of it as *goodbye* goodbye. Nothing ever really goes away."

"Daddy, please don't talk to me about reincarnation right now." She clicked over to MannyBoy27's messages, ready to fabricate an excuse to hang up with her parents so she could cry. All of it—the slow, lonely night, this news—it was getting to her. She could say she had a ride request.

"It's not the woo you think it is," Ken said. He puffed out his cheeks and then blew the air from his mouth. "Say you're buried and you eventually decompose and become part of the dirt around you. A seed falls and grows in the dirt you're part of, right?"

"Right." Cassidy rubbed the bridge of her nose.

"So maybe a little tree grows and a deer comes by and eats some of the leaves. A hunter kills the deer and brings it home to his family. Maybe his wife is pregnant, yada yada yada."

They both laughed at the *Seinfeld* reference and the air pressure in Cassidy's room seemed to lighten.

"That's all a really physical version of reincarnation. The matter is literally being transferred."

"I can buy that, but—"

"But why is it so radical to think consciousness, or parts of it, get transferred too—become part of that tree or that deer or that baby?"

"Hm."

"Even if not, though, there are other ways consciousness goes on. Part of me is in you. Part of Grandma Jane, too."

"Okay," Cassidy said.

"Just come home," Ken said. "Please."

"I'll think about it."

They hung up and Cassidy took her phone to bed, tucking it under her arm like a teddy bear as she fell asleep in her T-shirt and lace, her room small and dark as a cave.

CASSIDY

SecreC: *Hey . . .*
MannyBoy27: *Hey babygirl*

Cassidy smiled. She kind of loved when he called her pet names. She'd rolled out of bed and shimmied out of her lingerie bottoms, replaced them with a pair of red vinyl booty shorts, and gotten set up to cam. She was planning to tell her room about her grandma, but she wanted to tell Manny first.

SecreC: *I just talked to my parents . . . got some bad news about my grandma*
MannyBoy27: *O no. What's up?*
SecreC: *She has dementia*

Cassidy paused and bit her lip, considering the balancing act. With some fans, directness was the best approach, but Manny liked to feel like he was doing favors for a friend. A notification told Cassidy that Manny was attempting to video-call her. She accepted and put on her best vulnerable sexy face.

"Are you okay?" Manny asked once they were connected. He was in the same plaid shirt he wore in his profile picture, and behind him, Cassidy could see the large floor-to-ceiling window beyond his desk.

"I didn't mean to bother you while you were working."

"You're never a bother, C."

Cassidy gave a sad smile that she hoped looked demure and flirty. Usually whenever she smiled, Manny couldn't help smiling back. He had told her once that her smile melted him and she loved seeing the truth of the confession. Now, though, he looked at her with concern.

Manny tapped a silver pen on a legal pad. Beside him on his desk sat a framed caricature drawing of himself and his two sons. In the portrait, Manny's forehead was huge. His sons wore Marlins caps and held up gloved hands drawn to be the size of their heads. "Are you going home to see your grandma?"

Cassidy blew air through her nose. "I hate going home." Not everything about her camming persona was fake.

"Why?"

"I hate seeing all the people I grew up with. They're all shitbags."

"They're probably all in love with you."

Cassidy snorted. "The people I grew up with are most definitely *not* in love with me."

Manny tilted his head. "I find that really hard to believe. Anyway . . . if you want some help with a ticket, you know you can ask me for anything."

Dammit. Cassidy had hoped for sympathy tips—money she could spend on clothes and food and stuff for her apartment—not airplane money.

"Thanks, Manny. You know I appreciate you."

"How much?" Manny grinned deviously and Cassidy smiled for real.

"This much," she said, and lifted her shirt, sticking her boobs out to make them look as perky as possible.

"Good girl," he said, inspiring the same thrill the words always brought to Cassidy's chest. He looked up toward the office door. "I should go."

"Okay, Manny."

"You'll be okay?"

"I'm okay," Cassidy said, and blew a kiss. Manny smiled and hung up. A moment later an email appeared, informing her that forty thousand American Airlines miles had been transferred to her account. Dammit.

JANE

JANE DIDN'T REMEMBER what she'd been thinking about when the aide had interrupted until later that evening. Resident bedtime was nine o'clock, which meant Jane lay on her side on the adjustable bed for hours before drifting off. She got most of her sleep during the day in the armchair. As she stared out at the dark room, it came back to her in an image—her mother lifting her hand to the back of her head as if she might faint when Jane had told her parents she and Ding were joining the war effort. Philip had set his book on the table.

"Not anything dangerous," Jane had said quickly. "The Civil Service Commission is looking for girls to do jobs while the boys are away. Typing and whatnot."

"And just where are these Civil Service jobs you and Ding are taking?" Arzella had asked, recovering. Her voice tilted slightly with Jane's cousin's name, making room for the *that damn* she'd left unsaid. Arzella never cursed, but you could always tell when she wanted to.

Jane swallowed. "Washington."

Philip and Arzella looked at each other, speaking their secret language of subtle eye movements. Philip nodded. "Jane, Washington is a long ways away, darling."

"And we need your help here on the farm," Arzella said. "Remember the homemakers pledge?"

Jane remembered the ad in the *Buckhannon Record*: *It's up to you—and to every housewife in America—to "hold the line." To hold it until our boys come back . . . That's what* you *can do. That's* your *war job!*

"Mom, you've been holding the line just fine. You and I both know I'm mostly in your way."

Arzella crossed her arms and tapped her foot. She should have been a schoolteacher with that look, though it had come in equally handy as a mother of seven.

"Ding is going for sure," Jane said.

Of course she is. Arzella shot the words silently at her husband.

"She's talked to Violet and Vernon?" Philip asked, and he and Arzella exchanged another look.

"Yes," Jane lied. Surely Ding would use the same line on her aunt and uncle.

"Well, you best be ready to buy your own things if you're off earning your own money. And Washington is expensive," Philip said. "It's not like Buckhannon."

Jane put a hand to her mouth to stop a squeal from escaping. She had won and she knew it.

Arzella shot Philip a lightning glare. Jane wondered, Had he misunderstood their silent code, or worse—ignored it?

Heck, Jane could practically hear it herself. *Six sons in the war and you're sending our daughter to the capital on her own? God help me. We'll be here working the farm on our own. Alone.* Jane tried not to think about how quiet the house would be.

"I'll make my own clothes, pay for all my own things."

Arzella shook her head and looked up, as if asking God for patience.

"I don't like this, Jane," she said to the ceiling. "I don't know if you're prepared for the dangers and temptations of a place like Washington. Especially with that cousin of yours in tow."

"Isn't that a reason for me to go, Mama?" Jane asked. "I bet Uncle Vernon and Aunt Violet would be happy to have me there to keep an eye on Ding."

They ate their breakfast in silence, Arzella shaking her head and Jane stifling grins the whole time. Afterward, she helped her mother clear the table and then ran back to her room, where she pored over the Civil Service papers for the hundredth time before getting dressed. As she buttoned her top button, she heard the door slam in the kitchen. She looked out her window and saw Arzella walking toward the water pump without her, a bucket in each hand.

A quiet knock on her door moments later made her jump.

"It's me, Jane," Philip's voice called from the other side.

"Oh. Come on in, Daddy."

Philip opened the door.

"What do you think about the FBI?" he asked, removing a pipe and tobacco from his overall pocket before sitting beside Jane on her bed.

Jane watched him with astonishment. Arzella couldn't stand when he smoked.

"What about the FBI?" she asked.

"Well, for working. I hear they need a lot of girls there now." He packed the pipe.

Jane gawked.

"What an honor, eh? The FBI." He produced a lighter and lit his tobacco, then took a long puff. "Fidelity, bravery, integrity. That's what they say, you know."

Jane nodded. Outside, the rooster crowed.

"I best get out to till," Philip said, rising then shaking his head in disbelief. "My daughter, working for the FBI. Now that's somethin'. You'll have to take the exam and all—get a good score—but that's never been a problem for you." Philip patted Jane on the back with a hearty thump, then left, the smell of pipe smoke trailing behind him.

She'd wanted to make him proud. She'd wanted adventure. She'd thought she would get both. Now, in the nursing home, Jane pulled her thin blanket up to her chin, apologized silently to her daddy as she had for seven decades, and tried to sleep.

CASSIDY

CASSIDY'S PHONE BUZZED from between her boobs where it had nestled while she slept. She squeezed her eyes shut to clear her vision, then laughed. Though she usually fell asleep with her phone, most mornings she found it at the foot of her bed or on the floor. She was still tired from camming the night before, but the memory of how much money she'd made eased her grogginess. She'd brought in close to five hundred dollars, even after the site took its 45 percent cut. She tried not to think about how much they claimed—about how sex work, an industry consumed largely by men and produced largely by women, was stigmatized and financially punished.

As she opened her still-blurry eyes, her bedroom appeared around her and she took in the pile of dirty lingerie at the foot of the bed, the white plastic trash can full of Del Taco wrappers, and the assortment of empty cups arranged on the nightstand—a tumbler from Target whose lip had melted in the dishwasher, a mug with *slut* emblazoned on its side in pink script, and several short glasses made foggy by hard water. The mess distracted Cassidy from the strangeness of the early-morning call and she answered before she could think herself out of it.

"What, Mom?" Cassidy answered. She swung her feet to the floor and stood, walking out to the living room, where her LCD side lights still stood on their tripods on either side of her desk chair, their legs like still cyborg giraffes.

"Cassidy!" Her mom's voice was high-pitched.

"What?" Cassidy was almost amused. Was she laughing? Was she drunk?

"Cassidy!" Paloma choked again, and Cassidy realized with a start that she was not laughing—she was sobbing.

"What is it, Mom?"

"Cassidy, he hit a deer. Honey, he swerved." Paloma's voice rose to a long, steady *aaaaahhhhh* that seemed to stretch on and on.

Cassidy's mind reeled as she tried to make sense of what Paloma was saying. She couldn't piece it together. Her mom had said "he." Not Grandma Jane. Grandma Jane was okay.

"Who hit a deer, Mom?" she asked, trying to calm her mother down enough to explain.

"Your father, Cassidy. He hit a deer. He's gone." She made the awful sound again—a combination of a cry and a yell.

"No," Cassidy said firmly, insistent on stopping the noise. Still standing, unmoving, legs apart in the middle of the living room, she shook her head again and said, "No."

It was impossible. He couldn't have swerved. She remembered his voice as he sat in the passenger seat, teaching her to drive. Cassidy, sixteen, had clutched the steering wheel tightly, giving the car the smallest bit of gas and then immediately pressing the break. She'd released the pedal a little at a time to inch forward. "You're going to have to be a bit bolder, sweet pea," Ken had said. "Defensive driving is good, but you've still got to have balls."

"Dad, that's such a sexist thing to say," Cassidy had complained, though she was entertained.

"Then have some ovaries. Don't be afraid of the gas. The brake is there. It's like with deer. You can't swerve. It's better to hit it head-on." He'd paused. "Well." He'd laughed. "It's not better for the deer."

He wouldn't have swerved.

Her mother's awful sounds pulled Cassidy back to the dark room. Paloma seemed to be trying to get herself under control. She was panting now, a sad moan escaping with each breath out.

"I'm coming home, Mom," Cassidy said. She had the miles from Manny. She could avoid everyone else and hunker down at home. At home she could prove he wouldn't have swerved. She could stop him. She shook her head, understanding that these were not logical thoughts, but her logic would not overpower the sense that they were true.

Cassidy hung up on Paloma, who was still moaning, then strode to the couch. There was so much to do. She needed a plane, a car. She'd have to tell her guys she'd be away for a while and ask Noeli to check in on her place and . . . She knew this was self-distraction—a way to keep the reality of what her mom had just told her from infiltrating her brain—but she carried on. There were things to be done.

Cassidy looked around the room. The light was just appearing between the cheap vertical blinds, illuminating her desk and laptop and the crumbs on the carpet. Cassidy stared until it all blurred into hazy lines. What was she doing? She tried to remember. What did she need to do?

Eventually, somehow, she managed to navigate to the American Airlines website. Somehow she found the customer service line and somehow her fingers called the number.

The last phone call she'd received was her mother telling her that her father had died. She considered this with a scientific distance.

Somehow, when a chirpy customer service representative answered her call, Cassidy managed to say evenly that her father had recently passed away and that she needed information about bereavement fares.

Somehow, when the agent offered their sincerest apologies on the loss of her father, Cassidy managed to say "Thank you" in a low, serious voice that sounded like it came from someone who *actually* had just lost her father.

And somehow, when the agent also apologized that the airline no longer offered bereavement fares because their online deals were already so deeply discounted, Cassidy managed to thank her sincerely and hang up without cursing.

Cassidy stared at the mobile version of the website, its primary colors and blocky graphics blurring and twisting. "My father died. My father died recently." She'd heard herself saying the words to the agent. Her voice had sounded so far away. "My father died. My . . . daddy died." She sat, staring at the screen, hearing the sounds of her breath moving in and out of her mouth, unable to move, even to blink her eyes.

Finally she managed to call Noeli.

"Are you seriously calling me right now? Like an actual real-life voice phone call?"

"My dad died," Cassidy said, her voice distant and dreamy, something detached from herself.

Noeli's first response was a small chuckle, as if Cassidy had told a joke, but she quickly corrected, her voice twisting in horror. "Oh my God. What?"

"He hit a deer. He swerved."

"Oh my God. Are you okay? Stay right there. I'll be there in ten minutes." The line went dead.

Minutes later Cassidy heard the Accord screech into the parking lot. She looked out the window and saw Noeli exiting her car, her curls flat from sleep, her mouth strange and ghostly without her usual red lipstick. Around her, in the predawn quiet, men in suits got into luxury sedans. The haze obscuring the mountains was thicker than it appeared in the afternoon, and if Cassidy hadn't known better, she could have mistaken the smog for low-lying clouds. Noeli sprinted up the stairs and Cassidy opened the door to let her in. A gray cat on the neighbor's stoop mewed.

"I'm so sorry, mija," Noeli said, wrapping her arms around Cassidy. Cassidy could feel the hard angles of her friend's collarbone through her soft skin, how small and fragile she really was. Cassidy curled against her.

Noeli let go and took a step back, looking at Cassidy's face. "Let's get you home."

"I have miles for American."

"Enough for both of us?"

"I don't think so. You don't have to come."

Noeli looked at Cassidy like she was stupid. "Of course I'm coming."

"It will be expensive."

"It doesn't matter."

Cassidy sank to the ground, unable to remain standing, and hugged her knees to her chest. Noeli squatted beside her and placed a small hand on her back. "You logged in?"

Cassidy nodded and Noeli took the phone gently from her hands. "Pittsburgh, right?" Cassidy nodded again and Noeli frowned at the screen, typed, and clicked for several moments and then looked up. "Okay. LAX to Pittsburgh this afternoon."

Cassidy was awed by her competence, her ability to function in a universe like this. She didn't feel like she could move.

Noeli stood and kissed Cassidy affectionately on the top of her head. "I'll pack you a bag." She handed the phone back to Cassidy and disappeared into her bedroom.

Cassidy couldn't bring herself to look at the phone, to face a world where she would have to tell people about this or talk to people who knew. She breathed a tiny molecule of relief. She hadn't thought about what she would post on social media. Instead her instinct was to delete it all, to hide. She took a breath, almost called instructions to Noeli about what to bring, then stopped herself. Logistics, words, preferences about shirts or underwear—they all felt so small beside the specter of life and death, she couldn't move her mouth to make the sounds. She would have to bring her laptop. If she went too long without doing a show, she wouldn't be able to make rent. But how could she ever do a show now? Like this?

Noeli returned ten minutes later with a nylon duffel bag and Cassidy listened to the sound of the material rubbing against her friend's leg, thinking about high school gym class, about hiding with Simon in the giant rolls of wrestling mats to avoid running laps. Gym class was during some of the only years she'd had with her dad—that she would ever have with him.

Her phone vibrated with messages from MannyBoy27.

You ok?
Hope you got your beauty sleep.
Let me know if you need anything.
I miss your beautiful smile.

Cassidy watched them appear one after the other but did not unlock the phone, instead waiting, motionless, for Noeli to come back and tell her what to do to be a person in this world.

PALOMA

HE COULDN'T BE gone. It was a cliché, Paloma knew, but still, Ken's absence felt impossible. His handiwork filled the entire house, his presence too tangible for mere memory. He had shaped her entire life—its every contour and setting, and now she was here, in the world he'd made, without him. She could not stop thinking about the day they'd met.

She'd been standing at the edge of the Charles Bridge, wishing she had a drink. It was so beautiful that she'd wanted, as she often did when looking down the long stretch of cobblestones that spanned the Vltava River, to take it in fully, to experience it with the intensity with which one experiences the past. As she stood, she'd considered the sweet company of nostalgia, how she much preferred it to the hazy half-real way she bumbled through the present. Paloma loved the blue-green tint that nostalgia lent the experiences of her life—the swell in her heart that accompanied reminiscence, her life's seasons pared down and imbued with heightened significance.

She would walk the bridge and appreciate the walk as she lived it. *You are here now,* she told herself as she took a single step. However aware she was, though, she could not call up the same aching wistfulness that nostalgia brought. The present was simply the present, unimpressive until it had passed, no matter how appreciative Paloma tried to be.

There were two exceptions. One was when Paloma drank. She didn't drink to escape, nor to forget. She drank to experience the moment she was living with the same sweetness with which she would remember it. The other exception was endings. At graduations and farewell parties, Paloma could call the sensations of nostalgia for the present to her body quite easily. What was the point, though, in recognizing the loveliness of an era just as it ended?

She wanted instead for her whole life to feel this way—significant, marvelous, full of meaning and connection, but stripped of the knowledge of imminent dissolution. She wanted for her life an endless carnival of substance and sentiment.

Paloma took another step, watching the stones as she walked. She could smell the earthy freshness of the river below. When she'd first arrived in Prague, the activity on the bridge had been organic and spontaneous. People laid out blankets, made pencil sketches, and put on odd little performances. Soon after, it had grown crowded and predictable.

On that day, two meters ahead of Paloma, a man stood behind a table, a huge crowd gathered around. "Step right up and see for yourself!" he called in heavily accented English. "The incredible, the one and only, the Veg! O! Matic!" The crowd oohed as he produced the gadget and proceeded to demonstrate its abilities. Paloma approached, hovering at the edge of the group to observe. While most of the onlookers' faces were awash with astonishment, several, she saw, were distressed. One man looked particularly ghostly—stricken. As Paloma drew closer, she heard him muttering to himself in Czech. She still had to translate the language in her head to grasp its meaning; she'd not yet started thinking in its chewy syllables.

"This is all. No destruction," he said. "They told us forty years, America would destroy. This is it. This is the West. A Veg-O-Matic." The product name, which he said in English, sounded vulgar beside the palatal consonants of his native tongue.

The man was right—something had been destroyed. Paloma could see the loss all around her. It had been a liberation, of course, but the inhabitants of Prague were grieving, too. All they had been told to fear for four decades had come to fruition, and they were learning that the years of scarcity, of hunger and strict adherence to the party's rules, had all been a game of make-believe. It had all been in vain.

Paloma wandered away from the crowd and floated farther down the bridge, her long skirt brushing the cobblestones. Away from the obscene capitalist demonstration, she regained her yearning to capture the ephemeral beauty of the place, and she was pleasantly surprised to find she was able to. The demonstration had done it, she understood with twin stabs of gratitude and alarm. This was an ending after all. She had come with the first wave of English teachers, before the country had held its first elections, when one could still run into a drunken Václav Havel stumbling out of the Golden Tiger. Now the feeling of freshness—the newness of freedom she had felt so acutely when she'd arrived in the city, was fading.

Paloma was thinking these thoughts when she saw him, directly under the statue of Saint Anne, with the holy infant balanced on her hip. A live pigeon rested on the Christ child's tiny stone finger, purring its commentary on the scene.

The position of the pigeon, directly over the man on the bridge, looked precarious. Pigeons, unlike Pražáks, were unconcerned with privacy. Paloma moved closer to see what this stranger was selling and to warn him. She approached his open suitcase. Inside were tiny gold charms—hybrid animals—a giraffe with a lion's head atop its long neck, a fish with the outstretched wings of an eagle.

"You should move this," she said in Czech. "If you want to keep it clean."

The man smiled. "Promiňte," he apologized. "English."

"Ah. I was saying you should watch out for the pigeon." Paloma pointed toward the bird.

"We have an agreement," the man said, winking. "Where are you from?"

"Long Island. You?"

"West Virginia."

"Wow. All the way to Praha," Paloma said, thinking that this fellow American may be as bewildered by the bustle of Prague as its native inhabitants, given his roots. He, too, might be overwhelmed by a choice of markets and sneakers. How diverse her own country was.

"These are pretty," she said, fingering a bird with the head of a cat.

"You can have that one," he said, and ran his fingers through a halo of fluffy blond hair. "If you'll go out with me."

He was older than Paloma, but he had a boyish charm, a stubborn immaturity. His thin plaid button-down was open at the top, revealing a mess of curls on his chest, slightly darker than those on his head.

"Did you come to Prague for the prostitutes?" Paloma asked. "Gifts don't usually come with conditions."

He grinned an openmouthed grin that revealed a golden molar, shook his head, and looked over his shoulder at the green Vltava. "Mostly for the beer," he said, turning back to Paloma and looking up at her coyly through his thick eyelashes.

"How much?" Paloma asked.

"Take it. No strings attached. Here's a chain." He used a small pair of jewelry pliers to open the charm's jump ring and attach it to a link.

"Thank you." Paloma clasped her fingers around the piece and felt the cool metal in her palm. "Ahoj."

She started to walk toward the fakulty, where her English lesson was due to begin in an hour. She had gone only a few steps when she paused and turned back to the man. "I was thinking of going out tonight. Do you want to come?"

He grinned devilishly. "Where?" he asked. "And when?"

"I hadn't made plans."

"Come to Beef Stew," he said. "In the basement of Radost. People read poetry."

"What time?"

"Nine? Ten?" He waved his hand as if time were inconsequential.

"Okay. Ahoj," she said again, and walked—past a caricature artist and past a man selling patches, key chains, and other trinkets bearing the logo of the Soviet Army.

A bit farther down, close to the bank, a man with a trumpet and a woman with an accordion played polka. The man lowered the trumpet from his lips and sang, "Hey!" The woman wore new Levi's, no longer a political symbol or a sign of youth and freedom. She set her accordion on the bridge and began to skip in a tight circle, her Texas trousers jumping, kicking, and spinning as if by themselves.

What had drawn her to Ken that day? She hadn't found him particularly attractive, and his presence, like that of most of the newer American arrivals, was presumptuous and intrusive. His gold charms were sweet, yes, but there was no shortage of creative art in Prague. She'd needed some fun, that was all—a way to relax. It hadn't been about him.

She arrived that evening at half past nine. The club was an unassuming building from the outside, a black matte facade with its name, RADOST FX, painted above the door in red block letters. Though Paloma had grown used to Prague's eclectic collection of buildings from across the centuries, she still smiled to see a Western-style dance club in such close proximity to a Soviet grocery, a row of prefabricated concrete paneláky, and a church with neo-Gothic towers.

"You're here!" Ken had appeared as if from nowhere, taking her hand and leading her inside, through the dance floor and past the café. "There's good food here. Like, real food!" he shouted. "You can get a salad."

She followed him to a black dungeon-like door, which opened to a stairwell down to the basement.

Paloma could still hear the muffled throbbing pulse from the dance floor as they descended. By the bottom, it was reduced to a low hum. Opening another heavy door, they emerged in a new dark world.

A reading group of twenty or so people consciously ignored Paloma and Ken's arrival instead paying exquisite attention to a waifish woman on a wooden stool reading from a piece of notebook paper. Some sat cross-legged on the floor, others lounged in plush chairs upholstered with zebra or dalmatian prints. Each hand held a beer and each head nodded along with the woman's poetry. Two years earlier, people meeting underground would have been talking about resistance, Paloma thought, then realized that two years earlier, an underground poetry reading would have been an act of resistance.

They found seats on a blue velour sofa, and a man in a turtleneck took the woman's place on the stool. "How long have you been in Prague?" Paloma asked Ken as the next poem began.

"Six weeks. You're an old hat here, I assume? Practically Czech by now?"

"Practically." Paloma liked how this man's easy smile created space to take herself less seriously.

"This is it, man," he said. "Prague is it. This is the place to be. I was in Key West, but I was over it. Tried Woodstock. Tried Colorado, but this is it. It's beautiful. People are hungry for it—for art, for music, for poetry."

Paloma nodded. "It is. And they are." He awakened something in her—an appreciation for the changes happening in the city. Through him, she could see the magic of it.

"Let's get out of here," Ken said, and she agreed.

It wasn't just endings that brought fullness and presence to experience, Paloma had thought as she followed him back up the dark stairwell. Beginnings worked too.

Now, Ken was dead. There would be no more beginnings for him. He was gone, however impossible that felt, and Paloma was filled with nostalgia not only for their days together, but for the moments after, however imperfect.

In spite of herself, her aching for Ken swelled into an aching for Prague, and she could not help but imagine what beginnings might lie ahead for her.

She thought of cafés whose umbrellas donned red Marlboro logos and trams covered in wraparound ads for Camels. She thought of the woman who'd worked at the front desk of her kolej, of her long denim skirt and her white T-shirt with the words *David Hasselhoff!* scrawled in marker.

Paloma had felt Czechoslovakia in her blood—Prague in her plasma—and arriving had felt like a homecoming. She saw herself everywhere in the city—in the way people walked and in their reserved, proud nature, in the hairline of the sidewalk fixers in their blue overalls. Even carved faces on buildings seemed to reflect the slope of her own nose.

In Prague, she'd felt she could play a part in history. Everything there was significant, weighty, and unresolved in the best way possible.

She had not wished death on her husband. Of course she hadn't. But the possibilities she'd felt back then—the feeling that she might do something unknown and significant—suddenly lay again at her feet.

JANE

JANE COULDN'T SLEEP, of course. Instead she thought of the walk from Philip's truck to the Civil Service exam for junior clerks. Ding had chattered the whole way across Wesleyan's campus about the dresses she would buy with her first paycheck. Jane had stared out at the large college quad, which stood empty, save for two women reading side by side on a picnic blanket. As a child, Jane had pictured herself so clearly as a college girl that when Arzella had sat her down at fourteen to tell her they didn't have the money to send her, Jane had thought she was joking. Her parents had valued education, prided themselves on being learned, and besides, no one had money. If Jane had been able to skip the junior clerk exam and instead plop down right next to the girls with her own textbook, she would have skipped the FBI for college in a second.

What would her life have been like if she had gone to college instead of Washington? she wondered for the thousandth time. When Jane slipped finally into sleep, she dreamed, as she often did, that she was back in the exam room. In her dream, a voice warned her not to work so hard, not to perform so well, but as always, Jane was incapable of giving anything less than her all.

Which of the following would come second if arranged alphabetically for filing?
A. *albatross*
B. *actionable*
C. *assessment*
D. *allied*
E. *arrested*

Jane knew her alphabet, of course, but she second-guessed herself as she moved to mark her answer. Had it said *second*? Had she missed one of the words? She reread the question, trying not to focus on the minutes passing. The bright pink bloom of a rhododendron tapped on the window.

There are four typists at the Better Company Office. Working together, they can complete the office's typing duties in ten hours. If the manager wants to reduce their time to eight hours, how many additional typists must he hire?

The paper was rough under Jane's wrist as she scrawled her calculations. The pencil slipped between her sweaty fingers. Were the new typists as efficient as the others? One by one, girls stood and exited the exam room.

Finally, shaking, exhausted, and uncertain, she handed her completed exam to the proctor. A church bell rang. *If you're out there, God, a little luck would be lovely,* she thought.

"You should receive your results in the mail in the next few days," the proctor said. Jane thanked him and rushed out to the hall, where Ding had been waiting, back against the wall, blowing a pink bubble. The bubble popped and Jane woke with a start, forgetting where she was. "Ding?" she called, but it was an aide who rushed in.

"Are you all right? It was a hard day. I can sit with you if you'd like."

Jane looked around, registering the chair, the walker, the wheelchair, the air conditioner. She was here, at the old folks' home. The exam, Washington, it had all passed.

"Yes, yes, I'm fine," she said, and the aide smiled and left. Something weighed on her—something awful, she knew—but she could not recall what it was. It was the dream, she told herself, just a bad feeling that lingered from the dream.

PALOMA

PALOMA LAY IN bed alone, without Ken for the first time in two and a half decades. There had been many nights she'd felt alone in spite of the warm body beside her, but now the absence of that body felt tangible, an eerie presence against her bare skin. She'd felt alone their first night together, in his apartment in Žižkov, which would later become *their* apartment in Žižkov, furnished only with a futon on the floor and decorated with stacks of notebooks and rows of empty beer bottles. She hadn't been surprised he lived in the rough working-class district. All of the artists and writers who hoped to be the next Hemingway lived in these concrete boxes by the television tower.

In the metro station on the way there, Ken had hoisted himself onto the shining metal median between escalators. Leaning back, he'd slid, as Paloma watched in horror and the Czechs around them made a show of suppressing their disapproving looks, staring straight ahead or continuing their conversations.

Paloma had been mortified—he had given them away. He was unmistakably American, and so was she by association.

Paloma had seen Ken's face, ecstatic with joy, for only a moment before he disappeared from view. At the bottom a few moments later, Ken was waiting for her, shaking and giddy with adrenaline. When he embraced her, she felt his heart drumming against her ear, flooding her with excitement in spite of herself. As much as a tram rocking wildly through the city at night, this man felt palpably like the freedom she had hoped to find here. Prague was on the verge, and so was she.

The metro arrived a short minute later. Inside the tidy car, a steady buzz filled the air, just like the murmur all around the city—the sound of habitual cynicism, people occupied and then occupied again, meeting a cautious optimism. Paloma felt that same tension between her and Ken.

Ken's apartment building was incredibly close to the tower. The structure's protruding concrete rectangles bubbled out like a bizarre Soviet spaceship, separated from Ken's window by only a small strip of grass, a sidewalk with some benches, and the street.

"Víno or pivo?" Ken asked, motioning for Paloma to take a seat on the futon.

"So you have learned some Czech!" Paloma sat. "Víno prosim."

After a few long sips, the futon became more comfortable and Paloma set her glass on the floor beside it, stretching out as she looked at the bare concrete walls. Ken lay beside her and, still holding his beer, put a hand on her stomach. Paloma left it there. He sat up then, and Paloma followed, allowing him to pull the shirt over her head and cup her breasts in his hands. He seemed to be observing them more artistically than sexually. Paloma kissed him, more comfortable as an object of desire than an object of aesthetic admiration.

They traveled that night through the air—still haunted by the ghosts of revolution, and backward through occupation, victory, occupation, and war, history turning on and on around them in repeating spirals. Somehow, even through all the tender intimacy, their journey felt solitary. They covered distances through the entangled movements of their bodies, but they did not meet. Paloma, though her body was satisfied, was left feeling sentimentality for something she had not quite experienced. She could not escape her own head, could not see Ken fully, and certainly could not show herself to him. She ached for a wholeness she was not sure existed.

Paloma fell asleep to the pulse of wine and blood in her head and her genitals. She woke before Ken, who remained snoring, one hand over his head, fingers folded down. She rose and tiptoed into the kitchen, which she could see in the morning light was sticky with beer and dust. The sun shone in the window, yellowing the walls and floor, and looking out, Paloma saw the highest pillar of the radio tower extending toward the sky like a middle finger. The optimism of the night before felt dulled and naive in the gritty reality of dirty linoleum, and Paloma could not imagine she would return to this filthy apartment. Still, she thought, it would be nice to have something to remember the starry-eyed dreaminess of it all, the way it had opened something in her. She wanted a talisman.

She found Ken's suitcase of charms leaning against the wall by the apartment door. She opened it and fingered his creations, impressed again by his craftsmanship. But she was not a thief, and besides, he had already given her a piece of jewelry. She looked around for something he wouldn't miss.

She opened a closet door and found a stack of books by naturalists and back-to-the-landers. Certainly, he would notice if any of these went missing.

She walked back to the kitchen, where she leafed through a notebook that sat on the counter between greasy crumpled paper and the remnants of late-night fried cheese purchases, but she couldn't find anything written clearly enough to read.

The shape of the scrawling was poem-like, but the letters were illegible.

Ken grunted from the other room and Paloma looked at him through the doorway. He rolled over onto his stomach, belched, and went back to sleep.

A letter, in an envelope addressed but not yet sealed, fell from between the pages of the notebook, and Paloma bent to rescue it from the grime below. With another glance at the dozing Ken, she removed it and unfolded the paper.

Dear Mom, it read, in handwriting much neater than what he'd used for his poetry. *Hope all is well on the farm. Prague is wonderful, everything I wanted, but I miss our mountains. Making lots of great friends and working hard on my poetry. Jewelry biz is tough. Not making as much as I'd hoped. If you can manage another loan, I'd appreciate it. Sending you one of my charms.*

Paloma tucked the letter back into the envelope and got dressed, further convinced this had been a one-night encounter. She had met so many people here who were wise beyond their years. Idealistic or not, she had no need for a grown man who wrote home to his mother for an allowance.

She had just reached the apartment's door when Ken rolled onto his side and then sat up.

"Are you leaving?" he asked.

"I've got to get to work."

"Thanks, Paloma. Thanks for sharing your beauty."

Paloma blushed and said goodbye, then made her way down the dusty staircase and out to the street. As she hurried toward the metro station, it began to drizzle, and she let the rain wash away the night as the petrichor filled her nostrils. She didn't need Ken's kind of optimism. She needed this.

Paloma thought about things she liked: the scent of new rain on dusty streets, the parts of Prague still unoccupied by its most recent, opportunistically optimistic invaders—the Prague that was sweet and musty in its sad beauty.

Now, in bed alone at the farm, she thought of what she'd liked about Ken: his ever-buoyant idealism, the sense that emanated from his body of work to be done—that doing that work, if he ever managed to *do* it, would create the world she'd been waiting for. Ken had been sure he knew Paloma, and though she had never opened her heart fully to him, she now missed his confidence, however misguided. At least with Ken she could pretend to be knowable and known.

Paloma curled into a ball and held her legs, feeling a strange reversal of their first night together. Whereas then, they'd been completely naked and vulnerable, their bodies close and their minds far apart, here, with Paloma in the fetal position and Ken no longer present in the physical plane, Paloma felt an intimacy with him she had only glimpsed at brief moments during his life. They had shared so much in spite of their emotional distance.

"It's all right, it's all right," Paloma repeated to herself as if soothing a child, not sure to whom she spoke.

CASSIDY

CASSIDY LET NOELI guide her to their rideshare, into the airport terminal, and to the kiosk where she checked them in. Occasionally Cassidy nodded in agreement or understanding, but mostly, she stayed still and silent, relieved to be freed of the burden of thinking.

She followed Noeli through security and counted the number of people ahead of them in line—twenty-four people with baseball caps and camera bags, saris and suits. She followed her to the gate and counted the number of seats—eighty-five. There were three cups on the rim of the trash can, two from Starbucks and one that still had boba in the bottom. The newsstand across the hall featured twelve magazines out front, celebrities and brides smiling from their covers.

She followed Noeli onto the plane. They took twenty-one steps to their seats, past a teenager in pajamas and an old woman muttering the rosary.

Cassidy found herself deeply, sincerely interested in these numbers and facts. There were thirty-four drinks on the tray on the flight home after her dad died, about half of them coffee. She was gathering data. It was cold, scientific research.

In Pittsburgh, finally, Cassidy's brain now numb from sheer exhaustion, Noeli retrieved their luggage from the rotating metal carousel and, stumbling under the weight of twin duffels, led them to the car rental desk, where a family of four was ahead of them, twin boys hanging off of their mother's legs while their father signed paperwork. Cassidy saw she had several messages from MannyBoy27 and a couple other guys on the site, but she couldn't fathom responding.

"I truly am sorry, sweetheart," the man at the desk said to Cassidy once the family had gotten their keys, and it took a moment to register that he was speaking to her. His accent clicked in her ears like a familiar command to a well-trained dog, and yet she couldn't help but hear the sounds from Noeli's perspective. "Ah troolee aym sahr-eh." She repeated the sounds in her head until they lost their meaning. *Ah troolee aym sahr-eh. Aah troooolee aim.* It was close to a minute before she realized both the man and her friend were staring at her, waiting for her to reply. Noeli shifted her weight from foot to foot and finally set the bags on the floor.

"Thank you," Cassidy said.

The car was quiet in a way that made it feel like they were underwater. Noeli turned the radio all the way down and neither she nor Cassidy spoke. They were high above the road in the massive full-sized SUV, and Cassidy could feel them hurtling ahead. The heater kept the car at a cozy seventy-six degrees, making it easy to forget the forty-eight-degree temperature outside. The trees gave it away—their branches were thin and spindly, the leaves already gone. Though signs warned that "Bridge Ices Before Road," the pavement was dark and dry. Cassidy struggled to remove her hoodie from under her seat belt and was struck by a sudden, intense wave of fear.

"D-don't," she stammered, and Noeli glanced at her in alarm. "If you see a deer, don't swerve," she added breathlessly.

"They jump out sometimes. Especially now, around hunting season. Just brake. Don't swerve."

"Okay." Noeli held the steering wheel competently, but Cassidy saw her adjust her grip, wriggle her shoulders to get comfortable again. She looked so small and out of place in this huge vehicle, surrounded not by the endless freeway, but by mountains, dark and close as a sweater. Cassidy watched the glowing mile markers zip by, one after another. She couldn't undo it. She couldn't turn back. It was already done. It had already happened.

Cassidy focused on her breathing, concentrating on the air going into her nostrils. It didn't seem to be reaching her lungs. Was there something wrong? Was she breathing wrong? She tried to slow her breaths, to bring a sense of fullness to her chest. The air seemed to go out the back of her throat. Outside, the trees whipped past. Cassidy's fingers began to tingle, then her hands and arms. She clenched her hands and flexed them, but the tingling remained. She was having a panic attack. She didn't want to have a panic attack. She didn't want her body to feel like this. She didn't want to do this.

A sign towered above the road like a specter: "Wild and Wonderful." Cassidy stared as they approached, lifting her head to watch as they passed under. *"Welcome to West Virginia,"* Noeli's phone announced. Cassidy was happy they had changed it back from "West Virginia: Open for Business," but her happiness felt distant, like she was witnessing it on someone else's face.

"Thank you, pocket robot," Noeli said jovially.

The hills changed immediately after passing the sign and the familiar surroundings comforted her for a moment before appearing to close in further. She was here. They were drawing closer to it all—to people who knew her, to the absence of her father. Her breath only reached her nose now. She felt dizzy and restless. She thought she might scream.

"Can we stop?"

"Right now? Are you okay?"

"I think I'm having a panic attack."

Saying the words aloud brought her anxiety to full force. She pant-cried with each breath, every part of her body buzzing with oxygen.

"Oh shit. Take a deep breath," Noeli said.

"I am," Cassidy tried. "I'm trying. I don't think I'm breathing right."

"Okay. It's okay. I'm right here."

"Please stop," Cassidy said. "Stop the car." She felt trapped—headlights approached behind them, slowing for a moment before moving to the left to pass. The ragged shoulder dropped sharply to the right before climbing again to a dark wooded hill.

"I can't stop right now, Cass. I don't think it's safe."

"Okay," Cassidy said. She could do this. She could choose not to panic. It was all in her head. A deeper part of her had already chosen *to* panic, though. Panicking would get her out of this car, off of this road. Panicking would keep her safe.

A green sign showed the mileage to different Morgantown exits; the closest, WV University, was two and a quarter miles away.

"Are you all right till Morgantown?" Noeli asked. Cassidy nodded and focused on the odometer.

Two miles. Her ears throbbed and she closed her eyes. It was worse, feeling the hills rushing past, unable to see potential danger. She put a hand to her heart to feel it racing. *One mile.* She scanned the hills for glowing eyes.

Had her daddy seen them? An image of her father in his Malibu appeared in her mind's eye. She heard him humming—Bob Dylan, maybe Steve Miller. What had he been listening to? Cassidy would want the people she loved to know exactly what she was listening to. She saw him reach toward the radio. She saw him look up to see a deer. She felt his surprise. She saw him swerve.

What part of the car hit the deer? What part of the car killed him? Did the hood crumple? Did the car roll? Cassidy saw the metal crush, moving into the space where Ken's body was supposed to be. She imagined the look of fear on her father's face as his body was thrown and mangled. Did he know he would die? Was he afraid? How much pain did he feel?

In college she'd read a theory—time was relative, as we knew. The afterlife, it posited, was a person's last moment of consciousness experienced eternally. If her father's last moment was fear and agony, would he experience it for eternity?

She shook her head and gripped the door handle. No, no, no. Daddy was in the grass and the trees and in Cassidy, just like he had said. But a voice inside Cassidy told her these were just comforting platitudes. But still, she told herself. The body made DMT. That was a fact. Even if the accident was awful, maybe his very last moment was peaceful. She exhaled a full breath, finally, as they exited.

In Morgantown, WVU kids stalked the streets like zombies, the men in cargo shorts and baseball caps hollering drunkenly at the women who stumbled up the hills in their heels, miniskirts, and tank tops.

"I thought West Virginia was rural," Noeli said.

"This is one of the bigger cities," Cassidy explained. "This is where I went to college."

"Ah." Noeli pulled to the side of the road and Cassidy watched the debauchery, remembering her time there. She had thought maybe college would be different, that maybe she would make friends and, for once, not be the weird kid. But there had been all the same cliques at WVU and worse, here, Cassidy didn't even have Simon. These men were no worse than the ones who watched her show, who begged her for tit pics or to tell them in detail what she liked about their cocks. And yet, the tenderness she held for her fans was absent here. She glared at the college men with contempt.

Feeling was returning to her extremities, but her joints were stiff and sore, her brain wrung out. Noeli asked her phone to direct them to a hotel and when they arrived a few minutes later, Cassidy shuffled into the room, curled up under the plaid duvet, and fell almost immediately into a heavy dreamless sleep.

She woke to the sound of Noeli splashing water onto her curls and scrunching them over the sink.

The room was grungier in the light—the forest-green carpet worn from years of visiting university parents' pacing. The floral wallpaper peeled at the top edges and the scuffed faux-cherry furniture bore multiple cigarette burns.

Cassidy dressed quickly, shedding the previous day's travels with her warm slept-in jeans. The new, fresh clothes were a promise—a new start, she told herself. She could do this.

Noeli turned and smiled silently in affirmation, placed the room key on the nightstand, and walked out to the SUV, hugging her arms in her thin black hoodie as Cassidy followed behind.

The towns tumbled past—Fairmont, Bridgeport, Nutter Fort. A lone Target on top of a hill. A Huddle House, its sign proclaiming "Pipeliners Welcome." Huge wooden crosses watching them ominously. The skeletal remains of a burned-out barn.

Finally they approached Weston. "This is it—exit ninety-nine, but take it slow. It's a big loop." Noeli nodded and Cassidy's stomach dropped as they rounded the swooping ramp.

In Buckhannon, downtown felt new. A Taco Bell had sprouted, new murals seemed to have seeped from the old brick buildings, and the old firehouse, where Cassidy was used to seeing volunteer firemen polishing their shining truck, had changed into a Community Bank. A lane-widening project caused traffic that tested Cassidy's patience even after half a year in Southern California.

Driving through Buckhannon felt like strolling through her own mind, like the streets were part of her neurostucture. The unexpected changes felt like discovering secrets about herself. She had driven these streets innumerable times, had run down them as a child following the B-U Band during the Strawberry Festival parade, had walked them with Simon after school in the rain and snow. How was it possible they could change without her knowledge?

After a man in a pickup truck slowed and waved them along on a left-hand turn, things returned to their trusty stagnant selves. A right at the sagging red house and there was Grandma Jane's place—blue-gray, two-stories, over one hundred years old, on the left. Noeli parked the SUV, and they both leapt the two feet to the cracked sidewalk, then climbed two wooden steps, holding on to the black iron rail. Noeli stood behind Cassidy, hands in hoodie pockets, on the small square porch as she reached for the old mechanical doorbell. As she pressed it, the doorbell swung off of its screw and dangled from its left side. A rectangular button jangled a bell on the other side of the door.

There was no sound from within the house. After a beat, Cassidy took her own keys from the front side pocket of her duffel bag and found her grandma's, labeled *GJ* in fading Sharpie.

Unlocking the door and poking her head inside, Cassidy was met with the familiar smell of must and Avon face cream. "Grandma Jane?" she called. No answer. She stepped into the house, Noeli behind her. The brown brick linoleum creaked underfoot. Cassidy peeked up the stairs on the left, which were carpeted with matted orange shag and darkened by years of cat fur from a cat who had passed away half a decade before. On the right, the living room, piled on all sides with books, was otherwise empty.

"Grandma Jane?" she called again, and walked down the hall into the dining room. As usual, the round leafed table was too covered in books, newspapers, and catalogs for use, as were the glider, the floral couch, the coffee table, and the writing desk. In the kitchen, counters were packed with cans of soup and vegetables, piles of clean CorningWare plates, and linens hand-embroidered with mismatched colors and patterns.

Where was Grandma Jane? She rarely left the house, save for Women's Club and Hospital Auxiliary meetings, and this emptiness felt different from a temporary outing. It was colder, Cassidy realized. Grandma Jane always kept the house stifling hot—the old wall heater working tirelessly to maintain a comfortable eighty-something degrees, but now there was a chill. Someone had turned the heat down.

"Could you call your mom?" Noeli asked. Cassidy suddenly felt self-conscious about the smell of stale cat pee and the piles of junk in every corner.

She looked at her phone. "I seriously have no service."

"Me neither." Noeli shook her phone and held it above her head.

Cassidy laughed. "I can use the landline," she said, suddenly remembering that they existed. She walked to her grandmother's elegant gold-and-white rotary phone and lifted the handle. When she realized she couldn't remember her mom's number, she scrolled through her contacts list to find it, suppressing how disturbed this made her feel. Grandma Jane probably remembered it and she had dementia.

Paloma answered on the first ring. "Hello?" She had pulled herself together since the day before and now sounded like her usual no-bullshit self.

"Where's Grandma Jane? We're at her house."

"Oh, uh," Paloma stuttered, caught off guard. "She, um. She's staying somewhere else right now."

Cassidy crinkled her forehead. "Where is she staying?"

Paloma cleared her throat. "Well, hello to you, too, Cassidy. Your father and I agreed it would be best for your grandmother if she had more intensive care."

"What does that mean?"

"She's at Serenity Care Home."

"You weren't going to tell me this?"

"Well, we were," Paloma started. "But then all this with your father."

"All this?" Cassidy scoffed. Her mother was already talking about it like it was some inconvenience her dad had caused. She probably couldn't wait to get out of this town. She was probably glad this had happened.

"Cassidy, you know what I mean. We were going to tell you once everything was settled. I didn't think you would go to her house first. I thought you'd come here."

"Where is this place?" Cassidy asked brusquely, and her mom, when she responded, sounded hurt. Good. She should feel bad. She listened to her mother's directions and tried to imagine the route. Buckhannon's roads were so much a part of her psyche that though she didn't know all their names, she could imagine the drive perfectly. Rain began to patter against the rooftop.

"Okay, we'll be there after we see Grandma Jane." Cassidy placed the heavy receiver into its delicate holder.

Cassidy locked the door and walked back to the street with Noeli toward the huge SUV, both of them hunching their shoulders to minimize contact with the raindrops. Cassidy navigated and Noeli steered, moving her whole body with the steering wheel. Her friend was so out of place in this car and in this town, but it was no more out of place than Cassidy felt in her own life right now. "Past these streets. Yeah, over the bridge. I think it's around here."

Below them, the Buckhannon River clouded with the rain, morphing into the milky green of a mood ring. Serenity Care Home stood on the left, exactly where Cassidy had expected it, a wide green field stretching in all directions beyond the squat brick building. Outside an apartment complex in a low bank across the street, a woman with a gelled pixie cut and a Mountaineers shirt hung clothes on a line. Cassidy wondered if she realized it was raining. Beside the woman, a toddler tried unsuccessfully to pedal up the short, steep sidewalk.

Entering through the care home's glass doors, they found themselves in a small entryway, walled off from the main home by another set of glass doors. A sign warned visitors not to proceed if they were experiencing symptoms of cold or flu. On a table on the right were a box of surgical masks and a large bottle of hand sanitizer. The small anteroom smelled of Softsoap, and Cassidy was transported to the summer she turned fourteen, religiously cleaning her new belly button piercing. When her dad was still alive. He had hated her belly button ring. He had hated the idea of his daughter as an emerging sexual being. What would he have thought of her now? Cassidy suppressed a small stabbing sensation in her lower belly.

After rubbing sanitizer into their palms, Noeli and Cassidy entered the home, where the busy nurses failed to greet them.

Directly in front of them, a lobby filled with couches and recliners faced a brick fireplace adorned with a large collection of jack-o'-lanterns and a TV tuned to the Hallmark Channel. None of the women were her grandmother, not that Cassidy expected them to be. Grandma Jane had lived alone for thirty years and had unfavorable opinions about most residents of Buckhannon. Cassidy doubted she'd been socializing much. Cassidy signed her name in the guest notebook on the counter and waited for a moment to see if anyone would direct them. When no one acknowledged their presence, she began walking down a hallway to the left, glancing at the whiteboards outside each room. It was like a dorm, if you ignored the names that decorated each board—Ruetta, Betty Sue, Lorna. They arrived at the board marked *Jane*, and Cassidy knocked quietly.

"Mmm, come in," Jane's gentle voice called out.

Cassidy opened the door and stepped in, almost stumbling with the grief of it. On the left was a large industrial-looking bathroom, wheelchair accessible, smelling of bleach. A plastic three-drawered bin labeled *Jane* sat next to the sink containing her grandma's shampoos and face creams. A plastic shawl hung on the wall, and Cassidy's throat tightened as she realized this was for the employees to help her grandma wash.

Jane sat in a plush maroon chair by the window. On the wall next to her was a framed picture of Cassidy from her WVU graduation. The bed across from her was covered in a coordinating maroon quilt. It wasn't a real quilt, though—not something someone had made, but something store-bought—a print made to look like a quilt. Cassidy hated it.

Jane sat, quiet and staring. She had no music playing, no crossword puzzle in her lap, no book at her side. Cassidy whimpered as she ran to her.

As she approached, Cassidy realized that the chair was a lift chair, bulky with wires and a remote control. She could not get close to Jane, not in the way she wanted to, without crushing her small frame. She could only lean over her in an awkward half hug. Still, Jane took Cassidy's head in both hands and kissed her forehead.

"Oh, I love you, darling," the old woman said. "How are you?"

"I'm okay, Grandma Jane." Tears stung Cassidy's eyes.

"Don't cry, baby."

"Sorry." Cassidy wiped her tears and sniffed, then returned to standing.

"Don't apologize."

"Sorry." Cassidy sniffed again and laughed.

Jane laughed, too. "Oh, I love you," she repeated.

"How are *you*?" Cassidy asked. Had anyone even told her about her dad? Would she remember?

"I'm fine, baby." Jane lifted a hand from the mountain of blankets piled on her lap and held her long dainty fingers in the air, raising her index finger slightly in a gesture that meant she wanted Cassidy to take her hand. Cassidy sat on the arm of the lift chair and obliged. If Jane didn't remember, Cassidy didn't want to remind her.

Grandma Jane's hand felt cold in her own. Her skin was so thin—translucent like wax paper, that she could easily feel each bone beneath it, and when she examined their clasped hands, she could see the bones as well. As the thought struck her that her grandma's skeleton was *right there*, Cassidy loosened her grip and allowed Jane to gently stroke the back of her hand with a thumb, something she had done since Cassidy was a child. She would age like this. She would grow weak and wrinkled. How long could she stay attractive enough for people to care about her? Would the men who showered her with attention drop her all at once or would they fall away like leaves as she aged?

The metal heater under the window began to roar, filling the room. Who had decided to put her grandma's chair right by the heater? It would have been her mom, no doubt. Grandma Jane didn't belong here.

Noeli stood, small and awkward, in the doorway, until Grandma Jane noticed her.

"Who is this young woman?" Jane yelled over the heater.

"This is my friend, Noeli." Noeli stepped forward and took Jane's free hand.

"Hello, darling," Jane said, and Noeli smiled warmly.

"I actually need to use the restroom," she said, leaving Cassidy and Jane alone. Cassidy tried not to think about her utilizing the gray handled seat that balanced above the toilet.

"I would trade places with him in a heartbeat, Cassidy. In a second," Jane said. "I'm so sorry, sweetheart." Jane's milky blue eyes filled with tears and Cassidy had to turn away. Her chest constricted and once more she found it hard to take a good breath. She wouldn't cry. Jane's thumb, still rubbing the back of her hand, threatened to thwart her efforts, so she pulled her hand back, placing it under her leg on the chair.

"I remember when my daddy died," Jane said. "I don't know which is worse, baby. Fast like this, or slow like he went." Cassidy hadn't thought about this—that this was something Jane had experienced, too. The deaths in her life—her parents, her siblings, her husband, all seemed so long ago that it was easy to imagine Jane hadn't actually had to go *through* them.

Her grandma's life, Cassidy thought, had the glow of a forties movie combined with the charm of an old-time mountain string band. Her mom's held the romantic haziness of Bohemia. What was hers? This was the first real thing that had ever happened to her. Everything up to this point, even her sex life, had been pretend.

Jane went on. Her eyes drifted out the window as she spoke—she was somewhere else. On the sill sat three plastic figures with solar panels on their bases—a hula girl whose hips swayed side to side, a daisy whose leaves bounced up and down, and a black cat who popped in and out of a jack-o'-lantern. "Daddy's cancer sharpened knives in his belly. He was in so much pain." She shook her head. "Mama prayed and prayed and Daddy got frailer and frailer, whiter and whiter. It was the same damn time they came to cut the tops off our mountains. Daddy sold the mineral rights, not thinking anything would actually happen, and then as he's lying there dying, these men in big machines come and barely speak to us, digging and digging—every day another layer gone from the hill and Daddy weaker and weaker. It seemed then like they were doing it to him—digging right into his insides, wasting *him* away."

Cassidy leaned her head against the back of the chair.

"Those years were such a blur. I got married, then your dad was here, and then my daddy got sick. We would sing and pray to drown out the noise. Even your dad sang the old hymns." Jane laughed. "They didn't even use that mine. Tore up our hill and left. We had a day of quiet and then Daddy asked Mama to stop singing." Jane sighed and closed her eyes. "She stopped and he was gone."

Cassidy was quiet. She looked at the paper calendar of events on the bookshelf next to them. Saturdays were "Ladies' Nail Painting," Sundays were Bible study, Wednesdays were bingo. After a whole, full life, how did someone end up here?

Jane spoke again and Cassidy returned her gaze to her hands. "You know Grandma Arzella was religious—she even thought playing cards was a sin. But I never believed, really, till then. I still don't call myself a Christian. I don't know if it was God, Cassidy, but it was something. It was love."

Noeli returned, her Chuck Taylors squeaking on the tile floor.

"Not now, please. My granddaughter is visiting," Jane said, and waved her fingers at Noeli.

"Grandma, this is my friend," Cassidy said. Was she supposed to correct her? Had she embarrassed her?

"Oh, right! Cassidy's friend. Finally." Jane smiled warmly. Noeli smiled back politely.

"We have to go see Mom." Cassidy stood. She kissed Jane's head and her white hair was so thin, Cassidy could feel the shape of her grandmother's scalp on her lips. She smoothed her own hair. "I love you, Grandma Jane. We'll be back."

"I love you too, darling."

Cassidy left before her grandma's warbling voice could make her cry, Noeli following behind. In the lobby, a father-son duo sang "Praise the Mighty Name of Jesus" and strummed matching acoustic guitars.

In the sloping parking lot, Cassidy hoisted herself into the giant car. "You like that music?" Noeli asked as she pressed the button for the ignition and stuck her face right in the path of the heat, letting the vent blow her curls, which had grown frizzy.

"God, my grandma must hate it here." Cassidy shivered.

"Why?"

"She hates religious stuff. I'm sure she feels like she's surrounded by idiots."

"Isn't she religious?" Noeli released the emergency break and backed up slowly. The SUV was almost as big as the parking lot. "I heard that story she was telling you."

Cassidy sniff-laughed. "Yeah, that was weird coming from her. Like prayer can actually keep people alive."

"That wasn't the point of the—"

"There'd be a lot more people alive if that were the case." Cassidy smirked.

"It's not stupid to acknowledge it's pretty fucking weird that *anything* exists at all. Science explains what *does* exist and how it works. If the universe was some other way, science would have to figure out how to explain that."

"But science has already explained that some things *don't* exist." Cassidy looked at Noeli as she backtracked toward the river. Was her smart, radical friend really arguing for the power of prayer? "For example, I'm fairly certain magical thinking has been disproven." They approached the bridge.

"You can't prove a negative," Noeli said matter-of-factly. "You know how I feel about all the crazy Catholic shit I grew up with, but the universe is still pretty mind-boggling. And my grandma has told me some wild stories about brujería her mom did. I thought your grandma's story was cool."

In the face of mortality, Cassidy's dad had resorted to Buddhism, her grandma thought prayer could keep people alive, and even Noeli was superstitious. Cassidy pinched her thigh through her jeans, wondering at how the world around her had turned absurd overnight. The river, still splattering with raindrops, was now a muddy brown.

JANE

JANE AWOKE TO a train whistle and bolted upright. She had to catch the train. She was supposed to be in the Capitol in time for dinner.

Stumbling in the darkness, she made her way to the dresser and began throwing clothes on the floor, searching for stockings.

"Jane?"

"I'm almost ready."

"Ready for what?"

"The train." Light filled the room, disorienting her. The maroon armchair, the walker, the wheelchair. This wasn't her room in the farmhouse.

"Jane, you were dreaming. There's no train to catch, honey."

The present rushed back, and Jane sat on the bed, embarrassed. "Oh, I . . ."

"It's all right. Try to get some sleep. You need anything?"

"No, no." Jane shook her head, trying to shake the confusion from her mind. The aide turned off the light. That morning in 1944 felt so real—more real than the scene around her.

She had hugged her parents, the engine steaming and huffing behind her, more massive than she had imagined. The colossal machine had seemed to Jane evidence of mankind's dominance over the natural world.

When John Henry was a little baby, she had hummed to herself, thinking of the tall tale—the man as large as an ox who challenged a steam engine and fell dead on his face. That was another example of what West Virginia would do to a person. But not Jane. She was boarding this train, and she was leaving.

Philip and Arzella, stoic as always, stood before their daughter, the train's metal reflecting cold and gray on their pale faces. Arzella's voice betrayed only the smallest of quavers as she spoke. "You be good now."

"Always," Jane assured her, hugging her mother again.

"Come on!" Ding called.

They boarded, shuffling to their seats.

"It's awful silly, isn't it?" Ding asked once they were settled. "That we didn't take the *Washingtonian* from Martinsburg. We've gone west to go east. It's just wacky, is all."

"I suppose it's a bit queer."

"You know what else is queer?" Ding asked.

"Mmm?"

"That you're going to work for the FBI, and I'm going to be stuck pushing a typewriter for the notification bureau."

"Ding, you failed your exam. You should be counting your lucky stars you've got an assignment at all."

"Well, you know what they say—if you can tell a typewriter from a tractor, they'll take you in Washington." She said it without a trace of embarrassment. It was why she'd be great for the notification department, Jane thought. Only Ding could manage to shrug at being sent off to type condolence letters.

"You want my theory?" Ding asked, opening her train case and reapplying her lipstick. She didn't wait for Jane to answer. "The proctor told the Civil Service Commission how pleasant

I am. I'm sure the men in that department could use a morale boost."

"You know, I bet you're right." Jane smoothed her own hair. It had always been this way—she, the smart one, and Ding, the beauty.

They arrived in Parkersburg and transferred to the *West Virginian*, which was packed with federal workers on their way back to Washington. The girls squeezed in next to two men in dark suits and a woman knitting. Across the aisle, four more Government Girls giggled and gossiped.

"Mr. Smith went to the party all alone is what I heard."

"Better than with his secretary."

"He wouldn't have thought a thing of bringing his secretary if he didn't have anything to hide."

Jane listened, enthralled.

When they arrived, finally, at Union Station, Jane's stockings sticking to her legs from the heat, the passengers rose as a unified mass and pressed toward the exits. They jostled past Jane, who began to panic as her cousin was swept away with the crowd.

She let the wave of bodies carry her toward the door as she clutched her train case to her chest. Outside, the passengers split and dispersed, her car mates immediately lost in a swelling ocean of hats and curls. Jane spotted Ding waiting for her just ahead, waving frantically. When she got close enough to reach her cousin's hand, Ding grabbed it and led her to retrieve their luggage and then to the sidewalk, where they could have a better view of the monkey house that was Union Station.

Taxi drivers in their caps leaned out of windows, surveying the crowds—folks elbowing one another out of the way to get their attention. The drivers slowed, reaching back to open their doors, and people poured in, piling one on top of the other, five or six to a car.

Jane and Ding stayed close as they scurried to the median between the rows of cabs. Standing on her tiptoes, wondering what to do next, Jane could see through the station's large arch opening to the cyclopic dome of the Capitol Building. They were to meet their boarder, Mr. Plunkett, outside, though how they would find one another in this swarm, Jane had no clue.

As they lugged their bags out of the station and into the warm Washington evening, Jane breathed a sigh of relief. The crowd parted and through the briskly moving slacked and nyloned legs, she saw a green Nash Ambassador parked, and in front of it, a green-shirted man holding a sign that read "Jane and Christine."

The girls ran to the man. He was older than their parents, round as an egg, and stylish. His bow tie seemed to cover what small neck he possessed, and he had topped off his ensemble with an olive-green bowler, which he tipped as the girls approached.

"Jane? Christine?"

"That's right," Ding said. "Mr. Plunkett."

"That'll be me."

He opened the trunk and put their luggage inside, waving off would-be tagalongs as the girls climbed into the back seat.

"I would give you the tour, but you know how it is with gasoline," he apologized as they set off.

"Oh, that's more than all right, Mr. Plunkett. We so appreciate your taking us in," Ding said. Jane found herself still speechless from the shock of the station.

"Well, I could certainly use the company," Mr. Plunkett said. "It's my own way of helping with the war effort."

A short drive later, Mr. Plunkett parked the Ambassador in front of a row house, and the engine puttered to a stop. "Welcome to C Street."

They got out, Mr. Plunkett helped with the luggage, and the girls followed him up several steps to the front door. "Now, it isn't much, but I've done my best to make it comfortable for you," Mr. Plunkett said, setting the suitcases down on either side of his loafers and inserting the key. The door swung open, he gathered the bags, and they followed him in. "I hope you'll make yourselves at home."

Inside, it was clear that Mr. Plunkett's green clothes and car were not a simple coincidence. The kitchen was entirely green—from the cabinetry to the shelves to the window frames. The shamrock room was something out of the Sears catalog. Two chairs—green, of course—were tucked neatly around a table with the wings folded down. The place was immaculately decorated. Flowers perched perfectly in their vases. Pristine china glimmered in an elaborate hutch. Jane had not realized that rooms this modern actually existed in the world.

A small space between the kitchen and the living room was cordoned off with curtains. Mr. Plunkett led them by, motioning to the makeshift room. "This is where I'll sleep." Jane realized he was giving them his room.

Mr. Plunkett squeezed up the narrow stairway, and the girls followed close behind. He puffed and heaved as he climbed. At the top of the stairs he paused and caught his breath before a large bathroom.

Jane and Ding gawked at the enormous soaking tub. There would be no more hauling buckets of boiling water out to the washtub, no more running back to the house like wet rats. Jane nearly moaned as she pictured herself in it, submerged to her chin in hot water straight from the tap. She looked at Ding, whose eyes were as large as saucers, and knew her cousin was imagining the same.

"I'm sorry the room is so small," Mr. Plunkett said as he opened the door to the right of the bathroom. "But you won't have to worry about sharing it with any other girls. I'm not taking in any more boarders."

"Thank you, Mr. Plunkett. We know how lucky we are to find something so private for forty-five dollars," Ding said.

"Let me know if there's anything you need, girls," Mr. Plunkett said before leaving them. Jane heard him breathing heavily as he descended the stairs.

Ding jumped into the bed, shoes and all, crossing one leg over the other and examining her heels. She lay back, arms behind her hatted head, the picture of luxury. Jane laughed and noticed the lamp on the night table. *Electricity.* Of course there would be electricity here! Jane nearly cried with the realization that she could read herself to sleep without fear of setting the house on fire.

"Let's go explore!" Ding said, sitting up.

"We should unpack and get some rest." Jane could hardly wait to get into that tub.

"And the Nazis should all be dead already," Ding said, dragging her down the steps, from the row house, and out into the street.

"Where are we going?"

"Anywhere! That's the point!"

They walked and they walked. They walked so much that Jane rubbed blisters on both little toes. Pained pinkies or not, she was enamored. Washington was alive—as bubbling with life as its mighty Potomac. All over, people were going somewhere, doing something. There was nothing static in the city.

Girls everywhere, loads of them from all over the country, bustled and hustled down the streets and avenues. That first day, they met girls from Ohio, Oklahoma, North Carolina, and Missouri, even one from California—all here for Civil Service jobs. They moved around the city in pairs and packs, the click of their heels on the sidewalks running together to create one long drone—a buzzing undercurrent to the honking horns and shouting bureaucrats, an overpowering, distinctly feminine hum.

It was true, what they said, Jane thought, about there being eight girls for every guy. The fact had reassured Arzella when Philip had read it to her from the paper. What the fact didn't convey, though, was the electricity of that dynamic in a place where there were boys at all.

Oh, it was wonderful to see boys again. Servicemen swaggered down sidewalks, cocky but awkward, and though the women fought over their affection, it was still the men who fawned. They looked handsome, every one. Even the ones who Jane could tell weren't really handsome seemed to be, in their heroes' uniforms.

As Jane and Ding passed a pair of sailors, there was a sudden swell—Jane felt herself lifted in a tide of flirtatious giggling. Before she knew what was happening, she watched Ding kiss one of the men on the cheek. His face turned red, Ding skipped back to Jane, and they kept walking, the boys carrying on in the other direction.

Outside, the sun rose and the room filled again with light, illuminating that wretched blanket. "Do you need help dressing?" A woman stood in her doorway. "Eggs and bacon for breakfast today. You don't want to miss it."

"Oh, no, thank you," Jane said. She had forgotten. She didn't need to catch the train. She was already in Washington and would be late for her first day of work if she didn't hurry. She needed her lipstick. Ding was to go to the Office of the Chief of Naval Operations and she was to report to the Department of Justice Building on Pennsylvania Avenue.

"Have you seen my Revlon?"

"Lipstick for breakfast? Who are you courting, lady?"

Jane blinked. She was back in West Virginia. She was old. "No, never mind. No lipstick. No breakfast for me."

"Would you like it in your room?"

"Of course. That will be fine."

Jane shuffled to the chair and sat down. The chaos of that first day had been terrifying.

"Excuse me, I'm looking for Room 5517," she had asked a passing worker, but the girl pushed past her without acknowledgment.

"Could you help me find Room 5517?" she tried again, and again she was ignored.

A man brushed past in a dark suit and slick hair. "Excuse me, sir." He walked by with long strides. Jane dodged the other passersby and found a spot against the wall to collect herself, staring at the rush of legs.

"Are you new, too?" The question startled her, and Jane looked up to find a petite woman with neat brown curls before her, clutching her small pocketbook tightly with both hands. Jane nodded, and the girl extended her right hand. Jane took it. "Where are you going?"

"The chief clerk of the FBI." Jane wondered if this was allowed; her letter had noted that its contents were strictly confidential.

She was relieved when the girl said, "Me too." They shook hands. "I'm Mary Sintsink, from Washington state."

"Singsing?" Jane asked.

"Sintsink," Mary corrected cheerily. "But don't worry about it. That's what everyone thinks when they first hear it."

Though she looked mousy, Mary was confident, and Jane happily followed her to the fifth floor, where they found a line of thirty other girls—the new recruits of the day.

Mary Sintsink took her turn in the office first and Jane listened to her report as she waited to be called in. "We don't stay here," Mary told her. "It's just for your oath of office. They'll give you an assignment afterward."

"What's yours?" Jane asked.

"Can't say." Mary winked. "It's a job of the hush-hush sort."

The clerk was a bored woman who barely looked at Jane as she administered her oath. "Identification Division," she said. "Armory, third floor."

"How am I to get there?" Jane asked.

"Promptly," the woman said, sending her on her way.

She arrived at the Armory tired but proud of her proficiency with maps. A clerk on the third floor poked her head out of a doorway and greeted Jane. "First day?" she asked. Jane nodded. "We'll need your prints, dear." Jane followed her into the small office, where the woman took all four of the fingers of Jane's right hand, pressed them onto a black ink pad, and then rolled them onto a card. Holding Jane's thumb, she did the same, then repeated the process on the left. She had clearly done this hundreds of times.

What if her prints matched a criminal's? The thought was silly, she knew. Fingerprints were as unique as a signature, but still she could feel the sweat under her arms. The clerk placed the card into a metal handcart along with several others.

Jane was beginning to realize just how serious this all was. She had just been fingerprinted to work for the FBI—*the* FBI, who helped ensure only those with the country's interests at heart could work for its government. She, Jane Walls, might stop a spy. Or her mistake could cost the world its war.

History had always felt to Jane like fate. Looking back, it seemed obvious that each war had ended in its own particular way. Each decade seemed a chapter in a book, written purposefully with its own styles, its own peculiarities, and its own happenings. Jane thought of free will as an invention of the present. As she listened to the clerk now, Jane saw for the first time that this era, too, would soon be past. Her dress, her shoes, this war would all fit neatly into the chapter, concluded one way or another, of now.

The clerk did not seem to notice Jane's trembling. She led Jane down a long hallway and opened one of many identical doors. "Ms. Bruce. You have a new classification girl."

Ms. Bruce, nearly six feet tall, smiled a toothy grin and motioned for Jane to come in. "Come along, love," she said, and the clerk left. Jane followed Ms. Bruce into the room. Inside were thirty identical desks lined up in long rows from wall to wall. In the corner of each identical desk sat an identical green banker's lamp. Under each lamp was the bowed head of a girl that looked nearly identical in the yellow light to the head of the girl beside her. Several of the girls looked briefly up at Jane and smiled, though most stayed hunched over their work.

Ms. Bruce spoke to Jane softly. "This is the largest fingerprint clearinghouse in the world. Helping it to function effectively and efficiently requires the finest caliber of personnel available. Congratulations."

"Thank you, ma'am," Jane said. This was her war job, not being a homemaker.

Ms. Bruce handed Jane a small magnifying glass on a gold ball chain and directed her to her own brown desk with its own green lamp, where she was given her own stack of cards and a freshly sharpened pencil. It seemed wholly irresponsible that they trusted her so quickly. Jane lifted the magnifying glass and looked down at the card. The smudged ink took shape, forming intricate patterns. Ms. Bruce showed her how to classify them according to their arches, loops, and whorls, and soon Jane was cooking with gas. A girl came by periodically to collect the classified cards on her metal cart.

After half an hour, the lines on the prints started to blur. What at first looked like a loop whorled back around at the last moment. Jane seemed to be finding lots of arches, which she remembered Ms. Bruce had said were present in only 5 percent of the population. She began to second-guess each thing she wrote. The pressure seemed enormous. Jane squinted harder and traced the lines with her fingernail.

Though it was grueling, the absorbing work made the day pass quickly. Jane forgot everything else as her world narrowed to the little desk and the cards in front of her.

Jane's eyes were crossing by lunchtime, and she sat in the grass alone and unwrapped her jam sandwich from its grease paper. All around her the other girls gossiped. Someone was getting married. Someone had baked a cake for someone else. The afternoon was just as exhausting but just as distracting, and soon it was time to go home. On the walk back to C Street, she saw fingerprint patterns in the sidewalk, the bricks of buildings, the leaves of the red maples and pin oaks that lined the streets.

When Jane climbed the stairs at Mr. Plunkett's, ready to sink into the bed, she found her cousin already there, sobbing.

"Oh, Ding! What is it?" Jane sat beside her. "Is it awful writing all those letters home to wives and families? Oh, it must be just awful."

Jane's shoulders ached. Her neck ached. Her bottom was sore from sitting, and her feet throbbed from the walk. It was nothing, though, compared to what Ding must have been through.

"No." Ding sat up and rubbed her puffy eyes. "That isn't it. The Pentagon is miserably hot, and the construction is loud. But really, it's the WAVES."

"What about the WAVES?" Jane asked.

"I'm the only civilian girl at the office and they can't stand it. Well, you know what? I think they're the active crops. Free with their favors, is what I think. You should see the way they cozy up to the officers."

"You mean to tell me you wouldn't cozy up to an officer if you had the chance?"

"That's not the point, Jane. There isn't an officer in the place to cozy up to. The WAVES have taken them all." She wailed, collapsing again among the pillows. Jane felt for her magnifying glass in her pocketbook, clinking up against her tube of lipstick. She rolled its metal handle between her fingertips and sat with Ding, waiting for her sobbing to cease.

"Breakfast is served." The woman entered with a kind smile and set the plate on the tray of Jane's walker.

"Is Ding okay? She was crying."

"Is that your grandbaby's name?" the aide asked. "I'm so sorry. This is so hard. He's in a better place now, honey."

Oh yes. It was not Ding she had comforted earlier in the day. She was remembering ages ago. It was Cassidy, her granddaughter. Oh yes. Her granddaughter. Oh yes. Ken.

CASSIDY

ROUTE 20 TOWARD the farm wound through tree-covered hills that darkened the midday road and through bright open valleys that were corn-studded in the summer but now stood stark and empty. Noeli and Cassidy passed a shack with old tires piled up outside, then sped past Turkey Run Road. Cassidy had ridden her bike up Turkey Run as a kid—it looped the back way around to Shumaker Hill, but she'd never been on the roads branching off of it. She had classmates who lived off of them, but none of them had ever invited her over. These routes were so real, and yet the specifics of them so unimaginable that to Cassidy they felt almost mythical.

They passed an antique shop with a wagon wheel out front and then Mt. Lebanon Church, where her great-grandparents had been married, on the left. Then, they sailed down the hill. "Right at the green sign at the bottom. There." Cassidy pointed. The trees on either side bent above them in a protective, supplicating arc. "The first left. Here, this driveway."

The gravel crunched under the SUV's tires and Cassidy's stomach rose into her throat. Her father hadn't designed the winding narrow driveway for cars this big. They passed over Sugar Fork Creek, where cattails had once towered and leaned from its soggy bottom. Cassidy, like Ken, had caught crawdads here, had watched tadpoles grow legs. Now it was little more than a muddy trickle, wet leaves from overgrown brush clogging its flow. Branches thin as pencils clawed at the windows.

Cassidy held her breath as they rounded the bend near the old chestnut stump, and willed the tires not to slide as they climbed the hill beside the pond. She could feel stones slipping from under them, spraying out behind. She concentrated on the dock she'd helped her dad build and then, as they mounted the hill and its black sandpaper rafters appeared, on the house she'd grown up in—its wraparound porch hugging its two broad stories, its wooden sides, untreated at her dad's insistence, water-stained, moss reaching up the sides like long fuzzy fingers.

Her grief highlighted its corners—its edges sharp against the background of the bare trees. She sucked in a breath.

Beside the house was her mother's garden, where Paloma grew tomatoes, pole beans, snap peas, and other vegetables. By contrast, the wood of the garden fence was stained and sanded—perfectly maintained. Beyond the house and garden, thick trees and grasses blocked the view of the old strip mine at the top of the hill.

Noeli parked the SUV in the place usually reserved for Ken's silver Malibu, which was conspicuously absent. They got out and climbed the three steps to the open screen door, Cassidy's legs shaking.

"Come in," Paloma called from the kitchen. As they entered, she abandoned the cheesecloth she'd been squeezing on a scratched wooden cutting board and wiped her hands on her red-checked cotton apron.

Cassidy stood frozen in the doorway, staring at the coatrack where her dad's jacket and brown snowsuit hung casually on the hooks as always. His gold watch lay on the shoe bench, still ticking.

Cassidy turned to look at her mother, whose walnut hair frizzed around her head. How could she go on, doing the regular farmwork? Paloma's sharp features softened at the sight of her daughter and a sad smile rose to her lips.

"Come here, sweetheart."

Cassidy went to her, let Paloma wrap small arms around her, breathed in her lavender lotion, the rosemary essential oil she added to her laundry, the nag champa smoke that lingered in her hair. Paloma was so *herself* that Cassidy at once felt like a little girl. She let her mom stroke the back of her head, rub her back, and whisper in her ear. "I'm so sorry." Her breath was as hot and sweet as the steam rising from the stove. "I'm so sorry you have to do this."

Cassidy tried to remember her father's smells, but couldn't. Paloma's overpowered everything. Cassidy pulled away. When she had kids, she decided, she would plant associations intentionally. She'd pick the most beautiful smells, and the most moving music for them to associate with their childhood.

"Mom, this is—" Cassidy started, but before she could introduce Noeli, Paloma had turned back to the kitchen.

"So sorry. Just a minute. I have to keep this milk at the right temperature."

Cassidy turned to Noeli and mouthed, *Sorry*. Noeli shrugged.

"You're Cassidy's friend?" Paloma asked, her back to the women.

"I am!" Noeli smiled, though Paloma couldn't see her. "You're making cheese?"

"I am. From the goats right here on the farm. Cassidy didn't tell you we had goats, did she? We'll have to sit down and talk when I can step away from this." But Cassidy didn't want to talk. She didn't want to hear any sentiments about her dad that her mom might try to bullshit. She didn't want to think about how her mom would toss her dad's papers that still littered the table into the trash, how she wouldn't think twice about it. Coming home had been a mistake.

Outside the window, Cassidy saw the tree she'd climbed as a kid, calling down to her dad to look how high she was. Beyond the tree was the briar-filled path past the chicken coop, where they walked together, stopping to see the sassafras and its three kinds of leaves. They'd heard a coyote howl on one of their evening hikes. Ken pronounced it "Ki-ote." She'd reveled in the secret language and movements of their relationship—in knowing that he loved her more than anyone else in the world and that she was the person he wanted to share his memories and knowledge of the land with.

Cassidy closed her eyes and watched the light swirl behind her lids, then opened them and looked at her phone. There was no service here, either, as she'd expected, and she didn't feel like asking her mom for the Wi-Fi password. Cassidy caught Noeli's eye and tilted her head toward the stairs. Noeli nodded and followed her, carrying their bags.

JANE

"HOW MANY PEOPLE will be there?" Jane asked her nephew Henry.

"I reckon a whole mess of 'em. A lot of folks really looked up to Ken."

Jane grumbled into the hand mirror Henry held up and slipped the pin of her brooch through her collar. She didn't like large social gatherings now any more than she had at nineteen.

After her first day at the FBI, Jane had been adopted by a quirky gaggle of gals in spite of herself. Flossie Henderson had been the social butterfly; Betty Brown, the queen of celebrations. Peggy Akins started every sentence with "Golly." Polly Duncan was the eager beaver, volunteering for every extra bit of work that popped up. Erma Harvey found a new beau every week and talked incessantly about her latest love, always convinced he was the one she would marry. Dotty McIntire lay for hours on the sidewalk, working on her suntan.

At the edge of their group was Claudine Wills. There were girls in the division who scooted their desks away when Claudine walked by. Jane's friends did her the decency, at least, of politely ignoring her existence, allowing her to sit silently on the perimeter of their group as they ate lunch on the grass. Jane had never met a colored person in Buckhannon. She related, though, to the feeling of being on the outside, and she smiled at Claudine whenever their eyes met. When she found herself alone one afternoon in the powder room with the woman, they made small talk, and Jane found they got on easily. Claudine had wanted to be a WAVE, she told Jane, but at the time of her graduation from high school, colored girls were not allowed to enlist. She regretted being in civil service instead but was making the best of it, she said in a cheery voice.

And so Claudine was the brave one. But who was Jane? The quiet one, she guessed.

Most of the girls went out nightly.

"I'll go if you do," Jane said to Claudine one day as they discussed their plans after work. The other girls grew quiet and turned to face the two women. Jane felt her face grow hot.

"Oh, I'll be at my usual joint on U Street, but thank you," Claudine said. A palpable wave of relief swept over the other girls.

Jane cringed but couldn't blame Claudine. She was uncomfortable with the idea of nightlife already. She wouldn't have subjected herself to the stares Claudine was sure to receive at a downtown club if her life depended on it.

Eventually, though, Ding talked Jane into going out.

"Take me out with your friends!" she implored. "I need some human contact."

"By human, do you mean male?" Jane asked.

"Could you blame me?"

As Jane anticipated, Ding was the life of the party. Even Flossie basked in the wind of her flapping red lips. Jane smiled at Ding's jokes and nursed her gin rickey while her mind turned constantly to her brothers, her parents, the farm. She thought of the post office and Murphy's five-and-dime. Jane didn't miss them exactly—she just couldn't stop thinking about them.

"Killer-diller!" Ding's voice broke into Jane's daydreams, pulling her from Buckhannon back to Trade Winds, a nightclub that managed to feel both classy and dicey at once. A large round mirror on the opposite wall reflected the scene back to Jane, and she watched her friends seated at the blue tufted booth drinking and laughing in its dim reflection. Roman-style columns gave the club a bacchanal touch and chandeliers lent an air of sophistication. Mauve curtains behind the bandstand twinkled with stars—a clever trick with the lighting. An army man stood by the table, and Jane realized with a start that he was looking at her.

"Ahem." He coughed. Had he asked something?

Ding nudged Jane in the ribs. "Of course she'd like to dance."

The other girls stared. Someone kicked her ankle under the table. But Jane could not make herself rise and take this handsome stranger's hand.

"Well, if she won't, I will," Ding said, and the soldier shrugged. Jane turned her legs to allow Ding past and watched as the young man led her cousin to the dance floor, Ding's delicate hand in his strong one, his head bent so they moved cheek to cheek. He twirled her to "Jersey Bounce" and held her close to "My Devotion." The solo saxophonist rose and then sat, two trombone players rose and then sat, and then finally a row of trumpeters rose, covered their horns with hat-like mutes, then lifted them to release the full glory of their brassy sound in a dizzying crescendo. Jane felt the music in her chest, lifting her, and then suddenly it stopped, the band all at once quiet as they cleaned their instruments. The soldier grinned and escorted Ding back to the table where Jane sat with the other girls, staring and slack-jawed. The man kissed Ding on the cheek and as he walked away, the buttons on his jacket caught the light from the wall sconces in a final gleam before he disappeared into the uniformed masses.

That was the end for Ding. Though she'd always been boy crazy, over the course of those two songs, six minutes or so, a charming stranger had created a hole in her that couldn't possibly be filled. Ding thought and spoke of nothing but men.

"I do like a confident fellow, but there is something so charming and sweet about a boy who gets nervous around you," she would observe over dinner. Other times, she'd remark, "Isn't it funny that men are thought of as the tougher sex, but they're the ones who want their dates to be soft and pretty? It's rather adorable, if you think about it."

While Jane's work numbed her, lulled her into a trancelike state that let her forget the war, her brothers, and everything else for some hours every day, Ding's new hunger was distracting in a different way—a more effective way, Jane knew.

On her day off, Jane watched as Ding kissed her lunch-and-swimming date goodbye at the front door and headed right out the back door to meet her dinner-and-dancing date in the alleyway that connected to Seventh Street.

Jane tried to broach the subject over drinks. That night, a jazz band from New York City gave Trade Winds a sweaty, swinging feel. "You've gone khaki wacky," she said over the music.

"It's my patriotic duty, isn't it? We've got to keep our servicemen happy." Jane couldn't tell how serious her cousin was.

"Golly, you are pretty," a boy said, approaching their table in his air force uniform. He sat beside Jane, and his friend, another airman, sat on the other side next to Ding.

As if they'd run drills, the airmen put their hands on the girls' legs at the precise same moment. Jane jerked her leg sharply away. Ding leaned closer.

"Where are you from?" she asked, as if this boy, who looked like every other boy she'd talked to these last weeks, was the most interesting man she'd ever seen.

"Des Moines," the airman said, taking a sip of brandy.

"Des Moines," Ding repeated, moving his hand farther up her thigh, almost under her skirt. Before he could breach her hemline, she grabbed his hand and stood.

"Let's dance," she said.

"Are you rationed, sugar?" the man next to Jane asked.

"I'm sorry. I'm not up for grabs."

"Engaged?"

"Something like that."

They sat side by side, drinking but not speaking. Though the gin made her feel progressively looser, Jane barely moved, fearing any incidental contact might give the airman the wrong idea. She finished her drink and got another, then another, as Ding danced on and on with the boy from Des Moines. The night faded into bebop and gin, jitterbug and jive.

"Wasn't that marvelous?" Ding asked as they tiptoed past Mr. Plunkett's makeshift room.

"Spectacular," Jane said.

She woke up the next morning with a pounding headache.

"Do we have to go?" Ding asked, apparently no better off.

"We have to go." Jane nodded.

They dressed slowly, exaggerating their misery. "You were really sauced last night," Ding said.

"So were you, able Grable."

Ding stuck out her tongue.

Jane reached for her lipstick and noticed something on the counter. It was a small gold brooch, no bigger than a penny, octagonal with three blue mountains across the center. Above the mountains were the letters *AEF*. Below them, it said *80 Div*.

"What is this?!" she demanded, holding the insignia in front of Ding's nose.

"Christopher Columbus!" she exclaimed. "I thought I dreamed this. It's the boy's from last night—his pin!"

"Did you tell him you'd wait for him? Do you know his last name?"

"It doesn't matter, Jane. Don't you see? It's not about really waiting for him. He knows that." Ding's eyes were far off and dreamy. "It's about the hope. He needs me—the idea of me." She snapped back to the present and looked right at Jane. "But his name's Dean Willet, if you must know. I always know their names."

With this, Ding had snatched the pin, squeezed it into her palm, and tucked it safely into her pocketbook.

Jane stood frozen, fingering the pin at her own neck. Where were they going again?

"You need a hand with that, Aunt Jane?" Henry asked.

"No, no. I'm fine. Thank you."

Henry set the hand mirror back on the tray of Jane's walker and cupped her shoulder with his hand. Jane looked up at him, her eyes meeting the grief in his, and she remembered. "Oh, Henry," she said.

Her nephew nodded. "I know. I know."

CASSIDY

PALOMA STARTED THE dented teakettle to boil and joined Noeli and Cassidy at the long wooden table. "Your father built this table," she said.

"I thought so." Cassidy stroked its surface as if the scratches and dents might contain a secret message. Pinterest would call it a "farmhouse table." The table, the Mason jars, the dented woodstove, this little home that barely held back the encircling wilderness—they were the archetype for a hipster trend. She'd never thought about it, but her family's house would make a decently unique camming background.

The kettle whistled and Paloma rose, returning with three steaming Fiestaware mugs in a shade Cassidy knew was named "sunflower."

"Your dad didn't want a funeral," Paloma said, lifting her tea bag up and down.

"Why are we having one?" Cassidy asked.

"It's more a celebration of life. A memorial."

"You didn't waste any time preparing."

Paloma ignored this and Cassidy stared quietly into her cloudy cup. She took a sip, then another. She had barely reached the thick clover honey at the bottom of her mug when guests began to show up, the gravel driveway serving as an arrival bell for each car. Ken's coworkers came first, walking up to the house in their blazers, skirt suits, and curled hair, large bouquets of carnations and deli trays in their hands. They looked out of place so dressed up in this remote setting.

"I'm so sorry for your loss," they said, each giving Cassidy a hug.

"Thank you," Cassidy said.

"I'm so sorry."

"Thank you."

"He was a wonderful man."

"Thank you."

"He would be so proud of you."

"Thank you."

It was just like camming. Smile and say thank you. Let everyone think you were who they wanted you to be.

Paloma herded the growing crowd out to the porch, where they huddled, speaking in low voices, occasionally glancing in Cassidy's direction with sympathetic faces while she and Noeli hunched together and whisper-laughed about everyone's hairstyles.

Grandma Jane arrived, shuttled by Henry, her cousin Ding's son.

"How are you, darling?" Grandma Jane asked Cassidy. She looked elegant in her own black skirt suit—a crisp white shirt under her jacket and an ornate diamond pin at her neck. She could wear anything she wanted and never look out of place. The feel of the farm adjusted to Grandma Jane, not the other way around.

"I'm okay," Cassidy said, taking her hands. "How are you?"

"I'm fine, darling. I'm fine."

Other cousins arrived then, loads of them. Cousin Lina asked Grandma Jane if she needed some water. Jenny took her arm and kissed her cheeks. Gregory talked to her about his homemade wine and said nothing about Ken or the memorial. Cassidy thought this was nice.

They all hugged Cassidy and told her they were sorry, then fluttered and fussed around Grandma Jane, who waved off all of their offers for help but never refused conversation.

"How is Maggie doing at that new school?" she asked her brother Cliff's boy, Craig.

"Didn't you say Macklin has a girlfriend now?" she asked her brother Billy's daughter, Hannah.

It seemed from people's responses that she might be a few months behind on the family news—that the latest events weren't quite sticking, but still, Grandma Jane was in the loop.

Eventually Paloma led the murmuring mass down the plank stairs at the back of the porch like a Pied Piper, her song-like voice beckoning: "Let's move this way, folks," and "We'll begin shortly."

As the line wound its way through the trees, Cassidy was struck by how quiet a group of nearly a hundred people could be, and by the volume of the nature sounds around them—the birds, scattering squirrels, wind in the leaves.

At an old maple, the line rounded into a large circle, clusters of people in unlikely groups—well-dressed work friends with old hippies, Cassidy's teachers with second cousins from out of town. Everyone stared at the ground between them, a spongy tapestry of brown and gray.

"We're here to honor Ken," Paloma announced with practiced ease. The circle stood at attention and Noeli elbowed Cassidy affectionately. Cassidy realized her jaw was clenched, so she wiggled it back and forth. On her other side, Grandma Jane held on to Cassidy's hand for balance on the uneven ground. "Ken and I met on the Charles Bridge, a moment of pure serendipity." Cassidy had heard the story a hundred times and her mind wandered. Could you call something you regretted serendipity? Wasn't everything serendipity? Paloma was just recounting the past, not saying a word about her feelings. "We wanted a child more than anything," Paloma went on. "We poured our hearts into having a baby." Cassidy looked around at the assembled group and searched their tearstained faces for genuine emotion. Had they absorbed the reality of it all more than she had? They were all rapt, watching Paloma. "Finally we returned here to West Virginia to reconnect to Ken's homeland." Cassidy wished her mom would admit how trapped she felt in Ken's "homeland." She wished she would say out loud that nothing Ken or Cassidy ever did was enough for her to be happy here.

Cassidy's thoughts were interrupted by the crunching of leaves. Simon was trying and failing to inconspicuously make his way down the hill, late as always.

Cassidy was surprised she hadn't noticed Simon's absence. If she were visiting under different circumstances, he was one of the few people she would have gone out of her way to see. Simon slipped behind her and Cassidy broke away from Noeli's elbow, stepping backward out of the circle to give him a quick hug. His flannel shirt and beard smelled like chimney smoke.

"Simon!" Grandma Jane smiled and patted his chest.

"Hi, Grandma Jane," he said. "Hey, Cass." He looked into her eyes, holding contact for several seconds, waiting as always for Cassidy's emotions to set the tone for his own. Cassidy nodded reassuringly and he nodded in response, then found a spot in the circle on the far side, near the local dance teacher.

The memorial attendees found their groove, and as one wrapped up their tribute, another stepped forward to speak. "Ken hated two-line headlines," a coworker said. His other colleagues nodded and chuckled. "So this week, I'm writing his memorial in the paper. I'm going to give him his one-line headline."

Cousin Henry and Paloma looked to Grandma Jane expectantly, but she remained quiet, holding tight to Cassidy's hand. Cassidy, too, wondered if she should speak. What would she say?

She could tell the story about waking up afraid, when he had walked with her up the hill to see the sunrise. The farm cat had followed, slinking back and forth between their legs, and Cassidy had marveled at the realization that the cat had its own rich life before she awoke each morning. Ken had held her hand as they hiked. When they'd reached the old strip mine, he'd removed his coat and spread it out on the grass for them to sit. They didn't say a word, just watched as the sun brought the farm to life, first the garden, then the house, and finally the path through the trees. When dawn had reached them, Ken stood and took Cassidy's hand, and together they walked back toward home, the chickens rustling awake, the goats standing sentry to the new day, the smell of oatmeal meeting them with Paloma at the door. That night at bedtime, Ken asked Cassidy if she'd saved a piece of their walk to keep with her as she slept. She nodded and told him she wouldn't be afraid. "There are things to be afraid of, sweet pea," he'd said. "But the dark ain't one of them."

Cassidy wiped a tear from her lower eyelash. She couldn't tell that story without it sounding cheap and contrived. Crying here would feel as fake as her cam show emotions. And besides, Paloma would probably comment on her use of the word *ain't.*

Cousin Henry spoke next. "We went hunting once, Ken, Granddaddy, and I. We begged and begged and finally he took us." He laughed softly. "Ken shot a squirrel and burst into tears."

The group laughed, as if they deserved moments of levity, as if Ken would have wanted them to laugh because of his zest for life or some shit. But he was fucking dead. There was nothing funny. Cassidy clenched her teeth until her molars ached. "Grandaddy was so nice about it," Henry went on. "Just put a hand on Ken's shoulder and said 'Let's go in.' We never went hunting again."

Cassidy only knew him as a dad. She didn't know him as a coworker or a husband or a cousin or a friend. She would never know most of the whole, big person. But, she comforted herself, none of the people here knew the most important parts.

"Ken always liked jamming to this one," said Ross, a friend of Ken's and Paloma's, with a curly red beard and playful eyes. He bent to open a case by his feet, a peeling Grateful Dead bear sticker on its top, took out a guitar, and strummed a few chords. Other people brought out instruments—a mandolin, a banjo, a fiddle, several more guitars. Ross started singing and others joined in, slow and quiet. Cassidy wondered how she hadn't noticed the cases until people started clunking open their gold latches and unzipping gig bags.

"Oh lord, won't you buy me a Mercedes Benz?" Ken's friends crooned. Cassidy didn't know the song or where to look. She thought about her dance shows, when the men would request songs she hadn't heard. INXS, Depeche Mode. She'd close her eyes and pretend to be really into them anyway. She couldn't do that here, with Noeli and Simon watching.

The song ended and the mandolin player started another, fingerpicking a familiar melody, and the banjo player broke into a fast clawhammer: *bum-diddy, bum-diddy, bum-diddy, bum-diddy*. The others joined until the forest filled with the twangy old-time music and slowly, something inside of Cassidy began to shift. Her heart swelled and she felt held. These people knew her through her dad, even if only a part of her. She felt carried by their voices, as if they lifted her up over the branches to see the scene from above, enveloped in their love for her father. She closed her eyes and relaxed her jaw.

"I'll fly away, oh glory," the words rang out, people's collective accents piercing the chilly air, vowels hitting palates before escaping, wrapped snugly in *y*'s and *r*'s. Cassidy could imagine they were in the West Virginia of one hundred years ago, the voices belonging to folks in suspenders and gunnysack dresses. The words rose up in her and she fought them, held them down. She couldn't sing. These were the parents of the (notably absent) classmates who'd linked arms and swung around to "Cotton-Eyed Joe" at the school dances where she and Simon had stood in the corner. This was the epitome of the state she had been dying to leave since she was ten.

A moment later, though, she was singing. The words came from somewhere deep within and emerged to join the rising and swelling around her, like an old gospel sing, like a barn raising, like a tent revival, like all kinds of things she'd pushed down and tried to forget. The bare branches of the maple tree swayed above them, providing quiet accompaniment. She was vaguely aware of Noeli beside her, and she tried not to think about the look of shock that was inevitably on her friend's face.

With eyes still closed, tears streamed down Cassidy's cheeks. She lifted her lids and looked around at the blurred faces. It didn't seem sad, suddenly, this culmination of Cassidy's father's life. It felt joyful and moving and like part of something that stretched as far back as time and would go on as long as people went on—a gathering, as people had always gathered and would always gather in places like this, where there were still woods to gather and sing in, honoring the joys and sorrows of human-hood.

For the first time in a decade and a half, Cassidy considered the possibility that some things about West Virginia might be good. Even though she'd reluctantly agreed with her mom about how stifling this place was, the possibility that she might be able to understand what her dad had seen in it made endorphins bloom in her belly.

The song transitioned into "Will the Circle Be Unbroken?" and Cassidy sang along to that, too, really going for it now, belting it out regardless of pitch, feeling the vibration of her voice blending with the others, the same deep buzz filling her body as the time she had chanted *aum* for a strip-yoga show. The song wound down and "Rock of Ages" began. Somehow Cassidy knew that this was it—this must have been the hymn her dad, Grandma Jane, and her great-grandma had sung to Granddaddy when he was dying.

She didn't know the words, so she hummed along, rocking back and forth, letting it consume her. As if it had been rehearsed, people began to break away from the circle and walk slowly back up the hill. The musicians played and walked and Cassidy hummed. She marched slowly, falling in place toward the back of the procession. It was holy, what had just happened, and she knew it. They all knew it. Everyone had felt the shift—when they'd created something bigger than all of them. Just like Grandma Jane had said. Cassidy didn't know what it was, but it was something. She'd been wrong. She'd been selfish and shortsighted. There were parts of her that fit here, no matter how out of place she'd felt. There was something in her blood.

And then, interrupting her rhapsody, Noeli nudged her again. "How'd you like that hoedown?" she whispered.

Cassidy had never felt so much as slightly annoyed at Noeli, but she suddenly felt physically violent. She clenched her fists. Cassidy stomped ahead, ashamed. Noeli was right. It was all stupid and she'd been stupid to get wrapped up in it, to let her grief delude her into thinking any of it had mattered.

"Cass!" Noeli called out, jogging to catch up. "Sorry, I shouldn't have joked." Cassidy stared straight ahead at the friends and family gathering on and around the porch.

"I don't want to talk about it right now."

"I thought you hated this place."

"That doesn't mean you get to."

Noeli took a deep breath and sighed. "Fair."

"It's fine. I need to say bye to people."

The goodbyes were quiet and intimate, much less awkward than the hellos. Cassidy received hug after hug and earnest commands to take care of herself as Paloma's homemade spoon wind chimes clanged gently from the beams. When folks said Ken would be proud of her, their words felt genuine and moving. She tried to suppress her guilt. She tried to believe them, but what would he be proud of, exactly?

"I love you," Grandma Jane said as she held Cassidy tightly.

After a long embrace, Cassidy finally stepped back. "I love you too."

Cousin Henry led Grandma Jane down the porch steps to his car, and finally only Paloma, Noeli, and Simon remained with Cassidy on the now cold porch. The spoons swayed silently, without touching.

Paloma lifted a watering can from the wooden planks and moved from plant to plant, watering each one gingerly. Without a word she rubbed Cassidy's back briefly before going inside, the screen door slamming behind her. Cassidy, Simon, and Noeli were silent.

"I'm kind of worn-out," Noeli said after a moment. "Think I'm gonna go chill for a bit."

"Cool," Cassidy said, and Noeli followed Paloma inside.

"Hey, Cass," Simon said. His blond hair stuck out in all directions like he'd slept on it.

"Hey, Simon." They hadn't spoken in months.

"Do you want to grab a drink or something?" It was very Simon to offer a normal, comforting activity.

"Yeah." This was what she needed. A drink with Simon would be grounding. "Let me tell my friend."

"She wouldn't want to go?" Simon asked, and Cassidy was suddenly aware of his accent, his gruff way of walking, the fact that he'd never even wanted to leave. She tensed at the idea of what Noeli might say about him later if they all went out.

"I don't think so," she said. "I'll go ask."

Cassidy went inside and found Noeli cross-legged on the couch, flipping through Ken's CD binder.

"I'm gonna go get a drink with Simon," she said.

"Can I change first?" Noeli asked. "I need to get out of this dress."

"You relax. Take some time for yourself." It was a line Cassidy used on fans all the time—a way of telling them she needed space without giving them the space to call her a bitch. She knew they felt entitled to her time, and she prided herself on outsmarting them. Noeli was smarter. She looked hurt. Cassidy knew better than to let someone else's hurt feelings manipulate her though. "I won't be gone too late," she said, and went back out to the porch.

"Let's go." She grabbed Simon by the sleeve of his flannel shirt.

CASSIDY

"WHERE TO?" SIMON asked once they were seated in his rusty red Ford pickup, lovingly nicknamed the Porsche in high school. It had been ancient when he'd gotten it at sixteen and Cassidy could hardly believe it was still running all these years later.

"Allburghers?" Cassidy asked. The restaurant and bar had been their go-to on school breaks. It was the only decent place she knew of to hang out, with its truffle oil fries and craft beers.

"It's closed," Simon said.

"Permanently?"

Simon nodded and started the engine, letting the Porsche warm up. "Yeah, I think the new Buffalo Wild Wings put it out of business."

"Ew," Cassidy said. "That sucks. People would really rather go to a chain?"

Simon nodded again. "Yup. It's the new hot hang."

Cassidy looked up at the rising moon, obscured by the bare branches of the trees that lined the pond, and considered the other options. There was another bar on Main Street, but she'd never been there. It seemed too trashy, even for Buckhannon, always getting shut down for serving underage kids and reopening a few months later with a new name. The best was Club Chemistry, the name hand-painted on a sign outside along with beakers and test tubes.

"Club Chemistry?" she asked.

"It got some big grant!" Simon said. "I mean, Club Chemistry didn't. Some guy did for the building. They're going to renovate it and turn it into an opera house again."

"Whoa!"

"Yeah!" Simon thought for a second. "We could go to Ledbetters." The bar, where they'd gone for Cassidy's twenty-first birthday, was known for its two-for-one bottle rocket shots and corner stage where fortysomethings did karaoke to Metallica.

"Even better," Cassidy said, really in the mood for some Buckhannon culture. "Let's do the K Lounge."

"Klounge!" Simon cheered, putting the Porsche into drive. He navigated down the driveway, onto Shumaker Road, and then left onto Route 20 for the five-mile drive into town.

Entering the Kanawha Lounge felt illicit. In a small screening area set back from the street, they rang a doorbell. An old man who had been there since Cassidy had first visited the place as a child, when they had turned all the lights on and used the large dance floor for a 4-H sock hop, looked them over through a peephole and buzzed them in. Stepping over the thin weathered doormat and into a large dark room, they were overcome by years of cigarette smoke that had accumulated with no ventilation. On the left were the bathrooms and a small rectangular gambling room that was somehow even seedier than the broader establishment. On the right was a U-shaped wooden bar, surprisingly normal if provincial. This part of the room looked like a typical dive with its neon Budweiser sign, a dark mirror, and a sad assortment of patrons. The Kanawha Lounge was a former movie theater, and some said a porno theater, but the theater area had been converted to a dance floor and stage, complete with shady booths along the back side walls and a disco ball that revolved lonesomely. The booths were so shrouded in dark and smoke that they were barely visible, but they were of no use for the everyday purposes of the Kanawha Lounge. Its visitors were content to sit close to the alcohol, or if they were particularly energetic, to play billiards on the other side of the bar. The patrons of the gambling room rarely left, sitting for hours in front of video poker, smoking cigarette after cigarette.

"Beer?" Simon asked, and Cassidy nodded. He leaned against the bar and the bartender sauntered over, then reached under the bar to retrieve two cold bottles of Yuengling. He set them in front of Simon and opened them with a nod, then turned back to his conversation with the regulars. He knew who paid his bills.

Simon handed Cassidy a green bottle and they clinked their drinks in a quick cheers. Cassidy prowled for a spot, eventually selecting two seats on the far side by the pool table. Not wanting to talk about her dad or address the awkward fact that she and her best friend had been abysmal about staying in touch, she introduced herself to the other man next to her.

"Cassidy," she said, unmoving, not wanting to go so far as to touch his hand.

The man, whose stringy gray hair was kept out of his face by an American flag bandanna, did not say his name. Instead he slurred a question. "Do you like the Eagles?" His eye contact was slightly off, veering somewhere to the right of Cassidy's face.

"I guess so?"

"The Eagles ROCK," a guy who looked to be in his late twenties with a bad goatee and a khaki Carhartt hat chimed in, egging him on.

"But do you *really* like the Eagles? Do you appreciate their full musical offerings?"

"Hell yeah, dude!" Bad Goatee Guy said.

The man stumbled away in the direction of the jukebox.

"Cassidy?" Bad Goatee Guy said now.

"Yeah?" Cassidy had no idea who he was.

"I knew I seen you! It's me! Michael McCoy!"

"Oh, hey," she said, feigning recognition.

"I always think about you and ninth-grade English."

"Oh yeah," she mumbled, amazed that this man could be her age. He looked so *old* with his creased forehead and scruffy chin, his dirty work bibs. She tried to picture him in her freshman English class and could not imagine what he could have looked like as a fourteen-year-old.

"Man, I knew you was goin' somewhere even then. What've you been up to?"

"I'm out in California. What about you?" she asked.

"I heard you was out there." He nodded. "Good for you! I'm just doing construction. Nothing too exciting, but it's a good job." She suddenly realized who he was. Michael McCoy was the kid who had sat behind her and quietly scrawled *dyke* on her backpack in green Sharpie. She hadn't realized it until the end of the period, when she was packing her things up to move to pre-calc, and Michael had already bolted from the room, laughing. When she tried to complain to Mr. Jack, he had shrugged and said, "I didn't see it happen. Your word against his." Cassidy had scribbled over the word in black, but she could still see it when she looked closely, until her mom agreed to buy her a new backpack the next year.

The Eagles fan returned as "Lyin' Eyes" began to blare.

"Wait a minute," Michael said now. "Did I hear your dad died?"

"Uh, yeah," Cassidy said. This was the last person she wanted sympathy from.

"I'm real sorry to hear that."

"Yeah, thanks."

"Your daddy died?" Eagles Man asked.

"Yeah," Cassidy said, looking to Simon for help.

"Our loved ones never really go nowhere," the man said. "I want you to know that."

Oh good, he was going to talk about Jesus.

"Your daddy will be here in you with everything you do, pretty lady. Now how 'bout a dance?"

"N—"

"Of course she wants to dance," Simon cut in, nudging Cassidy off her stool with a gentle pat on the back. Cassidy glared at him, not really mad. She did want to be distracted.

The Eagles fan held her at arm's length, middle-school dance style, and Cassidy was grateful. She wanted to be disgusted by him, wanted to laugh at him. Instead she noticed how kind he was being to her. He was no grosser than many of the men she took her clothes off for online, and many of them were far ruder.

"I know it's hard, honey. It'll get easier," he said, and she smiled. "Our parents love us in a way we spend our whole lives trying to re-create. You married?"

"No," Cassidy said.

"Good. My wife's a bitch. She's in Virginia." His breath reached her now, sweetly alcoholic.

"Ah." Cassidy nodded, looking to Simon. There it was. She was done now. Simon grinned and tipped his beer.

"Dang, this song is fuckin' genius. You like the Eagles?"

Cassidy looked at the man's hand on her shoulder. "Oh, what's your ring?" she asked. She wanted to be kind to him, too. She'd become an expert at redirection, feigned interest, and nonjudgmental listening.

"That there's custom-made," he bragged. "It's silver. A girl touchin' her coochie."

Cassidy swallowed hard and called to Simon. "You hear that, Simon? He has a custom ring of a girl touchin' her coochie." She imitated his accent and then felt bad, hoping her dance partner didn't realize she was mocking him. Simon did a spit take with his beer, jumped down from his barstool, and scratched the back of his neck.

"My turn, pretty lady," he said, inserting his arm between Cassidy and the ringed man.

Reluctantly, the Eagles fan stumbled back to his seat. "You like the Eagles?" he asked Michael. Michael laughed and patted him on the back. The man slid off his barstool once more and headed toward the jukebox.

Cassidy and Simon danced ballroom style, one hand clasped, Simon's grip firm and confident, until the bartender called out to them, asking if they wanted another drink. They both nodded vigorously, Simon releasing Cassidy's hand to jog to the bar for the beers. Rather than continue dancing, they took their bottles to the wall and leaned against it, side by side.

The song ended and another began, and though Cassidy didn't recognize it, she had an idea whose back catalog it was from. She relaxed, feeling the familiar tingly warmth of alcohol.

After a couple of slow swallows, Simon spoke. "Lindsey and I broke up," he said. "I didn't know when to bring it up. Didn't feel like the right time at your dad's thing, but . . . yeah."

"Oh man, I'm sorry, dude."

"It's okay. I dunno. It's fine. For both of us. I don't think either of us really cared, so you know. That's why it's fine."

"I guess that's probably better then." Cassidy took a sip.

"I think it was . . . we were the people left, so it made sense to be together, but yeah. I don't think either of us really cared about each other romantically, and it didn't make sense to do the long-distance thing when she left."

Cassidy nodded. They'd never quite seemed like they fit together, Lindsey with her preppy collared shirts and boat shoes, Simon with his torn jeans and band T-shirts. And while Simon's family was rough to say the least, Lindsey's was refined. She lived with her grandfather, who had been a sociology professor at Wesleyan, somewhat famous for his involvement in the civil rights movement. Simon, on the other hand, was the adult in his household. His mom and younger brother refused to act like the grown-ups they were. Even in high school, his mom depended on Simon's income from his job at Burger King.

"So, what have you been up to?" Simon asked, eager to change the subject.

"I don't know. Work is weird. Southern California kind of sucks." It was a relief to say it aloud.

"You're still doing the—"

"Yep," Cassidy interrupted. She sipped her Yuengling. "How's work for you?"

"I actually got a grant too."

Cassidy turned her head to face Simon. "What kind of grant?"

"They're giving me some money for the cooperative farming thing I've been doing. To vary the crops and expand distribution."

"Simon, that's amazing!"

"Thanks." Simon blushed.

"How much is it? Can I ask that? Is that rude?"

"A hundred thousand dollars." Simon tried to suppress a smile.

"Holy shit—*what*?" Cassidy stood up straight and opened her eyes wide. Simon grinned. "So what are you doing for it? What's it for?"

"We'll be working to get healthy food out there on a larger scale. We want to create a replicable model."

"That's amazing! I'm so proud of you."

"Thanks, dude," Simon said.

Cassidy swirled what was left of her beer in awkward ovals and watched it splash against the green sides. "You stayed and you're making a difference. You're doing something with your life. I ran away and all I have to show for it is a shitty apartment and the 1,253rd spot on a second-tier cam site."

"1,253rd? That's pretty good! There are probably a ton of people on there."

Cassidy checked Simon's face for a smirk, but he was wide-eyed and earnest. "Hey, what time is it?" she asked.

Simon looked at his phone. "Almost ten."

"Ah, I should get back. Noeli—"

"Right. Are you two . . . ?"

"No," Cassidy said.

They downed their drinks.

As they walked out to the street, the cold air hit Cassidy's lungs and she felt like she could breathe again. At night these streets were even more *her* streets, changes and all. They belonged to her. They walked back to Main Street, where Simon had parked in front of Thompson's Pharmacy. Even before the new murals, Main Street had presented a sort of civilized facade. You could walk it and ignore the side alleys that led back toward the railroad tracks. As a kid, these side alleys had seemed dangerous to Cassidy, littered with empty single bottles of beer and the occasional drunk. She still probably wouldn't go down one herself.

Simon drove Cassidy back to the farm, the volume up on the tape that had been stuck in the Porsche's cassette deck since high school—the Ramones' *Greatest Hits*. Leaning back in her seat, Cassidy breathed deeply. Simon slowed carefully before each turn, then accelerated just the right amount. High beams on, Cassidy's gaze fell again on the empty cornfields by Turkey Run, the antique mall, and Mt. Lebanon Church. The familiar sights seemed more vivid under the harsh light. Had she ever really looked closely at them? Simon clicked the lights to low when they got to the long driveway, and Cassidy could feel the presence of every other being in the dark—a thousand eyes that seemed to watch them.

Simon stopped in front of the house. "See you later, bud."

"See you." Cassidy opened the door and jumped out. She stood on the porch, shivering, and watched him turn around. Simon waited, making sure she got in all right, so she waved goodbye and opened the door as quietly as she could.

Inside, the house was still. Their tea mugs, left on the table from that afternoon, were surrounded by cards, flowers, and trays of cookies.

The flowers brought a lump to Cassidy's throat. Her dad would have hated them. It was something they shared, their distaste for cut flowers. The bullfrog in the pond let out a loud *uuuurp* and Cassidy wiped her tears and tiptoed upstairs. Quietly, she passed the closed door of her parents' room and peeked her head into her own. The neon-painted walls were subdued in the dark. A Tegan and Sara poster smiled creepily. It looked preposterous and completely out of tune with her life. Her dresser and desk were dark outlines along the walls, which led to the twin bed where Noeli was already asleep. Cassidy lay down on the zigzag rug, which she'd spread on the one-layer wooden floor in high school in an attempt to soundproof her room, so that her parents couldn't hear every move she made from the kitchen below.

She gazed at her friend, still and small in sleep. One day, her body would get old and die. One day, Cassidy's own body would get old and die. How could people find bodies sexy? They were so fragile.

PALOMA

PALOMA TRIED TO imagine sleeping with someone else. She'd been casual about sex once, a lifetime ago. Her last fling had been with Jan, her boss at the university, a short red-haired man with round gold-rimmed glasses, who dressed in oversized corduroy jackets and baggy pleated slacks.

Ken had woken her that morning with a phone call.

"Ahoj." He'd said it ironically, like the word was a joke between them.

"Ken?"

"Paloma, I can't stop thinking about you. Let's get married."

If Paloma had had a drink, she would have spit it. Instead she stammered, "I've g-got to go."

"Don't hang up on me," Ken begged. "I know I'm an old man to you. And I know you think I'm immature. But I want to be a father. I have to be a father. All of this, it's nothing if I don't have a family. I thought I sensed something of that in you, too. Was I right?"

She considered his question. She hadn't planned to see Ken after their first night. Their continued affair was one of convenience. But did he understand her desire to assimilate more than she did herself? Paloma wanted to be part of this place.

Was it nothing more than the human desire to settle, to find a mate, to procreate? Maybe, at least partly.

"Paloma?" Ken asked again. "Can we talk about it?"

"Sorry," she said. "I, uh. Let's get a drink." They made plans to meet back at Radost that evening.

Paloma had to get some air. She left the kolej in a daze and wandered the city, stopping occasionally to lie on a bench or touch a centuries-old building, but she could not absorb the city and its spirit as fully as she desired. *How do I make you part of my body?* she asked the city, but the city was as silent and brooding as she. Finally, like a homing pigeon, she found herself in the place she knew best—the fakulty, where Jan was busy grading.

"Enough work," he said when he saw Paloma. "Time for lunch?"

Paloma nodded. "That would be nice." Jan locked the office and the two walked side by side to a small pub and each ordered a beer and a plate of utopenci.

"This dish means literally 'drowned man,'" Jan had said before taking a bite of his pickled sausage.

Paloma loved his accent, the way he, like other native Czech speakers, approached English words, accenting the first syllable no matter what. She felt almost guilty for robbing her students of this charm when they started using correct pronunciation and sentence structure. "You'd think a dish with that name would be covered in sauce."

"Is not about dish. Is about creator."

Paloma was confused. Czechs were not a religious people. "The creator?" she asked.

"Yes. Created in Beroun." Jan swallowed. "Was very popular at his pub, but one day? Drowned." Jan shrugged, as if this was not so uncommon for a pub owner in Beroun. "Drowned man. Is still very popular." Paloma took a bite of her own utopenci, feeling the soft sausage and the crisp onions melting together in her mouth. Only a Czech dish could be morbid, pungent, and sexual all at once.

When they'd finished their drowned men, Jan raised his studious face to Paloma's and brushed the hair from her eyes.

"You need to blow off steam, yes?" he asked. "Why you came to office on weekend. It is . . ." He paused, thinking of the phrase in English. "No string attached. No puppets." They both laughed, Jan at his own joke, and Paloma at how Czech it was. It was that essential Czechness that put her over the edge. She kissed him and they took the metro back to the fakulty.

Even drunk and near naked, his red hair standing out sharply against his thin pale thighs, Jan was conscientious, moving student files carefully aside, not pushing or tossing them. This, too, was very Czech, and Paloma felt her chest grow hot with desire as she watched him prepare their makeshift lovers' bed on the floor of the office amid stacks of papers and textbooks. His conscientiousness gave way quickly, then, to an intensity—a passion. He whispered, half Czech, half English, hot and breathy in her ear, and it was those sounds, the dry seriousness tinted at the edges with an absurd humor—those sounds rather than any physical sensations that brought her to climax. It was less a night with Jan and more a night with what he represented—a stubborn intellectualism; an everyday revolution; a humble, soft-spoken heroism; a connection to a place and a history.

Now, like then, sleeping with someone would be about place. Paloma didn't want to fuck West Virginia. But this loneliness—she didn't want that, either. At that moment her cell phone rang, the screen lighting up with the name of her friend Margaret, as if Paloma had summoned her.

"Hello?" Paloma answered.

"I wanted to check in . . . and also to talk about something."

CASSIDY

THE SUN WAS already high in the sky when Cassidy woke, bright light pouring through the curtainless windows. Cassidy grimaced and peeled herself from the rug, putting a hand to her face to feel the imprint it had left on her cheek. She stood and peered out at the bare tree branches. As a child, she'd loved how her room felt like a tree house. Cassidy's tongue stuck to the top of her mouth and she felt the slightest bit dizzy. She hadn't even had much alcohol. She must be dehydrated. The thought of water made her queasy, but she knew it was what she needed. Her phone said ten thirty. She was still on California time.

Her room felt small in the light and she was surprised at how close her head was to the ceiling. She padded softly across the rug and stopped at the shelf of knickknacks by the door, picking them up, one at a time—a miniature ceramic bear that Simon had given her once for her birthday, a painted wood thimble of her grandmother's. Grandma Jane had tried to teach her to sew, but Cassidy had gotten frustrated and given up. Still, Grandma Jane had let her keep the thimble. "You might come back to it someday," she'd said. "You never know."

Cassidy was amazed at how these trinkets retained their power—how holding each one could produce the same physical sensation in her belly that it had for years. She picked up an arrowhead she'd found on a walk with her dad. "I used to find these when I walked these woods with Grandaddy," he'd told her. If it was sharp enough, she would let it draw blood, she thought now, poking the point into her finger before putting it back in its place. The last time she'd held it, her dad was alive.

Downstairs, Paloma was awake and Cassidy watched her from the stairs as she watered each of her plants—tall aloe vera and spindly spiders—with a small terra-cotta pot. She walked briskly from one to the next, no nonsense. Paloma was not the kind of person to stop and chat with a plant.

"Good morning, Mom," Cassidy said from the bottom of the stairs.

"Oh!" Paloma turned and smiled. "Good morning. Did you sleep well?" Cassidy nodded. "Do you want some tea?" She nodded again.

Paloma set the watering pot on the coffee table and wiped her hands on her high-waisted jeans. These, too, were more practical than stylish. Paloma didn't care that high-waisted pants were trendy. Cassidy doubted she even knew. Paloma wore and did what she liked. Cassidy followed her into the kitchen.

The teakettle set, Paloma sat at the long table and placed one hand on top of the other on its surface. Cassidy sat across from her, her own hands in her lap.

"There's something I need to talk to you about," Paloma said, crossing her legs and pursing her lips. Cassidy gritted her teeth. "Talks" with her mother were never fun. They always involved some advice or suggestion Paloma meant as well-meaning but came across instead as criticism. "It's nice to finally meet Noeli."

Cassidy sighed. She knew this was where this was going.

"I know I'll make it out to see you in California at some point. I just wish you had picked the Bay Area. Southern California is such a joke."

Cassidy ran her tongue over her front teeth.

"Okay." Paloma sighed. "Cassidy . . ."

She was going to ask if she was dating Noeli, give her the talk for the millionth time about how she would love Cassidy no matter what. Paloma had been trying to get her to come out since eighth grade, when she mentioned casually that she hoped Cassidy was a lesbian because the sex talk would be easier. But Cassidy didn't want to discuss her sexuality any more now than she had then, especially not the fact that it had all taken place on camera. Paloma was less open-minded than she thought herself to be.

"I'm leaving the farm," Paloma cut into her thoughts.

Cassidy bit her cheek and let out a small yelp. She'd expected this, but so soon?

Paloma nodded sadly, as if it were something she couldn't help.

"I'm moving in with Margaret. She called last night. Hank is leaving early for college. Jean and May might join us next year when their kids leave."

"Wait. You're leaving the farm but you're staying in Buckhannon?" This, she hadn't expected.

"Yes. You can have it if you want. Your dad would have wanted you to have it."

"You want me to move back?" Cassidy asked with a laugh that came out as a snort.

"If you want to." Paloma stood to get the tea, and then set two steaming mugs on the table in front of the still silent Cassidy.

"You, of all people, think I should move back to West Virginia? I thought you hated it here. I thought you wanted me to leave, to get out."

The wind outside blew a spiral of leaves into the air and the spoons jangled.

"I did want you to leave," Paloma said. "I wanted you to experience something else. I didn't want this to be the only kind of place you knew. But this is a nice place to come back to."

"Is it? Or would it just make you feel less guilty than selling off land that's been in the family for generations so you can have an extended sleepover with your weird girlfriends?"

"I hated some things, you're right. I hated the food. I hated the racism, the ignorance, the intolerance. It was a big change, coming here from Prague."

"And you hated Daddy." Cassidy snorted again and a headache crept across her eyebrows.

"Cassidy, I've been lonely for so long. I was never in love with your father, but I didn't hate him." Paloma paused and Cassidy gaped at her, a look of disgust on her face. Paloma sighed but maintained eye contact.

"But why did you stay? If you didn't love Daddy." The words were bitter and Cassidy wanted to unsay them. What kind of monster told their grieving daughter that she didn't love her father? How dare she make Cassidy repeat it? She pushed her mug away and folded her arms.

"I stayed because I found a home here, Cass," she said. Cassidy cringed at the shortening of her name. That was for other people to call her. From her mom it was trying too hard. "I made friends and I made our home into a place where I wanted to live."

Cassidy pictured her mom in her garden with her Beatles shirt on and a batiked bandanna around her head. She pictured holiday potlucks with the other hippie families in town. She pictured weekend breakfasts, a stack of whole wheat pancakes, Mom pouring maple syrup from the sticky top of a Mason jar.

Paloma lowered her ear toward her shoulder in a pleading tilt of her head.

Something in this tilt softened Cassidy for a moment, and then enraged her. Breathing slow, heavy breaths that lifted her chest up and down, she tried to control this anger, tried to separate it from her grief. It was impossible. Her feelings felt magnified, distorted, twisted into shapes that were larger than life.

"How can you do this? To me? Now?" she asked, trying to control the volume of her voice. She wanted to mimic her mom's tone—the measured, sharp one.

Paloma picked up a spoon from the table and wrapped the string of her tea bag around it, squeezing the bag and letting the excess tea drip into her cup. She set the spoon and spent tea bag on the table, and the drops that fell enraged Cassidy further. How dare she let tea stain the table Ken had made for them with his own hands?

"Cassidy, I know it's soon—"

"Don't keep saying my name like that. Cassidy! Cassidy!" she mocked, losing control. "My *father died* this week. And you want me to be happy for you because you can finally be free of him." She stood, scraping the chair's legs on the wooden floor.

"Cassidy, I'm not expecting you to understand."

"Understand what? That you're selfish? That you couldn't have even waited a week to tell me this?"

"Cassidy," Paloma begged, tears in the corners of her green eyes.

"Stop saying my name!" Cassidy shrieked, bringing her hands, fingers flexed and spread wide, to the sides of her face.

"I'm sorry," Paloma said. "But I need you to at least hear me out."

"Hear that you're a selfish cunt?" Cassidy yelled. It was too much, too far, she realized as soon as the words flew from her mouth.

"Shut. Up." Paloma's volume was low, each word its own sentence. The words burned and cut through Cassidy. Never in her life had her mom said anything like it. The shock of it silenced her and she sat down shakily, her eyes stinging with tears.

Cassidy knew that what Paloma had not said was even worse. She was disappointed in Cassidy. She was hurt.

Just then, Noeli stumbled groggily down the stairs and Cassidy and Paloma both attempted to compose themselves. Paloma brought her tea to the kitchen and stood by the sink, holding the mug close to her lips without drinking. Cassidy turned to her friend. Noeli read the room instantly and widened her eyes.

"Do you want to get breakfast in town?" Cassidy asked in a tone that was more *I need to see you in the principal's office* than *Care for a leisurely brunch?*

"Yes. Definitely. Sounds great."

"Great." Cassidy brought her mug to the kitchen and placed it, still full, in the sink without looking at her mom.

"Are we going like this?" Noeli asked, nodding toward Cassidy's yoga pants and baggy sweatshirt and her own red-and-black flannel.

"Yep," Cassidy said, slipping her shoes onto her bare feet and taking her dad's jacket down from the hook. Noeli followed obediently as Cassidy put the jacket on and headed out the door.

Cassidy pulled the jacket close around her and smelled a familiar must. The scent was comforting at first, and then horrifying as she realized, with a jolt in her chest, that he hadn't left all the way yet. She thought of what the Eagles fan at the bar had said—that her dad would always be with her, but she knew he was wrong. He wasn't all the way gone yet, but he would be.

They'd barely gotten to Route 20 when Cassidy exploded.

"My mom is moving in with her weird hippie girlfriends and giving me the farm. What the *fuck*?"

"Wait, she's giving you the farm? Like to have?"

"I think you're missing the point," Cassidy tried again. "My *mom* just told me she's leaving the house my dad built for us while I'm here visiting for my dad's *funeral*."

"I can see why that's upsetting, but, Cass, she's *giving* you the farm—like a house and land that will be yours."

"But it won't be mine. It's all lip service. She knows I'd never really move back. She'll end up selling it. I will officially have no real home." Cassidy accelerated, flying up the winding hill by Turkey Run, her anger eating up her anxiety. "It's fucking insane. Am *I* fucking insane? Why does nobody else seem to think this is fucking insane?"

They passed a small building on the left of the road near the Pringle Tree that used to be one of Ken's favorite diners. It was a gambling place now, and even at eleven a.m., the small lot was full of pickup trucks. A bit farther over the hill, a young couple stood beside a camper with a sign that read "Metal for Sale."

"Could you rent out the farm and have some income? Or do an Airbnb thing?"

Cassidy let her rage boil up and over without speaking, her face turning red but her mouth staying silent. Noeli didn't understand. She breathed, letting oxygen slow her heartbeat until her anger was replaced by a general sense of sadness and annoyance and a larger sense of loneliness. In town, she parked the car in the same spot Simon had parked the night before.

Three large parties waited in the church pew benches that lined the entryway of C.J. Maggie's. Cassidy stood by the podium and stared at the antiques and oddities lining the walls—old Buckhannon street signs and maps, string lights shaped like chili peppers, an old sled. The hostess arrived and seated them at a high-backed booth tucked into the back corner of the restaurant. The Spin Doctors' "Two Princes" played loudly and waitstaff passed every few seconds with heaping plates of fries, gigantic burgers and sandwiches, and salads that could feed a family.

After a minute or two, their waitress, a woman Cassidy had known since kindergarten, arrived. Cassidy snorted under her breath and shook her head as she recognized her. "Oh my gosh, is that Cassidy?!" the woman squealed. "I heard about your dad, sweetheart. I am *so* sorry. How *are* you? Aren't you in California now?"

"Yeah. Thanks."

"What can I get you to drink, honey?"

"I'll take a lemonade."

"Iced tea," said Noeli.

"Coming right up! It is so good to see you, Cass! I really am so sorry." She hurried away.

"Our waitress," Cassidy said, "is the person who first told everyone in high school I was a lesbian."

"Oh shit. She was weirdly friendly."

"Yeah, for someone who started my four-year nightmare, right?"

The waitress returned quickly to deliver two huge drinks and the women avoided eye contact as they thumbed through the large menu. Noeli took a drink of her tea. "Oh my God, it's pure sugar," she said.

"What did you expect?" Cassidy laughed.

"Unsweetened."

"Not in West Virginia."

"Right, the South."

"West Virginia isn't the South," Cassidy said as the waitress returned.

"Are we ready to order, folks?" she asked.

"No breakfast?" Cassidy asked.

"At eleven o'clock, young lady?" the waitress teased like she was twice her age.

"All right, young lady," Cassidy said. "I'll have the eggplant parm, easy on the parm."

Noeli ordered half a turkey sandwich.

"You've got it. I'll put that in right now." The waitress winked and Cassidy stared at the metal bucket light hanging above the table. The restaurant used to have paper and crayons on each table and people had used them to write and draw on the inside of the lamps. *Laura* was written with a flowery wreath around it. *Ellie was here!* was in big turquoise block letters. *Zander likes farts.* Cassidy's eyes started to burn from the light, so she looked instead at the wall, the shape of the lightbulb still visible in her vision over the drywall and exposed brick. Noeli quietly drummed her nails on the table. Her black nail polish was almost all the way gone now.

The waitress came back with their food.

"If that's easy on the parm, I wouldn't want to see hard," Noeli said before taking a bite of her sandwich.

"It's weird eating eggplant at what feels like eight in the morning."

Noeli grunted in agreement, a large bite of turkey in her mouth.

"It was *so* nice to see you," the waitress said when she brought them the bill. "I really am sorry about your dad."

"Mmhmm. So nice." Cassidy left what she hoped was an insulting tip before following the shiny wooden floor back out to the cold bright day.

"What's Stone Tower Brews?" Noeli asked as they exited.

"What? Where?" Noeli pointed across the street to a chalkboard-style hand-lettered sign.

Cassidy shrugged. She was intrigued, so, jaywalking, she crossed the street, Noeli jogging to catch up. A West Virginia–shaped decal declaring "All Kinds Are Welcome Here" in rainbow letters decorated the glass door. Cassidy rolled her eyes. In a small entryway before another glass door was a poster stating "Hate Has No Home Here," flyers for local artist pop-ups and community theater shows, and a recruitment poster for the army. Noeli glanced around and, finding them alone, quickly reached up and ripped the army poster from the wall, crumpling it and shoving it in her pocket.

"One of these things is not like the other," she said with a small smile.

Inside, the place was packed. Wesleyan students sat alone with laptops. Groups and couples chatted animatedly over plates of food. The Stone Tower logo was spray-painted in white over the newly wood-paneled walls. The whole place looked very metropolitan.

Two large monitors over the L-shaped counter displayed names of craft beers and their origins, and large silver coffee-making appliances took up the space behind the glass on the long side of the L. At the register, Cassidy picked up a menu listing the food and drink offerings. A chalkboard announced the day's special was vegan tacos. "We should have eaten here," Noeli muttered, and, despite Cassidy's sense of loyalty to C.J.'s, a place she'd been going since she needed a booster seat, she had to admit the idea of a place in Buckhannon advertising vegan anything was pretty incredible. And they had breakfast! Still, she was relieved they had already eaten.

"You don't want tacos in West Virginia," she said.

"Oh, there's Wi-Fi," Noeli said, looking at the chalkboard and grabbing her phone.

"I'll have a chai with soy please," Cassidy said. "And?" She glanced at Noeli.

"I'll take a pour-over of whatever you recommend."

They sat at a booth by a low table and Cassidy took her phone out to connect to the Wi-Fi. Hundreds of notifications across several apps popped up, an even split between totally inane crap, messages from her fans telling her how horny they were, and sympathy messages flooding her status bar. Overwhelmed, she swiped them away with one motion, ignoring them all, then opened the cam site back up and told MannyBoy27 she was okay and sent a couple other bigger tippers a tit pic she'd taken in California, the night before her mom had called with the news about her dad. She could hardly look at her own happily oblivious face.

Cassidy rose from the booth and checked the counter, where their drinks were waiting in mismatched mugs. She retrieved them and set Noeli's in front of her, then sat down to sip her chai. She could feel the warm liquid move down her throat to her stomach. Cinnamon stuck to her tongue and she took another sip to wash the gritty feeling away. Noeli's drink sat, untouched, on the table.

"I'm sorry I was being insensitive," she said. "I know how important that house is to you, even if you don't want to live there. You're not insane. This is really fast and pretty messed up of your mom."

"Thank you," Cassidy said, and took another sip of her chai to cover the tears accumulating in the inner corners of her eyes.

JANE

SOMETIMES THE NURSING home cafeteria reminded Jane of Washington, the old women just as boy crazy as the girls at the Armory. Today they were giggling about a new male resident. Rumor was, the old man, with his hunched back and dead wife, still had his real teeth. Their excited gossiping brought Jane back to the day after Ding had claimed her first pin, and they'd both gone to work with tremendous hangovers.

The pile of cards waiting for Jane had stared back from her desk menacingly. She'd felt queasy. After an hour of staring at the inky lines, she'd thought she might chuck up her breakfast.

Jane needed water. Squeezing past the tight row of desks, she stepped out of the doorway and headed for the drinking fountain.

The water was cool and life-giving. Jane's cells awakened as the liquid calmed her parched throat and settled her gin-pickled stomach. As the reborn world sparkled back into focus, Jane froze, and then furiously wiped a dribble of water from her chin.

Not today. Her nylon seams were crooked, she had barely fluffed her hair that morning, her lips were their natural peachy color. Not today.

Several yards away in the training lobby, two dozen seamen in their white undress uniforms stood between Jane and her desk. A woman at the front of the group was giving them a tour.

Jane lifted her chin and walked through, avoiding eye contact.

"Hey, cookie," a sailor whispered as she passed. Jane blushed but kept her head high.

As the sea of men parted, Jane managed not to look at or speak to any of them. Wisps of hair flew around her face, and she fought off the urge to hold her hands over them. She was aware of the slight tilt of her gait, the heavy thud her round calves gave her steps, and all of their eyes on her backside.

Back in the room, Ms. Bruce struggled to keep control of the other girls, who could barely contain their whispers. The news had gotten through: *Sailors in the lobby!*

When Jane sat, Erma leaned in closer. "Any Casanovas?"

Jane shrugged.

"All right, girls. Who's thirsty?" Ms. Bruce asked in resignation. Thirty hands shot into the air.

"Okay, one row at a time. And make it quick." She pointed to the row on the left, and the girls scampered to the fountain. From the doorway, Erma turned and saluted the rest of the room, and even Ms. Bruce couldn't help but crack up.

When the first row returned a few minutes later, giggling and pink, Jane's row rose. Jane considered staying in her seat and finally getting to her work, but in the end, she decided she might as well get a look from the safe camouflage of prettier peers.

The boys were rowdier than they had been earlier, riled by the giddy girls. Their tour guide had given up, and the scene was a madhouse, everyone scrambling to talk in the brief moments before Ms. Bruce declared their time up. Girls scrawled their addresses on scraps of paper as date plans were confirmed.

Jane listened in awe to the symphony of flirtation.

"Bonkers, huh?" a voice spoke into Jane's ear, and she turned, expecting to see a sailor. Instead of a white cotton hat and jumper, she was shocked to see an officer's khakis. The lieutenant grinned from under his cap. The creases on his uniform were crisp as crackers.

In spite of his rank, he looked incredibly boyish, in large part due to his blond hair, which was really closer to white. His blue eyes were playful and searching.

"Wacky," Jane agreed.

"I don't go for this whole game," he said. "Too old for it."

"So you aren't angling for a date with me?" Jane felt suddenly coy.

"I didn't say that. But don't tell the kids." The man tipped his head toward the younger men.

"I was planning to tell Hoover," Jane said.

"Come on, ladies. There's work to be done," said Ms. Bruce, poking her head out from the doorway. "I have a feeling we won't be beating any records for productivity today."

"Where do you stay?" the officer asked.

"I'm too busy to date," Jane said. "It's important work here, you know."

"Critical," he agreed. "Eight o'clock? Tomorrow?"

"I don't think so." Jane's chest constricted as the corners of the lieutenant's sky-blue eyes drooped.

"This weekend," he said as she backed away and began squeezing through the crowd.

"Next week," he called, and Jane gave him an apologetic smile as Ms. Bruce placed a hand on her shoulder, shuffling her back toward the room.

Jane relayed the story to Ding at dinner.

"You didn't even ask his name?" Ding shook her head. She was distracted, rummaging around in her bag.

"Why does it matter?"

"It would do you good to go out with a nice guy." Ding opened the mouth of her bag wide, practically sticking her head inside it, reminding Jane of Jonah and the whale.

"How do you know he's nice?" Jane took a bite of creamed spinach.

"It would do you good anyway. Get your mind off of things."

Ding dumped the contents of her pocketbook onto the table, the small air force pin plinking and bouncing. Another pin, round and gold, emblazoned with *US*, landed beside it.

"There it is," Ding said. "I was worried I'd lost it."

"Is that an army pin?" Jane gawked. "When did you get that?"

Ding smiled. "On my lunch break, from Tony Prickett. That's his first and last name, mind you."

"Your new fiancé?"

Ding stuck out her tongue.

"Anyway. I'm meeting a marine tonight. All I need now is an anchor clanker."

Jane shook her head. "You are exactly why I'm not going out with the officer."

"What about you, Jane?" The voice startled her out of her memories and she looked up from her tray of green beans and chicken at the woman speaking. Jane was at the home. The old women were scheming about the new resident. "Why don't you talk to him?" the woman prodded.

"No, no. That's all right," Jane said. "I'm not interested."

CASSIDY

WHEN CASSIDY AND Noeli got back to the farm, Paloma and her hatchback Versa were gone. They stayed gone through the afternoon and into the evening. When the sun started to set and Cassidy's stomach started to growl, she scavenged through the kitchen and pantry but came up with only the most basic of ingredients—grains, flours, vegetables, powdered seitan. It was a kind of magic, how Paloma could turn these into meals and Cassidy hadn't learned it. Cassidy's magic was the microwave, sometimes the toaster oven, the frozen foods section at Trader Joe's. Until now, she hadn't realized how reliant she'd become on conveniences.

As a child, Cassidy had sometimes cooked with Paloma, and she remembered how her mom had eyeballed the ingredients. She wasn't even sure there were measuring cups in the house. In the dorm kitchen years later, when Cassidy tried to follow a recipe for broccoli casserole, she didn't stress too much about measuring perfectly. A little more or less couldn't make that much of a difference, she figured, and imagined the picture, captioned "Domestic dorm life," she'd take of the finished product. The whole thing was a mess, bubbling over the sides of the pan and crusting over in the bottom of the oven. When

Cassidy stubbornly decided to eat it anyway—she wasn't going to waste the fourteen dollars she'd spent on ingredients—all she could think was that it tasted like farts.

"Do you want to go back to Stone Tower for dinner?" Cassidy asked, waking Noeli, who was napping on the couch.

"Yeah, why not? I want to try those vegan tacos."

"Or you could try . . . something that isn't the tacos," Cassidy said.

As they made their way down the driveway, they had to pull over onto the grass to make way for Paloma, who was returning. Paloma raised her hand in a hesitant wave as they passed—a small peace offering. Cassidy returned it.

"We shouldn't stay out too late," Noeli said as they turned onto the road. "Our flight's at one tomorrow."

"Oh shit, that's tomorrow?" How had she lost track of the days? They felt different here—longer and shorter at the same time. Longer, without filling every moment with work or her phone or binging shows. Shorter in that she could see the time passing in front of her, see the fleetingness of it, and see how little she'd spent with Grandma Jane. On the one hand, she wanted to get out of here and back to her normal routine. Though she hated to admit it, she missed the sense of safety and affirmation her show gave her, how she knew she would log on each evening and be flooded with dopamine. On the other, the knowledge that everything would be different the next time she returned made her feel slightly panicked. What would it be like, visiting her mom on her pseudo-commune? What would it be like when Grandma Jane . . . She just wouldn't visit. Once Grandma Jane was gone, she'd have no reason to ever return.

"Hey, could you wait to eat? I want to go see Grandma Jane," she said.

"Of course," Noeli said. "I'll give you some time alone with her. I have an audiobook out from the library that I need to finish anyway."

The parking lot at Serenity was so dark and so empty that Cassidy wondered if visiting hours were over. The door said eight, though, so she entered the little receiving area. There was the Softsoap smell, there was the second glass door, there were the names scrawled in the little notebook. Cassidy felt a pang as she saw that only a few names had been scribbled between her current signature and the one from a couple days ago.

The TV in the lobby was still on the Hallmark Channel and two old women stared from recliners as another in a wheelchair slept, her head resting against her chest and her hands folded palms up in her lap. At nighttime like this, the home reminded Cassidy of Christmas Eve—that peaceful twinkling warmth. Some of these people might not make it till Christmas.

Passing each doorway in the dark hall, Cassidy made out small, sad sounds—a toilet flush, a man repeatedly clearing his throat, a recording of an evangelical preacher declaring that in Jesus, there was no death. Through an open door on the right Cassidy saw a nurse in pink scrubs perched on the edge of a bed, feeding a woman in a wheelchair. The woman's toothless mouth was open like a baby's, and when the nurse touched the silver spoon of yellow pudding to her lips, they trembled around it, trying to take it in. The nurse tipped the spoon up to deliver its contents and then dabbed the woman's mouth with a small napkin. The woman's tongue flicked in and out, trying to taste more.

Grandma Jane's door was slightly ajar, and when Cassidy knocked, it opened farther. "Hi, Grandma!" she called loudly. She tiptoed two steps in, remaining behind the door. There was no answer. "Grandma Jane?" Cassidy said again. Met with more silence, Cassidy stepped around the door and into the room. The hula girl, the daisy, and the Halloween cat were still in the darkness.

Grandma Jane lay on the small bed, facing the wall in the fetal position. The shape of her body was visible beneath the thin synthetic quilt. She looked like a baby.

Cassidy coughed and Jane stirred, opened her eyes, and rolled onto her back. "Oh, hello, darling," she said, sounding tired and weak but not particularly embarrassed. Cassidy retracted into herself, imagining how it must feel to get so old that it was normal for people to see you sleeping like that, at your most vulnerable. People thought getting naked on camera made her vulnerable, but Cassidy didn't feel weak when she was exposed like that. Naked wasn't weak. Naked, on your own terms, feeling people's need for you through the screen, was powerful. Alone, sleeping, feeble—that was weak. Cassidy sat on the edge of the bed next to Jane, who she remembered walking blocks around town, who brushed off hardship with a wave of her hand. That was the real Grandma Jane, she reminded herself.

"We're going back to California tomorrow," she said.

"Oh goodness. Already? Safe travels."

Would she remember that Cassidy had visited?

"Daddy's memorial was nice."

"Mmhmm. Yes, it was."

Did she remember it?

"There's a new place downtown. We're going to have dinner there."

"That sounds lovely. Have fun, dear," Grandma Jane said.

Would the rest of Cassidy and Grandma Jane's conversations be small talk? Would they ever talk about anything significant again?

"Why didn't you ever leave?" Cassidy asked, startling herself. "Why didn't you get out of Buckhannon?"

Grandma Jane sighed. "Oh, darling, I tried. I did."

"What happened?"

"I went to Washington, during the war." Jane's eyes stared up at the acoustical ceiling.

"What did you do there?"

"I worked for the FBI. Ding and I were Government Girls. You should have seen us."

"Did you lose the job when the men came back from the war?" Cassidy had heard about how the Rosie the Riveters had been kicked back to the kitchen with little more than a thank-you. Women's labor, as usual, was relied on but never valued.

"I left before that," Jane said, shaking her head against her too plump pillow. "I got into some trouble and had to come home."

Cassidy took Jane's hand. "What kind of trouble?"

"Oh, Cassidy. I don't like to talk about it much. The war was not a pleasant time in my life. My brothers were all abroad. Everyone was scared." Her eyes were clear now and she looked back at Cassidy. "Sometimes you just have to make the best of things."

But this was intolerable. Her grandma didn't have to tell her everything. It was clear she didn't want to. But Cassidy couldn't stand the injustice of it, whatever it was. Grandma Jane had been making the best of things her whole life. She couldn't end her story like this.

"Come with me, Grandma, back to California. We can find a home for you out there or you can stay with me. That would be even better." Cassidy was talking quickly now, without thinking.

Jane smiled and closed her eyes. "I'm too old to go anywhere, darling. You live your life, you hear me?"

Cassidy looked up to avoid crying. She wanted to tell her grandma that nothing she could have done would shock her, that nothing she had done could make her deserve this. She wished she could tell her about camming, about loving women, but she worried that instead of making Grandma Jane feel better, it would make her more ashamed, like her granddaughter had been a disgrace too.

"I don't know if we'll be able to come over before we go back to Pittsburgh. I'll hug you goodbye now."

Cassidy leaned into Grandma Jane's chest and breathed her in. When she lifted herself again, she had to wipe her cheeks.

"Don't cry, darling," Grandma Jane said. She struggled to sitting and propped her pillow against the wall behind her, the quilt bunched in her lap.

"Okay." Cassidy nodded, wiping her eyes to catch the tears before they emerged.

How could she leave? How could she handle another phone call?

"Don't cry or you'll make me cry." Grandma Jane laughed, dabbing at her own eyes.

Cassidy laughed too and dried her eyes for real. "I love you, Grandma Jane," she said.

"I love you too, Cassidy. Buh-bye."

"I love you," Cassidy called again as she walked toward the door. She pulled Ken's coat around herself, but she already felt him seeping out of the seams. She was walking away from the only thing she had left of her father.

"Bye bye, I love you," Jane called out, as if she were saying it first, waiting for a response.

"Bye, I love you." Cassidy walked out the door before her grandma could respond. It was like this on the phone, too—impossible to get in a final "I love you." Jane would just keep going.

Cassidy rushed past the rooms, not wanting to be burdened further by other people's tragedies. She dashed past the front desk, avoiding eye contact with the sleepy nurse behind it.

Outside, the cold air made her ears ache.

She hurried to the SUV, climbed in, and buckled her seat belt, rubbing her arms and letting the heat penetrate her skin.

"Are you okay?" Noeli asked as she turned off her audiobook.

Cassidy rubbed her hands together and blew into them, her breath forming a hot mist.

She looked right at her friend. "What if I stayed?"

JANE

CASSIDY'S VISIT HAD soothed Jane's irritation at the memory of the officer. Oh, Cassidy. It was true Jane had been given much in this life, but life had also taken so much away. She tried to focus on sweet Cassidy—that she was here in Buckhannon for a little while longer—but Jane could not hold the knowledge long. Her mind kept returning to 1944.

"Finally!" Ding had said as she hung her freshly washed hose over the side of the bathtub. "Working for the navy and this is the first time I've managed a date with a seaman."

"You've really made it," Jane said, scrubbing her own undergarments at the sink, the soap bubbling on her fingers.

"I had to wait for a fresh face, is all. Someone those dad-blamed WAVES hadn't corrupted. Oh!" Ding put her hands on her hips. "Did I tell you he's a lieutenant?"

"But it's more important that he completes your collection."

Ding ignored her and retrieved her trinkets from the ring dish by the sink—her air force and army pins, and the recently acquired tie clip from her marine. "Billy Grable," she said, staring at it fondly before putting them all in her pocketbook. "It's good luck to keep them with me, don't you think?"

"Oh, I'm sure of it." Despite using lukewarm water to wash their delicates, the bathroom was stifling, all the moisture hanging in the air like a heavy blanket.

Ding shrugged. "You know I'm susceptible to uniforms."

The girls got dressed and Jane helped Ding with her hair until the doorbell buzzed.

"Come meet him, at least. You'll see. He's heaven-sent!"

Jane trudged down the stairs after her cousin and stood behind her as she opened the door.

Standing coolly on the doorstep was the officer. Her officer.

"You!" Jane yelled over Ding's shoulder. "Of course it's you." Disdain fell over her face like a storm cloud.

"You," the man repeated, his mouth agape.

Ding was oblivious. "Jane, this is Owen. Owen, this is Jane."

"It's very nice to meet you." Owen extended his hand, looking right past Ding.

"I thought you weren't interested in the dating game," Jane said, leaving his hand hanging in the air and placing her own on her hips.

"You left me so lonely, what choice did I have?" Owen grinned his puckish grin. Jane crossed her arms and raised her eyebrows.

"Oh!" Ding exclaimed. "This is . . ."

Jane nodded and Owen smirked.

"What a coincidence!" Ding said. "You have to come, Jane. Come out with us!"

"Yes, Jane. Come out with us," Owen said, still looking only at her. Jane's heart fluttered, but she stood firm.

"I will do no such thing."

"Have it your way." Ding took a step out the door, and Owen moved aside to let her pass.

"Please, join us," he insisted. Jane glared at him. Though it required effort to stay angry as she took in his sleek gray suit and matching fedora, Jane was determined.

Ding flounced out to Owen's waiting Highlander, but Owen lingered, giving Jane a last, pleading glance with his oceany eyes. Jane stayed planted in the doorway until finally Owen turned, jogging down the steps to open the car door for Ding. Jane closed the door behind him with a slam just late enough to see Owen's longing look in her direction. She tried not to imagine how good the breeze would feel in his convertible.

They were two good-for-nothings, anyway.

When Ding returned hours later, tromping up the stairs, Jane pretended to sleep. She had no interest in seeing whatever souvenir Ding had weaseled from Owen.

When the Baby Ben alarm clock rang the next morning and Ding continued to snore, Jane huffed but did not wake her. *Let her be late for work,* she thought.

When they returned from work that evening, and Jane noticed the dark circles ringing her cousin's eyes, Jane said nothing. Ding deserved to be exhausted.

It wasn't that Jane was mad at Ding, per se; she just saw no good reason to speak to her.

Ding was a grown woman with a war job and it was about time she stopped depending on Jane and started taking responsibility.

Ding, in turn, huffed her way around the house. She did not take kindly to being ignored. The girls moved in their own circles around the city, limiting their intimacy to the hours they spent in their shared room, breathing each other's breath in deep slumber.

One night, as Ding snored away, Jane lay awake and pouted. Ding couldn't even let her keep the idea of Owen. She hadn't even wanted to go out with him. She'd just wanted a nice dream that was all her own.

How silly she'd been to pout. Life hadn't taken those last carefree times with Ding from her. She'd taken those herself. *Cassidy,* Jane reminded herself. She'd been thinking of Cassidy. But she couldn't remember why. Still, the image of her granddaughter comforted her.

CASSIDY

CASSIDY HADN'T THOUGHT the words through, let alone the idea. It came rushing up within her and then out of her mouth. "What if I moved here and lived on the farm after all? I wouldn't have to pay rent, so I'd have almost no expenses. That's almost two thousand dollars a month I wouldn't have to spend. I could still cam, but there'd be less pressure."

"What would you do with your apartment?" Noeli asked. "Sublet it?"

"I don't know. Maybe you could help me find someone?"

"I guess I'll return the rental car myself." Noeli looked at Cassidy with skepticism and concern.

Cassidy's heart was beating fast. Was she actually considering this? "Yeah, that would work."

"Should you think about it for a while?"

But Cassidy was surprised at how sure she felt, especially since a day ago the thought would have made her snort. The idea of staying in West Virginia had seemed absurd until it came out of her mouth. This wasn't high school. She could choose who she wanted to be around. She'd stick to Simon and Grandma Jane. "No. I'm staying. At least for now."

She pictured the palm trees, the warm weather. If she went back, she would chicken out. Noeli frowned and Cassidy tried not to think about how she'd be leaving her, too.

"I'm going back in to tell my grandma." The excitement tingled in her limbs.

"I'll come in." Noeli took the keys out of the ignition.

The SUV's doors clicked open. The salt on the sidewalk crunched under their feet as they hurried back into the building, into the entryway and the heat. They smelled the Softsoap. They skipped the sign-in. Cassidy flew down the hall so fast, she didn't hear a single sound other than her wet Chucks slipping on the tile. She knocked on the door but didn't hesitate behind it.

"I have news," she said as they burst in, their presence filling the small room. Jane was in her chair now, reading a Deepak Chopra book.

"What is it, dear?" she asked, looking up.

"I'm going to stay. In West Virginia, on the farm."

"Oh, how wonderful, darling!" Jane said, rising slowly and with effort. Cassidy rushed to close the space between them and gave her a long hug.

"How wonderful," Jane repeated. Cassidy focused on her face and not on Noeli's hunched shoulders behind her. As her heart rate returned to normal, she could feel how hungry she was.

"Okay, dinner for real now," she said. "I'll see you soon, Grandma Jane."

"Okay, dear. Buh-bye."

"I love you, Grandma."

"I love you." Jane smiled.

Cassidy walked backward toward the door. "I love you!" she said, and exited, Noeli behind her, hands squeezed into her pockets.

"Eeeee!" Cassidy squealed quietly, back in the hallway.

Noeli smiled a half smile. "You're cute when you're excited," she said, and they walked out together into the cold. Cassidy grinned back and gave a little jump, then had to catch herself as she slipped on ice on the way down.

"I'm okay!" She laughed.

The river was starting to freeze now, Cassidy saw, as they rounded the bend before the bridge. The muddy water was still, and frost reached like fingers from the shore. Other thin patches of white dotted the expanse on both sides of the short overpass, telling the town it was time to stagnate for a while.

There was more stagnation up ahead at the end of Marion Street, cars waiting for a state road worker to turn his sign from STOP to SLOW, so they went around, turning right onto Barbour Street and passing Simon's old house—the one his family had lived in before his mother lost her job and his dad moved them out to the trailer. The front porch was falling apart now and tricycles littered the yard.

What would Simon think about her staying? Cassidy stifled another squeal.

JANE

CASSIDY WAS STAYING. Jane never thought she'd live to see the day. But tragedy did things to people, changed them, encouraged rash decisions, just like it had for Ding.

Her cousin had lain facedown on their bed, sobbing, kicking, and pounding her fists against the pillow.

"Ding?" Jane asked. The wailing continued, so Jane sat beside her, careful to stay out of firing range of her size-six feet.

"Ding?" she tried again. "What is it?"

The kicking and pounding relented, but Ding remained facedown, unmoving. Jane put a hand cautiously on her back.

"It's Dean!" she wailed, finally.

"Dean?"

"Dean Willet!" Ding screamed into the pillow. "My fiancé!" The last word melted into a pitiful sob.

It rushed back to Jane then—Trade Winds, the airmen. He had given Ding the air force pin, her first conquest.

"Oh, darling." She rubbed Ding's shoulders. "How did you learn?"

Ding sat up and looked at Jane, her makeup running down her cheeks in dark meandering rivulets.

"His name came across my desk. No one could have known since I hadn't added him to my list. Oh, Jane, it's just awful. He was just here. We were just dancing. And now . . ." She trailed off. "And the worst part of it," she continued a moment later, "I had to type up the letter to his parents myself. I couldn't stand the thought of letting those nasty WAVES see me cry."

"Surely they would have understood."

"I couldn't give them the satisfaction. And besides, it doesn't matter now." Ding dried her eyes and put on a brave face. "I signed on with the Cadet Nurses."

Jane dropped her hands to her lap.

"I'll start my training next month."

"Ding! What if they send you abroad?"

"I won't have to worry about that till I finish training. But after that, I hope they do. I want to do something, Jane. *Really* do something."

She was brave. Everyone laughed at silly ole Ding, but she was really, truly brave.

"Where will you train?" Jane asked. The story and all its implications were coming together slowly, one word at a time, like in her daddy's crossword puzzles.

"Here in Washington," Ding said, and a cool wave of relief washed over Jane's insides. "But of course I'll have to move to one of the nurse residences." The wave congealed, leaving Jane with a belly full of rancid jam.

"I'm sorry," Ding said. "I'm sorry for everything. I should have stayed home with you when Owen—"

Jane cut her off. "No, I'm sorry. I wasn't mad at you. It was him, of course. And I should have gone with you and had a good time. It's just like me, isn't it—refusing an invitation and then sulking around the house for a week?"

"It rather is," Ding said, and Jane swatted her thigh. They both burst into giggles and then collapsed into a hug.

"I'm proud of you," Jane said.

"Can you believe I got in?" Ding asked. "When I put my mind to it, when I wasn't thinking about boys, I found I knew all that stuff, deep down."

So Ding had beauty and brains. Jane was the plain, old, boring one. Still, it felt good for things to be back to normal, her cousin blabbing a mile a minute. Jane tried not to think about the quiet that would return when Ding moved out, or how she would pay the rent alone.

Downstairs, the buzzer buzzed. "Ooh!" Ding squealed. "It's for you! Now, don't be mad."

"Be mad? Ding, what did you—"

Ding pulled Jane down the stairs, walking backward as she smoothed her cousin's hair. "It was torture not to tell you. On that date, all he talked about was you—'Does Jane like her job?' 'Is Jane always so serious?' It was tedious at the time, of course. And I didn't get my pin, but—"

"Ding! You didn't!"

"Life is so unpredictable, Jane. You have to take these chances when the—"

"Absolutely not." Jane planted herself firmly on the bottom step.

"I won't hear any more about it. This is my first good deed of many." She rushed to the door.

"I left my bag upstairs," Jane said.

"Take mine. It's fully stocked," Ding called back.

She would look ridiculous standing there when he came in. She stepped from the stairwell and stood behind her cousin, just like the first time he had come.

The door opened and there, smiling widely, was Owen, as handsome as she remembered. He removed his fedora and bowed his head to the girls.

"Hello, Jane," Owen said.

"Hello, Owen."

Ding beamed.

"Can I take you out?"

"I suppose I could go out." Jane put one foot in front of the other—testing for land mines.

"Have a lovely time," Ding told them, shoving her pocketbook toward Jane and knocking Jane's bottom as she pushed them out the door.

Jane blinked as Owen led her down the steps to his convertible. Jane put a hand to her chignon. Her pins were already coming loose. Inside, Jane marveled at the car's modern interior. Owen was like his car: fast, open, extravagant.

"Where are we going?" she asked, suddenly self-conscious about her simple work dress. "If I had known we were . . ."

"Don't worry, sweetheart. I just had to see you. I haven't stopped thinking about you," Owen said. "It was like lightning, when I met you at the Armory. All those other girls clambering around, and you . . ."

"I was hungover."

"You aren't hungover now, I take it?"

"Of course not."

"And you're just as beautiful. And just as smart."

"This is a beautiful car," Jane said.

"What did I tell you? Smart girl."

They set off and Jane allowed herself to relax a bit as the wind rolled over her skin. It was a luxury in this city not to sweat your brains out.

"I'm from Washington State," Owen said. "Since you're curious."

"West Virginia," Jane said.

"And how long have you been in the navy, Owen?" Owen said in a high falsetto. "Well, Jane, since you asked, I've been in since before the war. I joined right after high school."

"So how old are you?" Jane asked.

"Worried you're out with a fuddy-duddy?" He laughed. "I'm thirty-two."

He wasn't a boy—he was a man.

Owen didn't ask Jane's age, and she didn't offer it.

"The Hamilton," Owen said, parking the Highlander smoothly as he gestured toward the building before them, its impressive facade made up of an enormous half circle of white stone. The delicate Art Deco design upon it reminded Jane of a peacock's tail. Owen got out of the car, met Jane on her side, and led her by the hand through the revolving door.

So this was how it felt when the world was suddenly in Technicolor. Jane twirled under the vaulted ceilings and nearly clicked her heels on the gleaming marbled floor.

"Oh, this is a dream," she exclaimed. Owen beamed, then led her to the bar.

The crowd—if you could call it a crowd at all; there was actually room to breathe—was older than Jane was used to. Several officers in their uniforms sat with women who looked much more sophisticated than Jane felt.

"What do you drink, doll?" Owen asked.

"Gin rickey," she told him, and he leaned against the bar, waiting for the barman.

As she waited, Jane observed the other patrons. The women, dressed entirely in silk, were pale as china dolls—they certainly didn't tan on the sidewalks like the simple Government Girls, except—Jane recognized her with a start. In the uniform circle around the bar, a woman stood out—a woman Jane knew!

"Claudine?" Jane exclaimed. The woman straightened her exposed brown back and turned.

"Jane!"

"I thought you stuck around U Street."

"And I thought you stuck around Trade Winds." Claudine smirked.

"My date . . ." Jane motioned toward Owen, who was chatting familiarly with the bartender.

"My husband." Claudine motioned toward the man next to her. "Congressman William L. Wills."

Jane's jaw dropped. How arrogant she had been, thinking she had been doing this woman some sort of decency, when in fact . . . Jane had felt sorry for her, when all along Claudine had probably been pitying the poor girl from the backwoods. Jane again smoothed her plain dress. Well, regardless, it was no excuse for the way the other girls treated Claudine.

Claudine smiled graciously. "Have a fabulous night, Jane," she said. Jane nodded, mute.

Owen returned and handed Jane her glass. Drink in hand, she felt much more comfortable. As the alcohol made its way through her veins, she eased into the atmosphere of haughty, cool merriment.

"What made you sign up for civil service?" Owen asked, and she recounted the story of the bubble gum ad.

"What made you join the navy?"

"My brother was in the First World War. My older brother. He didn't come back."

"I'm so sorry." Jane placed a hand on Owen's arm. When he clutched it with his own, she pulled hers away.

"And I nearly didn't either," he added.

"What do you mean? You aren't going overseas with the boys from the Armory?"

"I've been overseas. I lost two toes in Midway." Jane was amazed at the lightness in his eyes, even when sharing this piece of information. "I could have gone home with a Purple Heart, but I wasn't ready. They have me running trainings here instead."

"You're a hero."

Owen blushed. "Want to dance with a hero?"

"Of course I do. But I could use another drink first."

"There's a war on, Ms. Walls, or have you heard? Gin may not be rationed yet, but . . ."

"Oh, you!" Jane laughed.

They drank and then swayed, cheek to cheek. Owen continued to shower Jane with his affections. "I've never met a girl like you. You changed me the first time I laid eyes on you."

When Jane found herself wanting to touch him, to be touched by him, to run her fingers through his blond hair, to let him kiss her, she resisted. How could she be so hypocritical? This was exactly why she had chided Ding.

But this was not some general need for attention. This was a need for Owen's attention. Jane discovered with a start that she wanted Owen to unbutton her dress, to slip it from her shoulders. Words from the papers ran through her mind—the accusations that Government Girls were more interested in hanky-panky than they were in their civic duties. But wasn't that just the thing? Didn't the women keeping the country's vital processes functioning deserve to be treated like adults? Didn't she deserve, after coming home with inky fingers and aches all over, after stopping potential saboteurs in their tracks, to feel *good*? Didn't Owen, after all he had sacrificed, deserve some happiness? Jane wasn't interested in hanky-panky. This was not hanky-panky.

When Owen told her, in a low, serious voice that he had a room upstairs, Jane found herself replying in the same register, "Take me to it."

In the room, just as swanky as the bar, Jane set Ding's pocketbook on the vanity and excused herself to the powder room. Staring at herself in the mirror, she thought of her mother and her mother's Bible verses. She was not her mother.

When she returned, she found Owen sitting on the chesterfield sofa, preparing to remove his shoes. Jane held her breath, nervous to see his mangled foot. They looked into each other's eyes as he peeled away the sock and tossed it to the floor. And then there it was—white scar tissue where his toes once were. Jane only wanted him more. She went to him and caressed his foot with the tips of her fingers. Owen pulled her to his lap and switched off the lamp.

Jane's memory faded with the light outside the home, and she dozed, worn-out from the happy news of Cassidy's return, and from unrelenting memories.

CASSIDY

CASSIDY STOOD OUTSIDE the entrance to the *Record Delta*, her arms full of her dad's office things. She hadn't realized it was so close to where Simon held his farm stand. She remembered when her dad had become the editor, when she was around eleven, and he had asked if she wanted to go to the mall.

"Yes!" she'd agreed, jumping from the couch and dropping *Harriet the Spy.* The mall was forty minutes away and going was a treat. Cassidy sat in front for the trip, something Paloma wouldn't allow for another three years or so, and Ken put on a Bob Dylan tape—*Blood on the Tracks.*

"It's funny, isn't it?" Ken asked as they listened to "Idiot Wind." Cassidy nodded. "But listen to the end."

"They're both idiots." She laughed. "Or neither of them are. Is he just mad at her?"

Ken smiled and shrugged. "We don't know."

At the mall, Ken told Cassidy he needed to buy a tie. "I'm the editor now," he said. "I can't be a schmuck anymore."

They made a game of it—Ken pulling the loudest, most ridiculous ties he could find from the department store racks and Cassidy nodding enthusiastically in approval. "Oh yes, certainly." They left JCPenney with a stuffed bag of paisleys and florals, stripes and polka dots.

"Pretzel for my fashion consultant?" Ken proposed.

Cassidy grinned. "Cinnamon!" She waited on a bench while Ken bought their treats, feeling very grown-up, as she always did in the presence of her father. Ken returned and presented her pretzel, warm and glistening with butter and sugar crystals. As she licked the sticky cinnamon-sugar mixture from her fingers, the napkin fell from her lap.

"Oh well." She shrugged, trying to imitate Ken's shoulder movements. "Not my problem."

"No," Ken said so sternly that she jumped. "We don't make more work for other people than we have to."

Obviously, this was a lesson many of Cassidy's fans hadn't been taught. She smirked to herself, thinking about all the awful comments and demands she'd received.

Fuck your ugly asshole now

This nasty cunt

Bet ur pussy smells like rat garbage

The last had actually made her laugh. The others would have stung had they not been anomalies amid the gracious praise and encouragement her regulars showered upon her. That was the difference between those comments and the ones she'd endured as a teenager. Online, people stood up for her. Online, the general consensus was that she was hot—that she was worthy.

But the assholes she'd grown up with weren't who she was staying for. She was staying for Grandma Jane. Simon had made a life here and she could too.

The farm stand stood just south of the paper's parking lot and consisted of three covered tables beneath a canvas canopy. Behind the table stood a silhouetted figure, waving at her. Cassidy walked a bit closer. "Simon!" she said when she could make out his face. She took Ken's stuff to the car and walked over.

Beyond the stand lay a field of long, flat yellow grasses, as thick and unkempt as the hair of some giant, marked only by the deep muddy tread of a tractor that had parted the strands.

"Where's Noeli?" Simon asked as Cassidy approached.

"She's back at the farm, packing."

"Well, I'm glad you could make it out to say bye. And to see the stand!"

"So, uh. Not bye. I'm staying?" Cassidy said, inspecting boxes of root vegetables that Simon had grown. He had turned seeds and dirt and water into food. She cringed again as she thought about how much more useful this was than the boners and ejaculate she helped manufacture.

"Dude! Here?" Simon asked.

"Yeah." She looked up and grinned.

"High five, bud!" Simon didn't raise a hand. Instead he tossed a purple-and-white sphere into Cassidy's hands. She fumbled a bit but caught the vegetable. "Celebratory rutabaga?" he asked.

Cassidy laughed. "Thanks."

"Dude, that's so rad," Simon said, smiling broadly.

Cassidy felt the vegetable in her hands, running her fingers over the ridged circles that interrupted its smooth skin. It felt unpretentious and uncomplicated, solid and wholesome, just like Simon. She threw the rutabaga back at him, harder than she'd meant to. He ducked and it landed in the grass behind him.

"Sorry!"

"It's cool," Simon said, laughing.

"Do you want to go to the river tomorrow?" Cassidy asked. "I want to do something fun."

"It's kind of cold for the river."

"Not *in* the river, dummy. Just to the river."

Simon laughed again. "Yeah, sounds great. Meet at my place?"

"Sure." It was good to have plans—things to look forward to.

Back at the house, Noeli was done packing and was lying on Cassidy's bed, staring at the Weakerthans poster on the ceiling. Quietly, Cassidy lay down beside her.

It was weird how music defined eras, but she never realized it until the era was over. Like in sixth grade when Cassidy got snowed in at Simon's house and had to spend the night and they'd listened to "Fireflies" by Owl City over and over, before Simon had stopped listening to anything that wasn't punk or ska. Cassidy tried to remember what she'd been thinking of as they sang along, but it didn't matter. It wasn't about the lyrics, it was about the music itself and who she was listening with. It was why adults were so into oldies. It wasn't about calling someone Al or only needing love. It was about being twelve or eighteen or twenty-five.

And now, when she listened to the Weakerthans, she'd remember when their song had come on in her car as she was driving Lyft and the drunken Noeli, who she learned later was coming back from a fight with Lupe, had slurred, "Holy shit. This is the Weakerthans. How is this the Weakerthans right now?" sparking their friendship. Her mind drifted to thoughts of California—to pink sunsets and wide clean sidewalks. She turned her head and looked at Noeli, whose chest rose and fell with each breath. What songs would make her think of now?

"I'll miss you," Cassidy said, her mania cooling. Noeli turned her head.

"Don't worry, I'll text you every time my mom does something shitty."

"So, several times daily."

Noeli smiled. "Seriously. You don't have to stay. I know you hated it here growing up."

"You hate the IE," Cassidy pointed out.

"At least there are other brown people there."

"True," Cassidy said. "But there are brown people in lots of places."

"Maybe I'll get out someday." There was hurt in Noeli's voice and Cassidy suddenly felt guilty, like she was abandoning her friend.

"Maybe I'll come back to California at some point."

Noeli shrugged against the sheets. "Maybe."

An hour later, after they'd hugged on the front porch and Cassidy had warned Noeli several times to watch for deer, she watched the SUV move slowly down the driveway and out of view.

"Oh, good. I didn't miss you!" Paloma ran outside and found Cassidy standing, staring out at the driveway and the pond beyond. "Where's the rental?"

"Noeli took it. I'm . . . I'm not going."

"Cassidy! That's . . . that's wonderful. I'm so glad you . . ." She stopped as she noticed her daughter's face.

"Oh, honey." Paloma's face softened and she stepped toward Cassidy, then pulled her close. Cassidy swallowed, and her throat felt pinched.

"Oh, honey," Paloma repeated, rubbing Cassidy's back. Her lavender-and-incense smell was dark and musky.

Cassidy cried in squeezed little gasps at first, little squeaks escaping her mouth as she scrunched her eyes tight and hid her face in Paloma's shoulder. She had to let the sobs out then, not for emotional release as much as to release the pressure in her throat. Holding it back hurt, so she let it go.

"You're loved." Paloma continued rubbing, her palm tracing wide ovals from one of Cassidy's shoulder blades to the other and then back around. One shoulder, the other shoulder. Left, right. Left, right. "You are so loved."

When Cassidy finally sat up, the pressure in her throat had dissipated, but her eyes felt tired and raw.

"Oh, Cassidy." Paloma wiped her daughter's face with the back of her hand. She was still wearing her wedding ring, a simple gold band, and Cassidy felt it, cool, on her cheek. Something about this was unbearable. It was the knowledge of impermanence—the in-between. She hadn't taken the ring off yet, but she would soon. And Grandma Jane—she was okay, but she wouldn't be. More tears appeared and Cassidy wiped them with her own hand.

"Let's sit. I'll make some tea." Paloma looked at Cassidy lovingly, like her daughter was still a small child, and led her by the hand to the couch, where Cassidy curled up in the fetal position, staring at the piles of books on the coffee table at eye level.

"Those were some of your dad's favorites." Paloma gestured toward the piles—a stack of Wendell Berry, several books about sustainable living and environmental issues, some poetry, and a few novels. She disappeared into the kitchen and returned a few minutes later with a green mug, the steam curling up from the exact center of its circular ceramic mouth. "I thought you might want them." Paloma set the mug on the coffee table next to the books.

"Maybe." Cassidy sat up and took *Lost Horizon* into her lap.

"You know you could have told me Noeli was your girlfriend. I've always tried to make sure you know I love you no matter—"

Cassidy cut Paloma off. "Noeli wasn't my girlfriend."

"Oh, I thought . . . with the tears . . ."

"She was my only friend, Mom. She's the only friend besides Simon I've ever had."

"Are you sure you aren't—"

"Yes, Mom. Jesus. I like women. But Noeli wasn't—"

"Oh, Cassidy!" It was Paloma's turn to interrupt, and she did so by pulling Cassidy into a suffocating embrace. "I'm so happy you told me. I've always had an inkling and I'm so glad you finally felt comfortable enough with me to say it. You know, I'm not strictly straight myself. I've always thought women were more aesthetically pleasing than—"

Why did Cassidy feel ashamed? Obviously, her mom was okay with it. But telling her mom, or being "out" in general, felt like sharing intimate details about her sex life. It felt like admitting to everyone who had secretly suspected it that she was, in fact, weird and dirty. But Cassidy didn't think those things about other queer people. It only felt embarrassing when it was about her.

As she thought of Noeli's mother, guilt joined her shame. Noeli was brave enough to be herself around her mom even when she knew she wasn't supportive. No wonder Cassidy never felt like a real part of the queer community. She didn't deserve to be. She wouldn't subject herself to the slightest bit of discomfort.

Cassidy wriggled away from Paloma's arms. "Did you hear anything else I said? This is exactly why I don't talk to you."

"I'm sorry," Paloma said quickly. "Yes, I heard you. I'm so sorry, honey. I'm so sorry your friend left, and that you have felt so alone."

Cassidy relaxed her jaw but steeled her reservation. She should feel grateful that her mom was accepting. She knew many people weren't so lucky. But Paloma's acceptance felt to Cassidy more about Paloma's own need to feel like a good person and less about real open-mindedness. She would never tell her mom about camming. She would never understand the real facets of her sexuality or her life.

"I'm fine. It's my choice to stay. It's just hard to say goodbye." Cassidy opened the book on her lap to a page marked by a folded piece of yellowing notepaper.

"He was rereading that one," Paloma said. "He read that one a lot."

Cassidy closed the book again and placed it back on top of the pile. She could feel the splintery heat of the woodstove in her lungs. Cassidy pulled out a thick bound journal tucked between *Watership Down* and *The Clan of the Cave Bear*. She could not bring herself to open it, and instead carried it with her across the room, to the large stereo system that occupied the space where most families would put a TV. Cassidy pressed the button and waited for the red light to flicker on, then pressed play and turned the volume knob up a quarter turn. Bob Dylan wailed "Mr. Tambourine Man" from the speakers. She walked back to the couch and sat down, hugging her knees to her chest and balancing the journal on top of them. This back-and-forth was worse than when Paloma had first called with the news. This was what she wanted. Why was she over the moon one moment and panicking the next?

Paloma stood and kissed Cassidy gently on the head. "I'm going to do some more packing," she said. "I love you, no matter what. I love all of you." She went upstairs, leaving Cassidy alone.

Once Paloma had gone, Cassidy opened the journal like a sacred text, handling the pages covered in Ken's handwriting with exquisite care. So much had happened in the last day. Had she really just decided to stay in West Virginia? Had she really just come out to her mom? Some pages of the journal were filled, the words jammed from corner to corner. Others had only a few words—poetry. His writing was hard to read, and

Cassidy had to work to make out each word. It felt wrong to read them, but she continued to turn the pages.

With effort, she deciphered a poem. *In California, even dandelions are strange*, Ken had written over and over, his line breaks and capitalization changing each time.

He was right. In California, *everything* was strange—even those things that seemed as natural and as non-alterable as dandelions took on a different quality. Or maybe it was the context. When unnatural crap was the norm, unblemished nature seemed strange. It was good to stay. This was a real place. It was where she should be.

Cassidy had never been a poetry person, had certainly never stopped to analyze a poem, but reading these now felt like receiving a secret message. She flipped a few more pages, until a title caught her eye, centered on the top of a page and written more neatly than most of the contents. *A Brief History of My God*, it said.

It was an essay, several pages long, and she struggled through interpreting it—a sketchy account of Ken's experience with religion and an explanation of how his own beliefs had evolved—as a kid, liking the songs at church, then as a young adult, trying drugs and expanding his mind.

At one time I knew there was a God. He went on to describe his take on reincarnation—the one he had shared with Cassidy just a few weeks earlier. The essay ended with a paragraph on Ken's embarrassment that the idea of God again seemed possible as he considered his mother's dementia.

Now, he knew. Despite her deep fear of death, Cassidy found herself, for a split second, jealous.

What had her father written about *her*? Cassidy wondered with a jolt. She glanced toward the empty steps and turned her back slightly, hiding the notebook from view in case her mother came back down.

Skimming Ken's handwriting for something in particular was impossible. Now the letters squirmed—her eyes were tired from working out the essay. She stopped every few pages and analyzed a word or two. There were political poems, a draft of an editorial about the pipeline, lots about sex and women and thighs and legs and breasts, but nothing about her.

Cassidy had gotten poetry from men online. One had written about her as *the girl with the crystal eyes*, and another had written a long free-form composition about the show she'd done in an Ariel costume. Her take on his favorite animated character, he'd said, had re-sparked his first hints of sexual longing and healed something long unfulfilled. Men declared their love for her in numerous thoughtful ways. They gave her nicknames and explained, in detail, how much her attention meant to them. But her own father, a professional writer, hadn't thought to compose something for her.

Cassidy wanted something cathartic—something she could keep with her, always, something she could get tattooed. She closed the journal with a soft smack and slammed it on the coffee table, then picked up *Lost Horizon* and threw it on the couch, watching it bounce slightly before landing in the crease between the seat and the back. She wanted to rip the pages out one at a time and scatter them on the floor, leave them there for someone else to deal with, but she could not make her hands harm the book. Instead she crossed the room in one long step, opened the door of the CD player with the Dylan disc still spinning, grabbed it from its shelf, and snapped it in half. Not satisfied, she broke it another time, then carried the sharp pieces to the kitchen trash and buried them under the plastic wrappers from the bouquets that were now wilting on the table, stifling a frustrated scream.

Cassidy muttered under her breath, "Where are you, Daddy? Tell me what you know now. If you have to be dead, can you tell me if it's all bullshit?" She heard no answer, felt no presence.

Fury reached down to Cassidy's tingling fingertips. She wasn't mad at her parents. She was mad that she'd ended up just as selfish and self-absorbed as they were. She was a piece of shit that lived for constant affirmation, that needed other people to call her pretty so she didn't feel bad about herself. She liked to think she was so empowered, so independent, but really, she was petty and pathetic, a needy little bitch. She slammed the trash can back under the kitchen sink, pivoted, and found herself facing Paloma.

"Cassidy, I am so sorry I said what I said earlier," Paloma said. "About my relationship with your father." The two women stood facing each other like a mirror, their shoulders sloping forward and their hands hanging at their sides. Even their heights were the same. "I hope you know that there is nothing you could do, nothing you could say, that could change my love for you."

"I know." Cassidy tried to step around her mom, but Paloma stopped her, placing her hands on Cassidy's shoulders, and the two looked directly into each other's eyes.

"You'll find your way," Paloma said.

"Okay," Cassidy growled.

They stood like that, breathing for a moment, until Paloma broke the stance.

"Are you done checking out the books? Come look at your dad's old school things. See what you want to keep."

"Fine." Cassidy stomped after her up the stairs. Kneeling before the pile of treasures Paloma had gathered, she fingered her dad's leather tool belt and remembered hanging off of it as he tried to work. She held his guitar pick over her head and watched the light filter through the tortoiseshell. She felt the smooth wood of his hand-carved fountain pen and the small heft of his pocketknife. His absence buzzed in all of them. "I don't need any of these," she said. All she'd wanted from him was a poem, or if there was a poem, better handwriting so she could read it.

PALOMA

HOW COULD PALOMA possibly explain her feelings for Ken to Cassidy? She'd been trying to parse them herself since the day they'd met. Even at their wedding, a small ceremony on the island of Kampa, below the Charles Bridge, Paloma had not understood the complicated mix of admiration and aversion she held in her heart for her husband-to-be.

She had loved seeing the bridge from the island. From below, the physical and intellectual behemoth, the heart of the city, seemed indestructible. She could see its building blocks, its powerful arches and huge pillars, sandstone green with algae where they met the water. Here, the reality of the thing was accessible. From here, Paloma could possess it.

The island was busy on that warm day; several people with bowl cuts and sneakers walked by the wedding, pausing to watch. Families picnicked nearby and a group of teenagers sat close to the river. One played "Let It Be" on an acoustic guitar as the others shared a single beer. Birds flew in every direction over the Vltava.

As their guests found seats on the grass, Paloma stared out over the water at a man in a rowboat paddling against the current. Sometimes it was easier to go where the flow wanted to take you. The back of the man's boat bonked against the bridge. Sometimes it was futile to fight.

Ken cared about Paloma. He wanted to make a family with her. She didn't have to search for whatever she was looking for anymore. She could finally settle. She'd come to this conclusion after a long series of dates with Ken, each of which had ended with a marriage proposal, and she repeated it to herself often as they made plans for the nuptials. At some point she had stopped distinguishing between his philosophies on home and him as a person. They'd been on the river when Paloma had finally accepted Ken's proposal, their small boat floating easily between island and city shore. She had been so tired of fighting, so tired of worrying and wondering what the world held for her.

The officiant cleared her throat and Paloma's heart beat hard against the charm Ken had given her the first day they met. The officiant was a friend of Jan's, a professor from the philosophy department who had been imprisoned for her political actions under the regime. At Paloma's request, she spoke of love as a means of resistance. At Ken's request, the woman read a quote from Carl Jung:

"This experience punctured the desired hole in her rationalism and broke the ice of her intellectual resistance."

Ken grinned at Paloma and she shivered, looking away from him and toward their guests. That was certainly what had happened, but she wasn't sure how romantic it was. Jan sat slouched in his oversized suit, stroking his chin thoughtfully. Jane, who had flown in for the ceremony, wiped joyful tears from her cheeks. Paloma felt a resolved, resigned sort of happiness.

Even then, before Cassidy, Paloma had loved Ken as her child's father. This *was* romantic, in a way that felt weighty to Paloma—a fateful way, rawer and realer than head-over-heels infatuation. She loved Ken for leading her to this place where she had discovered her ability to make a home out of sheer will. And she loved Ken for dying, for letting her go. This was not something she could ever say aloud, especially to Cassidy, but somehow, she hoped her daughter could understand this love that was not love. Perhaps Cassidy might even grow to love her mother because of it, and in spite of the ways she felt Paloma had failed her.

CASSIDY

CASSIDY THOUGHT ABOUT her goodbye hug with Noeli as she tramped up the holler to the double-wide trailer that Simon's dad had secured to the ground with concrete before leaving Simon, his mother, and his brother for a linesman job in Colorado and never returning. She could still smell the green apple scent of Noeli's curls.

Their trailer was in the center of an arching row of ones just like it, all cemented to the earth, each with their own unique pile of junk in the yard—rusting car bodies, broken baby jumpers, an old washing machine.

Simon's mom opened the door.

"Hey, Cassidy honey. How're you doin'?" She smelled just as Cassidy remembered, like old cigarettes and Bath & Body Works Sun-Ripened Raspberry.

"I'm all right, Beth. How are you?"

"You know, same old shit." She threw a skinny arm out, gesturing into the once-mobile home. Indeed, the home looked like it always had—boxes of Camel Lights stacked high on the kitchen counter, the small sink overflowing with dirty dishes. Stacks of *Us Weekly* lay scattered on the floor in the place a coffee table might be in another home, and filthy ashtrays were everywhere—the floor, the table, the arms of the love seat and recliner. There was something different about it though—a quality of disarray that Cassidy couldn't quite place. It had always been dirty—the kind of place that made her feel older than she was when she hung out there as a teenager, but this was different. She noticed something else, then. Scattered among the cigarettes, the magazines, the ashtrays, and the dirty dishes were empty pill containers, many on their sides, their tops long gone, others stacked neatly in lines, the way a child might lay out blocks.

Cassidy looked back to Beth and saw her arm, still outstretched, was mottled from the middle of her forearm to just above her elbow by a pale gray bruise. The sudden realization of what this meant made Cassidy gasp. Before she could stop herself from staring, the sight of black crusting scabs in a neat line starting just under the bruise and moving down toward Beth's wrist brought a wave of nausea. Cassidy had to look away.

"Is, uh, Simon here?" She felt heartbroken for Beth, this woman she had known since she was twelve, who had felt like a coconspirator at times, sneaking her Doritos though Paloma wouldn't buy them, who had given her and Simon the privacy they needed as teenagers to make this space feel like a sanctuary. Even among the outdated decorations—the creepy porcelain dolls on tiny rocking chairs; the sagging couches; the large wooden gun cabinet, empty since Simon's dad had left, save for a .22 and two BB guns, one Simon's and one his brother's—the trailer had felt homey and welcoming. Now the atmosphere had shifted to sad and stifling.

"Simon!" Beth called, her voice gravelly.

Simon appeared behind her, looking apologetic, his hair combed neatly to one side. He looked so out of place—so responsible and handsome and clean.

"See you later, Mom," Simon said, practically closing the door in Beth's face.

"Hey," she called out, pushing it back open. Her fingers were spindly and her nails dirty. "You aren't going to bring your brother?"

"He doesn't want to come," Simon said.

"Robbie!" Beth called out.

"What!" a voice growled from the direction of the bedrooms.

"Get your lazy ass out here."

Simon's older brother, Robbie, slumped into the room, his wiry frame hidden by baggy Levi's and a stained gray hoodie. His eyes looked hollow, big gray circles seemed to make up the majority of his face, and he clutched the top of a two-liter of Mountain Dew.

"Do you want to come to Sago?" Simon asked in the same tone a child would say "I'm sorry" if they had been forced to apologize.

"Why the fuck would I want to go to Sago?" Robbie turned back around, disappearing again.

"Bye, Mom," Simon said, closing the door hard.

Cassidy waited for Simon to speak first, but he said nothing. He turned up the music and "California Sun" rattled through the Porsche's old speakers.

"Wait, this is on the *Greatest Hits* album?" Cassidy asked.

"Nope." Simon grinned.

"You got the tape out?"

Simon's smile widened as he nodded.

"And you put in another Ramones tape?"

Simon smirked.

"It's bad, Cass," he finally said when the song ended. "Both of them. I don't know what to do about it."

"They're not your responsibility."

"Who else's responsibility would they be?" he asked.

"Their own."

Simon snorted.

Cassidy wanted to argue, to insist he take a stand, do something, get them help, but she had read the indictment lists in the *Record Delta*. How much help would it do Beth and Robbie to get arrested?

She looked at her friend in awe. He was so solid, so steady, so calm in his quietness.

"What was the movie with the brothers we watched for an ice cream party once?" Simon said, changing the subject as he turned onto Sago Road, toward the river.

"I think it was just called *Step Brothers*. 'Did we just become best friends?'" Cassidy said in her best Will Ferrell voice.

"Yep!" Simon quoted, and they high-fived, cracking up. Their hands lingered for a moment on the center console before Cassidy pulled hers away. She was surprised at how little anxiety she felt on the long drive.

Simon followed the winding curves of the road until they reached a small turnout. There were no other cars—not surprising, given the season, and Simon and Cassidy got out and began walking along the old railroad track.

On the left, the thawing river babbled. Cassidy glanced up the hill to their right at a hulking piece of mining equipment and imagined the miners—people she knew, who she saw at Sheetz and Walmart and C.J. Maggie's—wearing helmets and coveralls, covered in coal dust, their headlamps shining into the dark like stars.

Simon carried a rolled beach towel tucked under an arm and his keys around his neck on a piece of leather. Cassidy carried a tote bag with her own towel, a change of clothes, and a granola bar. Simon led the way slowly, balancing occasionally on the track like a beam, sometimes walking beside it. It was always a kind of meditation, this trek to the river—a passage from one world to another.

"You all right back there?" Simon asked.

"Yup." The rocks under the tracks pressed through the rubber soles of her shoes. When they reached the clearing down to the usual spot—the Buckhannon River green and wide and dotted with rocks ten feet across—they climbed carefully down the sloping bank. She turned her feet sideways, like her dad had taught her, to give herself more surface area and stop herself from slipping.

Once at the water, they stepped their way across smaller stones and big tilted boulders to a shelflike slab directly in the sunlight. There, they spread their towels on the flat rock and lay on their bellies, side by side, soaking in the warmth.

"Isn't it weird how when other people hear 'Sago,' they just think of the mine disaster?" Cassidy mused.

"I don't think most people think of anything when they hear 'Sago,'" Simon said.

"That's weird, too. But yeah. I don't know if I'll ever have that be my primary connection with the place. It's just . . . here."

Simon nodded, thinking. "It's hard to imagine that happened in a place so beautiful," he said.

Cassidy opened her eyes and looked at the far shore. The river was lined with thick pines on either side and the water made a constant bubbling sound.

"Can you believe that fucker ran for state senate?" Simon asked.

"The coal guy? With all the safety violations? Yeah, that's ridiculous."

It was strange talking West Virginia politics with Simon. In high school they'd often discussed national stuff, global stuff, and what Cassidy saw as "big" issues. Punk music had radicalized him about those, and Cassidy always figured he knew what he was talking about, but local or state affairs had never made their radar. Simon had worn a Free Mumia shirt for most of junior year; a history teacher sent Cassidy to the back of the room when she called him out for referring to Japanese people as "Orientals." Local stuff had seemed insignificant—removed from the important things happening in the world.

How had they not realized it was the local stuff that mattered? Cassidy thought about her classmates' relatives trapped underground. She thought of the scabs on Beth's arm and the dark circles under Robbie's eyes. It was all connected. If the rest of the country weren't so dependent on coal, West Virginia wouldn't have to mine it. If the War on Drugs weren't such a fucking joke . . . Cassidy rolled onto her back and stared up at the sky, which was unobstructed by trees from this vantage point in the middle of the river.

"Cass," Simon said. He pushed himself up to seated and stared over at the far bank. Cassidy watched him, lifting one arm to shield her face from the sun. "Were you with Noeli? Was she your girlfriend?"

"No. She was a friend."

Simon took several deep breaths, biting his lower lip. Finally he squeezed his eyes shut. When he opened them, he looked determined. "Cass, I've been in love with you for a long time," he blurted. She propped herself up on her elbows and let him continue.

"I know this probably isn't the time to tell you. I know. With your dad and everything. And I know you usually like women anyway."

Cassidy sat up all the way now, listening.

"Cass, I would be so good to you."

"Simon," Cassidy started. She didn't know what to say. He'd always been more like a brother than anything else. Here with him now, though, hearing this, she noticed how handsome he was. He had lost the chubby cheeks that had made him look younger than his age for so long, and he'd become lean and muscular from working in the gardens. Cassidy thought about his compassion and loyalty, caring for his family, how steadfast and dependable he had always been. He was so familiar and so safe. At the same time, there was something new and intriguing about him. If she had met him online, he would have been a breath of fresh air—a break from old, hairy men.

Maybe she should kiss him.

Simon had changed since Cassidy had been to Buckhannon last. He was more confident, and there was something about being here, too, in Buckhannon, and here, at the river, on this rock. There was a gritty sensuality—a realness. This place had a tangible physicality that seemed to amplify Cassidy's sense of *body.* This wasn't pretend. It wasn't an act.

She really should kiss him.

She almost did it. She almost leaned in, tilted her head, and parted her lips. She could see it playing like a movie in her mind. She would kiss him. They would kiss, on *this* rock, in *this* town, and it would mean . . . something.

"Simon," Cassidy said again, and his face perked up, like it had when she'd given him a NOFX CD for Christmas in ninth grade. That was it—she couldn't see him from an outsider's perspective. He would always be the kid she grew up with, regardless of who he was now, and he would always be part of here, of Buckhannon. The weight of Buckhannon, of all of it—of her dad and her grandma and her mom's hippie friends, of how Paloma had said she'd never loved Ken, of the mine disaster and Simon's mom and brother, and just all of it. It was crushing. Pretend was light and free. Real was suffocating.

Buckhannon was more than a place now. It was a mass, pressing down with all the heaviness of all of those awful things.

It was a place where the unthinkable could happen, and Simon was too much a part of it.

"I'm so sorry," she said, and looked away from him, toward the pines on the shore.

Simon's eyes creased at the corners and his lips turned down, but he nodded, holding his tears at bay, and lay back down on the rock.

Cassidy lay down and grabbed Simon's hand as they stared up at the clouds. Simon had never cared what other people said about her. Cassidy showed her most private parts to men with Confederate flags in their profiles, told men whose wives thought they were showering that she wished she could suck their cocks. She could do this for Simon. He deserved it. Cassidy rolled over and took Simon's face in her hands. She kissed him, then unbuttoned his jeans. The river flowed around the rock where they lay, parting and bubbling, always moving, moving, moving.

JANE

JANE HAD BEEN so happy after the Hamilton. She'd wanted to skip, to click her heels. She'd drowned herself in work, not for the usual purpose of numbing her melancholy, but to pass the time until she could see Owen again.

"Are you bringing anyone to the picnic?" Flossie asked, making the rounds with her clipboard.

"I'm having trouble narrowing it down," Erma said.

Flossie shook her head. "Well, narrow it down. I'm putting you down for a guest."

"Golly, I'm not sure," Peggy wondered aloud. "How does anyone make plans for three days away?"

"I'm sorry. I'm unable to attend," said Claudine. Unsurprised, Flossie made a note on her clipboard. Claudine winked at Jane.

"And you're bringing Ding, I suppose?"

Jane cleared her throat and looked at the floor. "I have another guest, actually." Her heart took on the lazy swing of a Glenn Miller tune and she blushed.

She looked up to see Claudine giving her a discreet smile before she looked away. The other girls demanded more information immediately.

"Only our second date."

"The Hamilton."

"It was marvelous."

"An officer, yes. Navy."

"Washington state."

Jane had not officially invited Owen to the FBI picnic. Rather, she had forgotten about it. The FBI picnic, suddenly, was child's play and Jane was a woman. Surely, though, Owen would humor her when she told him she was obligated—he had picked their first date, after all.

Owen arrived promptly at her doorstep at eleven o'clock that Sunday, as he'd promised when he'd brought her home from the Hamilton. He was as handsome as always, and Jane invited him in, then sat him at the kitchen table with a glass of water. "I hope you didn't make any grand plans," she said. She felt confident, beautiful even—it was her first premeditated meeting with Owen, and she'd been up since six getting ready. Her hair was freshly curled, her girdle and slip were washed. Her fingernails were a gleaming red.

"Only the grandest plans for you," Owen said.

"Can it wait?" Jane asked. "My friend Flossie is the organizer for the FBI's annual picnic, and I promised—"

Owen choked on his water.

"Well, goodness! Are you all right?" Jane asked as he wiped his mouth, eyes darting around the room.

"Quite." Owen coughed again. "Quite all right."

"Anyway," Jane said. "Don't tell me a game of baseball doesn't sound lovely."

Owen took a deep breath and cleared his throat again. He stroked his chin, his eyes now resting on a high corner of the room, above the stove.

Jane was struck with horror as she realized why he was hesitating. His toes. Owen couldn't run. How could she have been so stupid?

"Jane," Owen said.

"Oh, Owen. I'm so sorry. I didn't mean to—"

"No, Jane, it's . . ." He put his elbows on the table and began to massage his temples.

"We don't have to stay long. We can make an excuse and—"

"Jane, I can't go to the picnic because . . ." He looked at the ceiling. "Because my fiancée will be there."

The tips of Jane's ears went cold, the frost wrapping across her forehead and on around the back, squeezing her head like a vice. She must have misheard him. He could not have said what it sounded like he said.

"Your fiancée . . . ?" Stars twinkled in the corners of her vision, and she had the sudden sensation of staring at the horizon at sunset. She'd gone to bed with him. Not only unmarried, but him engaged. The darkness sank a bit lower and Jane was sinking now, too.

"Jane!" Owen shouted, jumping from his chair and catching her before she hit the ground. The light returned with a blinding flash.

"Get. Your. Hands. Off. Me," Jane hissed, prying herself from his embrace. She wobbled a bit, standing, and steadied herself on the table.

"I'm sorry." Owen sat down again. "I suppose I thought you knew. Or had an idea, in any case."

Jane threw her freshly manicured hands in the air. "Why on earth would you think that?" Because a girl with any sense would have known.

"Hell, Jane. Don't snap your cap."

"Snap my cap? I'll snap something!"

"Jane," Owen said in a low voice, glancing toward Mr. Plunkett's curtained room. "I thought you were going steady with someone, too. Or at least that you weren't that serious."

"And whatever gave you that idea? Our time together in your room?" She'd given herself so freely; of course she'd come across as a floozy.

"The pins in your pocketbook," Owen said. "I saw them when you got your lipstick."

"That was Ding's pocketbook!" Jane shouted. "Those are Ding's dad-blamed pins."

"Oh. Well. I wasn't trying to jerk you around. Listen. I know you're a good kid."

Jane thought the bobby pins might pop right off her scalp.

"I can't believe you snookered me into this. How many other girls?" Jane asked. "Since the war started. How many other girls?"

"You're really going to put me through the wringer?"

Jane laughed coldly. She was already putting herself through worse. She was the Government Girl they wrote about in the paper. Maybe she should have had a curfew. She pictured her mother busying herself with housework and trying not to worry over her children, her brothers saving the world, and her, here, disappointing everyone.

Owen looked at his hands resting on the table, ashamed.

"I meant it," Owen said. "I meant everything I said. I've never met a girl like you. Even Mary—"

"Mary who? What's her name?" Jane demanded. What poor girl had she done this to?

She knew, somehow. There couldn't have been a more common name. There must be a thousand Marys of marrying age in Washington. But somehow, Jane knew.

"Sintsink," Owen said. "Mary Sintsink. Our families are good friends back home. They were vying for years for us to—"

Jane thought back to her first day with the FBI and the mousy, friendly woman who had rescued her in the busy Department of Justice building. She had been so sweet—so unbearably, unconscionably kind.

"Give Mary my regards," Jane said, leaving Owen at the table and storming up the stairs. It was quiet in the kitchen for a few minutes and then, from her room, Jane heard the sounds of a chair scraping the floor, keys jangling, and the front door opening and closing.

She would go back to being the picture-perfect FBI girl. There would be no more men for her, no more fooling around.

Ding was in their room, studying her new Cadet Nurse manual. "No picnic?" she asked.

"Not unless we wanted to run into his fiancée." Jane sat next to Ding, hanging her head.

"Oooh, I'm going to give it to that fathead."

"Don't bother. I'm such a schnook."

"You are not," Ding said, leaning her head on Jane's shoulder. "It's different here than in Buckhannon. It's different when you don't know everyone and their business. You wouldn't have gotten snookered into this at home."

"There aren't men like him at home either."

Jane squeezed her eyes shut. "Would you like me to paint your nails?" She opened her eyes to see an aide sitting across from her, holding a plastic caddy of polish, clippers, and files. Jane looked at her fingers. She'd painted them this morning, in preparation for the picnic. But her nails were unpolished, their ends uneven. She reached up to touch her hair and found it thin, uncurled. She looked up at the woman with confusion.

"How about pink?" The aide held up a small bottle and shook it so the ball inside rattled. "Or do you want to do green? Go really wild."

"No, no." Jane wrinkled her nose in disgust. "Pink is fine."

CASSIDY

DOWNTOWN, THE FLOWER boxes on the corners, which in summer burst with reds and whites and purples, were bare, and Cassidy felt just as stripped of color. However much men's appreciation made her bloom, actual physical touch from a man, she had confirmed, did the opposite.

Simon, on the other hand, could barely contain the glow from behind his beard. He held Cassidy's hand tightly on the center console and she gritted her teeth to stop herself from pulling it away.

"There's a protest downtown," Simon said. "Against an anti-trans bathroom bill the city council's discussing."

"Sure, I'll go," Cassidy said, though Simon hadn't asked. She was desperate to get out of the car. Her clothes seemed to cling to her body in all the places Simon had touched, as if his fingers had made her sticky. She itched all over. They parked and walked to the courthouse.

"We are here to demand that Buckhannon be an inclusive, welcoming space for people of *all* genders," a waifish young woman said, her voice booming through a megaphone almost as big as she was. The small crowd—a few college students, a few professors, and a dozen or so other community members—cheered.

The woman's front teeth were rotting and the edge of a stick-and-poke tattoo peeked out of her sleeve.

"Faggots!" called a gangly kid as he drove by in a rusty truck, *FARM USE* spray-painted on its side. Cassidy was drawn instantly back to high school. She could hear the same word mumbled from the mouths of the jocks as she and Simon walked by their table. The offenders never looked up when they said it, just hunched over their yellow trays of rectangular pizza so that all Cassidy saw was a row of blue-and-white varsity jackets, like something out of a bad teen movie. The rednecks were bolder. When they yelled "faggot" and "dyke," they swiveled to reveal the fronts of their camo vests and squeaked their Red Wing boots on the tile floor, leaving black scuff marks.

Cassidy thought of the waitress, of Michael McCoy. There were so many ways to be cruel, and her classmates had mined the depths of them.

Everything in Buckhannon was a caricature of itself. People said "seen" instead of "saw." They walked around with snaggleteeth and heroin scabs, and the worst of it was that they thought *this* was normal. They thought *Cassidy* was the weird one, that there was something wrong with *her.* How could Cassidy live in a cartoon? But her dad hadn't been a cartoon. Grandma Jane wasn't a cartoon. Simon wasn't a cartoon.

She took a deep breath. It was all symptoms of poverty. People here were oppressed, too. Being ignorant dickheads wasn't entirely their fault. But the competing truths made her dizzy.

"Hey, can you take me home?" Cassidy asked.

"Oh." Simon looked confused. "Sure." They hurried back to the truck and Simon drove toward the farm while Cassidy kept her hands in her hoodie pockets and stared out the window.

Her dad had given her all these ideas—don't swerve, don't leave extra work for people—and look how that had turned out for him. Look how it was turning out for Cassidy. She wondered, for the first time—Were her daddy's ideas just ideas? Had he been full of shit? He'd tried so hard to love this place that she'd convinced herself she should, too, but the town was as cruel as it had ever been.

Her dad was gone. Without Noeli there, making it feel more like a vacation, she felt it more acutely. She was barely speaking to her mom. Grandma Jane was in a nursing home. She'd made things weird with Simon. She was alone. Traversing the long gravel path felt symbolic. She was trekking into the depths of herself, journeying deeper into the wilderness.

The untreated wood of the house was wet at the bottom, discolored. This would be her responsibility. Another fucking idea that didn't work in practice. Ken was so insistent about his principles and now, she realized, she was stuck with it all.

Cassidy knew she should kiss Simon goodbye before hopping out of the truck, but she couldn't bring herself to lean close enough to smell the nutty coffee aroma that hung around his beard again. Instead she said goodbye with a quick wave and tried not to notice Simon's bewildered face as she turned around to close the front door. She stood behind it, head leaning against the wooden panels, and listened to him drive away.

JANE

"LET'S GET YOU a fresh panty liner. Lift your bottom for me, honey." The nurse pulled down Jane's sweatpants and underwear, another of the indignities of this place, as if the incontinence of old age weren't horrid enough. She thought back to Washington, to the mortification of buying feminine hygiene products as a young woman, and to what had come of it.

A pile of Series E bonds had lain on the night table, fanned at precisely the right angle to reveal, in triplicate, Jefferson's disapproving face. Jane had flipped the bonds facedown before tying the bow of her red rain bonnet under her chin, securing the hood over her curlers, and setting out for the bus stop.

She would focus on her work, as she had every morning for the last week. She would put all her money, whatever wasn't absolutely necessary, into war bonds. Her feet slipped in her stacked-heel Oxfords, and she cursed herself for not having listened to Ding when she'd declared heels "impossible" for working girls. The bus, of course, was late. Raindrops plopped like gravy all around.

In the powder room, Jane vied for space in front of the mirror. The girls were crowded in, rain bonnets strewn across the chairs, removing their curlers.

"Oh!" Erma cried dramatically. "My female pain is just horrible."

The voices faded to the back of Jane's awareness. *Female pain.* Jane willed herself not to look, again, at the sanitary belt and pad in her pocketbook. At the drugstore two days prior, she had lingered by the boxes of Tampax. It would be more convenient, she thought, now that she needn't worry about the consequences of wearing something . . . internally. But the thought of placing the box beside the register, a clerk studying her conspicuously naked ring finger, mortified her.

She should have bought the Tampax. The universe was playing a cruel joke on her. She had forgone the convenience of tampons, embarrassed at what she had become, and now she was being punished, made to wait and worry.

The pad and belt sat unused, coiled like an elastic snake at the bottom of her purse, through the weekend. Jane watched Ding model her Cadet Nurse coat and hat, a lovely outfit to leave in. Later, they sat together in the small victory garden in the back and drank Coca-Colas, their foreheads sweating as much as the bottles, but Jane's undergarments remained perfectly dry.

On Monday, Jane left for work a half hour earlier than usual, stopping by the drugstore and lifting the Tampax from the shelf. She tucked the box under her arm, avoiding the other customers as she walked to the back of the store. The thrumming lights shone directly upon her head. Anyone who saw her would know she was unclean, that the Tampax couldn't sully her because she'd already been defiled.

"I don't know what they expected, turning you village girls loose," the clerk, an old man with sparse gray hair, said as Jane paid. Hot tears filled her eyes, but she did not respond. He shook his head and handed Jane her change. "Practicing your welcome on everything in trousers."

Jane hated this man for his accusations about her morals and his assumption about her background, however right he may have been about both. Jane snatched the box from the counter and ran out the door.

Full of hope—she had paid her penance now, hadn't she?—Jane rushed up the Armory steps and threw open the door to the restroom. Claudine was inside, applying her lipstick in the empty cavernous space.

"You're here early." Claudine's voice echoed and she smiled, smacking her lips and turning her head, viewing it from various angles.

"So are you." Jane's own lower voice fell flat.

"It's better than snide remarks from the girls who think I should use the smaller bathroom."

Jane nodded. People were just awful. Was anyone in the world truly decent?

"What's your excuse?" Claudine asked. Satisfied with her lipstick, she'd moved on to patting her already perfect curls.

Jane considered lying. Instead she burst into tears. Her sobs bounced across the walls, amplifying the sounds of her misery and shame.

Claudine turned from the mirror and gave her a look of such kindness and concern that Jane spilled the whole story.

"Do you promise you won't tell?" Jane asked when she had finished explaining.

"You've kept my secret, haven't you?"

"Thank you."

"Does he know?" Claudine asked.

Jane looked at the floor and shook her head. "I don't know how to get in touch with him."

"He's at the Hamilton every weekend." Claudine placed a cool hand on Jane's arm. "I'll give him a note to meet you."

"All done," the nurse said, and Jane lowered her bottom back onto her bed. She rolled to her side and lifted her eyes toward the window, letting herself dissolve into the motions of the hula girl's swaying hips. It was easier, sometimes, to pretend you weren't in your own body, your own life.

CASSIDY

CASSIDY CAMMED WHEN Paloma was out, using the jenky old webcam on the family desktop, the old woodstove in the background, just as she'd pictured it. She hadn't packed lingerie, so her shows were straightforward. When she reached each tipping milestone, she removed an article of clothing. When she met her goal, she masturbated. All her regulars joined; they were happy to have her back, and Cassidy did her best to fill them in without bumming them out. She accepted their sympathy graciously and they tipped her more than usual, though she knew her video quality was subpar.

She'd missed camming. She'd missed private chats with MannyBoy27 when she showed him her wedgies, CraftyCrotch's stupid jokes, and the ridiculous strings of emojis TitZoomer sent when her boobs finally came out. Cassidy wasn't fooling herself—she knew it filled a void, one that had begun to spread since before she could remember, since the first overtly loud whispers and darted glances during middle school phys ed. But did it matter why she liked it, especially when so many people spent decades at jobs they hated? At least these people made her feel good about herself.

Oh. My. God. Fuck, C. I adore watching you cum, MannyBoy27 messaged her after a show. She'd missed this most of all. No matter how many times he saw her naked, Manny always acted like she'd blown his mind. She loved imagining him in genuine awe, stunned by her beauty. But Cassidy hadn't really climaxed. She hadn't been able to since she'd slept with Simon.

Thank you, M. I adore you watching me. Cassidy pulled her pajama pants on just before Paloma opened the front door. *Gotta go . . . Night, love.* She pressed the PC's power button and ran up the stairs before she had to talk to her mom.

There was a twinge in the middle of the night, a tiny twitch in her abdomen that woke Cassidy for the slightest second. When she rose the next morning, already hoping Paloma would leave so she could sign on, she wasn't sure if she had dreamed it.

Cassidy peed, and when she wiped, she saw the toilet paper was tinted the slightest bit pink. When was her last period? She stared hard at the green-and-white striped panties around her ankles as she tried to remember.

She watched herself in the mirror as she brushed her teeth. When she'd graduated from college, Paloma had made a comment: "You're getting your adult face." At the time, Cassidy hadn't been sure what she'd meant, but now she saw it. Her features were sharper, the skin on her forehead less plump. Instead of dark circles, her eyes had white rings under them where the skin looked paler and thinner. Is this how she usually looked? Was her grief aging her? When was her period? Why did she feel sadder now than she had at the memorial?

"Can I borrow the car?" Cassidy asked her mom.

"Sure. What are you going to—"

Cassidy stuffed the keys in her pajama pants pocket and was out the door before Paloma could finish her question. It took longer to find a parking spot at Walmart than it had taken to drive there, as if every person in Buckhannon had gone to the superstore at once.

An elderly greeter with a short white perm hunched on a stool near the sliding doors in a yellow windbreaker, staring at the ground, and Cassidy remembered a documentary she'd seen about how poorly the chain treated its employees. The interior of the store was overwhelming, the blue-and-white walls rising what felt like hundreds of feet into the air, giant signs announcing Rollbacks, an incessant beeping pulse from the cash registers.

For a few minutes Cassidy was mesmerized, forgetting why she was there. The refrain that had been playing on repeat in her head all day—*When was my period? When was my period?*—faded under the beeps. She wandered, gawking at the pink camouflage T-shirts in the children's clothing section, fifteen-foot aisles packed with bulk paper towels and Dixie cups, the flashing lights of the electronics section. The Walmart had opened when Cassidy was small—the most exciting thing she could remember happening in Buckhannon. In middle school, her parents had dropped her off in front of the entrance to hang out with Simon. They would loiter for a while in the CD section and then walk from aisle to aisle, making fun of the people they saw. In high school, Simon drove them himself and they did the same thing. They'd spend their allowance on a huge tub of ice cream, drive back to Simon's, and share the whole thing while watching a movie.

When was her period?

"Cassidy?" The voice interrupted her thoughts and she looked up.

"Oh my gosh! I thought you were in California."

Though she couldn't remember the woman's name, Cassidy recognized her instantly, particularly her eyes, which looked like they could belong to a friendly cartoon chipmunk. She had gained weight and Cassidy was surprised at how much she now looked like an adult woman. She had *definitely* gotten her adult face, but her eyes had remained the same. Two dirty kids hung off the sides of her cart, which was packed to the top with Coke, Pop-Tarts, and frozen chicken nuggets in the shape of dinosaurs.

Cassidy wondered if it was too late to pretend she hadn't heard her.

"Yeah, uh. I'm back," she said. When was her period?

"Well, that's great." The woman smiled with her whole face. "I hope I see you around." Cassidy remembered a sense of sweet innocence that the woman had always conveyed. It was still there.

"Yeah." Cassidy forced a smile that she hoped seem just as genuine, relieved the conversation had been short.

The woman rolled toward the produce section, and Cassidy hurried toward Health and Beauty. She passed shampoos, deodorants, and tampons, recognizing at least three more faces as she walked. It was like a fishbowl, or a snow globe, here, everyone walking around thinking they were living independent lives. They thought they were as separate as people somewhere big, but they were all here, together, entangled. People in Buckhannon moved around from downtown to Walmart, to their schools and houses, and thought they were living real lives, but they were all trapped here together.

Cassidy arrived then, in front of the pregnancy tests, various shades of pink and white under fluorescent lighting. She stared for a moment before becoming self-conscious, imagining someone *else* from high school approaching her while she contemplated the merits of First Response versus EPT. Hastily, she snatched one that guaranteed results "6 days sooner" and clutched it to her body as she darted to the self-checkout line, avoiding looking at the shining eye of the security camera as she paid. Stuffing the test into a bag, she took her purchase to the bathroom at the front of the store.

The large accessible stall was thick with air freshener. Cassidy pulled down her pants and sat on the toilet as her mind narrowed to this moment—dirty tile floors, the bag crinkling and floating to the ground, her fingers ripping the box. She read the small print of the instructions: *five seconds in urine, three minutes for results*. There would be two lines or there would be one. How was she supposed to collect the pee? Her eyes moved back to the box and she shifted to one side of the toilet, lifting her other cheek and holding it under her.

She moved quickly, still reaching awkwardly under herself, to extract a few drops of urine with the dropper before it all soaked through the soggy, torn box into the toilet.

"Dammit," she cursed as a drop spilled on her jeans.

She squeezed one, two, three, four, five drops onto the test window. There would be one line or two.

She shoved the dripping box into the metal trash can, set the plastic stick on top of the lid, and waited.

One Mississippi, two Mississippi. One line or two.

At "ten Mississippi," Cassidy wiped and stood.

Eleven Mississippi, twelve Mississippi. She pulled up her pants and underwear.

Thirteen Mississippi. Fourteen Mississippi. She leaned her back against the door and squinted at the test, unable to see the little window. She wouldn't look early, she promised herself. If she looked too soon, there might be a second line that wouldn't have been there otherwise, and that would make it true by virtue of being seen.

Thirty Mississippi. Thirty-one Mississippi. Thirty-two Mississippi. She retrieved the bag from the floor and balled it in her fists.

Thirty-three Mississippi. Thirty-four Mississippi. By the time she reached sixty, the idea of doing it two more times seemed unreasonable. She rushed across the stall to the trash can and looked down. One line or two.

Two. There were two lines. The line that indicated a positive was a garishly dark pink. If Cassidy were in a movie, she would buy another test. She'd buy ten different tests and stare at them all in disbelief. But she wasn't in a movie, and she didn't need another test. She knew it was true.

She was surprised that a small part of her fluttered with something like excitement. It wasn't at the idea of pregnancy. It definitely was not at the idea of a baby. It was the drama of something *big*, the same manic tingle that had gripped her when she'd first decided to stay. But Cassidy didn't need big. There'd been too much big lately. This wasn't even going to be big. It wasn't going to be fun or exciting. It wasn't going to be anything except sad and expensive, and maybe painful.

Cassidy uncrumpled the bag in her hands and put the test inside, then stuffed it into the trash can on top of the pee-soaked box. She swung open the door of the stall. As she reached for the metal handle of the bathroom door, she hesitated and dropped her hand to her side. With one eye on the door, Cassidy rushed back to the stall, pulled the bag out of the trash can, retrieved the positive test, and put it in her pocket. She stuffed the bag back into the trash and speed-walked out of the stall, out of the bathroom, and out of the huge store.

Cassidy didn't think about her period. She didn't think about babies. She didn't think about her body. She thought about the classmate she'd seen and how she had aged, how she looked like a real adult—how she *was* a real adult. Cassidy was a child. She'd done nothing and she would do nothing, even if she'd fooled people here by moving to California. But now she was back, with nothing to show, and she had to take care of this before they knew the extent of her failure. She'd ask Manny for the money tonight.

Even more humiliating was Paloma, who'd been witness to Cassidy's failures forever. Every time she threw a fit over something dumb. Every time she got a B when Paloma would have gotten an A. Cassidy suddenly remembered the first time she'd masturbated, holding her breath, determined to be silent, thinking of Gwen Stefani in the "Rich Girl" video. Afterward, with the blood rushing in her ears, she'd been sure her mom could hear her in the kitchen below. Paloma kept all of it, every mortifying thing, barely restrained in her voice even when she praised her. Her acceptance was all an act to show how tolerant she was of her disgusting, embarrassing daughter.

Cassidy couldn't tell her. She wouldn't tell anybody.

CASSIDY

THE UPSHUR-BUCKHANNON HEALTH Department was committed to protecting the privacy of the poor and the perverted. The blinds of the unassuming brick building were always shut, adding to the sense that only shameful things happened inside.

When Cassidy was sixteen and had refused, in spite of much prodding, to come out, Paloma had taken her to get birth control. "I don't need to know if you're having sex, Cassidy," she'd said. "But they do."

Cassidy felt just as embarrassed to be here now. A receptionist whose name placard read *Mary* greeted her from behind a window in the wall just to the right of the door, smiling a bored but kind smile as she pointed to a clipboard. "Just a first name is fine," she said.

Cassidy wrote *Dee* and placed the clipboard back on the desk with a small clatter, then found a seat and tried not to make eye contact with the other waiting people, instead staring at the wood-paneled walls.

A woman on the other side of the room twitched her pale legs and Cassidy looked at her shoes—old jelly sandals, the glitter long faded. The hem of her jeans only reached her anklebones. The woman was impossibly skinny, her ribs showing through her tight white T-shirt, a large yellow stain at the collar. Cassidy glanced at her face, which was pale and sallow. Her greasy hair was pulled into a messy ponytail and she was staring off into the distance, her dark eyes serious.

Another woman, probably in her sixties, sat a few seats down in an oversized Garfield sweatshirt and gray sweatpants. Beside her, a little girl of about four stared at a phone, her eyes zombielike. "Okay, Clarissa, give me that back now," the woman said, taking her phone.

"But, Mamaw," the girl protested halfheartedly. The older woman proceeded to look at the phone herself and the little girl, resigned, jumped down from her seat and bounced over to Cassidy.

"My name's Clarissa."

"Hi, Clarissa." Cassidy looked to the receptionist's window. Mary was filing.

"What's your name?" the little girl asked. Up close like this, Cassidy could see how dirty she was—a layer of snot and grime covering her cheeks, her nose crusty, some kind of red rash on the side of her neck, her filthy fingernails untrimmed.

"Dee," Cassidy said, breaking eye contact. She'd almost said *C*, the name she used on cam. Why was it harder to lie to a little kid?

Clarissa scratched her head vigorously and scrunched up her tiny nose. "My mamaw comes here every day," she said.

"Oh yeah?"

"Yeah, we have to check her blood pressure. We walk over cause we live in the apartments on the Island." She motioned in the direction of the railroad tracks, to the part of town surrounded by a loop of the river.

"Oh."

"Why are you here?" the girl asked.

"Clarissa, that ain't none a' your business!" her grandmother shouted, and the child shifted her weight, more annoyed than embarrassed. She scratched her head again hard, and Cassidy nearly jumped out of her seat when she looked at the child's scalp and saw it was so infested with lice that her stringy black hair appeared to be moving, the strands covered in small white nits.

"We're ready for you, Brenda, honey," a nurse said, opening a door next to the receptionists' window, and Cassidy exhaled in relief as the older woman rose slowly and the girl followed her back.

They emerged again after a few minutes, and the little girl waved to Cassidy as they exited through the glass door to the parking lot. Cassidy waved back, wanting her wave to mean something—to help the little girl somehow, but she knew it wouldn't. She scratched her own scalp as, outside, it began to rain.

The woman in jelly sandals was next. "Shawntell," the nurse announced, looking at her clipboard. She was in the back longer, at least ten minutes, and was still there when the nurse appeared in the doorway again and said, "Dee?"

Cassidy followed her through the door and down a long hall, where the nurse then directed her to a small exam room. Posters on the wall advertised a medical debt relief program, an opioid recovery group, and a single mothers' support circle. Though she was better off than most of the patients here, Cassidy knew the nurse saw her as a charity case, like everyone else.

She climbed the metal step to the table. Its papered surface crinkled as she sat, and she felt the plastic test in her pocket poking her.

"What are we here for today, honey?" the nurse asked.

"I, uh, think I'm pregnant," Cassidy said.

"Why's that?"

"Because I had a positive pregnancy test."

"Are you on any kind of birth control?"

"No." She was like every one of the dumb teenagers who came in.

"Okay, honey." The nurse wrote something on her clipboard. "Can you go to the bathroom?"

"I think so."

The nurse pulled a specimen cup from a cupboard and directed Cassidy to a bathroom across the hall. How many women had peed in cups here? She could hear the ghosts of their prayers in the hum of the air conditioner.

Cassidy returned with the cup, warm now, and the nurse took it out of the room. Cassidy didn't count this time. She didn't need to. She felt calm and purposeful, waiting for what would happen next.

"You are definitely pregnant," the nurse said when she returned a few minutes later. She asked lots of questions, then—sexual partners, health history, last missed period.

"I don't remember," Cassidy said, and the nurse frowned. "So I . . ." Cassidy paused. "I was hoping there was a pill. The, uh, medical abortion." She looked past the nurse at a model pelvis.

"We don't have that here, honey. We have Plan B, but that's for just a few days after unprotected sex." Her tone was kind, with no hint of judgment.

Cassidy's eyes snapped back to the nurse's face, down to her Minnie Mouse scrubs, and then to her own hands in her lap. "So," she started, her heart beating in the small dip of her throat.

"The closest place is in Charleston. The only place in the state, actually."

Cassidy gaped. The blue-white lights overhead made the room sparkle, giving her a sudden feeling of dissociation. Charleston. It was going to be a whole thing.

"Is there anything else I can help you with?" the nurse asked kindly. "I can get you that number if that's something you need."

"Yes, please." Cassidy rose from the table, her legs slightly shaky as she stepped back down to the floor.

Charleston was two hours away. What did people do if they didn't have a car or couldn't take time off of work or had other kids? What did teenagers do? She walked unsteadily back toward the lobby, wondering what she could tell Paloma and Grandma Jane. What could she tell Simon? She couldn't ask him to come with her. He had enough to deal with with his mom and brother. She couldn't be another burden to him, another problem he was responsible for. Could she really ask Manny for the money? She couldn't tell the other guys, that was for sure. This wasn't a sexy problem, and even if Manny sent her the funds, it would break something between them, acknowledging that she'd had sex for real—the illusion that he was something special in her life. It would give him the wrong impression, though, because the reality was that Cassidy was totally, utterly alone.

The nurse came out to the lobby and handed Cassidy a number on a Post-it. Cassidy thanked her and left, cold rain pummeling her on the way to the car. By the time she'd buckled her seat belt, the drops had become flakes. Instead of going home, she sat and let the car warm up as she made an appointment, thanking gods she didn't believe in for the half bar of service that let the call go through. She would go straight there, enjoy some time alone, check out some bookstores, maybe go to a nice restaurant. She'd buy herself a shirt from Kin Ship Goods, the "304 for All" one she always saw on Instagram, and if anyone asked, she'd say it was a spur-of-the-moment vacation. Cassidy hung up and checked her bank account, finding $474, which was enough to cover the pill, but not enough for rent in Rancho if Noeli couldn't find a subletter soon. She sighed. She'd worry about that in a couple of weeks. She really didn't want to divulge the tiny secret she held behind her pubic bone to Manny.

Everything around her felt so tenuous, so shaky, and now she was going to lose someone else. No, it wasn't even a "someone" yet, she reminded herself and tried to picture her classmate with the dirty kids and the dinosaur nuggets. It was a bunch of cells. She had no obligation to a bunch of cells. Cassidy pressed her palms into her eyes and saw snowflakes in her vision that matched the ones outside.

She opened her eyes and turned them toward the rearview mirror, but she couldn't see her face until the dark sparkles dissipated. It emerged looking stunned and tired. "I'm going to Charleston to have an abortion," she told herself aloud, then started the car.

She dreaded all the stuff they would make her do before, the ultrasound and counseling. It would be easier in California, where she could go to a local clinic. But she wasn't in California; she was here. Cassidy imagined what it would be like to leave—to say goodbye to her grandma, to carry this pregnancy across the country on an airplane, to go to a Planned Parenthood in a strip mall that looked like every other Planned Parenthood in every other strip mall, to go back to her apartment that looked like every other apartment, and start doing shows every night again like nothing had happened. She would be empty. She would be so far away.

In the still-cold car, Cassidy could feel the presence in her belly—a conspicuous *something* that contrasted with the chilly air blowing through the vents. It wasn't someone, but it was something. Cassidy's toes were cold. Her arms were cold. Her nose was cold. Her belly was warm. She touched her palm to the car window and the cold went through her like a jolt of electricity. She was chilled to her very core now, frozen, except for that spot, a pinprick in her lower belly. Grandma Jane's words surged through Cassidy on the wings of this jolt, through her palm, up her arm, across her chest, and through her body—*It was something. It was love.* There was part of Cassidy's daddy in this baby.

The snow swirled faster now, filling in cracks of color—a coloring book in reverse. A leaf hanging over the parking lot drooped under the final snowflake it could hold. Cassidy put the car in drive and headed toward Charleston.

It felt like Christmas as Cassidy drove through Buckhannon; everything was so quiet and still, the snow falling. It felt like Christmas in that tangible way—the way you feel in your stomach—the warmth of a fireplace and the anticipation of presents all mixed up in the cold air. It was strange how excitement and nervousness felt the same in her body. She slipped a hand under her puffy winter coat, the one she'd had since high school, which had hung untouched on the hook by the door since she'd returned from her final semester at WVU, and let it rest on her lower abdomen, just over her seat belt. She'd left Ken's jacket at the farm. His scent had left it already.

The snow let up as she drove west on 33, out of Upshur County, and into Lewis, where she passed an almost abandoned strip mall. A Go-Mart, a tractor supply store, and a Shoe Show were all that remained. Once there had been a movie theater. Ken had taken Cassidy there to see *Nacho Libre* and they'd both cracked up the whole time. Once, there had been a little salon where Paloma had taken Cassidy after months of begging for a belly button piercing, one more failed attempt to fit in. Once there had been a Fashion Bug where Jane had taken Cassidy to find an outfit for the New Year's party she and Simon had planned, where they'd stayed up until midnight eating Wheat Thins and a cheeseball and pretending to be fancy.

Now the lot looked huge and lonely, so full of potential and the absence of what used to be there. Cassidy told herself she couldn't seriously be considering the idea of having a baby. If she had a baby, she would be like this lot—a shell that used to hold whatever else she could have done.

Past the shopping complex, Cassidy took the swooping entrance ramp to 79, and the snow thickened again, descending in sheets as she made her way south. Cassidy slowed as the downpour obscured her vision. The interstate was almost empty. Cassidy slowed further, then further, down to a crawl, barely ten miles an hour.

She would have to tell her mom, not to mention Grandma Jane.

The right thing would be taking a pill and being done with it all, but Cassidy had never wanted the right thing. She thought again about the lack of access and the restrictive laws and how effective they were, how this was precisely their purpose—to make women reconsider. She didn't know whether to be mad at the laws or mad at herself for being a sucker.

But maybe they were right. If she was going to change her mind with time, maybe people should take more time. She pictured Noeli before her, hand on her hip, getting ready to rant. Noeli would tell her that if she had been able to take the pill, she would have been relieved. She should have been able to take the pill. It was the time to think that even made it a potential someone—that made it a dilemma. Cassidy promised herself that even if she had this baby, she would never be thankful for laws that made actual someones' lives more difficult.

There was no one else on the road now. As the snow floated down and the lines on the road became less and less visible, she tried to concentrate on driving, but her mind reeled.

It wasn't the money. She wouldn't have to worry about rent. She could grow a lot of their food, like Paloma. But no, she had to be real. She'd killed her succulent. She could make enough camming for food that they wouldn't starve, but how would she cam pregnant? Sure, there was a market for it, but the idea felt gross. It wasn't the childcare. Paloma could babysit, like Grandma Jane, but that would mean not only telling Paloma, but making peace with her, and asking for a huge, never-ending favor.

It was just all of it. Cassidy exhaled. How could she be the weird mom at her kid's school? She wasn't as thick-skinned as her own mother—she knew that from her own time in school here. It would be living the nightmare all over again. But worse, how could she tell her kid that she'd been in California once, that she'd given up a different life? How could she make a life here as a single mom that didn't feel like giving up?

JANE

JANE HAD THREE blankets on her lap. She shivered and watched the rain. Hard rain always brought her back to the day she'd told Owen.

Outside, Washington had been drowning in fat drops. Inside, Owen had hunched over in his chair, as if he had been shot in the gut. "Jane . . ." He sat up and reached a hand toward her.

Jane told herself not to go to him, but she couldn't help herself. She took a step closer, and he touched her arm. For a moment, under Owen's piercing blue gaze, with his tender, softening face and his hand gentle on her arm, Jane thought that it would be all right. This could be the beginning of their story. She could smell him—the salty, bready smell of him.

"Jane," he repeated. "There are ways to deal with this sort of thing." A sudden screech of furniture against the floor screamed out from Mr. Plunkett's cordoned space. Owen lowered his voice. "I know a lieutenant in the hospital corps who's here for another week—"

"Get your paw off of me." Jane shoved his hand away. "How dare you try to sweep it all under the rug! No need to consider the danger to me, is there? No need to worry about me breaking the law."

"I know this is all my fault, Jane, but I can't be part of this."

"You can't be part of this?" Jane snapped. "You damn well shouldn't have been part of this from the beginning, because I don't have much choice in the matter now, do I?"

They were quiet for several moments.

Jane couldn't go back to Buckhannon pregnant. She imagined the look on her mother's face, Arzella lamenting to God, making quite sure Jane could hear her. She imagined the smug looks and whispers that would follow wherever she went around town.

She couldn't stay in Washington pregnant. She imagined Flossie, Erma, Peggy, and the others as her dresses grew tighter and tighter. She imagined trying to survive in the city without her paycheck or her roommate.

Jane clenched her fists. "Take me to the hospital corps lieutenant." She looked Owen straight in the eye.

If she was no longer innocent, she could at least be strong.

Without a word, Owen stood and walked to the door. Jane followed him down the slippery steps to the street, where he opened the Highlander's passenger-side door. It was the first time she had seen it with the top up—closed off, private, uninviting. Jane did not thank him, just sat, swung her legs inside, and put her handbag on her lap. Jane looked up at Owen, and he closed the door behind her.

The heat was oppressive with the windows up so they opened them, raindrops spinning toward them like torpedoes. It was seventy-five miles of drizzle on Route 222. As the rain beat her face like sewing needles, Jane considered that this is what it was like to be a sullied woman.

Owen slowed before a gated complex and eased toward the entrance, where he showed his credentials to the seaman on duty.

Inside, several sailors worked on a dummy ship. On land, the vessel looked pathetic, like an oversized children's toy. Owen parked his car beside the ship and held up a finger to indicate Jane should stay put, before walking over, and waiting for someone to notice him.

"Lieutenant!" a man called down, spotting Owen.

"I'm looking for Lieutenant Dickens!" he shouted back.

The sailor disappeared below the deck and returned a moment later with a man of about forty who smiled jovially when he saw Owen. Lieutenant Dickens hopped down to land and the two shook hands. They spoke, turning occasionally toward Jane, motioning toward the car. The men's hands never seemed to stop moving. When they weren't pointing in her direction, they placed their hands on their hips, crossed their arms at their chests, or stroked their chins.

It occurred to Jane that she was nothing but a problem for them to resolve, a thorn in Owen's side.

At one point, Lieutenant Dickens shook his head and looked at the ground. Owen leaned in closer and said something into his ear. Dickens looked up at him, sighed, and the two men approached the car.

"This way, Jane," Owen said, opening her door. She got out, unable to meet Dickens's eyes. He didn't look at her, either, tapping his foot impatiently instead. The rain had stopped.

Fear gripped Jane suddenly and she froze, wishing she had told Ding. The useless anchor, draped off the side of the dummy ship, seemed attached to her own leg. She was unable to move.

The two men stared back at Jane, and she felt from both of them a curling, angry disgust—a grimy, thick hate that she understood was not about her, not really. She represented something to them. She was the caricature—the loose-moraled, red-lipped seductress.

Clutching her handbag and wishing with all her might that it was her cousin's hand, Jane followed the men away from the ship to the long brick barracks, featureless save for hundreds of windows. It was empty inside, the boys busy training. On the right sat long rows of neatly made bunks. Dickens turned left, toward darkness and disorder.

Owen followed Dickens, and Jane walked a step behind, past the still-wet showers, past the toilets, one still burbling, and into a large furnace room. The walls of the room were unfinished and pipes of all sizes snaked from ceiling to floor and wall to wall. Two shovels leaned against the far wall next to a metal pail, beside which was a small attached room filled with coal, likely mined in West Virginia. It had probably taken the same B&O route as Jane.

"Excuse me," Lieutenant Dickens said, leaving Jane alone in the dark room with Owen.

"I can go," he said, not meeting her eyes.

"Don't you dare," Jane commanded, and Owen put his hands in his pockets.

How different this silent darkness was from that at the Hamilton. This room was not meant for luxury or joy, but for utility and necessity. It had the same lonely feel as the root cellar back home, and in spite of its warmth, Jane felt a chill.

Dickens returned with a small gray towel and a bag of medical supplies.

He cleared his throat. "You can take off your undergarments and lie down." He handed the towel to Jane.

"Turn around," she said, and both men obliged.

Apparently, Jane undressed for strange men now. The worst they could say about her would be true. Jane removed her underwear and lay down on the small towel. She thought of her innocent excitement as she had stitched her dress on her mother's machine and wanted to cry as she realized the coal dust would ruin it.

"All right," she said.

The two men towered over her and she closed her eyes, humiliated. A bobby pin poked the back of her neck. She was determined to be angry and dignified, not scared or embarrassed.

Dickens crouched down before her and without warning, placed his rough hands on her thighs.

"Oh!" Jane's eyes shot open and she pushed back with her feet away from Dickens, hitting her head on the wall. She told herself again not to cry.

"Stay still," Dickens muttered, his voice gruff.

Jane squeezed her eyes shut again, cracking them open just enough to catch a glimpse of something long and sharp. She closed them. She thought of home, of her mother and father, of the stench of the pigs and the flutter of the chickens' wings as they moved to roost each evening. She thought of the soft petals of her mother's violets and the dusty pages of her father's books. Suddenly sharp pain shot from her bottom to the very top of her head, extending, it felt, even to her soul, which seemed to hover somewhere just above her crown. She howled now, in agony, and Owen cringed.

She told herself she deserved all of this.

"Stay still," Lieutenant Dickens commanded, and Jane froze, the pain scorching her from tail to top. She felt rough fingers and then something dry. "I'm packing you with gauze," Dickens said. "You might feel some cramping, but you'll be fine."

Jane tried to stand, but the room shifted as she moved. Owen took her arm and she leaned on him—a grotesque parody of their first dance. Together, they hobbled back past the showers and dormitory, and back past the grounded ship. Jane felt the seamen staring, pausing to wonder at the suddenly weak woman, escorted away covered in blood and coal. Lieutenant Dickens acknowledged Owen with only a "Sir" before returning to the ship.

Owen delivered Jane to Mr. Plunkett's house, where she closed the door without a word. At the top of the stairs, she found Ding waiting. Ding took one look at her, from her disheveled head to her soiled dress and bare, bloodied legs, and pulled her into a long, tight hug. Tenderly, Ding helped her undress, then led her to the bath. She helped Jane step into the bath, which was supposed to have been their haven. Ding sat on the edge of the tub as she ran warm water.

Gently, quietly, Ding washed her cousin. She would make a good nurse.

On the first day, Jane stayed in bed. She felt hazy and heavy, her legs made of lead.

On the second day, she felt hot, feverish, confused. They had treated her like an animal, like one of her mama's pigs.

On the third day, she sent a telegram. *Daddy*, it read. *I got myself in trouble. I'm sorry. I know what I am. No trouble any longer, but may need to come home*. She felt guilty, sending it this way. Her mother, especially, would worry herself sick at a telegram, with her brothers away.

On the fourth day, the walls breathed, moving in and out—a carnivalesque squeeze-box accompanying the big band pulse in Jane's head.

On the fifth day, Mr. Plunkett's telephone rang and Ding helped Jane down the stairs. The telephone, its surface as shiny as West Virginia coal, its cord, a noose—the telephone, like the telegram, was only for bad news. How adept mankind had become at delivering dreadful messages.

"Come on home, honey." Jane could still hear Philip's voice crackling on the line. "Come on home."

"Jane!" Ding's voice rang through the darkness, and Jane blinked her eyes open to see her cousin's startled face staring down at her from above.

"You fainted." Ding knelt, putting a hand to Jane's forehead. Below her, the floor was hard. Jane looked at Ding's eyes, which wouldn't stay still long enough for her to focus on. All of Ding's boys, but Jane was the one on the floor. Who would have thought Ding was the smart one? Kisses and promises didn't put you on the floor.

Mr. Plunkett's heavy footsteps reverberated toward them.

"You're burning up." Ding rushed to the bathroom and returned with an armful of cold wet rags. Jane stood, brushing off her skirt, but when she straightened fully, she fell again, landing on her arm so that she cried out in pain.

"Mr. Plunkett!" Ding called, and the *pat pat pat* of his footsteps on linoleum gained speed.

Jane felt a starry purple darkness descend. She awoke in the hospital.

"Hello, dear," a nurse said kindly as she fussed with an assortment of syringes arranged on a metal tray. Her dress and stiff cap were glaringly white. "You're in the septic ward. You've had an infection, love. And a sprained wrist." The nurse never stopped moving. Satisfied with the placement of the syringes, she bustled to another woman's bedside, administered something orally to the girl, then at the next bed, examined a moaning woman's bloody underwear. In one steady movement, the nurse lifted her bottom, swiped her clean, and replaced her garments with a fresh pair.

"An infection," Jane repeated, looking around. Her whole body throbbed like a foot trying to push out a splinter. All around her were metal-framed beds occupied by girls in various states of infirmity. They had all gone through it. They'd all gotten themselves into a worse fix trying to get out of one.

For a week Jane slept, ate, and stared at the ceiling. There were hardly any visitors to the septic ward. Who would want to visit them? Its occupants did not speak to one another. What could they say? How could one talk of such disgrace?

Jane dozed, stared, and worried. What would her mama do if she didn't get better?

"It really is a miracle," a cheerful young nurse said as she administered Jane's daily dose of penicillin. "You're very lucky to have it."

Jane smiled politely and envisioned the miracle mold coursing through her veins, destroying whatever horridness had entered in the furnace room. In her mind, the drug wore red, white, and blue. But even this wonder of modern medicine could not destroy the darkness Jane felt inside. The war had won. That was its purpose, wasn't it? War sought to destroy the human spirit—hope, connection, and innocence. The war had won.

At the beginning of the second week, the doctor, whom Jane had never met, decided she was well enough for visitors. Less than an hour after a nurse informed her of this fact, Ding strode through the doors of the ward in a fur pillbox hat and snood.

"New hat?" Jane asked.

"Indeed. I asked myself why I wasn't entitled to a little happiness."

"You certainly are," Jane said.

"As are you, dear. How are you?"

"Infected."

"Still?" Ding teased in a dry tone. "I would have thought this whole ordeal would have got you off the fellow."

The girls smirked and then quieted.

"You had a caller," Ding said, sitting at the foot of the bed. "A Mrs. Wills."

"Claudine!" Jane said. Claudine knew all about her. She was mortified.

"Yes, that was it. She came around after you didn't show up at the Armory. She seemed to know the situation." Ding paused and gave Jane a quizzical look. When she remained silent, Ding went on. "Anyway, she told me to tell you that when you're ready to work again, her husband is on the hunt for a new secretary."

Secretary for a colored man. Jane imagined what folks at home, and even the girls at the Armory, would say. And so what? Claudine was a lovely person and a far better friend than most of the girls at the Armory. If she got looks for working for a kind, successful man, maybe it would make up for a portion of the detestable things she'd done.

Ding patted Jane's leg and looked around the room.

Here Jane was, worried about judgment for crimes almost no one knew about while Claudine and her husband faced judgment every day for the way they were born. She could learn a lot from Mr. Wills, she figured. When she thought of starting a new job, though—a new building, new people, new responsibilities, all in the city bustling with optimism, ambition, and servicemen, Jane knew what she must do.

"That's so kind," she said. "If she comes by again, please give her my very sincere thanks. I don't imagine I'll be taking her up on it, though."

"Whyever not?" Ding asked. "You know as well as I that in this city, connections—"

"It's time for me to go. Back home, I mean. This city has chewed me up and spit me out." Jane shook her head. "Mama will be happy to know she was right."

Ding looked aghast, blinking several times and then straightening her hat. "Why didn't you tell me?" she whispered, finally.

"About going home?" Jane asked. "I've barely been conscious."

"Not about going home. About . . ." She drew a handkerchief from her purse and covered her mouth.

"I didn't want anyone to know," Jane said. "I didn't want anyone to know what I was."

"You know I would never think any less of you. I love you more than anyone, Jane."

It was true, Jane knew. Ding would never in a million years have allowed her to lie on a dirty towel in a coal-covered furnace room. She would never have allowed her to fester for days in her room if she had known her malady was more than lovesickness.

"I'm sorry. I should have told you," Jane said.

"And I should have known." Ding bent and began brushing Jane's hair with her fingers. "We'll just have to eat our 'shoulds,' won't we?" She took her tube of Revlon from her pocketbook and applied it to Jane's parched lips, then stood back to admire her work. "You'll be the most stunning woman in the hills."

Behind the hula girl, in her room at the nursing home, the rain was trying to turn to snow. Jane touched her shaking fingers to her dry lips and pulled another blanket onto her lap.

CASSIDY

THE TRIP TO Charleston usually took two and a half hours, but Cassidy had already been driving for four. Finally the gold dome of the state capitol building shone like a promise up ahead. Cassidy couldn't help gaping out the window.

Mesmerized by its sheen, Cassidy drifted to the shoulder of the road. *Bopbopbopbopbop*—the tires bounced over the rumble strip and Cassidy pulled to the left to correct. As she did, she felt the back tires slip to the right. *Ice,* she thought, surprised at her lack of panic. There were cars, buildings, she was slipping. She simply noted the objects and sensations around her, turned the wheel to the right, and felt them glide. *Crunch.* She sat motionless now, the peaceful feeling of surrender to the unknown interrupted by the sidewalk. Cassidy was too stunned to move.

Then, all at once, the fear set in. She could have died. What if a car had been coming the other way? She wouldn't have even known to be scared. She would have let it happen. She wondered for a brief moment if she *had* died, or maybe been grievously injured, and this was her brain's way of coping. No, she was here. She was okay. She reached for her seat belt and bumped a tender spot on her chest where it had locked and tightened around her. The baby. How hard had the seat belt hit? How protected was the baby? Jokes about punching pregnant women in the stomach sprung to her memory.

Her phone interrupted. *"Your destination is on the right."*

Cassidy exited the navigation and turned the car around, making a U-turn in the middle of the street. She traced her steps back through downtown Charleston and back onto the interstate.

The world had transformed in such a short time, the hills now sunny and radiant, a different planet, and Cassidy thought of nothing but her uterus, searching and searching for the warmth she'd felt on the drive down, noticing every twinge and bracing for blood. Her mom had told her the story of her repeated miscarriages once, to Cassidy's horror. Paloma had meant to show Cassidy how wanted she was. Instead the whole story had felt like a guilt trip: *I wanted other children and all I got was you.* Now Cassidy felt destined to repeat her mother's history. She should have empathized more when Paloma had opened up.

Cassidy drove straight to the health department, where inside, the waiting room was empty, and the same nurse who had confirmed Cassidy's pregnancy led her straight back to the exam room and produced from a closet a wheeled ultrasound machine. Cassidy had not even taken off her coat, and as she lifted the puffy nylon, it bunched under her chin, making it difficult to see the screen.

"I see a fetal pole and a sac." The nurse paused for a moment, moving the wand through the jelly on Cassidy's abdomen, pressing firmly at different angles. "And there's some cardiac activity." She smiled and Cassidy exhaled.

"Thank you." She jumped up before the nurse could hand her a wet washcloth and instead wiped the jelly from her stomach with her shirt and ran back down the hall and out to the car.

She called Simon and started talking before he could finish saying hello. "I'm pregnant. I know, it was stupid. I should have told you I wasn't on birth control or anything. I mean, you probably should have asked or used a condom or something, or maybe it was dumb that we hooked up at all, but—"

"It wasn't dumb."

Cassidy cringed. "But I'm pregnant and I went to Charleston for the abortion pill, but I realized I don't want to get rid of it. I know it sounds crazy, but—"

"It doesn't sound crazy, Cass." Cassidy realized Simon was crying.

"Are you okay?"

"I'm more than okay. This is . . . I don't have words. What do you need? I'm here. We'll do this together."

Cassidy paused, Simon's joy sobering her. She'd given him the wrong idea. "I don't need anything. Thanks, Simon. I'm totally good."

"You can stop camming. You know you don't need to do that anyway."

Cassidy's jaw clenched. "I like camming."

"Oh. I know. I just meant . . ."

"Hey, Simon," Cassidy interrupted. "I have to go. I'll talk to you soon." She hung up and started the car.

The snow had mostly melted on the farm, but there was still enough to outline a dark bare rectangle where Paloma's car usually rested. Inside, Cassidy took off her coat and shoes and went upstairs.

She was good. It was true. From the second she had peeked over her coat to see a tiny pulsing on the ultrasound screen, the thoughts that had been tightening inside her chest for weeks had begun to unwind, the spiral turning the other direction, leaving behind a sense of calm and well-being. There was so much more to think about, so much more to figure out, but for now, she was overcome by a sense of relief and certainty. It flooded her body like alcohol, warming her. It cooled as she thought back to her conversation with Simon, but she told herself she would deal with him later. She would explain that it wasn't personal. He would understand.

Cassidy was at Walmart the next day, shopping for prenatal vitamins and trying to hold on to the feelings of excitement and possibility, when she crossed paths with a young mother who could not have been older than herself. Three kids buzzed around the scrawny sallow woman, who looked exhausted, overwhelmed, and something else that Cassidy recognized—lonely. Two of the children screamed and hit each other, then retreated to either side of their mom. The third, a baby, wailed in the car seat that swung from the mother's elbow, its mouth opened wide in rage: *Please pay attention to me*.

"Do you want me to whoop your ass?" the woman yelled, her face contorting, transforming into something ugly and sinister.

The older kids ignored her and continued their bickering.

"I swear, I will whoop both y'all," she threatened.

Cassidy watched, needing to know how the scenario played out. The saga continued, its players unaware of her investment.

The woman's hand snatched a pair of dirty overalls and she hit the oldest child, probably six or seven, hard on the side of the head. He yelped and then quieted, sulking. She reached out then for the other child, maybe four. The little girl bolted and cowered at the end of the aisle.

"Don't you run from me, Savannah, you little brat." The mom approached the child and towered over her. She lifted her hand high and hit the girl on the bottom in a swooping practiced arc. The little girl collapsed on the tiled floor, sobbing, other shoppers rolling their carts by as if nothing were out of the ordinary. Cassidy could not tear her eyes away from the young mom, whose face was both vindicated and ashamed. She turned to her baby, who had quieted, as if scared she would be next. The woman's face softened, and she gazed at the infant sadly. *How long before I have to beat you?* Cassidy imagined her thinking.

She could see herself in this young woman—her loneliness in the midst of upheaval, her desperation for one minute where things were not in a state of chaos.

How do I know? she wondered, the thought a wrecking ball to the backs of her knees. *How do I know I won't be just like her?*

Cassidy's Chucks squeaked as she pivoted, striding out of the monolithic store without the vitamins. Though Paloma was waiting at the farm for her car, Cassidy sat frozen, her hands resting flat on the front of the steering wheel. When she started to shiver, she put the key in the ignition and took out her phone. There, waiting for her, was a message from Noeli, a dumb video of a cat's meows replaced by someone saying "Hey." It was the first she had heard from her friend in days, since before the trip to Charleston. She must have driven by Stone Tower just slowly enough to catch their Wi-Fi and let the message come through. Cassidy chuckled, put the phone in the center console, and leaned her head back and giggled, the sounds morphing into slightly maniacal laughter. Her body shook with it, until the convulsions turned into loud sobs.

"Fuck, fuck, fuck, *fuck*," she said out loud, squeezing the steering wheel so hard that her nails cut into her palms. *"Fuck!"*

It wasn't that people were wrong about West Virginia. The stereotypes were all around her. Here was the poor mother beating her children. There was the racist old man. She was angry at all of them herself. But now she saw them as people. She was angry at them because she knew they could do better. Outside, people reduced them to this. They didn't see the old man put his arm around his friend. They didn't see way the mom looked at her baby. No one saw that Cassidy could have been one of them too. That they could have been, themselves.

Cassidy picked the phone up again and saw she had a full bar. Before she could talk herself out of it, she called Noeli. She didn't want to message somebody. She didn't want to distract herself with dumb videos or with errands or with whatever else. She needed to hear someone's voice—someone outside of the whole mess.

"Hey," Noeli said, picking up after the first ring. "I found a subletter!"

Cassidy's mind could not register the relief she knew she should feel. "I'm pregnant." She giggled again. "I'm, uh. I'm having a baby." She was full-on laughing again, and Noeli was silent.

"Holy shit," she said finally.

"Yep." Cassidy sounded alarmingly jovial.

"You said you're, uh. You're having the baby?" Noeli asked carefully.

"Yes." Cassidy stopped laughing.

Noeli didn't argue. She didn't try to talk Cassidy out of anything. She sat listening, her quiet presence tangible even through the phone.

"But I'm freaking out. It's Simon's and—"

"I figured."

"He said he's in love with me. And I shouldn't have given him the wrong idea by sleeping with him and now he really thinks—"

"How was *that*?"

"I'm definitely a lesbian. But now he's all excited about the baby and it's even more of a mess. I am literally about to be a young single mother in West Virginia, and I saw this mom at Walmart just now—"

Noeli cut her off. "Did you just say you were in Walmart?" She said the name as if testing an unfamiliar language.

"It's the only big store here."

"Go on." Noeli sounded amused.

Cassidy launched into the story of the woman and her three kids.

"Cass, do you seriously need me to reassure you that you aren't going to beat your kids?" Her voice was dry but comforting, and as soon as Cassidy heard it from her friend's mouth, she knew how ridiculous it sounded. She laughed again, this time in relief.

"I guess not," she said.

"Can we get back to the bigger issue, i.e., that you had sex with a man?"

"Are you hungry?" a voice asked in the background on Noeli's side. It sounded like Lupe, Noeli's fickle fuck buddy's judgmental vocal fry prominent even in an innocuous question.

"Hey, I have to go," Noeli said. "Are you okay?"

"Yeah, I'm fine," Cassidy assured her, flustered at the abrupt change in Noeli's attention.

"Okay, cool. I'll call you soon so you can figure out the paperwork for the apartment."

"Okay," Cassidy said, forcing herself to sound put together. "Bye." She hung up.

Cassidy took a deep breath and put the keys in the ignition. She had to return the car. She had to tell her mom. But she had to tell Grandma Jane first.

At Serenity, Cassidy pushed the door to the entryway open tentatively. She was here alone now, and she took her time sanitizing her hands and signing in. As she walked toward Jane's room, she imagined her grandmother's possible responses. Would she be disappointed? Would she cry?

Jane smiled as Cassidy entered, and set her crossword book in her lap, the cover folded back to keep her place. Cassidy rolled a wheelchair in front of Jane's recliner and sat down. She reached out and took Jane's hands in her own, like her grandma had done so many times with her.

"I'm having a baby," she said, smiling a little in spite of her nerves.

"Oh, Cassidy, that's just wonderful! Come here." Grandma Jane motioned for Cassidy to come closer. Cassidy stood, letting the wheelchair roll backward. It felt like the car on the ice.

She knelt before the recliner, feeling oddly like a churchgoer. This was her religion, Grandma Jane's love. Cassidy placed her head in Jane's lap and her grandmother stroked her hair, her long fingernails scratching her scalp.

"After I got pregnant, my daddy told me, 'Jane, come on home.'" Cassidy breathed in the scent of fabric softener on her khaki slacks. "There was never anything but love with them. With Grandma and Granddaddy," Jane continued. "You know I love you being here, Cassidy. I love you just like that." She sighed. "And you know I love the idea of a baby. But you have to be sure you want to be here. You have to be really sure about everything."

Cassidy lifted her head and met Jane's pale blue eyes. "I don't know," she said.

Jane held Cassidy's chin in her palm and took a deep breath. "It's okay, darling. It's okay. I didn't keep the first baby."

Cassidy's mouth fell open. "That baby wasn't Daddy?"

Grandma Jane shook her head and pressed her mouth shut, trembling. "I'm still ashamed, darling. I did what I had to do, but old feelings stay with you, no matter how things change. But you don't have to feel ashamed, Cassidy, no matter what you do. I want you to know that."

Cassidy nodded. “I want the baby, Grandma. But I don’t know if I want to stay here.”

Jane gripped Cassidy’s chin tighter. “You don’t have to feel ashamed of that, either.”

Back at the farm, Paloma was rushing to get dinner on the table. “I told Margaret I’d be there by now,” she said. “May wants to smudge my room to clear the space. I know it’s a little woo-woo, but it’s important to her.” She sat down.

“Sorry.” Cassidy sat, then picked up her fork and examined its prongs. A log fell in the woodstove. “I’m having a baby,” she said as she speared a piece of tofu.

“Excuse me?” Cassidy wasn’t sure whether Paloma really hadn’t heard her or if she was angry.

Cassidy brought the tofu to her mouth and chewed it slowly without tasting. She swallowed. “I’m having a baby.” She lifted her chin to meet Paloma’s gaze.

Paloma sat, stunned and speechless, a state Cassidy could not remember seeing her in before. She dropped her fork to the table. “Oh, Cassidy. I’m so glad you’ll be here. That you’ll be home.”

Paloma stood and rushed around the table in a swoop of scarves and maxi skirt. She bent toward her daughter and hugged her, tight. Cassidy remembered telling her mom when she had first gotten her period. She’d been scared then, too, and had a vague sense that Paloma might be mad at her. She had waited until they were making their way down the driveway to a school awards ceremony.

“I think I might have gotten my period,” Cassidy had said. Without a word, Paloma had stopped the car, gotten out of the driver’s seat, opened the back door, and given her a hug. “Congratulations,” she whispered before returning to her seat and continuing their drive.

Now, as then, Cassidy realized she needed to adjust the story she told herself about her mom. She was hard to please, yes, but she could be good about the big things.

In Paloma's embrace, Cassidy felt nothing but love, just as Grandma Jane had described, but still, as Paloma went back to her dinner, no longer annoyed, no longer in a rush, her grandmother's words rang in her ears. As Paloma gushed about having a grandchild, about the circle of life, about the wonder of women's bodies, Cassidy thought of her grandma. *You have to be really sure.*

"And without even trying," Paloma wondered aloud, shaking her head.

Was Cassidy as happy as her mom that she would be here?

"Fertility is the closest thing to a miracle that exists in this world," Paloma said. Outside, the spoon chimes tinkled.

Was this really her home? Her dad was gone. Her mom was moving out. What about when Grandma was gone? She shook the thought from her head and focused on Paloma's lips.

"It's early, but oh, Cassidy. I'm so excited. Who is the father? I can't believe I didn't think to ask."

"Simon."

"Of course it's Simon!" Paloma put a hand to her heart. "But I thought you liked women?"

"It's complicated."

"I understand." Paloma nodded serenely. "Life usually is." Her phone rang from the kitchen and she rose to retrieve it. She returned a moment later, beaming. "Speak of the devil. He's subscribed us to the CSA at no charge."

"Wow," Cassidy said through a mouthful of tofu. "That's really nice."

"What a sweetheart," Paloma said. "He called me Mom. He's a good egg, Cassidy."

Cassidy blinked and swallowed, but she didn't answer.

PALOMA

"IT'S SO NICE you'll have the house. So much space for the baby."

Paloma thought of the Žižkov apartment she'd moved into after her wedding, how every morning, Ken had packed his charms and headed to Charles Bridge, just as the neighbor next door set Dvořák's Symphony no. 9 on the record player. He'd returned each evening with a few crowns to the sounds of *Rusalka*. Paloma, for her part, went diligently to the fakulty, prepared lessons, taught classes, and graded papers while humming the Czech composer's melodies, then came home to sweep, scrub, and cook to the folky rhythms of *Slavonic Dances* blaring through the thin wall. She was not betraying her feminist values, she told herself, because she wanted, for herself, to make the space homey. It would be more of a betrayal to become an archetypical nagging wife, to demand that Ken change his free-spirited ways.

Her teaching money was enough to live on—not extravagantly, but enough. When her fellowship expired in August, just a few months away, she planned to apply for a full-time position directly through the university.

"I broached it with Jan," she told Ken, laying out the potatoes and cabbage she'd purchased from a student who grew them in her garden. Next door, *Rusalka* ended and Serenade for Strings in E Major began.

Ken studied Paloma. "What did he say?"

"That it should be no problem. I'm the only one who's stayed on for so long. He'll talk to the department head himself."

"What if you stopped when your fellowship was up?"

"Why would I do that?" Paloma laughed. "And what? We'd live on your income?"

Ken looked hurt. "Well, what if we had a baby?" He wasn't joking.

"I'm twenty-five. And we'd have no money."

"And I'm thirty-four," Ken said. "You've known from the outset it's what I wanted."

"I didn't know there was such a timeline for it!" Paloma took the two potatoes to the sink to scrub, turning her back to Ken.

"I don't want to be an old father," Ken said. "I want my mom to know my children. What if we want more than one?"

Paloma placed the potatoes on the chopping block and began to slice. She'd sliced thinner since getting married. She'd gotten quicker and more precise. What else about her had changed?

"My mom will send us money. She's said so. We wouldn't have to worry."

Paloma pictured the slight, emotive woman and did not doubt that she would be enthusiastic about supporting them if they had a baby, but she could never accept such support. She did want a family—it was what she had realized, eventually, while she and Ken were dating. It was a beautiful image—her, Ken, and a child in Prague together. It felt, she realized, like arriving.

"I want a baby." She continued to slice the potato. Ken crossed the kitchen and put an arm on her lower back, his enthusiasm coursing through his palm and into her with a buzzing heat. "But I want to keep my job."

"Okay." Ken immediately started rushing around the apartment, clearing beer bottles, washing dishes, as if, now that it had been summoned, an infant might arrive at any moment.

In fact, Paloma did get pregnant right away. She found out just days before her new position through the university began.

"Absolutely fucking wonderful!" Ken cheered, and she had to agree. Pregnancy suited Paloma, and she walked through Prague glowing with the knowledge of her own fecundity. She felt fuller, smoother, more vibrant. Everything she did—preparing meals, meeting students, selecting a new winter coat, burned with thrilling purpose. Though the city grew more marred by graffiti, she understood now that everything—the vandalism, the American entrepreneurs, all of it—fit into the picture of history. There were no mistakes. It all just was.

Paloma ignored her knowledge that Jane was sending money, though it was obvious whenever a new check arrived; Ken's optimism was at its highest, and she would always find some new extravagance in the apartment—a new guitar one time, another, an expensive bottle of wine. If she didn't acknowledge the gifts, she told herself, she was under no obligation to feel indebted by them.

As the weather turned colder, the air again grew thick with coal smoke, and ash fell down to the streets alongside the snow. She had never found it pleasant, but with her pregnancy, Paloma found her body reacting to the smog even more violently, and she retched when it reached her nostrils. She ran from the fakulty to the metro, hand over her nose and mouth, trying not to breathe the dirty air. Once safely underground, she released her hand and took several cool, sweet breaths. The baby kicked inside her—the first time—and she gasped a small "Ohhh!"

Just as they had when Ken slid down the median (which had metal spikes now—the joy of it had become too tempting for a critical mass), the other people on the escalator ignored her.

Then one day, soon after—it was Thanksgiving in the States, she realized on her race to the metro—her bag knocked the back of her knee, causing her to slip on the slick sidewalk, and she tumbled to the cobblestones. She looked around, expecting the same stoic ambivalence, and was surprised to find several passersby bending over her with concern. They helped her to her feet and upon noticing her belly, which had started to round, spoke in Czech so frantic that even her years of immersion left her grasping for meaning. Paloma found herself being led to a hospital and laid back on a table.

"I feel fine," Paloma told the doctor in Czech. "Dobre." He looked impressively like the Czech composer their neighbor was so fond of—wide forehead, furrowed brow, and a long mustache in the shape of an inverted V.

He frowned and motioned for her to put her legs in the cold stirrups at the foot of the bed. After a thorough examination, satisfied that Paloma and the baby were well, he dismissed her with a warning. "Bud' opatrný," he intoned in a low voice, and she understood this perfectly. "Be careful." She rode back to Žižkov determined not to tell Ken about the incident.

She had no choice when she saw his look of alarm. "Where were you?" he asked. "I was worried."

"I was at the hospital." She told him the story.

"I knew the coal was bad. I've been thinking about it for weeks." Ken shook his head, angry with himself. "Coal haunts me across the world."

"It wasn't the coal. It was the wet street."

"But you were running because of the coal," he said. "We should get out of here. I don't want you and the baby breathing this air. It's not good for either of you, and now this."

But Prague was where she'd learned to be free. Prague was where she was going to arrive. She looked out at the smog clinging to the television tower. Was this arriving? Hiding for months, waiting for sun and clean air? She thought of her students, of her obligation to them, and had to admit that as her position changed and the revolution grew more distant, her work had grown more and more demanding and her students less and less heroic. It was possible for the first time in years to imagine leaving.

"Where would we go?" she asked, and, as if he were ready to sweep her away with him at that moment, Ken's eyes danced, and their blue grew brilliant.

Paloma was struck by jealousy. Cassidy would arrive without even trying. But Paloma's envy dissipated quickly as she remembered her daughter would arrive *here*, with her, and there would be a baby. It was more wonderful than Paloma ever could have imagined.

CASSIDY

I'M A MESS, Cassidy messaged Noeli from the living room couch. Paloma had left for May's purification ritual, which would involve sage, which was contraindicated for pregnancy, but not before making Cassidy a spinach smoothie and holding her palm on Cassidy's belly for what felt like several long minutes.

Simon is calling my mom "Mom" and it's highlighting everything else stifling about here. Even he's stifling now. Ugh.

Noeli responded: *Do you think you'll come back?*

Cassidy imagined the temperature in California. Noeli was probably in a T-shirt. Which one would it be—"Harm Reduction Now" or the Selena tee she'd stolen from her mom?

I just signed those sublet papers, Cassidy said. She wanted to be in West Virginia. She felt like she *should* be in West Virginia. But she also didn't feel like she physically *could* be in West Virginia if she was going to have this baby. If she stayed right now, she knew she would be stuck, and she wasn't sure she wanted to be stuck. She'd be with Simon and she'd feel squirmy every time he touched her. It would be easier to say she was leaving than to stay and explain that she didn't want to be with him. She could either be a mom or be in Buckhannon, but she couldn't do both.

You could always stay with me for a bit while you get on your feet.

Really? Cassidy asked. She hadn't been angling for a pity invite and now she felt awkward. It was so appealing though, the idea of Noeli taking her in like a little pet and guiding her back into being a fully functional adult in the real world of California. *Would your mom be okay with it? And your grandma?* she asked.

Abuela loves literally everyone except my asshole dad, and my mom would seriously be over the moon to have a baby in the house. She's been telling me she wants grandkids since I turned eighteen.

Cassidy laughed. *Really though?* she typed. *Like really, the reality of it? I live in your house, and in a few months there's a baby there?* She typed furiously. *Because "on my feet" might take a while. I'm going to have a BABY, remember? Just making sure you're actually thinking this through and not just being nice.*

Yes. The formality of Noeli's reply felt strange and serious. She hadn't said *yep* or *yup* or *yeah*. *Yes*, and with the period after it, even, was a different animal. *We'll figure it out. You can always do Instacart if you don't want to drive rideshare again.*

Oh right. She wouldn't have an income if she didn't want to do sex work while pregnant. She groaned, considering it, but she knew it would be better than lolling around here, dependent on Simon's crushing generosity. *Wow. Okay. Thank you. You're incredible. I have to figure some shit out here. I'll talk to you soon*, she sent.

The four-hundred-something in her bank account went to a new plane ticket. The soonest flight she could get was a week away, which meant she had a week to help her mom pack up her dad's things. She had a week to tell Paloma and Simon she was leaving. She had a week to get okay again about leaving.

Paloma returned early the next morning and Cassidy met her at the door, more nervous to tell her she was leaving than she had been to tell her she was pregnant.

"Good morning!" Paloma said. "Let's have some tea. Oh, I'd better see which herbs are safe for early pregnancy. How about another smoothie?" The cold hovered around Paloma, clinging to her jean jacket and the Nordic wool socks she wore under her Birkenstocks.

"Mom, I can't stay. I'm so sorry." This was the closest she'd felt to her mom in years, since she was a little girl, and she was ruining it.

Paloma's face fell. "What do you mean?" she asked, and folded her arms across her chest, considering her daughter.

"I'm overwhelmed here. Everything feels like it's pressing down on me." Cassidy paused. How could she explain it without hurting her mom's feelings? She looked at Paloma and could not remember what she'd looked like when she was younger. Her baby, she realized, would only remember her as older, too, would never know she'd wanted to stay but couldn't without crushing Simon. Parents gave up so much for children, she suddenly realized. And what did children really know of it? What did they owe their parents? Would her baby owe her anything for giving it life? Did she owe staying to her own mom?

"I see." Paloma walked right past Cassidy, her Birkenstocks still on, up the stairs to her room. Cassidy stayed put, fighting the urge to follow her and apologize. She didn't owe her staying, she told herself. Her mom wasn't even staying. On camera, she'd gotten good at telling herself she didn't owe people more than what they gave her. Still, the guilt sat in her abdomen right above the embryo.

Paloma returned a few minutes later, composed again. "I can help you with Daddy's stuff," Cassidy offered. "And figure out how to get the house listed and everything." She forced herself not to look around, not to think about the mornings she and her dad had spent on the porch reading poetry or about the endless year of seventh grade, when Cassidy would sit with Paloma at the table working on math homework. She tried not to think about the piece of scrap wood attached between the two levels of floor from when Ken had given her wood and nails to occupy her, and she'd nailed it to the floor. Ken had laughed and said it could stay. She tried not to think about her old cat, Elsa, who had hidden in the crawl space under the stairs to have her kittens, or how she had sat in there for weeks feeding the tiny mewling mouths with an eye dropper when Elsa had wandered off after. Each space seemed to call to her, asking her to remember.

Paloma nodded. "It's fine. There's no rush. I'll take care of it."

PALOMA

PALOMA DREAMED OF her grandchild dancing in the woods. She woke and remembered Ken in Prague, dreaming of himself as a child running through the same forest.

"I'm tracking an animal, but I can't quite catch up to it." He'd held Paloma's hands as he spoke.

"West Virginia," she said, understanding. "I know your mother wants us there."

"We can live off the land. I'll build our baby a tree house. We'll get goats, chickens, have a garden."

Paloma sighed. Ken had pushed the issue relentlessly since her fall and his gusto was growing on her. Trees, wilderness, self-sufficiency, community. It all sounded beautiful. "Okay."

Ken threw open a notebook, retrieved the pen from his shirt pocket. The ink had bled through, leaving a deep stain at his breast. He started writing.

The next day he took Paloma by the hand and led her to the glass phone booth down the street. He punched the numbers from his calling card onto oval buttons and smiled at Paloma, pressed against him in the booth. Their breath formed condensation on the walls, and she wished she could take off her shawl, but there was no room to move.

"Mmmm, hello?" his mother answered. Her voice reached Paloma as if from another world.

Ken cradled the receiver in the crook of his neck, and told Jane everything. Outside, the coal smog hung low. In here, Paloma smelled only the sweet scent of pilsner clinging to Ken's suede jacket.

"Oh, darling," Jane said through the static. "Come on home. Both of you."

She'd resented Jane then, though she'd been grateful for her welcome. Her words had felt presumptuous, as if Paloma, too, had been off on a silly adventure.

Had Paloma failed to take Cassidy's life in California seriously? She had pushed her daughter away again. Paloma rubbed the bridge of her nose and willed the image—the joyful child among the trees—to dissipate.

CASSIDY

CASSIDY PUT OFF telling Simon until it was too late. She'd wanted to do it in person, but every time she imagined her friend's broken face, the way his lips would turn down under his beard, how his eyes would pool with tears, her determination vanished, and now she was on her way to the airport while Simon was going about his day, clueless.

Finally, as signs for Pittsburgh began to appear more frequently along the highway, she clenched her jaw and checked for service. She had some. *Hey, so . . .*

Before she could finish composing a text, several appeared from Simon—ones she'd been out of range to receive before.

I know you aren't getting messages but I need to put this somewhere.
My heart is exploding, Cass. I wish you could understand how happy I am, how long I've wanted this.
This feels like a dream come true.
We're going to be a real family, a good family. We're going to love this baby so hard.
I promise I'll always take care of you.

They went on. Cassidy squeezed her eyes shut. She had to tell him.

I can't stay, Simon. I'm so, so sorry. You are so important to me, but I'm going back to CA. I'm so sorry.

Her phone rang immediately, and she cringed as she answered. "Hey." Paloma glanced at her from the rearview mirror and Cassidy looked away.

"Cass, what's wrong?"

She kept her voice low, shielding her mouth with her hand. "It's too much. West Virginia, with my dad and everything. I need some space and time to process."

Simon was quiet, then finally said, "I'll come with you. It makes sense it's too hard to be here. Give me a week or so to—"

"Simon, no." Cassidy cut him off. "I don't want . . ." She heard him inhale sharply. "I don't want you to leave your CSA work. Seriously. Stay."

"But—"

"Listen, we're at the airport. I have to go." Cassidy hung up before he could answer.

Her phone rang. She ignored it.

Paloma pulled to the terminal curb and got out to help Cassidy with her things.

"I'm fine, Mom," Cassidy said, trying to shake the pit in her stomach from her conversation with Simon.

"You don't need to be bending and lifting." As Paloma clicked open the trunk and Cassidy watched her from the sidewalk, embarrassed, Jane managed to open the heavy car door and pull herself up from her seat using the handle above her. She stood between the car and the curb, shaking, unable to lift her foot to step up. Cassidy rushed to her and held her hands, and Jane carefully hoisted herself to join them on the sidewalk.

"That took some serious core work, Grandma Jane," Cassidy said, and they both laughed. Cassidy tried not to think about the havoc a baby belly would wreak on her abs. When she got back to sex work, she'd be a MILF, no longer "barely legal."

As they stood together with the trunk still open, the eyes of airport security an invisible timer on their goodbyes, Cassidy struggled to maintain the nonchalant demeanor she'd been careful to preserve. Paloma eased Cassidy's arm into her duffel straps. How many times had she helped Cassidy slide into a backpack when she was little? You never knew when you'd have more parenting to do. Cassidy's throat tightened, but she willed herself to subdue her tears until she got to her gate. Paloma hugged her.

"I'll come out when the baby arrives," Paloma said into Cassidy's neck. Her voice was low and warm, reassuring. Cassidy nodded. "I'm not going to sell the farm yet," Paloma said. "We'll wait until everything is a little more settled."

Cassidy nodded more vigorously. "Thank you," she whispered. Around them, cars pulled to the curb, released their passengers, and drove away.

Cassidy turned to Grandma Jane, who reached up to grasp her granddaughter's face in her hands as she always did at greetings and departures. "Ooh, I miss you when you're not here, darling, but I know you have to go," she said.

"I don't have to, Grandma Jane. I don't *have* to." Cassidy's brow furrowed in panic as she looked at her grandmother's smooth pale cheeks.

The last little while, the sense of settling into a routine, taking care of meals, sleep, errands, had deluded Cassidy into a sense that they were back to being a daily presence in each other's lives. It would always be trips now, always be visits. Their time together would always be numbered in days, would always be tainted by the date on the return ticket.

"You have to," Jane insisted.

"But what if you don't remember?" Cassidy squeaked.

Jane wrapped her arms around Cassidy and rocked her, and Cassidy smelled her Avon perfume. All around, planes took off and landed, people coming and going, beginnings and endings.

"I could never forget, Cassidy," she hummed in her ear. "I could never, ever forget."

JANE

IF CASSIDY WANTED to leave West Virginia, Jane wanted her to go. As Paloma pulled away from the airport curb, Jane thought about another trip home—one she'd taken years ago.

Jane had been stoic as she stood before the *West Virginian*, while Ding wept great heaving sobs into her handkerchief, rivaling the women around them saying goodbye to husbands and boyfriends setting off for the war.

"But why are you going?" she asked for the hundredth time. "Now that you've . . ."

"Lost the baby," Jane finished for her. "That's the story."

"Morning glory," Ding said through loud sniffs.

It was hard to tell what was worse, Jane thought—having an illegitimate baby or not having one after all. She couldn't face the capital any longer now that it had had its way with her.

"I need a fresh start," Jane said, as she had all the other times Ding had pressed her on it. "I can't look anyone here in the eye." Behind her the train sweated and puffed and Jane could feel it like a magnet, both pulling and repelling her.

Ding sighed and kissed her cheek. "Write me," she said.

"All aboard!" the porter shouted.

"I promise."

Arzella and Philip met Jane in Clarksburg, and Jane was amazed at how quaint the station seemed. She'd been gone only a few months, and yet everything appeared to have shrunk. Her parents, too, seemed bumbling, impossibly attached to each other, embarrassingly provincial.

"With this behind you, maybe you can find a good boy to marry and be happy with," Arzella chirped as they set off for home.

"Maybe." Jane watched out the window at the farmhouses and cattle. Blue stars hung in curtainless windows.

"Of course, losing a baby is a tragedy. I lost my share, myself, between the seven of you. But I think God was looking out for you, Janey."

Philip changed the subject. "Wait till you see the house," he said. "We got lights!"

The poles loomed tall as the Ford arrived back at the farm—stilted statues, arms outstretched, the wires reaching between them like tightropes at the circus. They seemed out of place—imposing. Jane had learned to take electricity for granted in Washington, but flipping a switch to illuminate her childhood home still felt like magic.

It reminded Jane of going to the movies. Inevitably, she would drink her Coke too quickly, wiggle in her seat for a bit, and then rush out to the lobby for the restroom. Though it never took more than a few minutes, she always felt disoriented for a time when she returned, as if she'd come back to a completely different picture. Back in Buckhannon, Jane was the only one around who had missed a bit of the story, and she felt herself scrambling to catch up.

She collapsed into her small bed, the familiar surroundings both comforting and stifling, equal parts womb and tomb. She slept, unaware that she had, in fact, been left out of an important bit of her own story.

"Jane, darling, you've got a visitor," Arzella called, rousing her from sleep.

Jane's heart fluttered. *Owen,* her dream-drunk state told her. He'd come to whisk her back to Washington, and no one would dare say a word with her on his arm.

But no, of course it was not Owen.

Maxine Potter, an old classmate of Jane's, sat at the kitchen table, her face as tiny and scrunched as always, her big surprised eyes taking up half of it. She wore a blouse two sizes too big.

"Jane, dear!" Maxine said, standing and scurrying toward her. "Ding told me all about your husband and your baby. I had to come see you. Is there anything I can do?"

Jane gaped. "What exactly did Ding tell you?"

"Oh, all about the boy you met in Washington, how you eloped before he went overseas, how you planned to do a big wedding when he came home. She said he was a big hero—what's that about him saving two of his friends? And how you heard he'd been killed the same day you found out you were expecting, and the grief of it all . . ." She trailed off. "Oh, I feel so awful, you poor thing."

"I . . .I, uh," Jane stuttered. When had Ding talked to Maxine? Who else had she fed this story to?

As the weeks passed, it became clear that word had gotten around. Everywhere, folks consoled Jane about the loss of her hero husband and poor baby—folks who really had lost husbands, brothers, sons. She almost began to believe the tale herself.

Ding, of course, had been trying to help. What Ding wouldn't have counted on, Jane thought, was the shame that overtook her whenever she remembered the truth. It stopped her in her tracks. One particularly bad day, Jane slunk to the orchard, eager to quell her shame with a golden delicious. When she arrived at her favorite tree, she smiled and greeted it like an old friend. "Hello there, girl," she said, reaching up to pick a fruit. She could enjoy simple pleasures, at least. The world could not take that from her. The apple, though, was covered in sooty blotches, its thin yellow skin marred by scabs and pits. Jane tossed it to the ground and tried another, only to find this apple more ruined by fungus than the last. She picked another and another, throwing each fruit to the ground as she saw its deformity. The tree was spoiled, just as she was spoiled. There would be no apple harvest this year.

Neither Philip nor Arzella said an unkind word. Jane, though, knew she was a criminal—a fugitive from justice. The G-men may not have known to flag her file, Jane thought, but God certainly did.

"Are you hungry?" Paloma's voice cut into her memories. "We could stop."

"No, no. Keep driving."

Paloma put a hand on Jane's leg, and they drove on in silence.

CASSIDY

"YOU LOOK ADORABLE," Cassidy said as Noeli helped shove her things into the Accord's small trunk.

"Always." Noeli winked and struck an exaggerated model pose. She had cut her hair and somehow looked even cooler than usual. It reminded Cassidy of the way characters seemed more attractive in the first episode of new TV show seasons because they looked a little different.

In the car, Noeli started the engine and nudged Cassidy's elbow with her own. When Cassidy looked at her, she smiled.

"Hey," Noeli said.

"Hey," Cassidy said back.

"How are you?"

"I'm actually really good."

"How's the creatura?" She looked toward Cassidy's stomach.

"Good, too." Cassidy smiled. She'd forgotten what Cassidy/Noeli-world felt like.

Noeli turned the stereo all the way down and stretched her small frame as high as it could go, as if it would help her navigate the airport's confusing layout.

"My mom said SoCal is a joke," Cassidy said, once they'd figured out how to exit. She peeled off the hoodie she'd worn on the plane. Noeli had put her own hood up, and her sleeves were pulled down over her palms. She had repainted her fingernails, red this time. Cassidy had never seen her wear red before.

"It kind of is," Noeli said, undisturbed. "I mean, it's a funny joke?" Cassidy laughed. "But really." Noeli grew serious. "A couple years ago I went to this Zen retreat for young adults."

"I didn't know you were into Buddhism."

"Yeah," Noeli continued. "I just went because it sounded cool. I don't even remember how I heard about it. I think Lupe was on their mailing list or something."

"Lupe was on a mailing list for a Zen center?" Cassidy asked. "On purpose?"

Noeli ignored this. "I remember one of the descriptions of Buddhist cosmology. There's this idea that there are all these different stages or cycles of the universe, and right now we're in the lowest—as bad as it gets." Cassidy listened. "So someone . . . a monk maybe? Someone was asking why he'd ended up here and not in a better time or place. I don't remember how he learned it, but he basically figured out he was here in the worst of the worlds to make it better."

Cassidy watched Noeli as she drove, tapping the steering wheel with her fingers, drumming to a song that wasn't playing.

"I don't think this is the lowest of the low," Noeli went on. "I mean, I know there are harder places to be. This place is definitely a dream for my grandma." Cassidy nodded and thought again of the little girl at the health department. "But sometimes I feel like that about here. I feel like of all the places in the world to be, why is this the one life led me to—like, seriously, with these freeways and the concrete and shit? And the fucking air quality? I don't know." Noeli shook her head. "I think I'm here to learn from it and try to make it better."

Cassidy was amazed at how similar Noeli's ramblings were to the interior monologue she'd been having in West Virginia.

"Even if the dandelions are strange," she said. Noeli tilted her head and smiled a little but didn't ask what she meant.

"Do you think we'll remember how this felt? When I first got here to stay?" Cassidy asked.

"I hope so," Noeli said. "I missed you."

It was so easy to fall back into their friendship. "I missed you too," she said.

"Come on, don't get sappy on me. Do you want to go home or should we do something?" The hairs on Cassidy's arms bristled at the word *home*, and her stomach fluttered.

"Like what?" she asked. After a nap on the plane and half a cup of coffee, she was feeling antsy and ready to start her new life.

"I dunno," Noeli said. "Want to drive around?"

Cassidy shrugged and turned the speakers up. The Weakerthans were on. "Hey, it's our band!" Cassidy said. "It's fate!"

"It definitely is. Oh!" Noeli perked up. "You haven't been to Amoeba yet!"

"Amoeba?"

"Yeah. It's the big famous record store in LA. I saw Sasha Grey there once. We should go while we're out here."

"Ooooh, now we have to go."

Amoeba's storefront had a funky retro California feel. A weird cylindrical something protruded from the top.

"This looks like what people in the sixties imagined the future would be like," Cassidy said.

Rows and rows of records from every possible genre sat between poster-plastered walls. The other shoppers were busy and purposeful—experienced record store people doing record store things.

"Do you even have a record player?" Cassidy asked, sifting through some albums and trying to look like she, too, knew what she was doing.

"Abuela does," Noeli said.

"Should I get this John K. Samson solo album?"

"I have that, actually!"

"Oh, awesome." Cassidy put it back and they kept browsing, drifting from aisle to aisle.

"Look at this." Noeli shoved a record under Cassidy's nose.

"Plastic People of the Universe," Cassidy read.

"They're from Prague, before the revolution. That's where your mom was, right? I just googled them—they used to get arrested by the regime."

"Wow." Cassidy took the record and flipped it over to study the back. "Should I get it? It might be cool to listen to stuff my mom and her friends there might have liked. It might make me feel a little less guilty."

"That would be pretty cool. Did you find anything?"

Cassidy showed Noeli the Bleachers album she'd been looking at. "He looks like a Jewish Buddy Holly," she said. "I'm kind of into it."

"You get that and I'll get this," Noeli said, taking the Plastic People album back and walking to the register.

Cassidy followed. These bands would be the soundtrack of this era, pregnant and living with Noeli. Cassidy was going to pay attention this time.

After checking out, they went back to the car. As they passed Pasadena, Cassidy felt herself slipping back to other old habits. All the chats she'd let idle between shows, all the men she'd dismissed by saying, *Sorry! Awful wifi here*, she pulled up now. *Back in Cali!* she told them. Almost instantly, she had several responses. They'd missed her. They were feeling frisky.

They couldn't wait to see her in a thong. What was she wearing now? Was she horny? Had she had any naughty fun lately?

"There's something else I want to show you." Cassidy looked up and realized they were almost back to Rancho.

"Yeah, sure. Where?"

"We're going hiking," Noeli said.

"Hiking?" Cassidy laughed. "You realize I'm pregnant and we're both wearing Chucks, right?"

"You're barely pregnant. It's a little steep but not for very long. I'm definitely not a hiker and I've done it."

Cassidy groaned. "We'll see."

Noeli exited on Haven and turned the car north, driving past Cassidy's old apartment complex, Tio's Mexican Food, and the community college with its tiered parking lots and brutalist architecture. When the buildings began to thin and they were in the foothills, Noeli parked and they got out. The air was wild here, all sage smell and chaparral; a lizard darted across their path as an eagle circled overhead. The mountains stood before them, enormous and dusty, snow powdering the very top. It was so different from the green of West Virginia's hills. These mountains were mean, but they were still beautiful.

"Is this an actual trail?" Cassidy asked.

"I think it might belong to the rich people who live up there." Noeli walked ahead.

Cassidy shrugged and jogged to catch up.

A hundred yards in and both women were panting. Noeli pulled a bottle of water from her messenger bag and offered it to Cassidy, who took a long swig.

"Thanks," she huffed. "Okay . . ." She blew a long breath out and willed herself to keep moving up the wide dusty path, but could not help stopping every few yards. "Okay, phew," she said again, when the incline began to level off. She leaned forward and rested her hands on her knees.

"Are you okay?" Noeli put a hand on Cassidy's back, breathing heavily, too. "I guess I underestimated that. And how out of shape I am."

"Yeah, barely pregnant is still pregnant," Cassidy said. "But also, I never exercise."

The women laughed but stopped quickly as they realized the amount of oxygen it required. Cassidy stood up and rested her hands on her lower back.

"Oh my God, you are such a pregnant lady with that pose," Noeli said, and Cassidy dropped her arms. She'd have to be conscious about how she moved so she could hide her pregnancy on cam as long as possible.

When they turned to face the side of the path, they found themselves looking out over a broad expanse of desert shrubs and trees. It was not the Rancho Cucamonga that Cassidy knew. It was green and peaceful. It was quiet. Farther down beyond the tangled flora was a wide panorama—a 180-degree view of the houses below. The whole Inland Empire was cradled here, held in the foothills like toys in a toy box, and Cassidy felt a tenderness creep into her chest.

She sat on the side of the trail, staring out over the bowl of houses and freeways beyond. Noeli sat beside her and rested her arms on her knees. "So this used to be Mexico," she said, extending one arm out toward the view. "In the 1800s, there was the Mexican–American War and California became part of the US. Classic settler colonialism. The US thought it could expand indefinitely and—surprise, surprise—people don't like being kicked out of their homes. So, of course, the US just killed people to get their way. Like the Wampanoag and the Pilgrims. It seems like West Virginia had lots of different tribes, all pushed out by settlers."

"You were reading about West Virginia history?" Cassidy asked.

"I was reading the Wikipedia page." Noeli laughed. "And you know all the warehouses around here? The Ports of Long Beach and LA are two of the biggest ways stuff gets to the United States from overseas, but land there is so expensive that they house the goods here. Two-day shipping is basically why the Inland Empire is such a shithole. It's political. Fontana used to be rural. It was a citrus farming area."

Cassidy listened quietly and wondered where this history lesson was heading.

Noeli paused and stared past the valley, out to the smoggy horizon. "I want you to know it's a real place. It's not this, like . . . pretend place."

"I know," Cassidy said quietly.

"It's not a joke."

"I know."

Noeli bit her lower lip and ran her fingers through her curls.

"I think I'll always be a person *from* there looking at here," Cassidy said, finally.

"You can be both," Noeli said. "You can be from there and from here."

"I don't know." Cassidy leaned back on her hands and looked up at the cloudless sky above. Even the sky was strange here—a hazy, milky blue rather than the piercing clear robin's egg she knew from West Virginia. "I feel like I'm in the hero's journey but without the return. Not that I'm a hero. Far from it." She thought again about her conversation with Simon. "But it's the one thing I remember from my freshman English seminar. All these great stories work the same way—*Star Wars*, *Lord of the Rings*. Going home after the big adventure is supposed to be the climax of the whole thing."

"First of all, the climax is the Resurrection in the hero's journey—the last big test before the return," Noeli said.

"Okay, Ms. English Major." Cassidy rolled her eyes and smiled at her friend.

Noeli grinned. "Also, *Lord of the Rings* and *Star Wars* are both boring bro nerd shit that try too hard to be deep."

"Fair," Cassidy said, and the women sat for a while in silence.

"I think there are other ways to return," Noeli said. "You don't have to actually go back."

"Like how?" Cassidy asked.

"So in the hero's journey, it's the Return with the Elixir, right? You bring what you found back to everyone at home. Like how my mom sends money back to my aunts and uncles in Mexico. Or think about scholars who go away to school but write about their home and send that knowledge back."

"Like you did." Cassidy looked at her friend. "What was your big paper on again?"

Noeli chuckled slightly. "Feminist poetry in the Oaxacan diaspora."

"You are way too smart to hang out with me," Cassidy said.

Noeli smirked. "But also, you tell your kids about home. Do you know how many times I've heard the song 'Bésame Mucho'? I know the life story of literally every single relative we have in Mexico even though I see them maybe once every five years. You make your home a part of your kids, too."

Cassidy nodded, pursing her lips. It was good, coming here. It was right to be near Noeli.

They sat for a long time, staring out over the scraggly trees, until the light started to dim and the valley lit up with millions of lights, shining like so many stars. A coyote howled in the distance and the women looked at each other, eyes wide before jumping to their feet and running down the path to the car, dust kicking out behind their rubber soles.

PALOMA

PALOMA TRIED TO remember if she'd ever told Cassidy the story of her miscarriages. She'd told her she'd had them, of course—that they'd struggled to conceive and to carry pregnancies to term, but Paloma was unsure if she'd ever told her daughter the full story. Maybe if she'd known, Paloma thought now. Maybe if Cassidy had known why they left Prague, how much Prague had meant to her, and that she had given it up to be a mother, maybe then Cassidy would understand her.

Paloma had told Jan she was leaving over a stack of ungraded papers.

"You are history from me?" he asked, putting his pen down and looking at her. His shoulders sagged, as if his jacket were too heavy.

"I don't want to be," Paloma said. "But the baby. And the coal." She wouldn't hear Czech-English anymore, she thought. Appalachian English couldn't be nearly as charming.

Jan nodded. "I understand. Just is . . . I always have problem to keep my friends."

"Me too."

"When will you go?"

"Tomorrow," Paloma said.

"Then what we doing working?" Jan asked. He stood, taking Paloma by the hand. In spite of his skinny arms and scruffy beard, Paloma thought of royalty at a ball, requesting a dance. Around them, dust floated and glimmered in the winter sun illuminating the room. Paloma breathed in the library fragrance of books and printer ink.

"I cough outside," she said.

"We won't go far."

The smog lifted as they exited the fakulty, as if by magic. They walked to the pub where they had gone on their night as lovers and again had utopenci, this time Jan with a beer and Paloma with a Pellegrino. The nostalgia was so sweet that Paloma felt buoyed by it, as if she might float out of the pub and across the bridge, over the castle, until she had flown far from the city.

"I wish for you radost, Paloma," Jan said after they'd sat and talked for several hours, extending a hand in a too formal gesture. "Joy. Thank you for all you do here for me and for Czech students. You will remember us?"

"Always," Paloma said.

The bell of the astrological clock chimed a farewell. Prague did not mourn its comings and goings.

Ken and Paloma boarded a train bound for Frankfurt. As Prague rolled away behind them, the thick and bready air in the compartment became a sharp acidic tang that entered Paloma's nose and straightened her back. The quiet clunky syllables around them grew clipped and barbed.

From Frankfurt they flew to New York, where languages jingled together like bells. Paloma remembered the sensation of disappearing into the manifold rumpus of humanity and felt something like tenderness until the excesses and victims of two centuries of capitalism assaulted her senses. A woman in mink brushed against Paloma's hand, the coat oily and ominous. A legless man opined on the ground beside her in a puddle of acrid urine, unacknowledged.

In Brooklyn, they met a friend of Ken's who sold them an old car, which they drove to Ken's hometown in West Virginia, where Jane still lived.

The drive was uneventful, though the jalopy they'd purchased, a ten-year-old white Pontiac Bonneville station wagon with wood paneling, refused to go more than fifty miles per hour. Paloma considered that this was a sadder version of *On the Road.* There was no vast American dreamscape. Unlike east to west, going north to south was turnpikes and backroads. Claustrophobia and nausea took turns with her psyche and stomach.

At the farm, finally, Jane threw open the door and embraced them both—a mountain queen in her kingdom.

"You're here! Oh, I'm so happy!" she exclaimed. "In! Come on in! Get yourself situated." She directed them to a rough sofa with mauve flowers and green vines winding in every direction on the worn fabric. Paloma marveled at the dirt floor. She had wanted the antithesis of materialism and here it was.

The farmhouse was cramped but homey. Jane handed them a plate of chocolate chip cookies and said, "This will be the fourth generation in this house, when the little one arrives. And I believe the eighth on the land. I can only imagine what my mom and daddy would have thought. I was thinking, this is all because of their love." She stared off wistfully, then took a cookie from the plate and sat across from them in a rocker. "So, I've rented you a place out in Adrian," she said, taking a bite and snapping back to the present. Crumbs fell to her lap, and she brushed them to the floor. "Of course, this isn't an excuse to loaf around, Kenny—"

"You—" Paloma started.

"Thank you," Ken said.

Paloma had known Jane was planning to help them get on their feet, but she had imagined them staying with her on the farm until they found a home of their own. Hadn't Jane just said the fourth generation? The news that she was renting a house for them did not seem to be nearly as surprising to Ken as it was to her.

"Thank you," she repeated.

It was the third night in the gifted home—a dilapidated two-story shack, really. There was no insulation, and they slept curled near the small woodstove. The farmhouse was small and cozy. This was tall and drafty. Paloma shivered, annoyed that she had left misery for something worse. They'd traded coal for wood smoke. Paloma reminded herself it was temporary, that soon they would get their own house and she would get to just be, in the present, with her family. Suddenly she felt something warm and wet between her legs. An earthy smell rose to her nose and instinctively she reached down. She stood, and a sharp pain seized her left side.

"Ken!" she called, and he jumped up beside her. Blood pooled at her feet.

They drove over twisting roads, past pastures of dozing cows, and Paloma wondered if their legs were shorter on one side from the hills, or if maybe, after some generations they were born that way.

They drove on through town, up the hill to St. Joseph's. A nurse who repeatedly called Paloma "honey" took her blood pressure and asked how many weeks along she was.

She started to answer in Czech, but stopped herself. "Almost twenty," she said.

"How heavy is your bleeding, honey?"

"Heavy. And clots." She didn't need them to tell her what was happening. The ultrasound only confirmed it. The kind, stern doctor searched for close to ten minutes before announcing that there was no heartbeat. "You'll have to deliver the baby," he said. "I'm so sorry."

Deliver the baby. The words came to her through the fog of his Appalachian accent so that she could not fully process what he was telling her. She was entranced with the way the vowels curved back around themselves, how his tongue floated and rolled where hers would have clucked and tapped.

The nurse inserted an IV before Paloma could ask any questions, and immediately she began contracting.

"I don't want to feel anything," she said, suddenly understanding, and Ken held her hand and nodded. He called for the doctor who called for an anesthesiologist, who inserted a long needle into the epidural space of Paloma's spine.

"I want it to be over. Take it out of me. Take it away. This can't be happening. This is why we came to West Virginia," Paloma cried. Ken held her hand and cried along.

The scene moved in front of her like a silent movie, doctors and nurses in blue scrubs and white masks moving about, busy, never quite looking at Paloma save for an occasional pitying smile. Each sad glance made her wrench forward with the renewed knowledge that her child was coming—she would see her soon, and she would be dead. *Dead.* All of the walks, all of the vegetables. They'd meant nothing. There was no purpose after all. When the baby emerged, impossibly tiny, from between her sprawled legs, she couldn't look. She did not want to hold her.

She would never get to sing to her. She would never get to brush her hair. How could she hold her and then give her away? "I can't. I can't. I can't," Paloma said. She'd thought she was arriving, but now she was stranded at sea.

The doctor had passed the motionless being to Ken, who'd held it tight to his chest, his back turned to Paloma, huddled and hunched in the corner, silently sobbing.

She should tell her the story, Paloma decided. She should tell Cassidy why she'd come here . . . and why she'd stayed.

CASSIDY

ONCE IN FONTANA, Noeli exited the freeway and made her way to a little house. This neighborhood broke the sepia filter spell of the Inland Empire's matching stucco box houses. Noeli's house was light blue with a short wire fence. Next door, a rooster strutted around a dirt yard, a menacing rumble emerging from behind its waddle.

"Come meet Abuela," Noeli said as they entered through a door on the side and walked into a small kitchen. Noeli hung their bags on hooks already crowded by her grandma's teal windbreaker and several designer knockoff purses.

Cassidy followed Noeli through the kitchen to a dark carpeted living room, lit only by the glow of the television and a single halogen light on a bendable arm, positioned directly over Abuela's head. The old woman sat in a reclining chair, a colorful knitted afghan over her legs, watching *The Price Is Right*.

"Abuela," Noeli said, and the woman lifted her head slowly. She was tiny with large brown eyes, piercing next to her dark sagging skin. Her gray hair was clipped into a neat bun. She was beautiful, and Cassidy could tell by looking at her, kind. "This is my friend Cassidy. Cass, this is my grandmother, Antonia."

"Abuela." Antonia smiled and offered her small hand.

Cassidy reached her own hand toward Abuela. The woman took it and squeezed, her skin just like Grandma Jane's—incredibly soft and thin, gliding over delicate metacarpals. Cassidy smiled, too. Abuela gently let go, her hand floating back to her lap.

This was where the soft part of Noeli came from, her empathy, her passion for social justice, the part that made her such a good friend.

Abuela returned her attention to Bob Barker, and Cassidy followed Noeli down a narrow hallway lined with dozens of framed photos—smiling faces of cousins, aunts, uncles, and who knew who else. As Noeli had explained on their hike, distant relatives were clearly an important part of the family. Cassidy paid attention as her friend pointed out the salmon-tiled bathroom, her room, and the extra room across the hall, which she had prepared for Cassidy—fresh sheets folded at the foot of a high twin bed.

"Make yourself at home, seriously." Noeli watched Cassidy for a moment and then left her to settle in. Cassidy allowed the door to stay open a crack while she made the bed. The room was clean and homey—a bowl of seashells on the nightstand and a decorative pocket watch on the windowsill. She climbed into the bed and fell asleep quickly to the sound of her friend typing six feet away.

Cassidy awoke part of the family. Whenever Abuela saw her, she gave Cassidy a conspiratorial look, her wrinkled face creasing in thousands of places as her thin lips turned up slightly. "I swear Abuela's eyes sparkle when she smiles," Cassidy said to Noeli.

"My abuela is a goddamn mystical being," Noeli confirmed.

Even Noeli's mom, Rosa, didn't seem to mind the intrusion. She put down her *Us Weekly* whenever Cassidy walked into the kitchen, reaching out to hold her belly and say a quick prayer to Saint Gerard, the patron saint of pregnancy.

A few nights in, after they'd cleaned up from dinner, Noeli excused herself to Rosa's room and returned with an oversized pack of playing cards.

"By the way, Mom, I do not even want to know about the lingerie, but you need a better hiding place for your weed."

Rosa glared at her daughter and Antonia crossed herself.

Noeli began dealing as the women returned to their regular seats around the table.

"How did this get in here?" Noeli asked as she turned over a card whose back was blue instead of red. A picture of a mermaid stared back at them all, a misplaced card from a Lotería set. "Con los cantos de sirena, no te vayas a marear," Noeli said in a low, raspy voice. "Don't be swayed by the song of the siren." She pouted her lips and set the card to the side.

"No drinks?" Rosa asked. Noeli pushed back her chair, stood, and selected a bottle of red wine from a cabinet above the sink. Snorting, Rosa stood, pushed Noeli aside with her hip, took down a bottle of cheap vodka, and poured herself a large glass.

"Anyone else?" she asked.

"Sí," Abuela said.

"Probably not okay," Cassidy said.

"Not to worry. I've got snacks for the pregnant lady," Noeli said. She set a bowl of potato chips in front of her, then popped the cork on the wine bottle and took a swig.

Noeli went through the complicated rules of the card game, and they began to play. As grandmother, mother, and daughter drank, they grew progressively louder and more rambunctious, the English in the conversation growing less and less frequent, until eventually Cassidy was surrounded by a sea of rapid Spanish. Cassidy laughed when the other women did, watching their faces grow more and more animated. She felt warmed by their glow.

Now two inches into her vodka, Rosa was bolder. She picked up the discarded mermaid and held it up to Noeli's face. "Oyes, Noeli? Do not be swayed by the siren." Noeli ignored her, but Rosa continued. "You've been swayed though, haven't you? Can't ignore the sirens." She had switched back to English, and Cassidy realized this was for her benefit.

"I guess not, Mamá," Noeli conceded, and Cassidy could see the anger in her eyes. This was where the hard part of her came from.

Abuela jumped in. "Rosalinda," she said sharply, looking at her own daughter. "Déjala. Leave her."

"Oh, I think I left her for too long," Rosa went on, raising her eyebrows and crossing her arms. "That's how she ended up this way. Marimacha," she hissed.

It was clear by the way Noeli rolled her eyes and leaned back in the wooden chair that this had been rehashed many times.

"Nonsense!" Abuela snapped, pounding her open palm on the table. "Our Noeli is who she is."

"Qué pena, though. I'll never have my own grandbabies." Rosa sighed.

Cassidy looked away, at the Felix the Cat clock ticking on the linoleum tiled wall.

"How do you know I won't have kids, Mamá?" Noeli asked. "And you could blame my jackoff brothers for that too, you know."

Cassidy was about to excuse herself to go to the bathroom, when a single knock on the door silenced everyone.

"Was that a knock?" Noeli asked, sitting up straight. The women listened.

Sure enough, it started again, several hard knocks in a row this time, unmistakably someone at the door.

Noeli stood and walked toward the door. "Speaking of jack-off brothers. Probably came back to get something and forgot their key." She stood on her tiptoes to peer out the peephole. "It's some white guy," she said, turning to face Cassidy.

"Because I'm the only person who could know a white guy?" Cassidy asked, and Noeli smirked.

Cassidy joined her at the door and looked out.

"What the fuck?" She threw open the door. "Manny?"

"Oh my God. Is this why you've been so distant?" The man stared at the small pooch forming at Cassidy's middle. He looked just like he did on-screen, down to the plaid shirt from his profile photo. "C, you should have told me."

"What the fuck are you doing here? How did you . . ." Cassidy took a step backward.

"The things I sent from your wish list . . ."

"Amazon hides my address."

"Well, sometimes, if it's through a third-party seller, they include the address on the receipt."

"This isn't the address where I got gifts." Cassidy shook her head. She'd been careful. She'd taken steps precisely so this kind of thing wouldn't happen.

"I went there first and they gave me the number of the person they talked to about subletting. I googled that and—"

"Okay, buddy." Noeli stepped up beside Cassidy. "Time to leave."

"Out," Rosa echoed.

"It's okay. She knows me. I help her out." Manny scratched his head.

"This is definitely not okay," Cassidy said. But even as she said it, she felt guilty. This was the man who had sent her hundreds, if not thousands, of dollars over the last year, had helped her pay her rent and fly back home. She knew intimate things about him and had confided in him, too. But that was all the distant idea of Manny—Manny as a brain, a disconnected mind, a bank account, not a real flesh-and-blood person.

"This is a fan?" Noeli asked. "That is some stalker shit. Jesus. You need to get the fuck out."

"Manny, I think you should go," Cassidy said gently.

Manny planted his feet firmly. "I just want to help. I was worried about you. I care about you."

Noeli reached for her phone, but before she could do anything with it, Abuela stood, holding a small beige sneaker in one hand. With the other, she reached for the broom propped against the counter.

"Lárgate de aquí y reza! Reza!" she screamed, moving toward the doorway. "Reza! Reza!" She seemed to grow as she shouted, transforming from her four-foot-eleven to at least the size of the man who was now cowering before her.

Manny put his hands in the air and backed up, but Abuela kept tottering toward him, shaking the shoe in the air and growing taller with each step. He kept stumbling backward, finally tripping on the welcome mat, his eyes wide with terror. Abuela slammed the door in his face and turned the dead bolt, then without a word, she left the kitchen. Her chair squeaked as she sat back down, and soon the familiar sound of her game shows made their way through Cassidy's racing thoughts.

"What did she say to him?" she asked Noeli. She was still shaken. She had been too stupid, too trusting. It didn't matter if Manny was harmless. He could have not been.

"Basically 'Get the fuck out of here. You better pray,'" Noeli said, and she, Cassidy, and Rosa broke into laughter, the intensity of the situation exploding into absurdity. Of all the things to scare a sizable man away, it had been the wrath of a minuscule grandmother. When Cassidy turned toward the living room—she wanted to thank Abuela—the old woman was already enveloped in her afghan, her large eyes closed.

CASSIDY

"HOW IS BABY shit so expensive?" Cassidy groaned.

She stood shoulder-to-shoulder with Noeli, looking up at a hundred-foot wall of strollers in the big baby store in Redlands, twenty minutes east of Fontana. Around them, stylish pregnant women with perfect baby bumps pointed to boxes for husbands, many of them decked out in scrubs, to lift into their carts.

"It would have been nice if your sugar daddy hadn't been a creep, but hey, at least this thing is fun." Noeli pointed the registry scanner at a wall of breastfeeding supplies. "Nipple shields! You definitely need some nipple shields." *Beep.* She scanned the barcode.

"Stop!" Cassidy said. "How do I delete something?!"

"You'll have to do it online later, I think."

"Great." Cassidy laughed.

"But nipple shields!"

"If I need nipple shields, whatever they are, I'll buy them myself. And by the way, pointing that laser at everything boob-related is pretty phallic." Cassidy raised her eyebrows.

"Hey, I'm gay. Gotta get my dick somewhere." Noeli held the scanner at her fly and pointed it at a box of breast pads. *Beep.*

Cassidy wrested the device from Noeli's hands.

"It's so weird that boobs—like, sexy boobs, are also for feeding little humans. Maybe it's good I'm single for this whole thing. I can't imagine someone watching me get huge, push a child out of my vagina, feed it from my boobs, and then want to have sex with me after." Cassidy shuddered.

Noeli picked up a jar of nipple butter and studied the ingredients. "I kind of think that's what makes bodies sexy."

"You have a lactation fetish? I've met some of your friends online."

"No, asshole." Noeli smirked. "Change, vulnerability, fertility. The whole reason boobs are sexy is because we want someone to feed our spawn. Big hips show you can push out a kid—"

"That's actually a myth," Cassidy interrupted. "I was reading something that said narrow pelvises haven't been a thing since people stopped getting rickets and doctors just say it to—"

"Right, but we evolved to have curvy hips as a signal about fertility. I guess personally I think about how bodies change and age and are capable of these amazing things. Getting to *touch* someone's *body* is so personal. It's what gets me worked up. The same skin they *live* in, and they're letting me feel it in such an intimate way."

"Wow," Cassidy said. "I never thought of it like that."

They walked slowly around the store, selecting glass bottles, a C-shaped nursing pillow, and an organic crib mattress. Everything was pastel pink, blue, or yellow. The eyes of cutesy bears, bunnies, and ducks watched them from onesies and walkers.

"How do you even pick?" Cassidy stopped at the giant wall of cribs.

"Which one is cheapest?" Noeli asked.

"Which one is safest?" Cassidy retorted.

"They all have to meet the standards, right?" Noeli asked. "The CPSCABCDEFG?"

"Awwww, were you reading about crib safety?"

Noeli blushed.

"You do care! She has a heart, ladies and gentlemen."

"It's true," Noeli conceded. "So, which one is the cheapest?" They found one and scanned it.

"I'm done for today," Cassidy said. "Can we go?"

They left the store and walked out to the parking lot the baby store shared with T.J. Maxx, Ross, Old Navy, and several other chains. "Redlands is actually kind of cool," Noeli said. Cassidy looked around the shopping complex skeptically. They found the Accord and instead of getting onto the freeway, Noeli drove them to a little downtown. There was a coffee shop, a children's bookstore, a comics shop, and several mom-and-pop restaurants.

In the center of the main street, a brick plaza held a huge Christmas tree, wrapped with lights waiting for the sun to set so they could twinkle.

"I wonder if it's like that everywhere," Cassidy said. The radio was barely audible, but she could hear carols crackling under the low static.

"Like what?" Noeli asked.

"I don't know. Like maybe every place can feel like you're in the worst part of the universe's cycles and like a sense of home is an arm's length away." Noeli listened. "Like here, it's so pretty, a lot of it, but it's distance, like physical distance—spending an hour in traffic to get anywhere, that makes me feel so separate from everything." Noeli nodded. "In Buckhannon, it's this sense that it's not where I'm supposed to be. If I'm there, there's still somewhere to go. I don't feel settled."

Noeli smiled empathetically, plugged the iPod back in, and turned up the volume. "Come on! Barn burner!" she said, skipping over No Doubt, blink-182, and the Jackson 5. "Yes!" She stopped on a song by Bleachers—"I Miss Those Days"—and turned up the volume.

"Ah! You downloaded some!" Cassidy said.

"I had to. They're so good!" Noeli turned the volume up more, until the windows hummed and rattled in their slots in the car doors. Cassidy sank lower in the seat and nodded along to the song, squinting against the warm, bright sun.

They drove through a residential area south of downtown and Cassidy watched as cute craftsmen and spacious Victorians rolled by, their yards filled with cacti and lavender, their porches adorned with rocking chairs and lined with Christmas lights. A woman in a fleece vest walked a Great Dane. Another, in a shirt that said Radlands, pushed a double stroller. They passed several Little Free Libraries and a large outdoor amphitheater where two young children laughed as they clambered over the chairs. Maybe a place like this wouldn't feel like the worst, Cassidy thought. This felt like a place where someone could feel settled. As soon as she'd thought it, Noeli turned the car around in the parking lot of a tiny grocery store with green umbrellas out front. Cassidy turned to watch two old men who stood by the entrance laughing and talking as Noeli exited and headed back toward the freeway. The mountains loomed tall, sharp, and brown to the north, marking the fault line.

PALOMA

PALOMA SCROLLED THROUGH Cassidy's baby registry. Anticipating this child's arrival, while knowing they would live so far from her, reminded Paloma of her efforts to get pregnant following her miscarriage. Every picture of a rounded belly, every onesie brought with it a stabbing pain.

After losing that first baby, Paloma had grown absorbed in becoming pregnant again. A baby, one she could hold, would erase all of it. She'd begun charting her cycle, measuring her temperature, and studying other more personal details that she'd never thought about let alone written down.

It had worked. Paloma was pregnant again two months later. Again, Ken was overjoyed and she felt triumphant. And then, a month later, she was no longer pregnant.

Would there ever be a baby? There had to be a baby. If there wasn't going to be a baby, she should still be in Prague.

"Acupuncture," Ken suggested one night in the drafty wooden house. Paloma's Czech shawl was draped over her shoulders as she fried potatoes for latkes. She hadn't made them for Hanukkah, but now she regretted it. She was feeling the slightest bit nostalgic for Long Island, for her mother, for sour cream and applesauce and oil. "Bob said you should try acupuncture. He said he'd do a session for us for free. You know Bob's wife is Jewish, too."

"Taste this," Paloma said, blotting a greasy potato pancake between some paper towels and then flipping it onto Ken's plate with a spatula.

"Mmm," he moaned. "Amazing."

Paloma agreed to the acupuncture. She felt nothing as the needles slid into her skin except a dull, heavy hum at each point. Her period arrived on schedule three weeks later.

Next was a homeopathic treatment administered by Ken's friend Jean, who told them at length about the distance training she'd done by mail. As Paloma felt the sugar dissolve under her tongue, she felt hopeful, but as her blood came the next month, she cursed her naiveté. There was nothing in the tablets. How did she expect them to do anything?

Bob's wife, May, pressed crystals into her palms and whispered the purpose of each stone meaningfully.

"Amethyst to come to terms with the babies who did not choose to join us earthside," she said. "Moonstone for fertility. Jade for cleansing. Jasper for everything. The supreme nurturer." Each stone's color was striking, surreal. Their jagged edges and smooth surfaces made their power seem possible.

Blood. Paloma remembered May's words. *The babies who did not choose to join us earthside.* Why had they all chosen to leave her?

Paloma became more determined. She'd left Prague to have a baby here. She was going to have a baby here.

She visited the health food store on College Avenue, its wooden door closing behind her as she stepped onto the hardwood floors and introduced herself. "Paloma! You must be Ken's wife," the woman behind the counter said. Her copper-red hair was cut in a short bob, and dainty round glasses balanced on her button nose. Though she wore slacks and a simple flowered shirt, she reminded Paloma of someone from an earlier time, a Beatrix Potter character, or Little Miss Muffet. "Margaret." She extended a hand.

"I'm interested in macrobiotics," Paloma told her, and Margaret directed her to a shelf. Situated among hand-thrown pottery, jars of incense, and assorted supplements were several books on nutrition. Paloma picked up *The Book of Macrobiotics* by Michio Kushi.

Paloma paid for the book and thanked Margaret, then sat in the Bonneville with the engine running to stay warm while she read the whole thing. When she'd finished, she smiled, set the book down on the empty seat beside her, and started back to the house. Ken was on board. He forwent his bloody steaks for pickles and sauerkraut. Instead of beer, he sipped herbal teas alongside Paloma. At dinner, they stared into each other's eyes and tried not to laugh as they made sure to chew their food thoroughly. A day on the calendar came and went. Paloma held her breath.

She began to feel superstitious about the rickety house, haunted by the memories of her loss, and so they moved out of the shack and squeezed into the farmhouse with Jane. Six weeks, seven, ten, and then twenty. She barely breathed at all during the twenty-first week, but it, too, passed. The baby moved inside her. Twenty-two weeks. Thirty. Forty.

And then she was in Paloma's arms, real for the first time. Paloma hadn't allowed her to be real until she could hold her, but here Paloma was, holding her. Now she was putting the baby to her breast, watching her suckle with lips like a fish. Now she was feeling her fine, downy hair.

Ken, his own hair mostly gray by now, wept as his wife placed his daughter in his arms. He held her just as he had held the one they'd lost—tight to his chest. "Thank you, Paloma," he said. "Thank you."

Visitors arrived. Not just Jane, as Paloma had expected, but Bob, May, Jean, and Margaret. It was not only Cassidy who had been born.

Paloma tried to get pregnant again. She charted her cycle and returned to macrobiotics. Cassidy nursed, rolled over, crawled. The three of them took long walks around the farm, Paloma balancing Cassidy on her hip. On one walk, Ken stopped, looking around in sudden recognition. "This is the old orchard. Mom said there haven't been apples in years." Paloma looked up. All around them, golden fruit hung like lanterns. Ken laughed and picked one, holding it out to Paloma, then selected one for himself. They walked together, the leaves crunching beneath their boots and the apples crunching between their teeth. It was so much sweeter than store-bought fruit. It was a good omen, Paloma mused, an unexplained renewal of fecundity. A few steps ahead, Ken finished his apple and tossed the core to the forest floor. Paloma took another bite, adjusting Cassidy, who was slipping. This time, she was met not by wine-sweetness, but a mealy decay. The inside of her fruit was rotten. Horrified, she spit out what was in her mouth and threw the rest to the ground. "Mama?" Cassidy asked.

"Yucky," Paloma said.

The state moped, grumpy about the dismal start of WVU's football season. Hope buzzed as the Mountaineers rallied, winning four games in a row. Blue and gold shone on every passing shirt and people smiled in the grocery store once again. Paloma missed her period. Though she'd never cared about football, she found herself holding her breath, caught up in the spirit of optimism.

WVU lost the Carquest Bowl, 21–24, and Paloma lost this baby, too. What cruel trick of fate would connect her luck to the football team's?

The last loss had been one of the worst. "Why you come to school with me?" Cassidy asked, and Paloma smiled at the similarities between Czech-English and toddler English. She removed her Birkenstocks and placed them next to Cassidy's pink patent Stride Rites in the cubby marked with her name. Paloma's wool socks kept her feet warm and she wiggled her toes, enjoying the feeling of envelopment and comfort as she stepped onto the colorful circle rug. She was five weeks pregnant.

"I'm a special guest today!"

Cassidy looked skeptical.

The teacher rang a small chime, calling the children to the rug for circle time. "Ms. Paloma, Cassidy's mommy, is here today to tell us about Hanukkah."

The preschoolers watched closely as their teacher stood and moved to the side, making room for Paloma to sit before them on the small chair. Several picked their noses. Paloma placed a menorah, candles, a wooden dreidel, and a small bag of gelt at her feet. Cassidy rose up on her knees for a better view of her mother.

"Hello!" Paloma said. "Has anybody heard of Hanukkah?"

The children squirmed and shifted but didn't raise their hands. Cassidy, too, was quiet.

"Hanukkah is a holiday celebrated in the wintertime by people who are Jewish," Paloma said. "There are Jewish people all over the world." She shared the story—how the Maccabees had taken their temple back from the king, who had tried to take it from them, and how the oil, which should have lasted for only one night, instead had lasted for eight. At this, many of the children gasped, and Paloma smiled. It was such a good age, three, wonder and amazement growing each day. Cassidy crawled around her classmates and snuggled next to Paloma's knees.

A little boy in the front stood and took a step toward them. Paloma smiled and met his gaze. "Did you have a question, sweetheart?" His large brown eyes met hers. Instead of answering, he reached out a hand. Paloma thought the boy was going to hug her. It really was a wonderful age. Instead of embracing her, though, the child began rubbing her head, more searchingly than affectionately. Confused, Paloma allowed him to do this for a moment, letting his tiny fingers tangle her hair.

Finally the little boy spoke. "Where are your horns?"

"I'm sorry?"

"Your horns," he said a little louder. "My daddy said that Jews have horns."

"You can tell your daddy that we do not." Paloma stood, taking his hand in her own and removing it from her head. She would always have horns here. Paloma took Cassidy's hand. "Let's go, sweetheart."

"But it's circle time."

"I know, baby." Paloma fought back tears.

"But after circle time is snack."

"I'll get you a snack."

Reluctantly, Cassidy stood and followed her mother. Paloma led Cassidy to the cubby for their shoes. She took her daughter's puffy purple coat down from the hook by the door and helped her zip up before slipping on her own leather jacket. She would pack Cassidy's coat away in the spring, and the next time the snow fell it would be too tight for her little body. Parenting held the kind of ever-present nostalgia she had hoped for in Prague. Every milestone, every season was both beginning and ending, and Paloma felt constantly aware of each moment's impermanence. Now that she had it, it felt like grasping.

They walked to the car, holding hands, and as Paloma lifted Cassidy into her car seat, she was shocked, as she occasionally was, by her daughter's heft. She was so . . . tangible. She took up so much space in the world already. She would fill this place—it couldn't contain her. Paloma buckled Cassidy in and kissed her on the head.

As Cassidy sang the chorus of "Jingle Bells" over and over, Paloma drove north on Route 20, but instead of continuing toward the farm, she turned west on Corridor H toward 79. In spite of the long battle against it, the Department of Highways would soon build the remainder of the Corridor.

Paloma had known it was inevitable, though she had signed all of Jean's petitions. When the people in charge decided to do something, they found a way to do it. Paloma thought suddenly of Jan, her colleague in Prague, and of her students there. They had resisted, and they had changed the world. But not here, Paloma thought. It would take more heroes than they had in West Virginia.

Paloma found it fitting that she was using the Corridor as her escape route. She was defeated too, an outcast here, even if she had fooled herself into thinking a few friends could make it bearable. If she stayed, they would probably burn her as a witch.

With Ken, she was the nag—constantly forced to bring him back to reality. With Cassidy, she was the enforcer. She was exhausted from keeping the endless balls of home and family life in the air—scrubbing toilets, worrying about money—while Ken enjoyed scheming with their daughter about elaborate tree houses, taking her on walks in the woods, and generally being the fun parent.

"We can talk to my mom." Ken dismissed Paloma's financial concerns, and then he did. Jane bailed them out, again and again. Paloma felt trapped in West Virginia and in the person it had turned her into.

She was on 79 now, going north. Though the hills were white, the road was clear of snow—dark gray with freshly painted yellow lines. They could go to New York, maybe. Not Long Island. Maybe the city. Maybe Woodstock. Paloma would figure it out. She took stock of what they had in the car—a change of clothes in Cassidy's bag, a wad of cash in the glove compartment, and a blanket and first aid kit in the trunk.

"Where we going, Mama?" Cassidy's little voice chimed from the back seat.

"I'm not sure, honey. It will be a little adventure."

"Is Daddy coming?" Something in her daughter's voice broke Paloma. As the bare trees whizzed by, she pictured the way Cassidy climbed onto Ken's lap and the way she squealed with delight when he tickled her. She thought of the way she nuzzled into his furry chest as he sang. She couldn't do this to either of them.

Paloma exited the interstate, then got back on, heading south.

"Change of plans. The adventure is at home."

Cassidy groaned. In front of them, a salt truck crept along, sprinkling the road, the crystals spattering their windshield. "Why it taking sooooo long?"

Finally, back at the farm, Paloma unloaded her from the car and held her hand as they crunched up the steps to the porch. "Let's paint," Paloma said, after they'd hung up their coat and jacket. Jane sat snoring in the recliner, her mouth open. Cassidy stared past her sleeping grandmother out the window at the snowy yard, the taller plants poking through so that the hills looked like white waves. "No," Paloma said with more determination. "Let's go sledding."

Cassidy perked up. "Sledding! Let's go! Sleddinnnnng!" She hopped from one foot to the other, then spun around in circles.

Today, Paloma would be the good parent. She took Cassidy's coat down from the hook again. She would be the good parent, even if Cassidy never knew how good. They tromped together through the trees to the top of the old strip mine. The incline would work well.

The bleeding started as Cassidy sailed down the hill away from her. Everything, it felt, was moving out of her grasp.

As the seasons carried on, Paloma no longer grew excited when her period came late, instead waiting for the day she would start to bleed again, heavy and painful. Cassidy began to read, sneak butcher shears from the kitchen drawer to cut her hair, and scream, "Go away!" at her mother. Paloma's life, and what she had hoped for it, slipped further and further away.

Paloma closed the baby registry tab. She opened Etsy, put a romper printed with the words "Mountain Made" into her cart, and had it sent to Noeli's.

CASSIDY

CASSIDY COULDN'T BRING herself to sign into the cam site after the incident with Manny. Whenever she locked the guest room door and sat down in the corner beside the bowl of seashells, which had grown dusty since she'd moved in, she found herself staring at her computer like it might bite, unable to stop thinking about all the men she'd shared little details of her life with—little details they might be able to piece together to find her. She listed her equipment on Facebook marketplace, trying not to think about how much she'd paid for it all new, and got an offer three days later.

She borrowed the Accord and met the woman in the parking lot of a place called Raspados Xtreme. Though it was winter, a line of people waited inside the shop to order shaved ice. Next door, the liquor store was even busier. On the other side of the lot was a party supply store, with a classic donkey piñata hanging outside and a sign that read Open, though the glass door was blockaded by a stack of plastic chairs.

"Cassidy?" a woman asked, getting out of her car. She was shorter than she looked in her profile picture, and younger, too. She couldn't have been more than twenty. Cassidy knew instantly that she was going to cam, and though she'd just met this woman, she felt protective of her.

"Reina?"

"Yes!" She was so cute and bubbly. Men would adore her.

"Okay, so I have the stuff in my trunk. Do you want to open yours? You can give me the money, and then we can move it over."

"Sounds good!" The woman smiled and Cassidy almost cried. She was so innocent and genuine. Or she was great at pretending. Either way, she'd do great on cam.

They completed the transaction and Reina waved. "Thanks again!"

"Yeah, thank you. Take care." Cassidy wanted to tell her more, like how it was worth it to get a PO Box and how she didn't owe shit to anybody, but instead she got into Noeli's car, counted her three hundred dollars, realized she should have done this before giving Reina the stuff, and tucked it in her bra, relieved it was all there.

From there, she drove to a used car lot, a gravel square no bigger than the eight cars parked there, sandwiched between a mortuary and a squat concrete "boxing club" she'd passed several times accompanying Noeli to the grocery store. Cassidy bought the jenkiest car she'd ever seen, even jenkier than the Accord. Something rattled from the minute she turned the key to the minute she turned it off, and something else seemed to drag on the ground when she went over speed bumps. The tinted windows peeled and bubbled and the clock blinked 00:00 no matter what Cassidy tried. Noeli laughed when she saw it.

"Look, it was three hundred dollars. What do you expect?"

"I thought it might have a bumper."

Cassidy's eyes widened and she went around to the back of the vehicle. "Oh my God, it doesn't have a bumper. I didn't even realize."

"It'll be fine. You're just going around Fontana. You don't even need to take it on the freeway."

But when Cassidy got her first Instacart assignment that night, she realized the car wasn't fine. Its trunk wouldn't open. She piled the customer's bags into the backseat and wondered what to do with the eggs. With a sigh, she got into her seat and set them on her lap. The customer turned out to be an old white man with a yard full of German shepherds who jumped and barked and growled when she rang the doorbell. The man watched Cassidy from the doorway as she made several trips back and forth with the groceries, then closed the door without a thank-you when she'd finished. When she looked back at the app, she saw he'd left her a two-dollar tip. She'd made twenty dollars total from the job.

The next customer ordered only a bouquet from the floral department and didn't tip. Cassidy made three dollars. The next ordered fifteen boxes of Fruit Loops, a bottle of rubbing alcohol, and a case of freezer bags. "There was a good sale," the woman said when she answered the door. She held a coffee mug that seemed to be full of orange juice. With her other hand, she yanked the first bag away from Cassidy and threw it on the couch behind her. "Do you want to come in for a bowl?"

"No, thank you," Cassidy said. She decided she was done for the day. People in person were just as weird as people online.

Back in the car, Christmas carols were on the radio, which worked surprisingly well, but "Have Yourself a Merry Little Christmas" and "Baby, It's Cold Outside" seemed totally out of place, in time and space, like the holidays were a play that Southern California pretended to be part of.

As she drove back toward Noeli's, the word *floating* kept weaseling its way into Cassidy's mind. There was nothing anchoring her anywhere—no relationship, no real job, no real money, no real home, no family anywhere close at all. Was bringing a baby into a life like that irresponsible?

Cassidy accelerated, closing the gap she had allowed to open between her and the SUV ahead, her breathing accelerating, too. She pictured the car slipping on the wet asphalt, slamming into the bumper of the SUV. There was nothing holding anybody to this life. A baby wouldn't anchor her. She drew closer and closer to the SUV. She was three feet from it, now two.

At one, she took her foot off the gas, letting the SUV pull ahead. When she eased into the driveway, she saw that the Accord was gone; she felt relieved. She didn't want to tell Noeli about her day yet, as funny as she would find it. Inside, Abuela turned from the old episode of *Family Feud* to watch Cassidy walk in.

"Siéntate," Abuela said, patting the arm of her chair. Cassidy obeyed. The old woman grasped her hand and held on through the commercials. It was like Grandma Jane was holding her hand through Abuela, Cassidy thought as she fought back tears. Abuela was her anchor here. She had to hold on.

When Noeli returned twenty minutes later and saw them sitting together, hands still clasped, she smiled and came over. As Cassidy looked at Noeli, her usual admiration gave way to a stark, stinging jealousy. Noeli was home here. Her mom was here, even if she was an asshole. Abuela was here and sharp as ever. Noeli complained about the admin job she'd had forever at the medical supply company, but it was still a real job and it was secure.

"Oil's on the counter, Abuela," Noeli said, oblivious to Cassidy's envy. She kissed Antonia's head from behind. As she did, she put her hand on Cassidy's arm and squeezed, pulling Cassidy and Abuela even closer together in her embrace. "You two are fucking adorable."

JANE

"HERE'S YOUR PAPER." The aide smiled and set the *Record Delta* on the tray of Jane's walker. The date on the top shocked her. Perhaps it was true, Jane admitted, what they said about her mind. She'd been slipping more and more. Still, 1944 was clear.

Jane had read the ad for the air cadet dance again and again: "Nice local girls encouraged to apply." She would meet someone and they'd get out of Buckhannon. Of course she'd wait for him here, but then after the war . . .

"Jane! Fancy seeing you," the secretary collecting the packets exclaimed. "I heard all about your time in Washington." She knew the girl, a long-necked brunette with a button nose, from high school, but she could not remember her name. "I really am so sorry to hear about your . . ." The girl's eyes darted around the room, landing on the black-shaded lamp on her desk. She let out a high-pitched sneeze. "Excuse me," she said. The sleeves of her shirt clipped into her pale arms, leaving a red ring around them.

It looked rather uncomfortable, Jane thought. "It's quite all right."

"The thing is," the girl said. She sneezed again, startling herself, jumping out of her seat a little. "The thing is . . . you're a widow, yes?"

Jane clenched her back teeth.

"Well, the thing is, we're to accept only girls who have never been married. I'm quite sorry about that, Jane. We just . . ."

"Of course," Jane said. "You wouldn't want to upset the boys."

"That's it. That's the thing. I'm very sorry. I'm sure you understand."

"Quite clearly. Thank you."

She walked straight to Stone & Thomas. Below the ad for the dance, there'd been one about the store needing a new girl for the makeup department. From FBI to makeup girl. Jane supposed whatever was left of her dignity was worth the humor of it.

She kept her chin up as well as she could manage, applying rouge to the crepe-paper cheeks of old women and doling out makeovers to teenagers before the high school's prom. She joined civic clubs too—the Women's Club and the rotary, the hospital auxiliary. The sense of sisterhood with a purpose was oddly comforting—the duty and meaning of her war work with the ease of a small town. Philip taught Jane, finally, to drive, and she shuttled herself to her job and various meetings. She may not have been happy, but at least she was busy.

The war ended and her brothers came home. Though they brought only eleven arms back with them, there was enough joy in the small house to grow eight new ones. It seemed an unbelievable miracle that all six of them had returned, and the farmhouse was loud and boisterous, full of battle stories and much teasing for Jane.

Downtown, people met on the sidewalk and slapped one another on the back, embracing on the corners. Jane held her breath as she passed houses where stars still hung in the windows, pillars of silence amid the general jollity.

Soon after, a letter arrived—a rare missive from Ding. The end of the war in Washington was unlike anything she'd ever witnessed, she wrote. It was a party, *the biggest party in the whole world.*

A knot tightened in Jane's stomach as she read, imagining all of them—Ding, Claudine, Flossie, Erma, even Owen, out yelling in the streets. It must have been wonderful.

"What's Ding say, Janey?" Billy asked, mussing her hair and kissing her on the cheek. Jane smiled. She would not trade being here, crowded in with her brothers, for anything.

"Just the scoop on Washington." Billy nodded and opened the door of the new refrigerator, taking out a jar of milk and downing it in three long gulps. Billy put the empty jar in the sink, belched, and walked away. Jane shook her head but could not suppress a smile—even this felt festive.

She turned her attention back to the letter. Ding would come home now that the war was over, surely, and she was eager for the details. What a reunion that would be! They would go to the pharmacies for old times' sake, and then Jane would show her the makeup counter. What a hoot! Jane couldn't wait until Ding saw that the farm had electricity.

She read on. *I'm not a duration girl, Jane. That's what I've learned,* Ding wrote. *I truly love nursing. I'm committed to completing my training, no matter what.*

Jane's heart sank.

And that's really what this letter is about, cousin. There's a bit of a "what." I've found myself in a situation. He's a nice boy, thank goodness, and we went to the courthouse straight away. You should have seen the line! We're certainly not the only honeymooners in the capital these days.

Honeymooners. Ding had gotten herself into the same mess that Jane had, but now Jane was here and Ding was married with a baby on the way. Jane's cheeks stung as if someone had slapped her.

Cal and I will get a house in the suburbs. I do hope you'll come when the baby's born. I'm sure to need all the help I can get, as it will be right in the thick of second-year exams.

Jane sat, stunned. She could hear two of her brothers wrestling in the yard outside, the others cheering them on. Ding was married. And pregnant. And staying. The war was over and things were returning, not to normal, but to a new configuration of it.

But what about her?

Jane had realized, then, that she had been thinking of her situation as "for the duration." Though she hadn't a clear picture of what would happen after, she'd felt certain that *something* would come up. She'd been in a holding pattern, flying in circles along with the rest of the world, but the world had begun moving again, and Jane had nowhere to go.

With a deep breath, Jane opened the paper before her and read about new restaurants, new laws, people she didn't know doing things she didn't understand. She looked up to the picture of Cassidy she kept tacked by her chair and remembered—what a glorious thing it was to remember the present—the baby. The world was moving along without her again, but Jane understood, finally, that this was all right.

CASSIDY

A SEVENTY-DEGREE CHRISTMAS gave way to a sixty-degree January. By fifty-degree February, Cassidy had reacclimated to the weather, shivering in her sweats as her belly grew and the baby moved and danced.

Cassidy watched in horror as her breasts swelled, blue veins bulging like spiderwebs across them, and as shiny stretch marks crossed her stomach like lightning bolts. She would never look the same again. But Noeli looked at her with fascination, wondering at the marvel of the human body and its ability to grow and change. As Cassidy struggled to tie her shoes one morning, Noeli knelt before her and took over. "Did you know your blood volume increases by forty to fifty percent when you're pregnant?"

By March the weather was warming again, and by May the extra resident in Cassidy's body left her sweaty the moment she left the air-conditioning.

After a particularly large Instacart order, Cassidy came home, sweaty from lifting and reaching, and found Noeli on the couch, her phone open to an article: "How to Be the Birth Partner Your Birthing Partner Needs."

She jumped when she realized Cassidy was standing behind her. "You must be exhausted! Sit down. Do you need anything?" Cassidy could hardly believe she'd ever felt jealous when Noeli had been nothing but amazing to her.

"I need a car with a trunk that opens so I don't have to reach across the seat all the time. It's getting hard to balance with my belly."

"Maybe you need to quit." Noeli stood and walked toward the kitchen.

"I'd feel too guilty not contributing anything. You already do so much for me."

"Work in the home is still labor. It's capitalism that devalues it," Noeli said. "It might be invisible in the marketplace, but I see it. No one ever scrubbed the baseboards before you moved in." Noeli poured a glass of water and handed it to Cassidy, who took a sip.

"That's just nesting. I don't really do that much around here."

"You're growing a human with your body. That's work, too."

Cassidy smiled. All Noeli did was give and give. A thought occurred to her, one she felt naive for never thinking before. What had Noeli thought about the word *partner* in the article she'd been reading? What did *she* think about it?

"Have we talked about middle names?" Noeli asked, interrupting her thinking.

"I don't think . . . *we* have. Hey, where's Abuela?"

"Out working in the rose garden."

"Ah." Cassidy took her water back to the couch and Noeli followed, sitting so close that their legs touched. Cassidy looked at Noeli's ripped black jeans and then at her own maternity leggings, the black stretched so thin, she could see her legs.

Noeli leaned her head on Cassidy's shoulder, and her curls tickled Cassidy's cheek.

"Theme party?" Cassidy asked, jumping up and causing Noeli to fall slowly sideways. Cassidy had to lean down and grab the coffee table to steady herself—she wasn't used to her current center of gravity.

"Always," Noeli agreed.

"Although . . ." Cassidy said, reconsidering. "This isn't going to be fair. Nothing's going to fit me."

"I'll give you a five-minute head start," Noeli offered.

"Okay," Cassidy agreed. "Theme?"

"Umm. Hipsters?"

"Too easy."

"Hipsters with superpowers?" Noeli tried.

"Yes!" Cassidy said.

"Go!" Noeli yelled, looking at the time on the clock.

Cassidy wobbled down the hall toward the closet and Noeli laughed.

"Shut up!" Cassidy's voice echoed behind her as she reached her room and began rummaging through clothes.

She felt weirdly competitive about this game, which they'd invented a couple of months earlier. Living with Noeli felt like the best kind of sleepover, Cassidy thought as she pulled clothes from drawers and flung them over her shoulder. The sleepovers from back before the other girls realized she was different and stopped inviting her. Noeli sprinted down the hall past Cassidy's door, tearing into her own room. Noeli got into the game, too, but she knew how to do it lightly. She'd be so good with the baby, Cassidy thought, picturing Noeli giving piggyback rides and singing silly songs. She threw on an outfit just as Noeli yelled "Time!"

Cassidy waddled into Noeli's room and saw her wearing a huge rebozo of her grandmother's draped around her neck like a giant infinity scarf. An enormous pair of sunglasses gave off a definite raccoon vibe, and she had combed her hair completely over one half of her face. They both cracked up.

"What's your superpower?" Cassidy asked.

"Drinking more pour-over coffee than humanly possible."

"Wow," Cassidy said. "I know we're having a baby together, but that was a little too much of a dad joke." She froze, realizing what had come out of her mouth.

Noeli laughed, unfazed. "Come on! I had five minutes! What's yours?" She looked at Cassidy's Modest Mouse shirt and the headband she'd pulled on top of her hair, making the bit above it poof up.

"Oh, my power?" Cassidy said, trying to sound bored. "You wouldn't have heard of it."

She couldn't hide her smirk as Noeli cracked up again. "Okay, you definitely win. Where's the hipsters-with-superpowers party?"

"You mean you didn't get the invitation?" Cassidy asked. "It was printed on artisanal recycled bacon."

"I get it! You tell better hipster jokes than I do!" Noeli bent her head to unwrap the rebozo from around her neck. When she looked up again, Cassidy was looking at her with wide eyes and a serious mouth.

"What are we doing?" Cassidy asked. The air-conditioner turned off, leaving the room even more still.

"What do you mean?" Noeli asked, still smiling. "You really want to find a party?"

"No." Cassidy removed the headband and her hair stuck up in awkward wisps. "I mean what are *we* doing? What is *this*?"

Noeli inhaled and lifted her head in a half nod of understanding. Her eyes darted back and forth from one of Cassidy's to the other. The air suddenly felt stagnant and hot. Outside, a woodpecker tapped an electrical pole.

"I don't know," Noeli said, choosing her words carefully. "Isn't it okay if it's a little . . . ambiguous?" She gripped the rebozo tightly, rubbing her fingers over its red-and-orange weave.

"Is it though? Is it ambiguous?" As Cassidy spoke, Noeli reached out to smooth her hair. Cassidy caught her hand at her head and held on. "I can't do much more ambiguity." She sighed. "Everything is ambiguous right now."

"That makes sense." Noeli tapped her thumb on Cassidy's fingers. "If it makes you feel any better, my feelings haven't been very ambiguous lately. Are your feelings? Are they ambiguous?"

"Very," Cassidy admitted. "But I don't like it." But her feelings were growing clearer with every second she looked into Noeli's eyes. Noeli laughed and Cassidy felt the *tap tap tap* of her thumb. Her baby responded—a *tap tap tap* to the right of her navel. "But I want something solid. And stable. I want someone who wants me now, even when I have nothing—even when I'm a mess." Cassidy felt her breathing sync with Noeli's as they clasped each other's hands tighter, waiting for whatever would happen next. She went on. "I want someone I can laugh with. I want someone I can talk to. I feel closer to you than anyone ever. I know you're always on my team. I love Abuela. I even love your mom." They both laughed and then returned to their slow, synchronous breathing. "You gave me a home when I had nothing."

Noeli dropped Cassidy's hand and hoisted herself back onto the bed. "Are you attracted to me?" she asked in a low voice.

Cassidy studied the woman before her with her dark eyes and pale skin, her ringlets, the sharp angles of her cheeks and elbows, and the smooth curves of her breasts and hips under her thin black T-shirt. She imagined what it would feel like to touch these contrasting features—hard and soft.

"I am." Noeli bit her lip and the baby kicked harder in Cassidy's uterus. The bed squeaked as Noeli stretched, then twisted, cracking her back. She twisted the other way and then faced Cassidy. When she reached out her hand, Cassidy took it. They laughed as they struggled to pull her onto the bed.

Once they'd settled, they looked at each other, their faces no more than a foot apart. Noeli's skin was almost translucent then, like notebook paper. Cassidy stared at the freckles that dotted her cheeks and nose, barely visible unless you paid attention like this—close. She looked like one of the "Celebrities without Makeup" photos where they all inevitably looked more beautiful somehow—pure and fresh. Cassidy was barely breathing.

Noeli leaned in to kiss Cassidy then, and Cassidy willed her not to stop. She wanted her nose to brush her freckles, to feel her red painted lips on her own. The moment she did, the moment she felt the sticky lipstick on her own mouth, any questions that remained disappeared.

It was like buttercream frosting, Cassidy thought, thinking of elaborate cupcakes and thick white sugar. "What if I tell my mom to get on with selling the farm?" she blurted. "What if we use the money to get a place together? Alone." Noeli tilted her head, her lips still soft and parted. "It could be really ours, and we'd be out of the suburbs and in a Real Place, and we'd both be happy, because we'd be here in SoCal, but we could be in a cool neighborhood and maybe even somewhere we could walk to cool stuff and have a community feeling. I don't know." Cassidy knew she was rambling.

Noeli kissed her again, harder this time. It was almost too good, like a guilty pleasure. Cassidy didn't know it could be so good.

CASSIDY

AS THEY ATE their cereal the next morning, Noeli brushed her leg against Cassidy's, giving her goose bumps that rose from the point of contact up the corresponding side of her neck. Noeli's jokester eyes sparkled with new amusement and Cassidy felt like the world could read it.

"I always feel the perfect amount of pregnant," Cassidy mused.

"What do you mean?"

"Whatever week I am in my pregnancy, when I see people who aren't as far, they seem so naive, like they're barely pregnant. And people further along seem *so* pregnant. It's kind of like when you're a kid and people younger than you seem so little and the ones older than you seem so mature. Like whatever age you are is the only normal age to be."

"I still feel like that." Noeli laughed.

Rosa shuffled into the room, surprising them both—it was unusually early for an appearance—and the women pulled their legs back under their own chairs like teenagers caught holding hands in the hallway. Rosa rubbed last night's makeup from her eyes and then paused mid-step to blink at them.

"Ahhhhh!" she squealed. "Finalmente!" Her hair splayed out from the pink band on top of her head in every direction, like a poorly maintained fountain.

Cassidy looked to Noeli, who looked as confused as she felt.

"Finalmente?"

"You two! Finalmente!"

"So you're cool with me being una marimacha now?"

Rosa's eyes glittered with the drama. "You're not una marimacha if you are with this one." She motioned toward Cassidy.

Noeli snorted. "Thanks, Mamá. I'm glad it just takes you loving someone else to accept who I am." Her tone was light.

Ignoring her, Rosa went to Cassidy. "My grandbaby!" she exclaimed, holding Cassidy's belly between her hands. Her tank top smelled like stale cigarettes. "Muah, muah!" she pantomimed kissing each side. Standing and turning, she walked to the cabinet, the bottom of each tan butt cheek peeking out from her gray cotton shorts. She rustled around in a box, retrieved a diet protein bar, and retreated back to her room.

"I really do need to get out of here," Noeli said through a mouthful of Corn Pops.

"I was a lot more worried about how she would react," Cassidy said. "How did she even know?"

"Una bruja. A witch." Noeli went back to her cereal, scooping another huge spoonful into her mouth.

"So are we?" Cassidy paused as Noeli chewed. "Together?"

"I mean, that's what that whole conversation was last night, wasn't it?"

"Yeah," Cassidy said, and it hung in the air between them, neither sure what to say next.

Cassidy took a bite of her own cereal and chewed it carefully. She stretched her leg out under the table again, and Noeli resumed caressing it with her own.

"Have you told your mom you're going to sell the farm after all? That you want to buy something out here?" Noeli asked, plucking a paper napkin from the green plastic holder between them and dabbing her bare lips.

Cassidy swallowed. "Not yet. I was totally browsing real estate last night when I couldn't sleep, though."

"Me too," Noeli admitted.

The similarity between Noeli's and Simon's lives struck Cassidy. Noeli was going to escape her mom and finally live like the grown-up she'd been playing since she was sixteen. And Cassidy would get a real home, one she picked, not one she ended up with due to circumstance or chance or because someone hundreds of years ago plopped a stick in the mud when they got sick of hiking. She thought of the headings on the real estate website: interior features, square footage, neighborhood info, schools. She would carefully weigh the pros and cons, and select the best possible home, consciously and intentionally.

Noeli brought her bowl to the sink, rinsed it, dried it, and placed it in the metal drying rack. Bending down, she kissed Cassidy softly on the lips, a familiar kiss now, the kind for departures and greetings. Cassidy felt a movement inside like a flower opening. The familiarity was thrilling and the baby responded to whatever hormonal reaction this was, flipping over and over.

"I'll see you after work," Noeli said. She took her lipstick from her bag, applied it, and blew Cassidy another kiss before heading out the door.

As it clicked shut, Cassidy tried not to think about the day that stretched before her. She should read the childbirth book. She should call her mom. Cassidy rinsed and dried her own bowl. When she turned around, Abuela was in the kitchen, holding on to the table for balance as she slipped her feet into her green rubber gardening clogs.

"Ayúdame?" she asked. "Snip, snip?" She pantomimed using a large pair of clippers.

"Sure." Cassidy put on her own shoes. She tried not to think about how much she hated working in the garden; she figured this was the least she could do for Noeli's family and all their hospitality. She followed Abuela out the door and watched as she stood on tiptoes to unlock the side gate to the backyard. Two pairs of shears, one large and one small, balanced against the back of the house. Abuela handed Cassidy the large pair and silently, they got to work deadheading roses.

Cassidy hadn't gardened since she was ten. Until that age, she'd enjoyed the attention of her mother, who often seemed so far away. In the garden, Paloma was present and patient, teaching Cassidy the names of the plants, how far to space them, how deep to push her finger into the earth for each seed. She showed her how to harvest and chop, which plants stored better in the refrigerator and which in the pantry.

As puberty brought breasts and a budding awareness that she was different, Cassidy grew more and more self-conscious, and soon the whole thing began to feel like another way her mom maintained perfect control. Paloma did it all so easily while Cassidy struggled. Her rows inched closer and closer together when she planted. When she harvested, she dropped onions and watched them roll away.

In this little rose-filled yard in Fontana, though, Abuela left things imperfect. Even in the middle of the suburbs, the wild seemed on the verge of intruding—the bushes just this side of unruly. The light smell of fresh petals was overpowered by the dry rotting ones. Pincer bugs crawled up and down stems and bees zipped from flower to flower.

But what was the point? Why would Abuela come out all the time to prune, to keep the weeds barely at bay, just for more roses to bloom so she had to do it again in a week? It was endless and thankless and . . . and then Cassidy got it.

Oh. She let the clippers fall to her side. That was the point. She turned to watch Abuela, who was shaping the plants with delicate snips, with perfect care and attention.

Cassidy felt angry with herself. Of course she hadn't seen it until she could imagine a trope—the wise old Mexican woman. Still, she couldn't stop herself from wanting to hear some wisdom in Abuela's voice.

"Why do you work so hard?" she asked. "Just to do it again tomorrow?"

Abuela paused, thinking, and Cassidy waited for her profound response. Finally she shrugged. "I like roses."

Cassidy laughed. "Me too." Abuela was no trope. She was her perfectly Zen self, all love and no judgment.

Inside, sun-worn and thirsty, Cassidy texted her mom.

How's the garden?

She sat back in the chair and took a long swig of ice water. The baby kicked as the cold reached her stomach. A moment later, when Paloma responded, *Still my little corner of our woods for now. Enjoying it while I can*, it seemed to Cassidy one of the wisest things she'd ever read.

I want my own corner, she typed back. She thought of the houses in Redlands, the land behind them. She could build raised beds and plant roses like Abuela's. *I'm ready for you to sell the farm. I want to buy out here.*

Later, when Noeli returned from work, Cassidy tried to explain her revelation. "I got gardening for the first time. It's about the present moment and enjoying the process," she gushed. She couldn't explain it in a way that didn't sound trite and obvious. "Also, I realized I like roses."

Noeli laughed and kissed her on the nose. “I love that you’re spending time with Abuela.”

Cassidy called Grandma Jane later that night. “You told me about the first baby, but why did you stay after? You could have left at any time, but you stayed your whole life.”

JANE

"WELL, DARLING," JANE began. It was past midnight, and she felt glad that her granddaughter knew she would be up. "I suppose one thing simply leads to another." It was true. She could not tell Cassidy anything more about the filthy furnace room. Instead she began her story later, when she'd gone devotedly to her job at the department store. At work, powders were soon out—Jane rubbed subtly shaded creams onto women's bright cheeks.

Victory Red lips slowly grew pinker. Movies grew more colorful, tight curls loosened, and cars began to resemble spaceships. It was as if the public wanted to propel itself as far from the war as possible, into a bright, shining future.

By twenty-three, she'd accepted her status as a spinster. "Oh, I'm perfectly happy without a husband," she told Mrs. Sharpo as she held out a palette of pinks and waited for the woman to choose.

"I don't see how, dear. Although I know you're still living with your mom and daddy. Myself, I need a man's—"

Jane set the creams back on the counter, picked up a tube of lipstick, and began applying it to Mrs. Sharpo's jabbering mouth in an effort to stop the racket.

Cassidy laughed at this part of the story. "That's hilarious," she said, and Jane smiled at her granddaughter's amusement. It was funny, Jane knew, because old women talking about sex was funny. Jane didn't mind being a joke if it meant she heard Cassidy's sweet laugh.

"I told Mrs. Sharpo I supposed I'd learned a little about self-sufficiency at the FBI. She was shocked I'd worked for the Bureau and told me they needed people to help with computer punch cards at the hospital—that I was the perfect candidate."

Just like at the Armory, Jane had lost herself in work. Though her back ached, and she often dreamed of rows of rectangular holes, she knew she was making a real difference. Jane felt she could spend her life this way.

The blizzard of '49 kept the whole county home, and Jane sat restless at her window, watching the snowflakes careen past like little dancers as her music box accompanied them, popping out the tinny notes of "The Teddy Bear's Picnic." The house was quiet, aside from the music box's song; four of Jane's brothers had married local girls, and the other two had taken an apartment together downtown. The snow surrounded the small farmhouse like a heavy quilt, insulating Jane from the world beyond.

The last flake had barely fallen when the announcements began. Jane, apparently, had been the only one facing the cold alone. Billy and Franklin were both expecting little bundles, and Arzella was overjoyed. It had been too long since she'd held a squalling baby to her chest and comforted it, she said.

"Of course, you'll be our go-to babysitter," Billy said.

"Aunt Jane!" Franklin declared.

The title filled Jane with bubbling giddiness. "Aunt Jane," she repeated. Suddenly she had an outlet for all the love she'd been holding deep within her chest. Every evening after work, she knitted hats and sweaters, blankets and socks. The clack of her needles became a rhythm to hum along to—sometimes jazz tunes, and at others, old hymns.

"And then there was the letter from Ding."

"What letter?" Cassidy asked.

Among the advertisements, a lunch invitation for Arzella, and the latest Sears catalog had been a letter postmarked from Arlington, Virginia. Jane tore into the envelope and extracted the peach stationary.

Dear Jane, she read. *I hope you are doing well back at home.* Jane's stomach clenched at this and she crossed her legs. Ding had not been "home" in half a decade. Could she even call it that anymore?

I'm writing to tell you that little Harry has contracted polio. Oh, Jane. I am terribly afraid. I fear in my heart, though I can't tell Cal, of course, that he won't recover, and I don't know what I'll do. I miss you something awful, cousin. I need you, the way I used to. Please write back as soon as you can. I am doing nothing but wringing my hands and missing you.

Jane placed the letter in her lap and put a hand to her mouth, her whole body convulsing with cries. As she wept, a hot throb arose in her index finger. From the corner of her eye, Jane saw a red globe of blood squeezing from a small straight cut. Just as Jane brought her finger to her lips, the phone rang out. Jane tasted iron and earth, and knew, of course, that it would be Ding.

"That's terrible," Cassidy breathed.

"Yes, it was awful." Jane realized she should not have told such a story to a pregnant woman. "But that's why I stayed. I had work here and people who needed me." This, too, was the wrong thing to say, and Jane again felt guilty instantly. "But you go on now. Get back to your life there. I know you're busy, darling. I love you." She hung up before Cassidy could protest, and pulled the awful blanket around her arms. To her own surprise, she was able to sleep.

CASSIDY

WHEN THE ACCORD returned the next day, Cassidy tried to force herself to stay put in her room rather than greet her girlfriend at the door. She had a girlfriend. In real life. And she was here. Cassidy threw her phone, which she'd been using to go back and forth between real estate listings and old pictures of said girlfriend, on the nightstand. She walked to the door, then made herself turn around and get back on the bed. She opened the as-yet-untouched childbirth book to a random page and waited for Noeli to come in.

"Oh, hi," she said as *her girlfriend* stepped into the room.

Noeli kissed her on the cheek. "Did you talk to your mom today?"

"I did! And look what I found!" Cassidy gave up pretending to read the book, letting it fall to the floor. She showed Noeli the latest house she'd bookmarked. "It's only nine hundred square feet, but it's not like we need a ton of space. It's walking distance to downtown. I'm imagining us walking all the time with the baby. Look at those floors! It was built in 1908!" She looked at Noeli, who was frowning. "What?"

"It's in Redlands."

"I really loved it when we drove around. The houses and the downtown. I can really imagine feeling settled there. It seems like the perfect place to have a family."

"A white family." Cassidy froze and Noeli sighed. "Redlands is adorable, but it's a bunch of rich white liberals. They're always voting down affordable housing measures because they want to keep their city's 'charm.'"

"But we could afford this one. The money from the farm is enough for a down payment where our mortgage wouldn't be bad."

"That's not the point," Noeli said. "They don't want brown people there. That's what they think makes their city charming. What they think distinguishes it from San Bernardino."

"Isn't it more about the crime rate? And the better schools? I looked at a few houses in San Bernardino, but—"

Noeli cut her off. "And you think crime rate and good schools is a separate issue from poverty and race?"

"No, but—" Cassidy felt defensive.

"I don't want to live somewhere that doesn't want me. Or only wants me if I'm with a nice, respectable white girl and have enough money. San Bernardino has groups doing real community organizing. Redlands has people raising money for their summer concert series."

Cassidy had read about the summer concert series. She'd thought it sounded nice. "San Bernardino just seems like a bigger Fontana when we've driven through. I don't want to live somewhere that feels like another shitty suburb. I want to feel like it's somewhere I chose."

"I'm sure you do." Noeli rolled her eyes. "Somewhere 'charming.'"

"I think if I'm buying you a house, I should get to say I want it somewhere nice."

The women shut their mouths in shock as the air seemed to leave the room. For a moment they stayed silent, contemplating the direction this would go. There seemed, still, to be a chance they could laugh it off, apologize, lie back and play with filters together on one of their phones. The moment passed and Noeli's face hardened. "Buying me a house!" she snorted. "So you think I'm what? Using you? Do you remember that you brought this up? Every single bit of it? And that I took you into *my* house, pregnant, without wanting anything from you?"

"This isn't about you using me. You're putting words in my mouth. This is about you pushing me to spend my family's money on a boring box of a house where we're going to get stabbed walking around." It was about more than that now, though, but there was no way for Cassidy to say this. In that silent moment, Noeli had flipped a switch, throwing up a wall between them. She had closed herself off. The angle of her eyebrows and the rhythm of her head movements mimicked Rosa's, and Cassidy realized that Noeli had avoided becoming her mother simply by circumstance.

No. Noeli was not Rosa. She was Noeli. Cassidy's Noeli. Cassidy took a deep breath and tried to cross the distance between them. "This is the land I grew up on, and we're talking about selling it for something that doesn't feel right to me. I don't know how to explain what a big deal that is."

"Because I wouldn't get it? Because we're immigrants? Because we don't have land that's been in the family for generations?"

"No, you're right. I'm sorry. You should get it more."

"I *should*, shouldn't I? But I don't because I'll never be as smart as Cassidy. Cassidy didn't go to a community college—she went to a *university*," she jeered.

"I didn't mean it like—" The bedspread felt scratchy under her fingers.

"Cassidy makes better hipster jokes than anyone. Cassidy is tortured, but it's endearing. Cassidy doesn't get in trouble, and even if she does, it magically falls back into place because that's how it is for women like *Cassidy*. It must be really fucking nice."

"Women like me?" Anger rose in Cassidy's throat like stomach acid.

"Yes. White women. You don't get to pretend you're not white because you grew up in West Virginia."

"I never . . . all I ever said about that was that I grew up without a lot of money. That I understand class struggles, and it's different in a place where there aren't a lot of people of color. Especially being Jewish."

Had Noeli been harboring all of this? What else did she hate about Cassidy?

"Being poor is different in a place where you have your own house and plenty of food and you know it."

"I know it's different. That doesn't mean it's—"

Noeli had collected everything Cassidy said and did and saved it for when she needed it. Even when Cassidy had thought they were friends, she was gathering resentments like eggs, waiting to break them over her head.

"We talk about your feelings constantly," Noeli said. "And you barely ask me how my day was. Of course it's only your feelings that matter if we're making a big decision."

"That isn't true," Cassidy protested. She frantically tried to replay their conversations, searching for moments that contradicted this assertion of her terribleness.

"It is true, Cass." Her use of the nickname conveyed exasperation rather than endearment. "But you don't realize it because you don't even *think* to talk about me. Speaking of which, you know how camming makes you feel so 'empowered'? You get to feel that way because you're white and you're making the choice to do it. You get to choose the parameters and only do things you're comfortable with. It's not like that for everyone."

"I know that," Cassidy said. "I know it's a privilege to be empowered by it. You know I'm in that advocacy group for sex workers—" Shame churned within her, swirling with embarrassment and anger.

"That's another thing." Noeli cut her off again. "You *love* being a sex worker the same way you love talking about how you grew up poor because it makes you sound so oppressed and cool. You know I could go over to Lupe's right now." Noeli's words were ice picks poking Cassidy. Cassidy saw a look of horror in Noeli's eyes, like she simultaneously hated what she was doing and delighted in it. "It would be *easy*. I could drive over to her condo and knock on her door and she would let me in and we'd argue for a couple minutes and then we would fuck. And it would be easy because she gets being Latina and she gets being a lesbian who's *out* and she gets how to interact with other humans like they also have feelings."

Cassidy winced, picturing Noeli with Lupe, imagining the names they would call her, knowing they would be right.

"Mostly though . . ." Noeli was looking at the ceiling now and shaking her head. "Mostly, she doesn't have so much *shit going on*!" Noeli screamed the last few words and leapt from the bed. As she walked out of the room and into the hallway, the rubber soles of her Chucks thudded rhythmically—*thump, thump, thump* toward the kitchen. Cassidy watched Noeli's curls bobbing as she went.

Cassidy sat, stunned, and put a hand to her belly. The baby turned, the hard edge of its foot moving across her abdomen in an arc from right to left, pausing at her belly button like it was tracing the line of the equator on a globe.

Thump, thump, thump. Noeli's Chucks came back up the hall, and Cassidy nearly cried in relief. The thumps thumped right past Cassidy's door, though, with a blur of dark curls, and Cassidy heard the door across the hall open and then close, then moments later the fuzzy sounds of riot grrrl from laptop speakers.

Cassidy picked up her phone, which was still open to the beautiful craftsman in South Redlands, with its cute blue pillars and yellow trim, the sunflowers growing in the front yard. The colors blurred together with her tears. She exited the real estate website and went to her contacts, blinking hard as the phone rang.

"Mom," she said when Paloma answered. "I need to come home."

PALOMA

IT TOOK SEVERAL seconds for Paloma to register what her daughter was saying. She'd been sure Cassidy would stay in California no matter what. Cassidy never admitted to her mistakes. She hated to be vulnerable. She'd been stubborn her whole life.

Paloma remembered a night when Cassidy was three or four. The sun had begun to set, the swings and slides fading into silhouettes in the dusk.

"Daddy! Fireflies!" Cassidy exclaimed as yellow bulbs blinked around them.

"Catch one!" Ken said. It took Cassidy a few tries, but eventually she managed to enclose one of the glowing creatures between her cupped palms.

"Now let it go," Paloma said.

"Nuh-uh."

Cassidy felt strangely unfamiliar to Paloma sometimes—this child she'd grown within her body, fed from her breast. Watching her in the dark, Paloma thought she looked like a miniature Jane. Where Paloma's hair was thick and brittle, Cassidy's was sleek and wavy. Where Paloma's long legs seemed to feed directly into her torso, Cassidy's child body was already rounding into a small bell. Paloma wondered if she had simply been a vessel to bring Ken's baby into the world. This flash of a thought disturbed her. *No,* she told herself. Cassidy was hers. She knew her like she knew her own limbs.

"Cassidy, wild things want to be free. You can enjoy it for a while, say thank you, and then let it go."

"It's my friend," Cassidy insisted. "I named her Amy, and she wants to be with me."

A bullfrog croaked in the pond. The crickets thrummed. Paloma and Ken walked back toward the house, Cassidy following behind. Inside, Cassidy's small murmurings continued until the insect's glow had faded to a pale yellow dot. "Let it out, Cassidy. Please. It's dying," Paloma said as they stood by the coatrack.

"It's not dying. It's sleeping," Cassidy said, her small face screwed up in anger at her mother. "She wants to sleep in my room."

Paloma could not know then how at twelve Cassidy would refuse her help with homework because she thought it was cheating, instead preferring to get an answer wrong, but she could sense that same unyielding sense of righteousness. She could not know that at twenty Cassidy would stop eating meat, or how at twenty-four she would get naked on camera for strangers because she preferred it to the indignity of driving for a rideshare service. She could not know these things, but still she could picture the obstinate, dogged core of Cassidy that led to each of these decisions. Paloma imagined it as a small glowing stone somewhere deep within her daughter.

Neither could Paloma have conceived then of the possibility that each of these choices, in their own way, might be right for Cassidy. Instead, as Cassidy placed the dying insect at her bedside and changed into the large Mickey Mouse T-shirt she wore as a nightgown, Paloma thought, *My daughter's stubbornness will be an obstacle for her.*

Paloma returned to the room thirty minutes later, when Cassidy had fallen asleep, her long eyelashes splayed down her smooth cheeks. This was when Cassidy felt the most like hers. Paloma put a hand on her belly and felt it rise and fall with each breath, as it had since she was a tiny baby. She kissed her sleeping daughter on the forehead and breathed in the warm scent of her hair, then lifted the firefly gently and took it outside, blowing it from her palm into the long grass behind the house.

In the morning, Cassidy awoke, frantic. "Where's Amy?" she demanded. Her little fists were balled at her sides.

"She must have flown away in the night." Paloma shrugged and dunked her tea bag. Cassidy looked at her mother, skeptical and angry.

Cassidy had come upon her stubbornness honestly, Paloma thought in the years that followed, as she beseeched Ken to put aside his pet projects. "You have to build the house. A real one."

Ken looked up from his seat on the floor and the tepee he was constructing. "I was thinking of trying to sell these," he said. "Feel this." He held an animal hide out to Paloma.

"A real house," she said, and though the thick white skin looked inviting, she did not reach out for it.

Ken put the hide in his lap and leaned back on his hands. "We'll get to it. How much do you think these could sell for?"

Far away, towers came down, and everywhere, flags went up. In Buckhannon, the stars and stripes often waved next to the Confederate banner and Paloma knew her neighbors' unity did not include her. She watched as Cassidy grew into a feral, wild thing, more and more independent. Her daughter roamed the woods, scattering yarn scraps and spotting them later in songbird nests. She sucked the pink-white fingers of clover flowers. She was native to this place in a way Paloma would never be.

"I don't need you to follow me, Mommy," Cassidy said one afternoon.

Thinking about the comment, Paloma was struck, to her horror, with resentment. How many hours had she spent braiding Cassidy's hair? Would her other babies have wanted her more? Why was Cassidy the one who was born, who "chose to come earthside"?

"Of course you don't." Paloma smiled and watched as Cassidy flew down Shumaker Hill on her purple Huffy bike, her two braids flying out behind her in the wind, leaving Paloma alone at the top.

Ken came home late that evening. "I'll put her to bed," he told Paloma. "You've had a long day."

"You've been at work all day. It's all right." Idleness made Paloma feel guilty, as if she did not deserve her daughter.

"I don't mind. Let's go, sweet pea." He patted Cassidy on the back. "Bedtime."

In the kitchen, Paloma sat before a cup of chamomile tea and listened to the muffled sounds of Ken and Cassidy talking and laughing. They didn't need her, either of them. She'd merely been a means for them to get to each other. She could disappear and they'd be fine. She took a sip of tea. She'd let it steep too long and it tasted bitter.

An hour later Cassidy awoke crying and Paloma rushed to her side, Cabbage Patch dolls pouting in the light from glow-in-the-dark star decals. "I don't feel good, Mommy." Cassidy's hair was plastered to her sweaty cheeks.

Paloma cupped her palm over Cassidy's forehead. "Oh my God, you're burning up. Ken!"

Ken stumbled into the room, groggy and disoriented. "What is it? What?"

"She's burning up. We need to get her into the car." Paloma could picture the emergency room, hear the beeps, picture them carrying her daughter away from her. She shouldn't have thought about the other babies. She was being punished for resenting her child.

"Paloma, it's a fever. Did you take her temperature?" He left and returned with a glass thermometer.

Paloma held Cassidy's hand as the mercury rose. Ninety-eight. Ninety-nine. At one hundred, it stood still.

"She's okay," Ken said.

"Okay." Paloma sighed. "We'll watch her." Ken stumbled back toward the bedroom and Paloma curled up next to Cassidy, the heat radiating from her daughter more effective than any woodstove.

Now, like then, Paloma wanted to cradle her daughter, to protect her from fear and danger. She wished Cassidy were small again, so that she might wrap her in her own body—envelop her with her love.

"Oh, baby," she said into the receiver. "Come home. You can always come home."

CASSIDY

CASSIDY REMINDED HERSELF of the positives as she packed, pulling underwear from the dresser drawer, balling it up, and stuffing it into her bag. She would be there for Grandma Jane. The baby would grow up in the woods. She'd get to play in the creek. They would garden together and with Paloma. She'd get over her distaste for goats' milk. Cassidy wondered how hard it was to raise the little fainting ones. This baby was basically going to have her childhood, she realized, and sighed. She'd loved her childhood. But would this baby have her adolescence, too? She couldn't think that far ahead.

Cassidy picked up a pair of black pleather flats that barely contained her swollen feet, then set them back down. She'd leave them here for Noeli.

She raised a small glass hummingbird to the window and watched the blue light filter through its delicate wing. She'd picked up the trinket at the Victoria Gardens Farmers Market and held it in her hand as she walked between the tents, careful not to bump into any of the hundreds of strollers and shaded wagons that well-dressed mothers pushed and pulled through the Disneyesque downtown of the outdoor mall. She'd made eye contact with the children as she passed them, clutching

BPA-free sippy cups and holding colorful silicon-covered tablets.

Cassidy was having a different kind of child. Her baby would not be like the girl at the health department, but it would not be like these children either, and for that she was grateful. She would give the hummingbird to her mom for her new home.

Across the hall, Noeli's laptop played the digital version of the Bleachers album they'd bought at Amoeba. Cassidy would give up every positive on the list if it meant Noeli would forgive her. She tried not to think about what Noeli was doing in her room, instead focusing on packing the few things she didn't want to leave behind. So much for making good memories with this band. Cassidy wondered what the memory of this time would feel like in her body.

Squeezing her last pair of underwear into the bag, she thought again about her childhood. It was the right way to have a childhood, it seemed. Another kind would be lacking. This was why parents signed their kids up for ballet, why they tried to re-create the holidays their parents created for them, and why they wanted their kids to attend their alma maters. It was why Paloma wanted so badly for her to be a lesbian. She looked out the window as a man selling corn from a rolling cart walked by, his skin thick from a life in the sun. It wasn't about living through your children, the way people thought. It was about your children living you—your life and experiences.

Cassidy understood that this was kind of fucked-up, but, she thought, it was a forgivable kind of fucked-up—an instinctual one. It was how people ensured the survival of their legacies. Every living species tried to reproduce by passing down its genes, its DNA. This was part of what made us human, though—the genes weren't enough. Everyone wanted their stories and experiences to live forever, too.

Of course, there would be things totally unfamiliar to her—some new sport or camp she couldn't imagine, whatever new technology sprung up, but in Buckhannon there would be other things that would not have changed since she was little. There would be the same rickety rides at the Strawberry Festival each May, the same drippy rocket pops at the pool concession stand, the same snowy hills to sled at the farm.

Cassidy pictured Grandma Jane and her childhood. In West Virginia, some things would be like they were twenty years ago. Still others would be exactly the same as they had been for her dad and grandma. In West Virginia, this child wouldn't just relive Cassidy's childhood—she would relive Ken's and Jane's, another positive. Cassidy wrapped the hummingbird carefully back in its tissue paper and box and put it in the laptop case she'd use for a carry-on. She zipped her bag with a satisfying *zup zup zup*. The positives would have to be enough.

CASSIDY

AS NOELI DROVE Cassidy to the airport, Cassidy thought of the last time they were there together—the hike on the way home, how vulnerable Noeli had seemed, and how close she'd felt to her. There was no trace of that vulnerability now.

Noeli turned the volume up on the iPod, which was usually on shuffle, but was currently playing a full Dresden Dolls album—angry, sad, carnivalesque. Cassidy's list of positives felt pathetic here in the car, where she could smell Noeli's apple shampoo.

As the music blared, Noeli drummed on the steering wheel with her fingers and stuck her tongue in her cheek.

"I'm sorry I didn't think about Redlands from your perspective," Cassidy shouted over the pummeling piano. "I was just so taken with how cute it was and—"

Noeli cut her off. "It's not really an apology if you make excuses." She closed her mouth again and ran her tongue back and forth over her teeth.

"I wasn't trying to make excuses!" Cassidy yelled. "Can you turn this down? Christ."

Noeli conceded with annoyance.

"I was just saying—" Cassidy's voice was still too loud, so she lowered her volume. "I was saying, I thought we both wanted to live somewhere that felt like a place worth living in." Noeli didn't respond. "And you're not apologizing either."

"So you were apologizing to try to get an apology from me?"

Cassidy was silent now. It *was* what she wanted—if not an apology, then at least some kind of resolution, but it was clear she wasn't going to get it. The baby's head was down now, pressing directly on her cervix, its feet in her ribs. She thought back to that morning in the living room, sitting on the arm of Abuela's chair, watching *Hollywood Squares*.

"I'm going back to West Virginia today," she'd said during a commercial.

The old woman had looked at her and squeezed her hand. "Vaya con Dios," she'd whispered as tears appeared in both of their eyes. It wasn't fair that Cassidy had to lose Abuela, too.

Large concrete letters—*LAX*—greeted them at the airport. Noeli navigated expertly now, driving directly to Cassidy's terminal, unbuckling her seat belt, and getting out. She walked carefully around to the back, opened the trunk, and lifted Cassidy's suitcase. It would be a lot easier, Cassidy thought as she struggled to hoist herself from the seat, if Noeli were an asshole.

"It's heavy," Noeli said, lifting the bag onto the curb.

"Yeah." For a moment their hands touched as they both gripped the plastic handle.

"I'll see you later," Noeli said, pulling hers away. Businessmen rushed past wheeling black carry-ons.

"Noeli, we can't leave things like this." Noeli was silent. "We can look at San Bernardino, maybe—" Noeli glanced at the time on her phone and Cassidy sighed. "Thanks for the ride."

"You're welcome."

"And for everything. For taking me in. For everything you've done to help me feel at home." Cassidy moved to hug her, hesitating in case she resisted. She imagined sparks, tearful apologies on both sides. Noeli didn't retreat, but neither did she return the embrace. It was cold and casual, barely acceptable for acquaintances.

Cassidy let go. "Noeli, I'd go anywhere for you. I mean it." But Noeli's curls were already bouncing toward the car.

Cassidy watched as Noeli reentered the Accord, waited for an opening in the traffic, and drove away. Heaving her suitcase of things that would no longer occupy drawers and shelves in Noeli's home, she sulked through check-in, then to security, where the TSA officer glanced at her belly and waved her out of the X-ray line and over to the regular metal detector.

Of course an apology didn't fix things. An apology didn't make Cassidy a better person. She'd broken Simon and she'd hurt Noeli, she thought as she waited for her carry-on to emerge from the scanner. She deserved to be alone.

There were people here who had just been on the other side of the world. Cassidy sat at the gate, thinking and watching the planes come and go. There were people here who would be on the other side of the world tomorrow.

She should call Simon, or at least text, tell him she was coming back, apologize profusely. She took out her phone, preparing to move the message from her mind to the screen, to send it through the ether to Simon's beat-up old flip phone, but halfway through, she paused.

What was she trying to accomplish? Simon would be better off not knowing. Messaging him would be selfish. Maybe she should text Noeli and try to apologize again, take her time, think over what she wanted to say. But Cassidy knew it was no use, that she'd fucked that up irreparably, too.

Still, she couldn't put down her phone. She wanted the dopamine, she realized, the excitement of doing something on her phone and watching it morph into possibility and affirmation. All around her, people were buried in their own phones, typing away.

Across the aisle, a Pomeranian rested on its haunches, its majestic coat puffed out like a lion's mane. Cassidy and the Pomeranian locked eyes, the only two creatures fully present in the moment. She could tell Simon about the dog. That wouldn't be misleading and maybe it would open things up for them to be friends again, she thought, beginning to form the text in her mind. But it wasn't fair to Simon and she knew it. She couldn't use him as her dopamine dealer when she had no intention of giving him the oxytocin he'd want in return.

For the first time in months, she checked her cam site messages. There were dozens of them, and they were full of genuine concern and care. Quietly, she took her things to the bathroom and closed herself in the stall, and then, taking a deep breath, hit broadcast. Her guys joined immediately and the chat box flooded with their messages.

OMG SecreC! is it really you?
It's a miracle!
She's back!
My prayers are answered.

Then, as they saw her surroundings, the messages appeared even more quickly.

A public show?
OMFG

Why did I jerk off earlier? I knew I should have waited
C, you are an angel

"Hi, guys," Cassidy said as quietly as she could. "I have something to tell you."

Please say you're staying
We missed you
We love you
Are you doing a crazy public show?
Where are you? Are you back in Cali?

"So . . . it's been a while and some things have changed." Cassidy tilted her phone down to point at her belly. She bit her lip and held her breath as she brought the camera back up to her face.

CONGRATULATIONS
U are so cute
Hottie Mama!
MILF
OMG great news!

Tokens began to roll in, and Cassidy laughed in disbelief. "Aww, thank you so much, guys." Tears appeared in the corners of her eyes. "I was so nervous to tell you." More tokens and more compliments appeared.

Don't be nervous, we love you
Happy for you
You're always sexy!
Baby bumps are hot

"Aw, you are all seriously so sweet. I have to go. But I won't abandon you like that again." She blew kisses and ended the broadcast, left the stall, and returned to the gate.

Cassidy shifted in the padded seat and put a hand to her belly. The baby was still, so she prodded her uterus until it squirmed in protest. As it kicked and pushed, Cassidy observed the people rushing past—coming and going, coming and going. Announcements from other terminals floated in and out of her ears without comprehension and the scent of cinnamon rolls wafted across the terminal, making her stomach growl. She still couldn't believe her fans had acted like she'd never left. They'd been right there waiting for her, and not one had said anything mean about her transformation. They had opened their arms and let her back in.

The Pomeranian sniffed the air and licked its thin lips and Cassidy thought of the classmates she would run into, her parents' friends, and the people at the courthouse protest. Everyone from Buckhannon would be so smug about her coming home. But, she resolved, she was going to become a better person. Grandma Jane would always let Cassidy back in. Paloma would always let her back in. Simon would always let her back in. And in a way Cassidy understood but couldn't articulate, West Virginia would always let her back in.

She would be there for the people who mattered. She would be less selfish, for her baby. The positives she'd listed earlier—family, space, history—weren't just a coping mechanism. Maybe West Virginia wouldn't always be the best thing for her child, but it was the best thing for now.

"Now boarding for Pittsburgh," the woman behind the desk spoke into the intercom.

"I'm coming now," Cassidy whispered, and rubbed her belly. "We're coming home."

PALOMA

AS PALOMA DROVE toward Pittsburgh, she thought of their family trip to the state fair. Ken had been sent to cover it for the paper, so she and Cassidy had spent most of the week alone together.

The building with heritage crafts had felt like stepping into a West Virginia of the past. They passed displays of apple-head dolls and toys made of wood and twine. Quilts hung on huge ropes from the high ceilings, separating the open space and giving it the feel of a carpet store. Paloma lingered over blown glass and handwoven baskets while Cassidy kicked at her tennis shoes, bored until Ken appeared behind them.

"I've got a few hours," he said. "Is it time for rides?"

"Yeah!" Cassidy cheered, and they skipped off toward the Ferris wheel.

Paloma took the crumpled fair schedule from her bag and unfolded it. An old-time Appalachian band was due to play at a small stage in ten minutes. She walked that way, past sunburned teenage boys in undershirts and Mennonites in suspenders and bonnets.

As she found a seat in the center of the metal bleachers, the musicians tuned their instruments. They were all old men at least in their sixties, except for the banjo player, who looked about twenty. Her braided hair fell down her rose-printed cowgirl shirt, almost to the banjo's rim, as she smiled in turn at the bassist, guitarist, and mandolin player. Paloma felt a pang of jealousy. She had been young and adventurous once too. Behind the band, salesmen hawked hot tubs and deck stains.

The musicians went right from tuning into "Country Roads," the young banjoist singing. A few old men in the front row slapped their hands on the thighs of their work pants, one even hollering "Woo, boys!" to the delight of the band. Paloma danced in her seat. Otherwise, the audience sat still, most more concerned with fanning themselves with their schedules or quieting their fussy toddlers with bottles of Mountain Dew than with the music.

The song worked itself into a frenzy. The mandolin player hunched over his instrument, and the woman's voice cut loud and clear through the humidity. The bleachers buzzed against her thighs, and Paloma leaned her head back and clapped, overcome. She tried to remember the last time she'd danced.

A hand on her leg startled her, and she thought at first that someone was coming on to her—someone as taken by the swells and dips as she was. It was Cassidy, though, her seven-year-old daughter, clambering up bleachers and pulling herself onto the aluminum seat, Ken behind her.

"Mommy, you're silly," Cassidy said. Paloma smiled, feigning good sportsmanship, but inside, she seethed. Though her daughter had said the words, it was Ken she felt angry with.

She had done her best not to judge the people who crawled out of the woodwork here. She remembered a woman with ratty hair and a crop top with SEXY bedazzled on the front, shoveling funnel cake into her powdered-sugar-covered face. She thought of the fourteen-year-old boys spewing racist shit behind the grandstand as they spit chewing tobacco on the ground. Paloma didn't care about any of the looks they gave her, in her Birkenstocks and Free Tibet shirt. But it had only taken an hour of rickety rides and adrenaline for her husband to turn her back into an embarrassment in the eyes of her daughter. She put her arm around Cassidy's shoulder and clapped her small hands in her own. She would teach her not to care what other people thought.

Cassidy resisted at first, leaning away and letting her hands go limp. After a moment, though, Paloma felt her daughter relax into her. Cassidy closed her eyes and nodded to the *bum-ditty* of the banjo. Paloma was satisfied. Her daughter felt it too.

Back at the Holiday Inn, Cassidy sat on the queen bed next to Ken, pointedly ignoring Paloma as she pulled pamphlets, key chains, and other swag from the booths in the exhibition hall from her goody bag.

Ken switched the TV on and leaned back under the stock painting of tulips to watch *Family Feud.*

Reluctantly, Cassidy jumped down and crawled onto the other bed next to Paloma.

"I don't want to go home in three days. Why would anyone want to go to Buckhannon?" she whined. "What is there to do in stupid Buckhannon?"

"Hush," Paloma said. "You'll make your dad feel bad."

Cassidy's face flashed with realization and then remorse. She settled on a stubborn pout as she looked over at Ken, who watched the heavy television set intently, not looking at either of them.

Paloma had seen her own negativity in her daughter then, her own entitled dismissal of the privilege of quiet farm and forest. Ken had unwittingly turned Cassidy against Paloma, but Paloma had realized then that she had unintentionally turned her daughter against the simple beauty of their land and home.

As she left West Virginia, gliding past the "Pennsylvania Welcomes You" sign, Paloma resolved to atone for these mistakes. Cassidy was giving her another chance and she would take it. She would help her daughter to be less invested in the opinions of others, and she would keep her own tendency to appear judgmental in check. Paloma would show Cassidy how loved she was and what a wonderful home West Virginia could be.

CASSIDY

STEPPING OUT OF the airport into Pittsburgh's early June air, Cassidy noticed humidity for the first time in her life. Growing up in this climate, she'd been oblivious—this was just what "hot" felt like. But after her time in the dry desert heat of Southern California, it felt like swimming.

Paloma stood beside her car, smiling. It was a different drive from Pittsburgh to Buckhannon than the trip with Noeli, the sun illuminating not only the emerald green of the now lush hills, but the modern office buildings and new construction. Dilapidated shacks still appeared in the hollows occasionally, but they were the exception, not the rule.

As they slid down the High-Tech Corridor, Cassidy wondered if the state could progress without being overrun. Could it change without being destroyed? Her friendship with Noeli apparently couldn't.

Her thoughts were interrupted by the mention of Noeli's name. "Huh?"

"I was asking what happened with Noeli." Paloma raised her sunglasses—which had been perched at the tip of her nose over her dollar-store reading glasses—to her head so she could get a better look at her daughter. "If you want to talk about it. Now that I understand your sexuality, I thought—"

"You don't understand my sexuality." Cassidy looked out the window as they crossed a long bridge—a winding river flanked by a valley of trees so round and full, they could have been a pile of green sheep stretched below. Her chest felt tight.

"I understand that it's fluid, honey. We're all somewhere along a spectrum."

"It's not just that." Cassidy continued looking out the window.

Paloma put a hand on Cassidy's leg, which began to shake with adrenaline. Soon the whole story came rushing out. "I like women. The Simon thing was a mistake. I am definitely not into sex with men in person, but I haven't been driving Lyft for a long time. I do cam work—getting naked on camera for money, for men, and it's not just a money thing. I enjoy it."

Paloma took a deep breath and nodded. She patted Cassidy's leg. "It would take so much more than that to shock me, Cassidy. You're fine. Totally fine."

Cassidy exhaled and closed her eyes. She'd been holding this for such a long time that she hadn't realized it had manifested as tightness in her shoulders. The reaction she'd anticipated from Paloma, the secret judgment she'd known Noeli held, her own confusion about what it meant about her sexuality—she'd held it all in her body. Now, finally, she felt it begin to let go.

"We need to switch your cell phone service to something that works here, but first I want a coffee drink," Paloma said as they arrived in Buckhannon—her code for "expensive coffee." Cassidy suspected it was also code for, "Let's cheer you up."

Downtown seemed to shine. Art met Cassidy at every corner, gazed at her from shop windows, poked up from the flower beds, and beamed from brick walls. It was charming, and in that moment, Cassidy was truly, deeply happy to be there.

She ached, though, in equal measure. Every mural, every cute shop, every young person with blue hair or dreadlocks—Cassidy wanted Noeli to see it all. She wanted to tell her more about her town's transformation, to brag about how her generation had been the one to transform it. She wanted Noeli to be here so she could convince her to stay.

Cassidy imagined Noeli here with her again, as her girlfriend this time, holding her hand as they looked at hand-carved chairs, sitting across from her and trying a flight of local beers. Cassidy put a hand on her belly and imagined it was Noeli's hand. When the baby kicked in response, Cassidy wanted it to be Noeli who felt it. Paloma parked and together, she and Cassidy walked down the sparkling sidewalk to Stone Tower.

"I wanted you to leave, Cassidy," Paloma said after ordering her coffee. The other customers at the coffee shop buzzed around, discussing the Community Theater, Riverfest, the band playing in Traders Ally the next day. Behind the bar, plates clanked and the espresso machine hissed. It was as vibrant as any coffee shop in California, maybe more so, Cassidy thought, because people were talking to one another, and not to their phones. "But I always thought you might come back someday," Paloma went on. She had said something similar during Cassidy's last visit, but it hadn't stuck like this. Then, it had felt to Cassidy like an excuse—a justification for leaving her daughter with the emotional burden of the farm. Now it felt like a celebration, a homecoming. "I'm so happy you're here," Paloma said.

"How do you live with it?" Cassidy asked. "All of the history? Especially when you weren't happy with Daddy?"

Paloma thought for a long minute. "I made this place my home," she finally said, her lip trembling. "Seeing you at home here made it my home. There are so many ways to love. You know, I had potential buyers out to look at the farm. They stomped around like they owned the place and talked about putting a deer head over the mantel and I was so relieved when they decided not to buy. I'm even more relieved you'll be there after all. The farm is important to me." She put her hands on Cassidy's belly and tears appeared in the corners of her eyes. The baby moved, as if on command. The baby, in fact, had hardly stopped moving since they'd arrived in Buckhannon. It was like something inside her had woken up, like she knew this place, too.

"Paloma," the woman at the counter called. They went together to get their drinks.

"Toasted coconut steamed soy milk," the barista said as she tucked her purple hair behind her ear. Cassidy thanked her and took a sip. The sweet liquid warmed her throat and then her belly and the baby kicked again, leaving a foot pressing against her abdomen. Cassidy took Paloma's hand and held it to the spot where the tiny foot pushed.

"Ooh hoo hoo!" Paloma squealed, the exact sound she'd made watching Cassidy on rides at the Strawberry Festival each May, like she was amazed but also a little nauseous.

They sat with their drinks at a little table facing Main. Across the street, painted strawberries still adorned the windows of Thompson's Pharmacy from the festival the month before. Cassidy no longer cared what anyone in Buckhannon might think about her being back, about her being pregnant, about her being queer, because she had the approval of the person who mattered, the person who had always mattered. They finished their coffee and went back out to Main Street. A couple windows down was the nTelos store, and Cassidy followed Paloma in. Inside the small room, the walls lined with bright new screens, Paloma asked the teenager at the counter for the latest model smartphone and told him to add it to her family plan. The acne-scarred boy handed a chic white box to Cassidy and she took the device from its packaging.

"If you like this one, I'll go ahead and get it all set up for ya," he said. Cassidy stared at the phone's screen, shiny and unblemished, and saw her image reflected back to her, whole. She'd forgotten what it felt like to see herself unfragmented.

PALOMA

AT THE HOUSE, Paloma went upstairs to sift through more of Ken's things. They'd built their relationship on the fact that they wanted children.

It had felt solid, at first—an ancient mountain, a centuries-old bridge. The ordeal of conceiving and the triumph of success had buoyed Ken and Paloma for a long time.

Though the wonder at their progeny never faded, the marvel of their collaboration in her conception did, and with time, wind and rain battered their hillsides and eroded their parapets. The largest threat—the gargantuan bucket-wheel excavator that threatened to strip the crumbling mine of their relationship—was the house.

Jane had given them the farm when she moved into town to be closer to the hospital, where she still volunteered. Caring for the land as her own, rather than in exchange for lodging, renewed Paloma's sense of purpose. The farmhouse was less cramped with just the three of them, but still Paloma worried about the safety of the outdated electricity and spoke like a martyr about her days potty training Cassidy in an outhouse.

Ken drew plans with stubby architects' pencils, and his line sketches sat in piles on every surface. Paloma moved the thin papers from the bed to the floor before crawling in to sleep, pausing to imagine how these lines, arrows, and numbers could transform into a three-dimensional structure.

"How's it coming?" she asked one morning as he scratched his beard over breakfast and studied the plans.

"It's coming," Ken said.

The next day he went to Home Hardware and priced nails, lumber, and drywall—jotting the numbers in the flip pad he kept in his back pocket. A week later he drove to the library and brought home books on structures around the world, everything from Iroquois longhouses to the hanok-style houses of Korea.

"Hay clay!" he declared triumphantly at dinner.

"I'm sorry?" Paloma asked.

"Hay clay," he repeated. "Insulation. It's straw and clay. It lasts for seven hundred years."

"Sounds great." Paloma passed him the green beans. How long would she have to hear about hay clay before he moved on to his next idea?

"Hay clay! Hay clay!" Cassidy chanted, then caught Paloma's eye and stopped. Paloma had noticed a change in her daughter lately—she'd grown self-conscious around her, as if she'd become aware of Paloma's secret moments of resentment. Cassidy seemed to understand that she was not just the sun of her mother's world but that she had to be. Paloma felt she'd broken her daughter. She'd failed at unconditional love.

"Hay clay!" Paloma smiled and tried to revive the chant, but Cassidy remained quiet.

Months later Ken was still making daily trips to Home Hardware, returning only with notes. In Buckhannon, flags still flew from every corner, but they'd grown faded and forgotten, part of the background. The town felt frozen, stagnant.

"How much research are you going to do?" Paloma asked one evening as Cassidy dozed beside them. Ken looked up from his book on Russian izba and the plans spread before him on the threadbare lilac sheets.

"As much as I need to. I was thinking of an outdoor sauna."

Paloma sighed. They would be in the farmhouse forever. Beneath her, something scurried in the root cellar, small claws scrambling over the dirt floor.

She tried to adjust her mood—closed her eyes, leaned back, and let herself imagine it—a log cabin, hay-clay insulation, and a sauna outside.

The next day, when he returned from work slightly later than usual, Ken did not slump into a chair with a book and plans. Instead he stood in the doorway and called out, "Who wants to help me unload?"

"Me!" Cassidy jumped up. "Unload what?"

Paloma followed them out. There, in the rusty bed of the old Ford they'd purchased after the Bonneville finally gave up the ghost, were several dozen boxes of nails.

Paloma looked at Ken, who grinned. Somewhere close by, a whip-poor-will sang.

"We'll have to dig for the foundation first, have someone come out to do the concrete. But I wanted to get something to mark the occasion." Ken lifted Cassidy to the truck's bumper, and she reached into the bed. As she lifted a box of nails, its contents spilled out of the flimsy flip-top box to the muddy driveway. The cascade of metal sounded like rain and she shrieked. "Don't worry, sweet pea," Ken said. "We're going to be spilling lots of nails."

They cleaned up the mess, and all three carried the nails to the shed, Paloma holding her stack close to her body. Their weight against her cotton shirt held a palpable promise. Once the truck bed was empty, Ken took two rusty shovels from their place against the wall and handed the smaller one to Cassidy.

"Ready?" he asked, and she nodded eagerly.

Ceremonially, they carried their shovels to a spot slightly up the hill, and together, moved a few shovelfuls of earth as Paloma cheered. After, the three went back to the house and feasted, the air around them light and jolly. The next day, Ken began in earnest, clearing the land and digging. Two weeks later two men and a truck came out and laid the concrete foundation. A month after that, Ken hammered the last nail on the rough framing.

Paloma tried to help, doing her best to follow Ken's instructions, but it seemed she could do nothing right.

"God*damn it*, Paloma. I need you to *hold* it!" Ken shouted. Her arms burned. "No, *hold* it." Paloma let the piece of drywall fall to the floor with a heavy thud and a puff of white dust that reminded her of coal smoke.

"Mommy?" Cassidy asked from the doorway.

"What?" Paloma snapped, feeling instant regret.

"Nothing." Cassidy slunk back out.

"I'm done, Ken," Paloma said. "You can build the damn house yourself."

So he did. Paloma invested more time in the farm—turning the goats' milk into cheese, yogurt, and small soaps, expanding the garden until it covered a quarter acre and provided a good portion of their family's food. Cassidy sat at Ken's feet and practiced hammering nails into wood scraps, excited at the responsibility of holding a heavy tool.

The house took shape, Ken's blueprints came to life, and despite his minimal experience in construction, Paloma had to admit the home was gorgeous. Ken became totally consumed by work and building and, with Paloma removed from both of these worlds, even raising Cassidy began to feel like less of a shared project. She was growing more independent, and her time with each of them required less consultation between parents.

Paloma felt herself grow anxious as the house began to transform from a sketch into a solid structure. It was Ken's dream she'd needed—the possibility. As the house took shape, she felt herself retreat from the real, permanent life here that it signified. The walls of the house went up with ones in her heart to match.

They painted Cassidy's room in the bright shades of neon orange and green that she chose and their own in a light bluebell. Paloma, in turn, grew moody and bitter, Ken, callous and insensitive.

On the first night they slept in the new house, Paloma, Ken, and Cassidy sat together in the living room, which smelled of semigloss and sawdust, and watched *The Simpsons.* Cassidy fell asleep between them and Ken gently removed her head from his lap and walked up the stairs, past the octagonal window. Paloma followed him to their new master bedroom, which felt huge; there was space for a rug beside the queen-sized bed, and the floor-to-ceiling windows overlooked the vast dark stretches of trees beyond. This sense of openness felt to Paloma less like freedom than like loneliness.

Their lovemaking, too, was lonely. Neither looked at each other, but kept turning their heads to take in their new surroundings. They were like wild animals, though their wildness had nothing to do with passion. They were like small rodents caught out in the open, anticipating threats in every direction. Paloma reached for the charm around her neck—the one Ken had given her in Prague, and found only a chain. When had it fallen off? She gripped the sheets instead, clinging to the real, reassuring linen.

When Ken had finished, he'd rolled over and fallen asleep. Paloma had stood, gone to the window, and strained to look skyward. The roof's eaves jutted out, preventing her from seeing the stars.

Now, alone in the room they'd shared, Paloma went to the window again and looked out at the sunlight sparkling on the pond, transfixed for a moment by beauty and nostalgia. She would not be fooled, though, by tricks of light and her sentimental mind. She was ready to leave this house.

CASSIDY

"CASSIDY?" PALOMA CALLED from upstairs.

Cassidy looked up from her grandmother's sewing machine, which she'd set up on the kitchen table. A dozen or so YouTube videos had helped her figure out how to thread the thing and several more had guided her as she sewed a crib sheet. "Yeah?" she called back. Cassidy studied the slightly crooked hem. It wasn't perfect, but she'd done it.

"Can you come here?" Paloma's voice had been softer around the edges lately, even when she was shouting from another room.

"Sure. Let me put this away."

Paloma's scent hit Cassidy like a wave as she entered her mother's large walk-in closet. It was concentrated here, the air saturated with lavender. Being in the master bedroom was strange. It had always been a grown-up sanctuary with an invisible line drawn in the doorway that Cassidy had crossed only for a reason—to ask for a snack or to tell her parents she was going outside—and left right after. Even as a little kid, startled by a nightmare, she ran in and clawed her way up the double-stacked futon to nestle between her parents' warm sleeping bodies, but there was an unspoken understanding that she would return to her own room before the sun came up.

"There's something I want to give you." Paloma opened her top dresser drawer and rummaged for a moment, moving fuzzy wool socks and lace underwear aside while Cassidy waited, still a little dizzy from dashing up the stairs. Finally Paloma retrieved a folded piece of notebook paper and held it to her chest as she breathed deeply. She looked into Cassidy's eyes, her own damp with tears.

"I loved your father when he was looking at you," she said at last, still clutching the paper, not quite ready to release it. Whatever this paper was, whatever it contained, was the part of Cassidy's father that Paloma wanted to hold on to, the part of him that had brought her to West Virginia and kept her here long enough to get attached. It was the part of him that she was mourning. Paloma's lip quivered as she held the paper out for Cassidy like an offering, her palm up and her head slightly bowed. Cassidy took the paper and her own breathing slowed. She didn't want to open it yet. She wanted to savor the feeling of there being something unread.

Paloma watched Cassidy eagerly, and so Cassidy unfolded the paper, opened its creases one at a time like a philologist unearthing an ancient text.

In the center, in Ken's scrawling handwriting, still messy, but more intentional than the pieces Cassidy had found in his journal, were a few lines—a poem. The room narrowed as Cassidy squinted at them.

I have fallen in the flooding river
all the things crowding my life
the teacups and trousers
the hammers and books
the cooking pots and garden rakes

are scattered on the surface.
There is so much to do to make this life perfect.
I gather all I can in my arms
and go under
regain the surface and try again.
Full of anger the water spews from my mouth.
And suddenly I see the frightened face of my daughter.
Comforting her, she carries me
to the shore.

Cassidy read the words once, twice, a third time. She couldn't bear to look at Paloma, so she stared at the notebook paper, imagining her dad writing the words. Paloma watched for a few moments and then quietly retreated from the room, sniffling, leaving Cassidy standing alone . . . and with her father.

How could she hold this herself? How could she not share this with Noeli?

JANE

JANE STARED AT the mashed potatoes on her tray and thought of Spudnuts. It had been Ding who'd insisted on the Spudnuts, Ding who'd ended up saving her after all.

Ding and Cal had arrived on the farm within a week of little Harry's passing, Ding collapsing into Jane's arms the moment they saw each other. The embrace was familiar, though Jane could sense numerous subtle changes in her cousin since she had last seen her. There was a roundness to her cheeks and hips, and an impatient edge to her sad voice. Her scent had changed too, Jane noticed. What once had been light and flowery had gained a deep, musty note.

Cal ordered a prefabricated Lustron home and when it was assembled, Jane stood with Ding and Cal in front of the surf-blue, square-sided, space-age steel structure. Cal put an arm around Ding and kissed the top of her head. "A fresh start," he whispered. It was the first time Jane had heard him speak.

Cal got a job at Sago Mine, and Ding joined the obstetric ward at St. Joe's. She and Jane got lunch together most days at a new joint called Kollege Kitchen. They were old ladies there—most of the patrons were students—but the food was good, the music was better, and the service was unparalleled.

They could go on like this, Jane thought, forever, and they did, as another five years passed, spinning by as on a turntable. Then one day, over a decade after they'd boarded the *West Virginian* for Washington, Ding dropped the news.

Standing behind Jane as she finished her last bit of work before lunch, Ding put a hand on her shoulder. "Thank God Kollege Kitchen is serving those Spudnuts now. I've got a terrible craving for something sweet and fried. I have lots of cravings these days."

Jane let her magnifying glass rest on its chain against her chest and looked up from the patient file she'd been encoding. "You have, have you?" She raised an eyebrow.

"Oh, let's not beat around the bush. I'm pregnant!"

Jane's face flushed, and she hid it in Ding's ponytail as they hugged. So she would be alone after all, doomed to sad aunthood. Another pair of little feet for her to run after on the weekends wouldn't make a difference, she supposed, but losing Ding again would be her end. She thought of her eight nieces and nephews lined up from tallest to shortest. At least someone needed her.

"It makes me miss Harry even more." Ding began to cry. "I remember the excitement like this with him and I'm . . . I'm terrified."

"Oh, darling." Jane pulled away, holding Ding's shoulders. "Let's get you some Spudnuts." They walked out of the hospital with arms around each other's waists.

The bell tinkled as they entered Kollege Kitchen, and students swiveled on their stools, then turned back to the counter and continued eating their hot dogs. On the jukebox, Frank Weir proclaimed himself a happy wanderer.

Ma Curtis, at least, was pleased to see them. "Hello, girls!" she chimed. "Spudnuts are here! We've really got 'em!"

"That's what we came for!" Ding grinned. They sat at two stools facing the ice cream bar.

"What is a Spudnut, anyway?" Jane whispered to Ding.

"A doughnut. Made with spuds."

"Now, they're five cents apiece," Mrs. Curtis said. "Six cents for cream-filled, or a dozen for fifty-five cents, and believe me, you'll want a dozen to bring back once you taste them."

"Just one for now, please," Jane said, not overly tempted by the thought of cream-filled potatoes. "And a hot dog with special sauce and onions."

"I'll take a dozen," Ding said, never one to pass up a deal, and Ma turned to fix up their orders. The bell tinkled again, and Jane turned toward the door, along with the rest of the patrons. A man close to her own age entered and tipped his tan fedora to Mrs. Curtis.

"John!" Ma beamed.

"I came to try the famous Spudnuts." The man grinned back. "Had to see if the rumors were true."

Ding and Jane gaped at each other. It was John Hinkle, Ding's crush from Thompson's Pharmacy, all grown-up. Though his voice had deepened, gaining a sense of competence and sophistication, it was unmistakably his. He had grown six inches in height, and much more than that in muscle, and his baby face was covered with stubble.

"And what rumors were those?" Ma asked him.

"That they're the best, freshest treat in Upshur County," John said, removing his hat and hanging it up along with his long tan coat. He sat on the stool beside Jane without glancing at her.

Ding elbowed her in the ribs. Jane coughed. "John?" she asked. "John Hinkle?"

He tipped his head slightly, trying to place her, and Jane found it suddenly hard to breathe. How had the gangly teenager behind the drugstore counter turned into this magnificent man?

"Yes?" John looked from her to Ding, and a smile of recognition spread across his face. "Hey, you two used to come into the shop a lot!"

Ding smirked. "Yes. I'm sorry about that. Married now. No need to run." She held up her ring finger and John laughed.

"How have you been?" Jane asked.

"That's certainly a big question for a decade."

"How about the highlights?" Janes said as Ma Curtis returned with their Spudnuts and Frank Sinatra began "Young at Heart." "It looks just like a doughnut!" she cried.

"What did you expect?" Ding asked. "A potato rolled in powdered sugar?"

John took a bite of his, and Jane took a deep breath before following suit, Ding close behind.

"Mmm!" all three said at once.

"The highlights I can do," John said. He had a speck of cream on his chin and Jane was surprised to find herself reaching out to wipe it for him.

"Thank you, miss," he said, unembarrassed. "The highlights are—I graduated, finally, and escaped the birds of prey." He looked at Ding and the three laughed. "Air Cadets at Wesleyan, met a girl at a dance, married, went to war, came back, got divorced. Any questions?"

"So I suppose you're a pariah now?" Jane asked.

John tipped an imaginary hat.

"Jane's a pariah too. A widow," Ding said, sticking her head around Jane and inserting it between them.

"I'm very sorry to hear that," John said.

"Actually," Jane said, making sure Ma Curtis was nowhere nearby. It was the first time she had said the truth aloud. "We weren't married."

"Well, I'm sorry to hear that, too. Sadder for the poor fellow."

"He didn't die." Jane took a bite of her Spudnut so she didn't have to look at John.

"Even sadder," John said. "Now he has to live without you."

Jane smiled close-lipped, her mouth full of cream, and swallowed. Ding gawked.

"Since we're both unattached, would you like to get dinner with me sometime?" John asked.

Jane took another bite, chewed, and swallowed. "I'd like that very much."

"You don't want your taters?" The woman across the table poked the gravy-covered mound with her fork, returning Jane to the present.

"You can have them," Jane said. Oh, John. She tried to bring the feeling of him back to her body. John had been so good to her.

CASSIDY

MARGARET LIVED IN a large ranch-style out on Brushy Fork. Beyond the manicured grassy hill where it sat was the forest, with more hills and valleys covered in pines.

As Paloma, Jane, and Cassidy walked up the front steps, a round graying woman appeared in the doorway and grinned. "My new roommate," she bellowed, and moved out to the recently built porch, which still donned lumber stamps on its wooden planks. Paloma beamed.

"I brought my home inspectors," she said, motioning toward Cassidy and Jane. She balanced the glass hummingbird carefully in one hand, the creature's wings lifted as if it might take flight.

"Come on in, ladies," Margaret said.

This was Paloma's house now. Cassidy took in the Buddha statue resting in the window and smiled as she entered, noticing bookshelves lining several of the walls. On the coffee table sat a blue-green vase of bloodroot and buttercups. Cassidy peeked through the living room into the kitchen and saw cabinets topped with Mason jars, old vases, and Blenko pitchers. Her mom would be happy here. She'd feel like Cassidy had at Noeli's.

Jane settled into a lumpy armchair and Cassidy sat near her on the floor, leaned close to the flowers, inhaled their breezy scent, and promptly sneezed. A muscle by her hip tightened with a spasm, a joy of late pregnancy. Abuela would love these flowers, Cassidy thought, remembering her day in the Fontana garden. Noeli had been so happy they were bonding.

"You two relax," Margaret said. "I wanted to get your mom's opinion on furniture placement." Paloma followed her friend down a hallway and out of sight.

Grandma Jane reached out and squeezed Cassidy's hand, her cool skin reassuring. "Your dad is here," Grandma Jane whispered suddenly, and panic tightened Cassidy's shoulders. Was she confused? "I can feel him. He's here with us." Cassidy sighed with relief and understanding.

Grandma Jane leaned toward Cassidy's ear conspiratorially. "I never met the love of my life. The romantic kind, I mean. Your grandpa, Grandpa John, he was wonderful, but he was never my soul mate."

Cassidy considered Jane's earnest face, her eyes crinkling at the sides as she smiled. Grandma Jane wasn't sad, just reminiscing.

"He was meant to be the father of my child, and I loved him, I did, but my family is the love of my life."

"You're the love of my life too," Cassidy said, running her fingers along the edge of the coffee table.

"Cassidy Christine," Jane chided, then chuckled as her eyes got a far-off look. "Ding hated her name. My daddy was the only one she let call her by it. Why your father insisted on giving you . . ." She paused, reeling herself back in, and looked at Cassidy. "You don't owe me a thing, darling, except your fearless, unapologetic happiness."

Cassidy swallowed the lump in her throat and nodded. From down the hall, music began to play, and Cassidy recognized it as Plastic People of the Universe, the Czech band.

"I'm glad your mother found happiness," Jane went on. "I want you to find that too, wherever you are. Here or California. It doesn't matter."

"Grandma Jane, I . . ." Cassidy swallowed. "I already found the love of my life, I think. Noeli?"

"Good," Grandma Jane said. "Don't you dare let fear or shame get in the way. You go after that love, darling."

Cassidy nodded, unable to speak.

"I told you your dad was here." Jane pointed to the middle of her coral sweatshirt. "Twice before he was *here*." She threw her hands in the air to indicate the world around them. "He waited for the right time, like you did. You had your own timeline for meeting us too. You were finicky—there were a few false starts. You've always had some trouble with decisiveness, haven't you?" Jane laughed and rubbed Cassidy's belly. "Your dad will be back again," she said knowingly.

Before Cassidy could respond, Paloma shimmied down the hallway to join them. Cassidy couldn't remember the last time she'd seen her mother's smile look so carefree. Her weight was on her toes and her arms floated as if in water. "Want to dance?" Paloma asked.

"Sure." Cassidy stood and went to Paloma. Paloma wrapped her arms around Cassidy's waist and their bellies touched, making them both laugh. For a moment Cassidy remembered being little, remembered laughing from pure joy, remembered feeling like her joy was entwined with her mother's, like they were one entity.

Paloma moved her hands to Cassidy's shoulders. "You look beautiful, Mom," Cassidy said. "And happy."

Paloma hugged her. "Margaret asked us to stay for dinner," she said as the song ended.

"I've got some serious Braxton Hicks going on. You stay though. I can get you when you're ready."

"Thank you, Cassidy. I'm sure Margaret can give me a ride." Paloma hugged her again and went back down the hallway to join her friend.

"I'm tired, Grandma Jane. I'm going to head out. Are you ready?"

"Of course, darling." Cassidy helped her up from the chair and Jane held on to Cassidy's elbow as they left the house and descended the steps. The moon was beginning to appear above the pines and the green all around them took on an unnaturally vivid hue in the twilight. Cassidy helped Grandma Jane into her seat and then buckled her own seat belt under her bump.

As they drove in silence, Cassidy thought about her grandma's words. Could she give Grandma Jane her happiness? Cows stood sleeping on the hills, their heads down.

After dropping Jane at the care home, Cassidy returned to the farm, where the absence of her parents' voices rang in her ears. She stood in front of the half-empty bookshelf where her father's books remained. Paloma had moved them from the coffee table back onto the shelves, but the side where Paloma's books had been—macrobiotic guides, Tom Robbins novels, biographies of John Lennon—was as empty as an abandoned shopping complex. It felt like Cassidy's mind. She was dizzy from the wobble between fullness and emptiness, contentment and searching.

Cassidy was tired, exhausted, really, her feet so swollen that when she flopped herself down on the couch, kicked off her shoes, and heaved them onto the coffee table, her toes stuck out like plump cocktail sausages. But there was no way she could sleep. Every noise, every animal's scrambling claws, every branch blown by the wind, made her jump, her head jerking toward the sound.

It had been the same, these noises, since she was small. As a girl, when Cassidy heard the tapping of leaves on her window, the knowledge that her parents were there protecting her had been all the assurance she'd needed to sleep soundly. Now she would be the parent, she realized. She would have to be the brave one.

She pictured herself with Noeli, holding hands and giggling as they tiptoed toward the window to look out together. How had she fucked this up?

A text lit up her phone screen and she scrambled to read it, visions of apologies spurring her on. It was Simon, though, asking if she wanted to get lunch tomorrow. She was the one who would need to do the apologizing.

I'm kind of broke right now, she responded. *How did you know I was here?*

Small town lol. And no problem. It's on me. C.J.'s? Noon?

No way. I'll make it work. Sounds good.

This was how she'd begin to smooth things over with Simon. She'd be totally forthright. As she thought about the promise of company and the hope of fixing their friendship, Cassidy's eyes closed and she began to drift, but when her phone buzzed a minute later, she nearly leapt from the couch, causing another bout of round ligament pain, the sharp pull on her side. When she recovered and looked at the screen, she saw she'd missed a call from a restricted number, almost certainly spam. But when the phone buzzed again, she felt nervous. Could it be the nursing home? Was Simon's number not registering for some reason? He'd probably changed his mind about seeing her. She would understand if he had. Her plump feet felt every fiber of the braided rug below them. She would wait and talk to him in the morning, she decided, letting her eyes close again.

When the caller called a third time, Cassidy answered. "Hello?"

JANE

IT WAS TRUE, John hadn't been the love of her life. John had been solid and sweet, and he'd made Jane laugh. She'd told him the truth—all of it, and he'd listened as if she were telling him she had returned a hat she'd found unflattering. Jane thought back to his proposal at the river.

"Red is your color, darling. There's no doubt about it." John stood back and admired Jane standing amid the trees in her baby-doll swimsuit.

"And black suits you perfectly," Jane said. John raised an arm behind his head, striking a pose in his trunks, and she could not help but notice the delectable lines of his abdominal muscles, the impressive breadth of his chest.

John took Jane's hand and helped her up to a rock in the middle of the water. There they lay side by side, soaking the delicious sun into their skin. Jane remembered rows of Government Girls tanning on sidewalks. A lifetime ago, it seemed.

Finally John propped his head on his elbow and looked at Jane. "Do you love me?" he asked.

"Of course, darling." It was true. She loved John the way one loves any pleasant thing in one's life—a kitten, a good book, chicken à la king. He was kind to her and her parents, he got on well with her brothers, and he always smelled pleasant.

"Do you think you would marry me?" John asked.

"I'm sure I would." Jane turned lazily to her back to sun her belly.

"Will you?"

Jane opened her eyes and saw that John had produced—from where, she did not know—a box containing a diamond ring, a baguette-cut accent stone at each shoulder of the center gem. He looked quite nervous.

"Oh, John," Jane said. "It's beautiful."

"I love you, Jane. I'll be a good husband. I promise you."

She could not quite believe that someone loved her—that someone wanted to marry her, knowing the truth of all she had done. She felt very, very grateful.

She looked at John's dark hair, his classically handsome face. John's face was the comfort of home. It was leaving and returning. It was the unconditional love of her parents, the promise of family. It was shared history, generations of solid hard work. It was West Virginia—dependable and reassuring.

A month later, family and friends arrived at the farm after church, and Jane and John said "I do" under a canopy of maples. Everything was sunny and bright.

The guests ate and drank and danced and laughed, and then went home, leaving Jane's cheeks thoroughly kissed, until only close family remained. Finally, when the summer sun lowered and little Henry started fussing, Ding added her lips to the pile, and whispered in Jane's ear. "You deserve all of this," she said, before she and Cal and the baby took off over the hill.

"I love you, Jane," Arzella said, holding her close and then kissing her forehead. Philip and her brothers each took a turn too. "You lovebirds get on now," Frank said, patting her on the shoulder with his remaining arm, then winking at John.

Jane's groom said his own goodbyes and opened her car door. Together, they rolled down the winding driveway, through the dense trees, holding hands.

"Stop," Jane said as they reached the gate, which opened onto Shumaker Road.

"What is it, my bride?" John asked, hitting the brakes and grinning at her.

"I forgot something."

"I'll turn around."

"No, no," Jane said. "I'll run and get it."

She had forgotten something, she knew it. She had the strongest sense that she was leaving something behind, though for the life of her, she didn't know what.

Shoes in hand, Jane stepped out and darted back down the driveway. The trees of her childhood enveloping her, she did not feel afraid or even alone in the dark. As she rounded the first turn, the dirt hard under her feet, she was met suddenly by a doe, no more than a yard away. Neither moved. The deer's tail stood straight up in attention, her sinewy body strong and confident.

Jane's blue eyes met the dark globes of the doe's, and Jane saw in that moment that they understood each other. She was a mother, this deer—Jane knew it. The doe inched closer and nudged Jane's midriff with her snout. Jane drew in a sharp breath of the fresh summer air, and her nostrils filled with the scent of crushed sassafras. She saw in a flash an image of her own stomach growing and growing, until a baby boy appeared, a thick blond curl smack-dab in the middle of his forehead. She was a mother too, or would be soon.

"Thank you," Jane said, and the deer lifted her head, then turned and walked into the woods to her waiting fawns. Jane took in another deep breath and surveyed the farm—the trees, the creek, the mountain, the ground, at once changing and eternal. "Thank you," she whispered again.

No, John had not been the love of Jane's life, but he'd brought her to Ken and to Cassidy, to the new baby she would meet any day, and he'd done it without judgment. For that, Jane had loved him. In the dark of the nursing home, she settled under the ugly blanket. "Thank you," she said, and closed her eyes.

CASSIDY

THE CALL WAS fuzzy, and Noeli's voice dropped in and out.

"Gas station . . . payphones still exist?"

"I can't . . ." Cassidy started but Noeli didn't seem to be able to hear her either. "Are you okay?" she tried.

"Fucking . . . service . . . fuck. Fine—" The call ended.

Cassidy sat back, both jarred from the mysterious phone call and relieved to be distracted from her own thoughts. She wouldn't let herself add hope to the mix.

Ten minutes later, when the familiar crunch of gravel made its way to her ears, and she peeked out between the dusty horizontal blinds to see the shadowy outline of an unfamiliar sports car making its way up the driveway, she scolded herself for the excitement that leapt to her chest. When the car drew closer and in the driver's seat appeared the silhouette of short, bobbing ringlets, still Cassidy refused to consider it. It was not until the head full of curls emerged atop a petite figure and walked toward the house that Cassidy allowed herself to try to reconcile the cognitive dissonance that arose when she tried to understand how *Noeli* could be *here.* She'd been too wrapped up in grief the last time to truly notice how out of place Noeli seemed.

It was as strange as if a palm tree had popped up among the maples, and yet here she was. Cassidy watched her swat at a mosquito and heard her cursing to herself, and she had to restrain her laughter. It came out instead as a hiccuppy sob, which transformed into heavy cries of surprise, joy, and relief. Noeli was so tough, so gritty in her own element, but here she looked so vulnerable. It made Cassidy love her even more, she thought as she ran to the door. "What are you doing here?" she exclaimed, throwing it open.

"Oh, am I the first brown person you've seen since you got back?" They laughed and hugged, tears still streaming down Cassidy's face.

"Come in!" Cassidy said, wiping her cheeks. She felt protective now, like Noeli might be swallowed by the woods or eaten alive by mosquitoes.

Inside, Noeli collapsed in a heap, propped her worn-out Chucks on the coffee table, and sighed. Cassidy watched in awe, still trying to process the reality of her visit and wondering what it meant.

"What a fucking pain," Noeli began, and Cassidy nodded sympathetically. "I went through my own hero's journey to get here." Outside, an owl hooted and something scampered under the window. Cassidy didn't even flinch. The interior of the house, which had felt so oppressively quiet an hour ago, now felt alive with Noeli's dancing voice.

"And then I got stuck in a ditch," Noeli said flatly.

"What!" Cassidy exclaimed. "How?"

"I don't even know, but I had zero cell phone service. Literally zero. So I stood on a hill and waited for someone to come help me."

"Oh my God."

"Yeah. Some old guy and his son got under the car with chains and pulled it out. It. Was. Terrifying," she deadpanned.

"But also kind of awesome? Can you imagine that happening in California?"

"No."

"Well, now I'm here and I'm pretty sure the bugs are trying to destroy me," Noeli finished.

"Wow. So now you're here."

"So now I'm here," Noeli repeated. "And Jesus, why am I so sweaty?" She paused. "It's pretty, though. I mean, from what I can tell. The drive was prettier with the leaves back." They both laughed again.

"It is," Cassidy agreed.

"Really, it's beautiful," Noeli said, serious now.

"You are," Cassidy said. "You look beautiful."

"Seriously? Because I feel like I'm swimming in my own body odor."

Cassidy kissed her. "Okay, you definitely do smell." She pulled away and they both laughed. "Do you want to shower?"

"Please." Noeli leaned in this time and they kissed again. "I'm sorry, Cass. For everything."

"Me too." She took Noeli by the hand and led her to the bathroom, then kissed her again before stepping in behind her. She watched Noeli, asking silently if this was okay. Noeli slipped off her jeans. Cassidy took off her own pants, leaving them in a pool at her feet. Noeli reached over and lifted Cassidy's shirt over her head, stopping when she was done to put her hands on Cassidy's belly. "It's gotten bigger," she said. Cassidy nodded and helped Noeli out of her hoodie and shirt. She'd worn the Selena tee. When they were undressed, Cassidy turned on the hot water.

How long was Noeli going to stay? Were they okay now? Cassidy's thoughts cascaded one on top of another as they stepped one at a time into the shower's stream. Her thoughts were eclipsed by the reality before her, every curl, every angle of

Noeli's body—her nose, her wrist—so familiar, so totally Noeli, and yet so new, like Cassidy was noticing them for the first time. They were here, their stomachs pressed together, without even clothing between them. Their barriers, their defenses, all had been stripped away, and they were here, in the bodies they lived in, naked and vulnerable and alive.

They helped each other wash, rubbing soap slowly over each of their curves and angles, until their skin was clean and soft between them. When they'd finished, they stood wordlessly under the water, holding each other, until Noeli began to shiver. Cassidy shut off the water with a clunk.

Steam rolled out behind them as they opened the door, wrapped in two of Paloma's light purple towels. Noeli's ringlets were damp now, longer and thinner, flattened down her back, and Cassidy marveled at the clean freshness of her freckles.

"This is what I need to wear in this weather," Noeli said, and they walked together back to the couch to sit, Cassidy draping her bare legs over Noeli's.

"I hated the way we left things," Cassidy said after a moment.

"I'm sorry," Noeli said again.

"I'm sorry too. I'm so sorry."

"I'm also fucking exhausted." Noeli let her body fall across Cassidy's lap and Cassidy stroked her damp hair.

"Let's go upstairs." Cassidy would have to wait to ask questions, to figure out where they stood. It was better, maybe. Not knowing might be better for tonight.

Still wrapped in their towels, they curled beside each other and slept, Cassidy pressed in close behind Noeli, her nose in Noeli's curls.

PALOMA

IN THE DARKNESS, Paloma looked around her new room, still decorated for a sixteen-year-old boy, a Bob Marley poster over the bed, a navy-blue beanbag chair in the corner. It felt unbelievable that Hank could be headed off to college when Paloma could still remember her friends announcing their pregnancies.

"There's something in the water," Jean had said, laughing.

"Our cycles are synced," May had said.

Margaret had raised a finger in the air. "It's the chasteberry supplements."

All three were pregnant, and all three had arrived at their monthly tea date in the back room of Margaret's store, ready to announce the good news.

Three sets of eyes turned cautiously toward Paloma, all aware of her struggles with fertility.

"You'll have to bring the babies over," Paloma gushed. "Finally! We'll all be mothers." The women exhaled with relief and talk turned to pregnancy-safe supplements and the best vegetarian sources of various nutrients.

As Paloma looked at each of the women's faces, she tried to picture the process happening within them—cells dividing, life building itself one day at a time. She was both jealous and overjoyed for her friends.

These were the people of her life. Until now, she'd thought of the people around her as ephemeral—minor. She'd always had the sense that she would do so much, meet so many people, that whomever she was with now would become insignificant. Penny Moscowitz had been her best childhood friend by circumstance. Growing up, she'd imagined that when she left Long Island, the girl would fade into obscurity, her stringy brown braids disappearing into the void, but in the story of Paloma's life, Penny was forever her first friend. Lovers, too, had felt trivial, expendable, interchangeable, but in the story of her one life, those were Paloma's lovers. And these were her true friends. These people right here. Gratitude and awe at their presence bloomed within her.

The months flew by and soon, while Cassidy grew ever more sullen and reserved, four babies crawled around on Paloma's wooden floors. Paloma fielded questions about breastfeeding, and her friends commiserated about teething and sleepless nights.

"He doesn't understand how exhausted I am," May said. "I haven't slept more than two hours straight in months."

"David has changed exactly one diaper," Jean said.

"Ken didn't change diapers either," Paloma said. "He's always been great with Cassidy, but he assumed that was my job. No discussion or anything." The other women nodded knowingly.

"We'll have a stronger bond with our babies, though," Margaret said. "They can sense all the time we put in. It's worth it."

Paloma kept her mouth shut.

Jean's fuzzy-headed daughter looked up at the four of them with her huge brown eyes, mirror images of her mother's. Jean lifted the girl to her breast, and she suckled as the women continued talking. May's twins, named after philosophers, scooted after Cassidy, who cooed back at them. Paloma bent and scooped Margaret's son into her lap.

"These thighs!" she exclaimed, squishing his baby rolls. "They're irresistible." She buried her nose in his soft blond hair. She'd thought people were making up the baby smell thing when Cassidy was born. She hadn't noticed it until it was gone.

Ken swung open the door, smiled at the women, set down his briefcase, and got down on all fours to grin at the babies. A familiar pang of guilt ran through Paloma as she wondered for the thousandth time what their life would have been like with more children.

The women said hello to Ken and goodbye to Paloma, explaining that they needed to get home to their own husbands. They scooped their pudgy offspring from the floor and left, a haze of exhaustion and joy trailing behind them.

Paloma stood and moved past Ken. "I need some things from the garden for dinner."

Outside, May struggled to get the twins settled into the car.

"Let me help you," Paloma said.

"Thank you!" May handed her one of the squirming boys, who relaxed into her arms. "I forgot to ask if you wanted to do a vegetarian Passover. I'll call Jean and Margaret."

"I'd love that." The baby gave Paloma a gummy smile as she lowered him into his seat.

May drove down the gravel path, and Paloma trudged over the damp ground to the garden, reached up to open the latch on the deer fence, and let herself in. The house door slammed and Cassidy came running out.

"Can I help?"

"Of course." Paloma tried to hide her surprise at seeing her daughter here voluntarily for the first time in months.

Together, they clipped spinach leaves and popped sugar snap peas from the vine. Cassidy didn't seem to notice the light dimming around them. The first sprinkles of rain pricked Paloma's skin, as small as the heads of pins.

"Go on back to the house," she said. "I'll be in in a minute."

Paloma watched as her daughter ran through the tall grass, up the wooden steps, and into the house that her husband had built. The sky was darker now, and she shivered in the chilly evening. A doe stood in the darkness beyond, watching, and Paloma watched back, filled with a calm contentment. The doe looked skyward and Paloma followed suit, the light rain moistening her cheeks. She watched as the sky filled with its million stars, points as small as the raindrops. The sky was black now, each star a perfect silver circle, and looking at them, Paloma felt her consciousness transported to another time, another body. It was the body she called hers before carrying and losing pregnancies, before birthing a baby, before nursing a child at her breast. Her mind, too, returned to one from long ago. For a moment she was Paloma, but not Paloma. She was young Paloma, looking out over the Vltava, the stars, transformed too—the twinkling lights of Prague.

Paloma closed her eyes and breathed in, arriving. It was not a singular occurrence in her life. She had arrived and arrived and arrived.

CASSIDY

"THIS IS *THE* Simon? Father of your baby, Simon?"

Cassidy confirmed and Noeli smirked.

"And we're having lunch with him." They'd risen in the morning and gotten dressed for their day, just as they'd done for months in Fontana.

"I have to make it better."

"So . . ." Noeli started. "Are we? Better?"

This was the closest they'd come to really discussing things and Cassidy wanted to keep the tone light, worried that if they talked seriously, the dreamlike quality of their reunion would be ruined.

"On my end, we're better. You battled mosquitoes and humidity for me."

"And a ditch!" Noeli added.

"And a ditch!" Cassidy glanced at the car's clock. "We're a little early. Can we stop and see Grandma Jane?"

"Of course."

She passed through downtown Buckhannon, drove over the bridge and around the corkscrew curve, then turned into the Serenity parking lot. Noeli followed her through the entrance and down the hall.

"Come in," Jane called when Cassidy knocked. They padded quietly into the room, Noeli a step behind.

"Oh hello, darling." Jane set her crossword on the tray of the walker beside her chair. In the window, the plastic solar-powered hula girl shook her hips.

"Grandma Jane, you remember Noeli? She came and surprised me." Noeli stepped forward. "Noeli, you remember your West Virginia abuela."

Noeli knelt before Jane and took her hands. "Hi, Jane," she said. "It's nice to see you again."

They looked into each other's eyes and Jane clasped Noeli's hands in return, shaking them as she spoke. "Grandma Jane. You call me Grandma Jane, darling." Her eyes glistened and her lips quivered. "Thank you, thank you, thank you." Noeli nodded, understanding.

"We're meeting Simon for lunch," Cassidy said hesitantly, not wanting to interrupt the moment. "So this is a quick visit, but I'll be back to see you soon."

"Of course," Grandma Jane said, and Cassidy and Noeli hugged her before turning to go. "Cassidy," Jane called before they could reach the door.

She turned around. Jane motioned for her to come closer, so the young women walked back toward the lift chair.

Fumbling in the pocket on the side of the chair, Jane pulled out something on a long chain. "I've been meaning to give this to you." She placed the small object in Cassidy's palm.

"Your crossword glass," Cassidy said.

"My fingerprint glass."

Cassidy examined the gold magnifying glass, rubbing the burnished metal with her fingertips. "Thank you," she said. Jane closed her eyes and smiled.

Cassidy turned to Noeli now and held the chain between her fingers, letting the magnifying glass hang. She took a step closer and lifted her hands. Noeli bowed her head and let Cassidy lower the chain over her hair as Jane watched with hands pressed together, fingertips at her lips, nodding.

Even with the detour, Cassidy and Noeli arrived at C.J. Maggie's before Simon, so they waited outside on an iron bench that sat beside a life-sized cardboard cutout of Lurch from *The Addams Family*.

"Uh?" Noeli asked.

Cassidy shrugged.

When Simon parked a few minutes later and climbed down from the Porsche, he glanced at Noeli and gave Cassidy a quizzical look.

"You remember Noeli from the memorial?" Cassidy said.

"Oh yeah, of course. Hey, Noeli."

"Hey." Noeli gave a small nod.

The exchange was charged, the words running between their mouths like electricity on exposed wire, crackling, intimidating. Rather than hug or shake hands, they both stared at a Little Free Library next door, the first Cassidy had seen in Buckhannon. A raised pickup truck roared by, deafening them. After a moment without eye contact, Cassidy and Noeli walked into the restaurant first, holding hands, and Simon followed awkwardly behind.

The tension began to ease as the hostess seated the trio in a booth and brought out giant cups of lemonade and sweet tea.

"Here's your diabetes, folks," Noeli said after she left. Simon smirked and Noeli looked pleased.

"I know I should be doing this privately," Cassidy said. "But I need to apologize. Simon, I'm so sorry I led you on and I'm so sorry I took off without telling—"

"It wasn't fair of me to expect you to be someone you weren't."

"It wasn't fair of me to disappear."

Simon smiled and looked down at the table.

By the time the fried zucchini arrived, Noeli and Simon loved each other, their rapport so natural that Cassidy almost felt like the third wheel. Their senses of humor played perfectly off each other, Simon deadpanning ridiculous comments, and Noeli almost spitting out her drink, slapping him on the back playfully.

After the waitress deposited silverware and returned to the kitchen, Simon produced a Sharpie from his pocket and added to the inside of the metal pail lamp above the table: *Simon and two lesbians.*

It was Cassidy's turn to almost spit out her drink.

"I never wanted to push you to be anything but yourself," Simon said. Noeli grinned and reached under the table to find Cassidy's hand.

With bellies full and hearts at ease, Cassidy, Noeli, and Simon leaned back and stared at one another until, eventually, Simon took a breath. "So, I'm leaving," he said, tapping his fingers on his cup and looking down at the table.

"Leaving? Buckhannon?" Cassidy stared.

"Yeah. I got an AmeriCorps position in upstate New York to build a community farm that starts right when my grant is up. I was going to turn it down to help you and the baby, but . . ." He looked at Noeli, who bit her lip.

"Simon, that's awesome!" Cassidy had recovered from her shock, but was now glancing nervously at Noeli while attempting to keep her smile plastered to her face.

"Thanks, dude. Yeah, so I've got to get busy now making everything here sustainable. Capacity building and all that. I don't want it to fall apart when I go. But yeah. This is great. You'll have your space from me and I'll have my space from my mom and Robbie. I'm excited." He blushed with pride.

"What are they going to do? Your mom and Robbie."

Simon shrugged. "Guess they'll figure it out."

Cassidy nodded. "I'm so happy for you. And proud."

"Thanks, Cass. And I was wondering . . ." He paused again to look back and forth between Cassidy and Noeli. "If you two would take over the CSA when I go."

"Totally," Noeli said, before Cassidy could answer. "I was wondering what I'd do for money here, and that is about the raddest job I can think of."

"Oh man, that's such a relief. I didn't want to put too much pressure on you with the baby, Cass, and if it's both of you, you'll still have time for camming."

"Yeah . . . totally." Did this mean Noeli was really staying? And Simon was really leaving? Cassidy tried to process the enormity of everything that was happening. "You'll be a part of this baby's life, Simon. I want you to know that." Simon's eyes grew teary and he nodded.

The waitress came back with the bill, and Simon produced his credit card, insisting everyone's meals were on him. Once he'd signed the receipt and they'd followed the waxed wooden floors out to the sweaty street, he ran back in to use the restroom and Noeli and Cassidy sat down on the iron bench again. Cassidy's thighs stuck to the seat, and she knew there would be a red imprint of the metal slats on her legs when they stood. They held hands.

"You really want to stay? You don't have to commit to anything. I don't want you to—"

"Your piece-of-shit car and the Accord combined only got me enough for a one-way ticket." Noeli laughed.

"Oh my God, you really sold the Accord?" Cassidy mimed a sad face.

"It was time. And besides, Abuela told me to." Noeli bit her bottom lip.

"She told you to sell it?"

"She told me to come." Noeli smiled. "She told me I was an idiot if I let you get away. I told her you moved back home and she told me to go, not to waste my life with my old grandma. She moved to the US for my grandpa and she said it was worth every bit of struggle."

"Grandma Jane basically told me the same thing." Cassidy laughed. "You don't have to do the CSA. I can take it on and you can find whatever you really want to do."

"Cass, the CSA is an amazing opportunity. You think I want to find another secretary job to work for the next decade? Besides, if I'm on board too, you can focus on your cam work."

"I don't know if I'm going to keep camming," Cassidy said.

"Well, you don't have to. But you can."

"I'm sorry I was such a privileged jerk about camming."

"I'm sorry I was a dick about it, too," Noeli said. "You are a sex worker, even if you're white. You're allowed to be empowered by it and acknowledge it's different for other people at the same time."

"Thank you." Cassidy squeezed her hand. "And I'm sorry again. I'm sorry I didn't think about why Redlands wasn't appealing to you."

"I'm sorry, too," Noeli said. "I'm sorry I didn't understand why this place meant so much."

"Can we stop apologizing now?" Cassidy asked.

"Yes, let's." Noeli leaned in for a quick peck on the lips. Her sun-kissed shoulders looked so soft that Cassidy had to reach out to feel them. How had she gotten so lucky?

"Sorry, didn't mean to interrupt you lovers." Simon had appeared in the doorway and the women scooted, Cassidy's thighs peeling up painfully. Simon sat.

"What's going on over there?" Noeli looked down Main Street toward the courthouse, where a small crowd was gathering.

"Hm," Cassidy said.

"Want to go check it out?" Simon asked.

"Sure." Cassidy stood before her legs could re-adhere. They walked past the pharmacies, where an antique armoire and found metal art decorated the windows; a new upscale eatery; and the Upshur County Historical Society, where several people sat poring over old photos and newspapers.

As they approached the crowd of twenty or so spilling out from between the white columns that flanked the courthouse's stone steps, it became apparent that the group was chanting. A few were holding signs. As they got closer still, Cassidy started to make out their words: "We love immigrants! You are welcome here! We love immigrants! You are welcome here!" Their signs read "Hate has no home here."

"Right on!" Simon declared, and high-fived a couple people. "I didn't know this was happening."

"You've got to check your email, kid!" a woman about their age with red hair and a septum ring teased. Cassidy recognized her from the trans rights rally.

"Simon!" A couple other people greeted him with hugs and high fives. He introduced them to Noeli and Cassidy. "I know these folks from the farming co-op." They wore band T-shirts and cutoff shorts that showed off their thigh tattoos. "Cassidy and Noeli are taking over the CSA when I go." Cassidy felt like the weird pregnant lady as she braced her lower back with her hands and smiled politely, telling people it was nice to meet them. Cassidy looked at Noeli, who looked impressed, smiling cautiously and chatting. Cassidy turned back to the red-haired woman and smiled, then waited with Noeli at the edge of the group while Simon made his rounds. Cassidy would be the new kid, even though she'd grown up here, but she'd be the new kid in a group of people who seemed like decent humans, and Noeli would be here, too. They would have friends.

"So how should we celebrate Noeli's arrival?" Simon asked after he'd said his goodbyes. "And my departure."

"Klounge?" Cassidy asked, laughing at the thought of her heavily pregnant self at the bar.

"Nah," Simon said. "Something low-key, I think." He patted Cassidy on the shoulder.

"Ice cream party?" Cassidy asked, feeling nostalgic.

"I don't want to deal with my mom or Robbie."

"We could do it at my house . . . our house." She smiled at Noeli. "New traditions."

Simon agreed. "I'll stop for the goods."

Cassidy took Noeli the long way back and decided on a whim to stop at Pringle Tree. "I want to show you something," she said.

She held her belly as she waddled from the car to the tree, feeling huge and trying not to imagine the animals that might be out there with them—mountain lions, coyotes, bears. Cassidy had never been afraid of wilderness as a child, even when she was alone in it. She would have to recultivate that comfort and teach it to her baby.

"This is Pringle Tree," she said. "Or the great-great-grandtree or something of the Pringle Tree." They walked through a never-ending swarm of various kinds of bugs.

"What's Pringle Tree?" Noeli asked.

Cassidy puffed; it was her turn to teach some local history, to defend her home as a Real Place. "These brothers, the Pringle Brothers, were deserters in the French and Indian War and hid in a hollow tree here for years."

"Years?" Noeli raised her eyebrows.

"Yeah, I'm pretty sure it really was years. We took a field trip here in fourth grade and learned about it, but I don't remember all the details. It was something pretty insane. I mean, they were probably assholes who were fighting the Native Americans, but at least they deserted, I guess."

"Damn," Noeli said.

They sat with their backs against the tree and Cassidy rested her head on Noeli's shoulder. Leaning closer, she could smell the sweat from the nape of her neck. "Abuela will be in this baby, too," she said. "And you. Everyone and everything. I want you to know you're a part of it."

Noeli's curls tickled Cassidy's forehead, and they sat up and looked at each other. Noeli's face held something like admiration, her brown eyes crinkling at the sides. Taking Noeli's cheeks in her hands, Cassidy kissed her, hard. The tree was rough against her back, the wet grass was starting to soak through her shorts, and the baby was dancing.

"We should go so Simon isn't waiting too long," Cassidy said, pulling away.

Noeli groaned, then stood and hoisted Cassidy to her feet. The soft grass and earth padded their steps to the car, and Cassidy thought of poison ivy, hoping they hadn't been sitting in a patch of it. She decided against saying anything to Noeli.

Simon arrived at the farm just as they did, and together, the trio ascended the wooden steps to Cassidy's home, which was both old and new, both unchanged and irrevocably different.

Simon swung the giant tub of Neapolitan ice cream for what was quite possibly their last ice cream party. Ken was gone, and Noeli was here. Inside of Cassidy, a child grew. This was life, she thought, in awe at the grace with which her companions accepted the facts of it. People got older. They became adults and things changed. They did their best to be here, with each other. For each other.

CASSIDY

"REALLY, IT'S AN estimate. Only five percent of babies show up on their due dates," Dr. Bassiouni said. She looked at her chart and then patted Cassidy on the shoulder.

"So, we just wait until the baby comes?" Noeli asked.

"Basically, yes. As long as things are looking good, and they are, there's no reason to induce."

"Induce?" Noeli crossed her arms.

"There are things we can do to encourage labor to start, but they won't do much unless the baby's ready. If we get to forty-two weeks and there's still no sign, then we can talk induction."

"Okay." Cassidy sighed. Dr. Bassiouni's frizzy black hair and oversized glasses were a reassuring presence. "I don't want to induce either."

At forty weeks and two days pregnant, though, Cassidy was ready to do something. "So how do you know if the baby's ready?" She jumped as the baby kicked her in the cervix, and she experienced what she'd recently learned was called "lightning crotch."

"Labor will start." Dr. Bassiouni chuckled. "But if you're really getting antsy, we can check your Bishop score."

"What's a Bishop score?"

"It's a way of measuring how effective an induction might be. It looks at a few different things related to your cervix—its position, how thin it is, how dilated, and also how low the baby is."

"The baby feels pretty low," Cassidy said. "I can feel it pretty much between my legs." Noeli's eyes widened and she backed up a step, as if this feeling might be contagious.

"That's good! Maybe it will be here soon! Really, I don't encourage induction until at least forty-one weeks. Everything tends to go much more smoothly if you let your body do its work, especially if you're thinking about having an unmedicated birth."

Cassidy sighed. "Yeah, I would like to." It was part of her resolve to be more selfless. She could handle temporary pain if it was for the good of her child. "I'm just ready."

The doctor laughed. "I'm sure you are! I'll see you soon. I promise." Five days sounded like ages.

"It's like a hotel here compared to hospitals in California," Noeli said as they walked the hallway back to the elevator. Cassidy had never thought about how quiet St. Joseph's was, the only sounds her plodding footsteps and heavy breathing. For being so low, the baby was doing a good job of crowding her lungs.

Downstairs in the lobby, she took a detour, stopping at the tiny glass-walled gift shop. "My grandma volunteered here for years and years," she told Noeli. "When the hospital stopped using punch cards, she retired, but she'd been coming here so long, she just kept coming."

Inside, balloons, mugs, and other breakable trinkets lined the glass shelves. "Don't knock anything over," Noeli teased, poking Cassidy's belly.

"I know. It's giant."

"It's like a torpedo." Noeli laughed.

Toys and stuffed animals sat on a low shelf under a wall of cards. "I used to sit here for hours and play with the toys. Grandma Jane always let me pick something to bring home. I had this neon-yellow Mickey Mouse airplane that made this annoying whistle sound. Now *that's* part of my consciousness forever."

"Let's get something for the baby," Noeli said.

As Cassidy surveyed the offerings, thinking about the airplane toy and about her resolution to consciously select music and smells for her child, she was hit by the realization that none of it really mattered. Who cared what toys her kid would remember? "How about that?" she asked, pointing to a fuzzy green teddy bear. If she'd learned anything about people, it was that they were all quirky and messy. The only thing that mattered was that there was love there, too.

Cassidy swung the bag as they walked out into the hospital's empty lobby and through the familiar glass-doored exit, feeling the same sense of excitement she had as a child, leaving with a new toy.

"You really feel ready?" Noeli asked as she drove back to the farm. Cassidy was uncomfortable behind the wheel now that she had to move the seat back to accommodate the baby.

"Ready to not be pregnant anymore. Not ready to give birth. Or to have a baby." She tried to shift her weight from her sciatic nerve, which protested when Cassidy stood or sat for more than five minutes at a time.

"Well, I'm glad I'm not the only terrified one," Noeli said.

"It will be fine." Cassidy rubbed Noeli's shoulder. "You're going to be great."

When Cassidy woke that night with her belly hard, she lay still, pillow between her knees, Noeli pressed against the wall beside her. After a few seconds, her belly grew soft again. A few minutes later, it hardened. There was no pain or discomfort; the muscles simply stiffened and then released. It was dark outside, but something in the quality of the stillness signaled the far side of midnight. Even the night animals had hushed, respecting the sanctity of the wee hours.

Cassidy remained in bed, eyes closed, telling herself it could be nothing, or it could be something and still take a very long time, but it was impossible to stay put. She rolled out of bed, went to the empty master bedroom, and sat cross-legged on the floor of her parents' closet with her laptop. There were hundreds of contraction timers online, so she opened the first one and began clicking the button on the screen each time her stomach tightened.

Six minutes, thirty-four seconds.

Five minutes, thirteen seconds.

Seven minutes, twelve seconds.

Six minutes, twenty-five seconds.

The intervals weren't long, but they weren't regular, either. Cassidy opened a new tab, and the muscle memory in her fingers was so strong, she nearly opened the cam site, despite not having broadcast for weeks. Instead she opened Netflix and pressed play on *10 Things I Hate About You*. Normally, Julia Stiles was a guaranteed distraction, but right now Cassidy could barely focus on her face, so she moved between trying to watch the movie and walking up and down the stairs, peering out the octagonal window at the coming dawn. Though the light was still a navy gray, insects began to sing their morning songs. The grass, bent as if it, too, had been resting for the night, began to spring to attention.

As Letters to Cleo played "I Want You to Want Me" and the credits rolled on the unwatched movie, Cassidy, on hands and knees before it, alternately arched her back like an angry cat and let her belly hang low to the ground like a hammock. Mid-cat, Noeli peeked her head in the door.

"Everything okay in here?"

"I think I'm having contractions." Cassidy looked up at her.

"Really?!"

"Yeah, I got up a couple hours ago. You should keep sleeping, though. It could be a while. Like, days."

"Okay . . ." Noeli watched her skeptically for a moment before backing out of the room. Cassidy heard the bed squeak and the covers rustle then settle.

As the sun began to peek above the strip mine, hanging heavy below the tree cover, Cassidy restarted the movie. Suddenly she sprung to her feet with more agility than she'd mustered in months. It was instinctual—her body needed to walk, and now was the time, before the humidity made it impossible. She tiptoed down the stairs and opened the front door as quietly as possible, then stepped out into the still-cool air.

She walked, just down the driveway at first. Then, setting out like an explorer breaking new ground, she lifted her right foot with effort from the gray-and-white gravel and turned at a forty-five-degree angle onto the unruly grass. Each step was a challenge, her muscles straining to move each foot forward. She kept going, though her hips began to ache. The grass tickled her ankles and as she went farther, her thighs. A firefly, not ready for the night to end, flashed three feet ahead. Another to her right answered and soon, above and below, to her left and her right, they flickered and danced, their secret signals a language not meant for her.

They flashed whether Cassidy was here or not and she felt awe at the honor of witnessing them. Insects flitted about her, emitting a low, constant whir. Each time her belly hardened, Cassidy stopped walking, put her hands on her abdomen, and breathed. With each one, the whir of wings heightened momentarily until it sounded like a rug beating against her ears.

Cassidy walked and walked as the sun rose higher and higher. She could almost feel the old farm cat there with her. She could almost feel her dad. Carefully, she trudged, one foot, then the other, until she reached the maple tree where her father lay. She was driven by something deep and internal, the process living through her, the baby directing. Lying next to the stone that marked Ken's resting place, the wet grass rose around her body. Pressing her cheek to the cool stone, she stared at the ground below. Layers of leaves pressed into the wet ground. Soft moss grew on roots and trunks. There were signs of life everywhere, and death. A dead spider, smaller than Cassidy's fingernail, lay unmoving under a piece of bark. Beside it, on a spindly fern, a small white caterpillar dangled from a glinting string, curling and twisting its way up to the plant, which was drooping ever so slightly with its minuscule weight. There were worlds here. Cassidy had forgotten them, had grown so accustomed to buildings and to concrete. Even the "outside" she knew now was manicured and sanitized. She had forgotten about the layers, the whole worlds that lived in each square inch. She would learn to remember.

Cassidy breathed in the scent of the dirt, earthy and wet, until she felt vitalized—ready. She wanted to see Noeli. As she rose slowly to her feet, she noticed the branches of the trees just ahead hung lower than they had only a few weeks before. Stepping closer she saw why. There were apples! The scene was surreal—Cassidy could not remember seeing apples on the farm, and these dangled like decorations at a woodland feast—and yet, Cassidy felt totally present. She reached out and picked a golden fruit, took a bite. Her mouth filled with the taste of honey. She moaned in pleasure and continued back toward the house.

As she walked, the contractions picked up speed and strength, but this did not slow Cassidy down. Her own strength and energy seemed to increase with the demands of labor, and she made it back in half the time her walk out had taken. She opened the door and stepped back into the world of people. There was her purple coat. There was her father's watch. In the bedroom, Noeli was sitting up and smiling.

"How are you doing? Are you okay?" she asked.

"Yeah, sorry. I should have left a note. I wanted to walk a little."

"I figured," Noeli said, and Cassidy sat beside her.

"Oh, whoa. That feels different, sitting."

"Are you okay?" Noeli put a hand on her shoulder.

"Yeah." Cassidy laughed through clenched teeth. "I think you're going to have to stop asking that. Maybe go back to sleep."

Noeli lay back down. "I'll try."

Cassidy tried to lie next to her, but reposing, she could no longer pretend the waves weren't uncomfortable. She jumped up and paced back and forth down the hall between her bedroom and the master, watched the scene with Heath Ledger on the bleachers, then timed a few contractions. They were regular now—five minutes apart. She went downstairs and tried to eat a strawberry.

Somehow the morning passed this way, walking from room to room, trying one activity for a few minutes and then giving up. The contractions weren't quite as painful as period cramps, as long as she kept moving, but they were more distracting. Cassidy's thoughts were consumed by the intervals, her life occurring in five-minute cycles.

Noeli woke up and watched Cassidy nervously for a while. "You need to stop looking at me," Cassidy said, and Noeli hid behind her own laptop screen, occasionally peeking up.

"Do you think we should go to the hospital?" Cassidy asked. She had no idea how much time had passed.

"Do *you* think we should go to the hospital?"

"I don't know. They hurt, but it isn't bad and they're still almost three minutes apart."

"Three minutes?" Noeli's eyes grew wide. "I thought the nurse said we were supposed to go at four or five."

"That's if you want an epidural."

"You remember it takes fifteen minutes to get to town and that you agreed to a hep lock and external monitoring? Are you going to be cool getting that all set up when you're . . . in the thick of it?"

"Oh," Cassidy said. She hadn't remembered—she'd been lost in the primal feel of it all, the sinking into herself. "Maybe we should go."

At that, Noeli snapped into action, grabbing the hospital bag, a big red yoga ball, and Cassidy's phone.

In the next moment, though, Cassidy knew they were not going to town. A contraction followed the previous one, almost on its heels, and it was different—very different, this time.

"Uhh," Cassidy half said, half groaned, and when she emerged from this world-dissolving contraction, she was surprised to see both Paloma and Grandma Jane there with her, beside Noeli.

"Wha—"

"I used your phone to call them while you were on your walk," Noeli said.

"Let's go, sweetheart," Paloma said. "I'll help you down the steps."

"I'm not getting in the car," Cassidy said as the next contraction began, with barely a break from the last one, and her world collapsed again. Moaning, she rocked side to side, and someone held her, rocking with her, dancing. She wasn't sure if it was her mom or Noeli, and it didn't matter.

"Let's go," Paloma said again when the contraction ended. "Before the next one starts."

"I'm not going," she managed to bellow before the next began. Her voice was low and raspy, animalistic. Cassidy felt the world around her close to a pinhole, like the end of *Looney Tunes* episodes. As the wave subsided, the hole opened and she took in the room around her—posters, furniture, Noeli's things so at home now in this familiar space. Noeli herself, pacing and biting her lower lip, unusually pink in its lack of red lipstick. "I'm not going anywhere," she breathed. "Ohhhh."

Her groans grew louder as the contractions grew closer and more intense. Her mind space felt like a physical space—one she had visited, a place inside herself that she knew. It was familiar, though she wasn't sure she'd actually been there before. "I don't know if I can do this." She looked at Noeli, her eyes as wide as a scared child's. "I didn't know it was going to be like this."

"You knew it would hurt," Noeli said, coming to her.

"I knew it would hurt, but I didn't know I would be *here*." Cassidy knew Noeli wouldn't understand what this meant, but it didn't matter. Noeli held her and Cassidy melted into her arms. As another contraction built, Noeli rested her forehead against Cassidy's so that they were nose to nose. As the tightening grew, crested, and then subsided, they looked right into each other's eyes. Somehow, like this, Cassidy managed to keep one foot there, in her room, even as the rest of her inhabited that strange yet familiar internal world.

"We need to call 911." Paloma's voice sounded far away, like a television in another room.

"I don't have service," Noeli said.

"Here, take my phone." Paloma handed it to Noeli.

And suddenly a deer. Its eyes black, flowers wildly strewn about its ears. It stared at Cassidy. "There's a deer. The deer is here," she practically screamed. "Am I dying?" She was frantic, thrashing, searching for Noeli. Her absence was stabbing.

"No, Cass, you're not dying," Noeli said softly as she returned and put a hand behind Cassidy's head, cradling it firmly. Paloma and Jane were both surrounding her now too, the arms of all three of them encircling her like the pattern on a wedding ring quilt.

The contractions continued, one on top of the other, each bringing Cassidy to the closed glass house inside herself, a place beyond thoughts of cars or hospital bags or any of the love she'd felt a moment ago. It was a place completely solitary, and yet totally raw and open, vulnerable to all the hurts she had carried one on top of another since she was three and the burden of memory had graced her with its double-edged gift.

In her mind, she saw the hotel room from their trip to the state fair. She could smell the old cigarette smoke clinging to the curtains, hear the screams from the Tornado and the Zipper echoing in her mind. She watched as her father turned his head away, upset that she'd said she didn't want to go back to Buckhannon. Grandma Jane had turned her head in the exact same way when she said she would have taken his place. "In a heartbeat," she had said.

Paloma squeezed her shoulders, tried to bring her back to them, but all Cassidy could hear was her mother's voice telling her she'd been lonely for so long. "I understand," Cassidy said aloud. "But what about me?" Paloma held her harder.

Each wave brought her back to that place—the one where all of these hurts lived, and all of her mother's hurts lived, and her father's hurts, and her grandmother's hurts, and every hurt that had been felt here for years and years and years and years and years. With each contraction, it rose around her, shattering the walls in a dizzying crescendo. All of it, everything, had been leading to this moment.

Then there were moments between, just long enough to fill Cassidy with love, its weight almost as heavy as the hurts. Her father's smile. Her mother's arms. Her grandmother's hands there with her, now.

She saw the flow of events in the world and in her life, continuous and legible. Her grandmother had grown up during the war, had worked for the war effort. The results of that war had led to the Soviet invasion of Prague and her parents' meeting. It all led to this moment. It was as if someone had written it, had known the whole story.

Only flashes broke through the ups and downs.

Noeli: "They said it would be about fifteen minutes."

Paloma: "Get some towels."

Cassidy, her own voice sounding far away now: "Don't you dare go anywhere."

Now, Noeli's arms were around her. Now, she was wiping the sweat from her brow. Now, Noeli's arms held her up. Now, their tears streamed together.

Suddenly it was time, and Cassidy knew it without questioning. She squatted, supported by Paloma on one side and Noeli on the other, and without thinking consciously about what to do, she pushed. Her body pushed without her telling it to, a bearing down that was not unlike the sensation of throwing up.

Grandma Jane brushed the sweaty hair from Cassidy's forehead and again the world came in flashes. The paramedics arriving. Noeli whispering, "I'm right here with you." Changing positions, all fours now. Bright lights—the sun streaming through the window. The deer again, this time benevolent, her eyes soft, encouraging, welcoming Cassidy to motherhood.

A flash of searing, stretching pain and then—and then he was here—pink, writhing, Cassidy's arms reaching back through her legs for him and sitting up on her knees, bringing him to her chest. His face in a halo of light. *This* was what he looked like. Of course. He could not have looked like anything but this. His face, so soft and perfectly round, his eyes closed tight against the imposing sunlight, two slits that seemed to span his whole tiny face, his mouth open in a perfect Cupid's bow, almost a smile. His tiny fingers flexed wide and then relaxed against Cassidy, his knuckles crescent moons.

"Hola, mi amor," Noeli said, her tears falling down on them both. Paloma and Grandma Jane, holding each other beside them, were crying, too.

The paramedic, faceless and sexless, stood in the shadow of the presence of Cassidy's child, who was really, really here, checking both her and the baby, then standing back. This child was holy; there was no other word for it.

They insisted on taking them in, just to check on them both. At St. Joe's they ran the usual tests, washed the vernix from her baby's hair and fuzzy shoulders, sutured Cassidy with two quick stitches, and produced a bottle of extra-strength ibuprofen.

"Wesley," she said, stroking her son's impossibly soft hair and bringing him to her breast for the first time. "Daddy's middle name. Wesley Antonio. For Abuela."

Noeli smiled and kissed Cassidy's forehead and then Wesley's.

"Let's go home," Cassidy said. She searched Noeli's face.

"We are home," Noeli said, putting a hand to Cassidy's cheek. Cassidy breathed in. She looked up at Noeli, whose doe eyes shone back at her, and then at Wesley, whose lower lip curled under in a sloppy latch. She spoke to them both. "I'm so glad you're here," she said, the notes of a hymn on her lips, salty.

ACKNOWLEDGMENTS

Thank you to Mommy, for everything.

Daddy, thank you for making me feel like a writer.

Thank you to my husband, Jer, for being proud of me and for understanding when I worked on the book instead of hanging out.

Thank you, Sadie, for reading and encouraging me, and for helping me work through my insecurities.

Thank you, Grandma, for modeling avid reading, for being so brave and adventurous, for believing in me, and for your endless love.

Thank you, Marc and Terry, for the babysitting and support.

Thank you, J, Eric, and Connor, for your pod-ship and enthusiasm.

Thank you to Liz Worth, for your early coaching.

Thank you, Diana, for reading and for your pride in me, and for your help with the Spanish.

Thank you, Amy Tenney, the Upshur County Historical Society, Cindy Gueli, and Bruce Damer, for your help with the historical research.

Thank you to Steve Soldwedel for your fantastic WWII-era knowledge and generous editing. Christopher Henckel, thank you for reading countless versions of the first chapter.

Thank you, Inkshares and Adam Gomolin, for making this possible, and thank you to everyone who supported my crowdfunding campaign, especially those who went above and beyond by encouraging me and telling people about the book.

Thank you, Matt Harry and Avalon Radys, for seeing my vision and pushing me to bring it forward. Thank you to Kaitlin Severini for your incredible copy editing, to Lauren Harms for the beautiful cover, and to everyone else behind the scenes who helped make this the best book it can be. Thanks to all of my Inkshares and Writing Bloc friends, especially Jacqui Castle and Cari Dubiel!

Thank you, Jonas and Josie, for being wonderful. You are my inspirations every day. I love you so much.

* * *

GRAND PATRONS

Aaron T. Williams
Andrew and Annie Harrington
Bonnie Yelverton
Bradlee A. Chidester
Callie M. Rubin
Carl D. Walls
Cherie Volosin Beeck
Christopher Newman
Daniel Rosenberg
Ellie Volosin
Eugene M. Herman
Heather Walls Pakala
Henry Melgarejo
Janelle Libertone
Jared Spence Dobias
Julie Smith
Kali Stewart
Kimberley A. Schorr
Leah A. Morehead

Marie Buckner
Max Freund and Cynthia Luna
Nick and Wendy Masi
Neuromancer Dude No Way!!!
Randi Yokota
Ray E. Lapoint
Robin Rosenberg Spence
Sadie Spence Stewart
Scott G. Parker
Susan Matelan King
Zachary Elliott

INKSHARES

INKSHARES is a reader-driven publisher and producer based in Oakland, California. Our books are selected not by a group of editors, but by readers worldwide.

While we've published books by established writers like *Big Fish* author Daniel Wallace and *Star Wars: Rogue One* scribe Gary Whitta, our aim remains surfacing and developing the new author voices of tomorrow.

Previously unknown Inkshares authors have received starred reviews and been featured in the *New York Times*. Their books are on the front tables of Barnes & Noble and hundreds of independents nationwide, and many have been licensed by publishers in other major markets. They are also being adapted by Oscar-winning screenwriters at the biggest studios and networks.

Interested in making your own story a reality? Visit Inkshares.com to start your own project or find other great books.